THE
SHAAR
PRESS

THE JUDAICA IMPRINT
FOR THOUGHTFUL PEOPLE

A PROMISE

A SHAAR PRESS PUBLICATION

FULFILLED

A NOVEL BY
MENACHEM KAGAN

Published by **SHAAR PRESS**
Distributed by MESORAH PUBLICATIONS, LTD.
4401 Second Avenue / Brooklyn, N.Y 11232 / (718) 921-9000

Distributed in Israel by SIFRIATI / A. GITLER
6 Hayarkon Street / Bnei Brak 51127

Distributed in Europe by LEHMANNS
Unit E, Viking Industrial Park, Rolling Mill Road / Jarrow, Tyne and Wear, NE32 3DP/ England

Distributed in Australia and New Zealand by GOLDS WORLD OF JUDAICA
3-13 William Street / Balaclava, Melbourne 3183 / Victoria Australia

Distributed in South Africa by KOLLEL BOOKSHOP
Shop 8A Norwood Hypermarket / Norwood 2196, Johannesburg, South Africa

ISBN: 1-57819-713-9 Hard Cover
ISBN: 1-57819-714-7 Paperback

Printed in the United States of America by Noble Book Press
Custom bound by Sefercraft, Inc. / 4401 Second Avenue / Brooklyn N.Y. 11232

I wish to dedicate this book
to four unique individuals
who have guided me and taught me
some of my most important lessons
in Torah and in life.

Reb Gershon Singer,
Rabbi Shmuli Schorr,
Dr. Aaron Glatt
and
Judge Leon Ruchelsman

have all shown me in their own ways
that we are only inhibited
by our false sense of the impossible,
and that true greatness
lies in never giving up.

AUTHOR'S NOTE

The ideas and themes presented in this novel are the result of my many years of wondering just what is meant by the ordinary Jew. History is taught as the story of nations, of great men and women. Rarely do we consider the role of the ordinary, of the millions whose lives have passed through time without memory or remembrance. We often attribute peerlessness and grandeur to the leaders and discount the rest. But the more I thought about it, the more I realized the opposite is true: Each Jew is unique, brimming with greatness. Simple adherence to ancient principles, a dedication to the Torah and a simple faith in a common destiny are the greatest expressions of nobility and magnificence imaginable. I came to this conclusion by observing my family, friends and even strangers. An early morning *minyan*, a late night *shiur*, a zealousness to carry on and continue our *mesorah*. This work is of my own creation but not my own invention.

ACKNOWLEDGMENTS

There are many people I must thank who have supported me and guided me and who in their own ways helped me toward the completion of this novel.

To Just Us: Tzvi, Avi, Donny, Nissy and to Avi Roth, my most enduring friends. To Rabbi Shalom Rosner and everyone at Congregation Bais Ephraim Yitzchok of Woodmere, who helped build a *shul*, a family and a place to call home. To Dr. Michael Oppenheim, Josh Szpilzinger and Mrs. Aliza Spinner whose help, encouragement and advice were indispensable to me. To Yossi Adest and Issachar Goldberg of Woodmere, and to Shaya Elefant and Berel Septimus of

Brooklyn Law School — it wouldn't have been the same without all of you. To the Rubinstein and Groner families of East 23rd Street, Flatbush, Brooklyn, whose thirst for literature finally urged me to pick up my pen.

To Davy and Tevie Kagan, whose resources and love of our family traditions have guided my priorities for as long as I can remember.

To everyone at ArtScroll who helped make this possible, especially Mrs. Charlotte Friedland and Mrs. Judi Dick, who fashioned a novel out of my original unpolished manuscript and who taught me how to be a better writer. To my grandparents, Mr. and Mrs. Alexander and Olga Spiegel; your early hardships and lives in a bygone world always inspire me. Your open home, your wide smiles and your loving affections always comfort me.

To Yitzchok Levine; your strength of character and commitment to my family are dear treasures to me.

To Susy Kagan; I have never forgotten your devotion and your unceasing belief that we can conquer it all.

To my grandparents-in-law, Mr. and Mrs. Lazer and Mina Rosen; your genuine love for the family is truly inspiring. All your joys are found in our successes and in our endeavors. To my in-laws, Mr. and Mrs. Sheldon and Sally Hirsch; for treating me like one of your own and for my greatest treasure of all. To Hilly and Ellie; for always listening, for your endless encouragement and unbridled support. To my brothers, Avi and Tuli; for your love of my family and for always being there whenever I need you.

To my father, Howard, and my mother, Blima; it has been a long time since a sad six-year-old birthday boy could not be cheered up. Your warmth and tenderness, your magical optimism and your boundless generosity are your most enduring traits, which I treasure and which I hope to vouchsafe for Sruly and Adina. I am always thankful for your confidence in me, your wisdom, honesty, sincerity and love.

Lastly, to my wife, Aviva; you have helped make our lives together the greatest chapter of any book ever written. You are not only my greatest inspiration, you are the co-author of my life.

The Holy City and its suburbs have become a disgrace and have been looted, all her treasures have been buried and hidden, and there is nothing left but this Torah.

– Rabbenu Gershom 'Meor Hagolah'

Blois, France 1171

We see troubles being renewed, and we think they are types of signs of salvation and redemption, for we are promised to be redeemed from the sorrow and disaster …

— Rashi to Isaiah 26:17

1

He took a long look as he applied the finishing stroke. He had been involved with writing this Torah scroll for much of his life. He replaced the quill where it was always kept beneath a sturdy wooden table and began to reminisce as feelings of nostalgia, pride and sorrow welled up within him. He had begun writing this scroll over seventy years ago. He had written others, many others, during the course of his life but none with the care and meticulousness invested in this one. It was his crowning achievement, his legacy, a bequest to his people. He had begun writing it to fulfill a promise he had made to a friend, long since dead. Over time the obligation was transformed and blossomed into a mission that consumed him.

He never forgot the promise, and as he studied the finished product, he recalled how it all came about. His thoughts took him back many years to the terrible events that had taken place during the spring of 1171.

Gavriel was fifteen and lived with his family in the small town of Blois, France along with some forty other Jews. Gavriel's mother had died almost six years earlier, when his sister, Chana, was born. Ill prepared for the unexpected responsibility of raising an infant, his father, Rabbi Shimon, found the task almost too great to bear. Rabbi Shimon was the spiritual leader of the town and was constantly called upon to address the needs of the congregation. He did not have adequate time to devote to his children and he feared they would grow up without the benefit of parental direction and guidance.

After the death of his wife, Rivka, he aged rapidly. His beard turned gray, then white, and he walked with a stick to support his ailing feet. He was prone to sickness, which left him tired and weak. He was fifty years old but appeared much older. Overwhelmed, he felt that soon all his infirmities would catch up with him and he would no longer be able to competently guide the community. Gavriel was still a youth, and too young to take over as rabbi; Rabbi Shimon longed for a capable and learned man who could succeed him.

The townspeople likewise were growing impatient with Rabbi Shimon and his deteriorating health. Though they had too much regard for him to ever say anything, deep-down they wished he would retire. They all respected him and believed he was a decent and learned man but his illnesses recurred so frequently they felt he was becoming ineffective. The tension between the rabbi and his congregants nearly erupted when Leah, the wife of Gedaliah the tailor, stormed into Rabbi Shimon's study one Friday morning to relate that she had witnessed several children walking with the aid of sticks and she believed they were mocking Rabbi Shimon's frail health. Rabbi Shimon, who was preparing his lecture for the following day, the Sabbath before Passover, looked up from behind a stack of books. He saw Leah, a short and pleasant and exasperated woman. This was just the sort of incident he felt he could no longer tolerate. The children's behavior was improper, that was certain, but he lacked the strength and the passion to care to do anything about it, to inspire the children to rectify these faults. Nevertheless, he knew he could not ignore the problem. It was his job and he was not permitted to shirk his responsibilities. Yet he wondered how long this could go on.

Rabbi Shimon seemed to be lost in thought and after a moment came up with a solution. He moved the pile of books aside, stood up and asked, "Would you like me to deliver a sermon about the evils of ridiculing other people, especially the rabbi?"

"Well, I believe that a few years ago you commanded greater reverence and the children never would have acted in this discourteous way," responded Leah, implying it was the rabbi's fault.

Leah blushed, turned away and avoided facing Rabbi Shimon directly. Rabbi Shimon sensed that Leah felt awkward and likely regretted blaming him for harmless child's play, which had innocently turned insolent. He was fully aware how the town felt, he was cognizant of his own inadequacies, but he never dreamed anyone would confront him, even in this circuitous fashion. "I understand, and the situation will be resolved," said Rabbi Shimon in a definitive and stern voice, without explaining what he meant. Leah, who by now was red with embarrassment, accepted his vague declaration, bid the rabbi the standard Sabbath salutations and departed.

Rabbi Shimon believed that Leah was sincere and was genuinely disturbed by the children's behavior. He also felt that she was probably more upset with his recent performance as rabbi. Rabbi Shimon was sure that other townspeople knew of Leah's visit and would expect him to address her concerns the next day. He understood that Leah's complaints went beyond the specific issue she had raised, and that this was a test of his resolve and dedication to his flock. He concluded that he would speak about this on the Sabbath. He hoped he could muster some of the emotion and inspiration he used to feel toward his congregation, find a replacement rabbi and retire to care for Gavriel and Chana, his two motherless children.

Rabbi Shimon immediately began preparing his lecture.

The next morning Rabbi Shimon walked unusually slowly to the synagogue. He refrained from using his walking stick on the Sabbath, and stopped every few moments to catch his breath. Rabbi Shimon and his children arrived a few minutes late and Chana quickly ran upstairs to sit with the women in the balcony. As she entered, Dina, the wife of Shalom the shoemaker, a kindhearted woman who was childless, motioned for Chana to sit next to her, as she did every Sabbath.

The synagogue was an old building yet it had a distinct style and was tastefully decorated. The main sanctuary where the men prayed was long and narrow, with rows of benches on either side of a central aisle. In the center, three steps down, was the well from where the cantor would sing and lead the congregation. The front of the synagogue contained the Ark, which housed the holy Torah scrolls. There were four scrolls and it was rumored that Rashi, the great sage from nearby Worms, had written one of them. Each scroll was covered with ornamental silk tapestries, with designs such as a shofar and a menorah embroidered onto the silk. On the front of the Ark hung a curtain with an exquisite design of two lions holding a depiction of the Two Tablets on which were written the Ten Commandments. All congregants who gazed at the curtain were to be inspired by the strength of lions, an allegory for the Jewish People, the bearers of G-d's law.

The synagogue contained seating for upwards of one hundred men but typically saw no more than twenty-five. The balcony was reserved for the women's gallery and held only a few rows of well-worn benches which were no longer used by the men. The women had an unobstructed view of the cantor's podium, the rabbi and the first three rows of the men's benches. Flowers were placed at the balcony entrance every Friday afternoon by the caretaker's wife, to beautify the otherwise dreary area.

Rabbi Shimon quickly took his seat at the front of the synagogue near the Ark, placed his prayer shawl over his head and shoulders and began to pray. Gedaliah the tailor entered shortly after Rabbi Shimon and started toward the rabbi as if he had something important to say but then changed his mind. Gedaliah too donned his shawl, sat down and prayed. As the synagogue began to fill, it became stuffy and hot. April was the month when winter officially ended and the long summer lay ahead. Passover was usually regarded as the dividing line between cold weather and warm and as Passover was only a few days away the heat portended an unusually long and hot summer.

The morning's prayers proceeded as usual but some of the congregants sensed a vague uneasiness in the rabbi's demeanor. Everybody waited for the sermon.

The entire town naturally expected the Rabbi to speak about the Passover holiday, if only briefly, notwithstanding the traditional

"Great" speech which the rabbi would deliver later in the afternoon. Rabbi Shimon, though, had other plans. He needed to reassert his authority as the town leader and would focus only on that one goal.

The time of the sermon was at hand and Rabbi Shimon was ready. He rose and moved to the center of the synagogue where he stood facing the congregation. He paused a moment, sighed and closed his eyes, a familiar ritual before each speech. He slowly opened his eyes and began softly. He recalled many of the miracles which had taken place for the Jews when they left Egypt and while they wandered in the wilderness for forty years. Some of the more imaginative congregants thought Rabbi Shimon would elaborate on those parables with stories, which contained even more fantastic and wondrous miracles than those recorded in the Bible. Those congregants, however, were quickly disappointed. Rabbi Shimon delivered a lengthy discourse regarding the staff Moses had used to perform many of those miracles and presumably to walk with as well. Rabbi Shimon spoke earnestly about this walking aid and said that he had searched throughout all of Jewish literature and could find no mention of any reference that belittled the staff. Rabbi Shimon mentioned the legend that this staff was originally owned by Adam, the first man, and that it had been passed down from generation to generation until Moses.

The Rabbi concluded his speech with a simple question. "If any of us sitting here today would have had the privilege to spend forty years with our great and holy teacher, and would have had the honor to watch him every day and to learn from his wisdom and kindness, would any of us have viewed his staff as a sign of weakness and incapacity?"

A frosy silence descended on the synagogue. Rabbi Shimon stepped from the podium. He studied the faces of the silent and awestruck crowd and knew he had struck a chord. He hoped he had succeeded and that they would rethink their attitudes and the lack of respect they had shown him lately. He promised himself to exert greater efforts on behalf of his congregation, at least until a replacement could be found. He further reflected upon the speech and believed it was one of his best in quite some time, the way he used to speak when Devorah, his wife, was still living. He wished she could have been there to hear it. He then looked up and smiled briefly.

Naturally, everybody was a little embarrassed by the rabbi's speech. They fully appreciated the moral of the message and were thankful he had chosen this subtle method instead of a more direct and blunt approach. The townspeople agreed that Rabbi Shimon had been slighted by them and resolved among themselves to be more understanding and more courteous toward him.

As Rabbi Shimon reached his seat, he heard a loud rustling sound resonating from the women's gallery. He looked up and saw Leah's face peering through the curtains, nodding in satisfaction and complacency.

Nothing more was ever said about the rabbi's abilities as leader of the congregation, nor his age or his ailing health, because two days later the community was plunged into an abyss of despair from which it never emerged.

2

Some people are born to greatness. They are groomed, trained and educated, destined to become kings, warriors or heroes. These are in the vanguard of history.

Others, many others, lead simple and uneventful lives. They are born of ordinary stock and struggle to break from the mundane, to soar beyond the humble lives where the whirlwind of history has tossed them.

Others still, mostly common souls, are thrust into the maelstrom of upheaval and precipitate great changes in the world. They are provincial citizens, ill prepared for an arena chiefly reserved for statesmen and nobles.

On Thursday, a few days before Passover, Yitzchak, the son of Eleazar, an honest and modest man from Blois, was returning home from a month-long journey. Yitzchak had traveled to Paris in an effort to buy silks, woolens and leather for a new business venture. He had missed all of the controversy surrounding Rabbi Shimon but would not have cared much as he rarely became involved with the concerns of the community. He was anxious to return home and spend Passover with his family.

It was late in the afternoon but Yitzchak hoped to arrive home before sundown, when traveling was difficult and dangerous. Not far from Blois he paused at the river to water his horse and rest for a few moments. He knew that his horse needed to rest and would never make it to town without water to drink. Yitzchak promised himself the stop would only last a short while and that he would still reach home before dark. He was already at the Loire, the outskirts of the Blois region; he could be home within the hour.

The water's current seemed unusually strong, almost turbulent. Yitzchak dismounted and led his horse to the water's edge. Someone else was already there. It was a soldier clad in old, rusty mail and his helmet bare of the customary richly colored plumes. Yitzchak scrutinized the man more closely and concluded that he was not a soldier at all but probably an illiterate slave who had stolen some old and useless armor from his master. The horse, on the other hand, was strikingly beautiful with a well-combed mane draped in lavish cloths with intricate designs and a coat-of-arms embellishing the saddlebag. The disparity in appearance between horse and rider confirmed Yitzchak's belief that the horse belonged to the man's master.

The slave saw Yitzchak's fringes and sidelocks, recognized a Jew, grunted and looked away.

Yitzchak, not wishing to engage the man and further delay his return home, avoided him entirely. He approached the brook, bent down to drink and the horse did likewise. Several costly hides concealed in his shirt inexplicably dislodged and fell into the water. The splash alarmed Yitzchak's horse and it neighed in fright. The slave's mount, startled by Yitzchak's horse's reaction, lifted its head from the water, backed away from the stream and retreated to a nearby tree. The reins were still firmly in the hands of the slave, who felt them jerk by the horse's sudden move. The slave drew closer to examine what had transpired. The river's strong current had drawn the hides too far downstream to be retrieved, and the slave merely observed a fleshy-looking substance float away. He pondered what it was that he had just barely glimpsed. It could not have been coins, a pouch that size would have sunk immediately. It did not look like food or anything else that came to mind and yet, it was heavy enough to startle both horses.

What was it?

What was the Jew hiding?

It was obviously something the Jew did not want found or he would simply have placed it in his saddlebag. No doubt this Jew was concealing contraband of some kind and the object, which fell into the water, was part of some wrongdoing. The slave recalled that the object appeared fleshy yet pale, almost white and ghostly. Once again, the slave wondered what it was. What appeared white yet plump and could produce such a loud splash? He could not think of an answer.

The slave continued to study the Jew and he drew his hand across his face to wipe his brow. His hand passed before his eyes and then the slave believed he had solved the mystery. What had fallen into the water was a dead body, a child's body! It was the only thing he could imagine which had the same texture, weight and pale color as the object he watched float downstream. The slave concluded that this was not an ordinary dead body, this child's body had been drained of its blood! How else to explain the ghastly and anemic complexion of the corpse?

The slave did not know why a Jew would kill a Christian child and then remove the blood but he had heard of this sort of iniquity happening before. He did not question that a Jew could commit such a horrible act and refused to accept that there could be some other logical, some more reasonable explanation. He gazed at Yitzchak and no longer saw an ordinary man, he saw a criminal, a murderer who deserved stern and swift justice. He could not allow the Jew to leave without answering for the crime and, fearing that perhaps the Jew might turn violent, approached him cautiously.

"What was that object which fell out of your bosom and landed in the river?" asked the slave abruptly.

Yitzchak turned to face the man, surprised by the question. Why the interest in his merchandise? Was he a robber seeking to steal his other valuables? Yitzchak was uncertain but wanted the slave to believe he was carrying nothing else of value.

"Those were some cheap hides I purchased in Paris," answered Yitzchak, calmly.

Hides.

Perhaps they were hides. It was a reasonable explanation, one that would account for the color and consistency of the item. But why conceal them in the bosom? It sounded contrived and implausible. The slave pressed on.

"Why did you not leave them in your saddlebag with your other belongings? Were they magic hides, part of some Jewish ritual? You are a Jew, aren't you?"

Yitzchak grew apprehensive. The slave obviously mistrusted him and believed there was more to those hides than Yitzchak admitted; his suspicions regarding Yitzchak's religion made that abundantly clear. What did the slave want?

The slave continued to move toward Yitzchak and quickly reached for a sword. Yitzchak shuddered at the sight of the sword and knew he needed to convince the slave immediately. "You may investigate if you wish. I purchased hides from Charles, the leather merchant, whose shop is located three streets from the Seine River," replied Yitzchak emphatically. He added, "I then hid them in my bosom to protect them!"

The slave remained unimpressed and refused to consider the explanation. He drew his sword and placed the tip at Yitzchak's throat. He shouted, "What is your name, you dirty Jew, and where do you live? If you do not answer me this instant I will kill you!!"

Yitzchak, who had never seen a drawn sword before, stood trembling. Why was the slave tormenting and threatening him? What had he done? Yitzchak did not want to delay answering this reckless and dangerous man and thereby provide him with additional reasons to be angrier still. He quickly responded, "My name is Yitzchak, my father's name was Eleazar and I live in Blois. I am a modest merchant and if you do not believe me you may check my bags which are laden with sewing materials and garments and hides I purchased while in Paris. You may take whatever you wish."

The slave opened one of the saddlebags, rummaged through it and observed all the goods. He was not interested in worthless needles and materials and remained convinced he had witnessed evidence of an unspeakable crime. He threw down the saddlebag and confronted Yitzchak.

"You claim that what fell from your cloak were hides, but I saw it. I saw what truly fell into the river. You cannot alter what I saw! My eyes do not lie and your assertions of innocence will not deceive me. I saw you drop a Christian child into this river!" The slave started to yell, "I saw you drop a Christian child into this river. The child was white, drained of all its blood! You filthy Jew, you killed this child and have taken its blood!! You will no doubt be using the blood of that holy martyred child for your Satanic practices! How fortunate I am to have seen this. Do you know who I am? I am the groom of Prince Henri, master and protector of this region. I am confident he will know how to deal with you. Begone now, filthy Jew!"

The slave calmed himself, placed his sword back into its sheath and approached his horse.

Yitzchak stood in a state of shock. Was the slave serious? The accusation was so preposterous, so outrageous that for a moment he believed that perhaps the slave was merely teasing him, a cruel joke, but a joke nonetheless. But Yitzchak heard the ferocity in the slave's voice and understood this was not said in jest, the slave meant every word. The slave had already mounted his horse, and would soon ride away. Yitzchak saw one chance to implore the slave, explain he had been terribly mistaken. He ran to him. "Please, my lord," pleaded Yitzchak, "I have done nothing wrong, you must believe me. I insist that what fell into the river were leather hides that might have looked like white skin. I assure you that I am speaking the truth. I have not harmed anyone!" Yitzchak fell to the ground and began weeping at the feet of the slave.

The slave kicked Yitzchak, who fell backward, then quickly galloped away.

The accusation had been made. An accusation which would be hurled numerous times throughout the centuries. An accusation which defied logic, reason and proof. An accusation rooted in hatred and ignorance. The first had taken place many years earlier in Norwich, England.

The slave had just made the second.

There would be others.

Yitzchak slowly rose from the ground, trembling uncontrollably as the allegations resonated within him. The slave could not have been serious, he could not have meant all that. Nobody could accuse another person of a crime this grave on such flimsy evidence. Surely he would return in a few moments to explain it had been an awful mistake.

Or perhaps the slave was drunk and by the time he was sober he would have forgotten the whole matter. That seemed more plausible, there was nothing to worry about.

But a few moments later Yitzchak realized he was deluding himself, the slave had not been drunk, just cruel and vicious. There was no mistake, the accusation would not be rescinded.

What would happen now?

Yitzchak was not sure. Neither he nor anyone he knew had ever been involved in anything remotely resembling this.

Would he be brought to trial? Face charges of murder based on the testimony of a common slave? Or would the slave just forget about it, too afraid to mention it and risk being punished for stealing his master's armor?

He did not know.

But if he were brought to some kind of trial and found guilty he would surely be put to death!

Yitzchak cringed.

Could that happen? Could the episode escalate to such dire and unfortunate consequences?

He felt sick.

Yitzchak wondered why it had been his destiny to encounter the slave and suffer the accusations of murder and cruelty. The Jews of Blois roamed the riverside all the time and nothing like this had ever occurred. Yitzchak did not know the answer but he did know that if he were to face some sort of trial resulting from the accusations of the slave and his master he would undoubtedly be found guilty.

Yitzchak knew that to survive he had to find a way to avoid all that. There had to be someone who could intercede on his behalf and convince the slave, and presumably the master, that this was all a terrible mistake and he was innocent of any wrongdoing.

Rabbi Shimon!

Rabbi Shimon possessed the esteem and dignity to influence even the most stubborn French nobles of his innocence. Yitzchak recalled that two years earlier Rabbi Shimon helped prove the innocence of Reuven the dye merchant after some local nobles accused him of stealing their wares. True, a charge of murder was far more severe than the accusation leveled against Reuven, but that incident demonstrated Rabbi Shimon's honesty and passion for truth, which left a lasting impression on all those present, Jew and Christian alike. Yitzchak was convinced that those same qualities could help him now in persuading the local nobles that no crime had been committed.

Yitzchak felt relieved that Rabbi Shimon might intercede on his behalf and exhibit the same zealousness for truth that saved Reuven. But he recalled the hatred and rancor which the slave had displayed and wondered whether anybody, even Rabbi Shimon, could soothe the slave's flaring and wild temperament. Before departing, Yitzchak stopped and prayed.

It was dark by now. The blackness of night seemed to augur the uncertainty and dread now hanging over his future.

Only a short time earlier he had been anticipating reuniting with his family and enjoying the approaching holiday. Now he could scarcely muster the strength to continue homeward.

In a slow, almost reluctant manner Yitzchak undertook the walk back to Blois. He lacked the enthusiasm and strength to mount his horse and hasten home. He led the animal instead, meandering through the fields that led to Blois. He thought of his four children, Yaakov, Shmuel, Shalom and Devorah, and his wife, Tamar. Were they safe? Would the slave involve them in his fabricated tale of ritual murder? Was anyone beyond the reach of these outlandish accusations? The outlook was terrifying indeed.

But Yitzchak kept returning to the same nagging question, the same mystery which tortures each soul in times of duress and hardship.

Why me?

Yitzchak continued home a broken and discouraged man, as if he had already been condemned to the gallows.

He slowly entered the city and feigned a smile as he waved to Gedaliah and Leah, who were standing outside, taking a break from the frenzied Passover preparations.

"It is good to see you Yitzchak, welcome home!" remarked Gedaliah. "How are things in Paris? Did you remember the special needles I asked you to purchase for me?"

"Thank you, Gedaliah, and yes, I remembered the needles," replied Yitzchak listlessly. "I also brought some threads that I purchased for a very good price, given their excellent quality. I thought you would want them; otherwise, I can make use of them."

"Thank you, Yitzchak, I will take them and perhaps we can go into business together soon!" Gedaliah chuckled.

Yitzchak told him he would bring over the merchandise later, as he was very anxious to see his family and did not wish to spend time rummaging through his bag. Gedaliah understood and thanked him again.

Yitzchak proceeded to his home and instantly smiled. He saw his youngest, Devorah, playing near the house. He marveled how much she had grown over the past month. Devorah heard someone approach and looked up. "Father! Father!" she shouted, running toward him. "I thought you weren't coming until tomorrow."

Tamar always told the children he would be returning later than expected so that any unforeseen delays would not cause the children additional unease. The boys were already wise to Tamar's trick and knew their father usually arrived sooner than expected, but Devorah was only five years old and was truly surprised to see him.

She ran to him, her long hair bound in ribbon bouncing up and down. She greeted him and nearly knocked him over with the force of her hug. She was particularly fond of her father, the way all children seem to be of the parents with whom they rarely spend enough time.

"I am so happy to see you, Devorah," said Yitzchak as he pried his daughter from his waist. "I brought you something special from Paris, but first you must close your eyes and open your hands and think of nice things." Devorah eagerly complied while Yitzchak removed a soft, green scarf from his bag and gently laid it across Devorah's palms. Yitzchak was relieved the slave had not stolen it and was certain the boor had overlooked it. Devorah felt a tingling sensation and opened her eyes and stared at the scarf, which was a color she had never seen before. It was the most beautiful and precious thing she had ever touched. She jumped into his arms and kissed him. "Thank you, Father, this is my favorite scarf in the whole world and I will only wear it on special times, like Passover." Yitzchak kissed her, set her down and told her to find the boys.

Inside the house, he found Tamar busily cleaning for Passover. She hated that Yitzchak traveled this time of year but understood that he had no control over when the fabric merchants sold their merchandise. She greeted him warmly but cautioned him she was too busy to discuss his trip now and that it would have to wait until later.

The hectic commotion of the home before Passover, and the gratification of seeing his loving family, allowed him to briefly forget the incident at the river, but the longer he sat alone waiting for the boys the more uneasy he became.

Moments later Yaakov entered. He was Yitzchak's eldest, a handsome boy of fourteen with wisps of facial hair, harbingers of a fullgrown beard within a few years. He was very strong, with large hands and a rough, angular face. Yitzchak thought the boy should train to become a ritual slaughterer since he would have no trouble controlling the animals. Yaakov did not oppose the idea but was too young to commit himself. At the present moment Yaakov was excelling in his studies and in fact had interrupted them to greet his father.

"Hello, Father, how was your trip?" He had grown in the past month and was almost as tall as Yitzchak.

"Fine, Yaakov, thank you for asking," said Yitzchak, concealing his true feelings. He wished he could confide in his son and draw courage from the boy's strength.

"Tell me, Yaakov, how are your studies?"

"Fine, Father, I have already mastered almost all of the laws of Passover and will be tested on them shortly after the holiday. I hope you can help me."

"I am certain I will be able to help you. It was wonderful seeing you, now return to your studies and tell Shalom and Shmuel that I will see them later as well."

Yaakov left and Yitzchak turned to Tamar, who was busy in the kitchen. Tamar pointed to an empty bucket, which Yitzchak quickly filled with water.

Over the next few hours Yitzchak had an opportunity to once again review what had transpired. By now Yitzchak had pondered every conceivable angle and concluded that any chance of escaping harm resided in the wisdom and skill of Rabbi Shimon.

At dinner, Yitzchak caught up with Shmuel and Shalom and the rest of the family, but was very quiet. He was preoccupied and it showed. He frequently spoke up when nobody was talking to him and once asked Shalom if he liked the green scarf. Tamar immediately sensed something was wrong and hurried dinner so they could be alone. After dinner, Yitzchak and the boys went to evening services. When they returned, Tamar told the children to prepare for bed, and Yitzchak wished them all a good night.

Yitzchak and Tamar were alone.

"What's wrong?" said Tamar, after she watched Yitzchak pace.

Yitzchak just stared at her without saying a word. He wondered where to begin. Yitzchak was no longer looking at her, he was looking beyond her. Looking into the unknown when a crisis engulfs a family and there seems to be no answer. Looking for a miracle, that one thing which could save him.

Finally Tamar remarked again, "Yitzchak, you have been very quiet and acting rather odd since you returned. You are not even looking at me now as we speak. Please tell me what is wrong." She continued, "If the purchasing did not go as planned, or if you were attacked and robbed on the way home, please, there is no reason to keep bad news from me."

Yitzchak knew he could not contain himself any longer. He looked at Tamar again and burst out crying. Through his tears he told Tamar everything that transpired at the river, how he had dropped the hides, how the slave had accused him of murdering a Christian child and how the prince of the region would be notified.

Tamar listened intently and wept too. They had been together as husband and wife for so long, but for the first time they were truly afraid.

She confessed that she obviously had not expected something this serious. She agreed that if Yitzchak was in danger then only Rabbi Shimon could save him. They decided not to tell the children, especially Yaakov. The news would only distress them. By now it was well past midnight, yet they agreed this could not wait, not even until the morning. Tamar woke Yaakov and told him they needed to see the rabbi on an urgent matter, and he should mind Devorah or Shalom if they awoke. Half asleep, Yaakov complied and wondered about the urgency.

Yitzchak and Tamar, in the middle of the night a few days before Passover, went to the rabbi, over matters of life and death.

3

Amaster and slave are oftentimes mirror images of one another. A master who displays kindness and compassion will have servants of like character. An angry and bitter master who rules with the whip will produce slaves of similar cruelty.

Thus, as the slave Philippe galloped away from the River Loire, he anticipated greeting his master, Prince Henri, and informing him that he had just witnessed a horrible crime committed by a Jew, Yitzchak, son of Eleazar of Blois.

Prince Henri was a tall man with the features and build of royalty. He had an imposing presence, powerful and fearless. He secured his position with his strength and treated his enemies mercilessly. He lacked the cunning and intelligence, though, to expand the boundries of his authority and control any further and conceded he would never be more than lord and ruler of the local squire. But he always dreamed of more power and hoped that someday he would be granted greater patronage and honor by the king.

Henri was relaxing in the garden waiting for Philippe to bring his evening drink. It was still too early for dinner, yet Henri was accustomed to imbibe at this hour, while the cook prepared the meal. Philippe was late and Henri was growing impatient. He stood up to await his servant's arrival. A few moments later Philippe hurriedly approached. He was carrying a decanter of choice wine and one of Henri's expensive crystal goblets, those used only on the most momentous occasions. Before Henri had an opportunity to even question the reason for such lavish celebration, Philip provided the explanation. Henri listened intently but wondered whether Philippe was telling the truth. Could a Jew have thrown a dead and bloodless child into the river? For what purpose? He had heard of a similar incident that had taken place in England, but that could not support Philippe's accusation. Slaves had tendencies to stretch the truth or fabricate entirely; Philippe himself had done so in the past. Could this be another of his wild and outrageous tales?

But what if it were true? What if the Jew did commit this horrible act? He would not be surprised, the ways of the Jew were known to be wicked indeed. If Philippe was telling the truth and the Jew killed a Christian child, then this could prove the moment for which he had been waiting. He could ingratiate himself with the regional leaders, rally the populace against the hated and vile Jews and position himself for further entitlements, possibly an expansion of his current area of control. Philippe's allegation could advance his position, and put an end to so many years of waiting and longing. But he had to be completely convinced that Philippe was telling the truth.

"Are you absolutely certain that you saw a dead child? Are you positive that what you say now is the truth? You have misled me before and that cannot happen this time. I cannot approach that Jew and accuse him of this heinous crime if he is innocent. That would cause me untold harm: I will be accused of being bloodthirsty and cruel and my plans for more power will surely backfire. If you are mistaken and I pursue it nevertheless, it could be my undoing! However, if the Jew is guilty, then I will unleash all the power and authority that I possess to insure that justice is served and I will receive great rewards in the process. But I must be thoroughly convinced that you are telling me the truth."

Philippe understood the seriousness of his charge. He was fully aware that if Henri's authority unraveled because of his error he would pay with his life. He believed that would never happen.

"I assure you my master, that I saw the body of a child fall out of the Jew's cloak with my very own eyes and I know that the Jew has murdered a Christian youth," answered Philippe with a decisiveness Henri had never heard before. "My master, if you allow me to tell what I saw to a council, I know I will be believed. I am certain my story will prove true. I would swear by all that is holy and I will accept any test to prove that what I say is true."

The slave did not elaborate on those truth-seeking methods, but Henri understood that there were various techniques that different priests utilized to determine the truth and accuracy of an accusation. The most popular procedure involved placing the accuser in a pool of water. While in the pool, the priest would observe whether the accuser stayed afloat or sank. Some priests viewed floating individuals as honest, while others interpreted their buoyancy as a sign of falsehood. Each priest had his own unique truth verification method whose accuracy could not be impugned. Henri had been waiting for Philippe to offer to undergo one of those procedures. If Philippe were to successfully pass that test, then he could proceed without fear of humiliation or defeat.

Henri, assured by Philippe's insistence he was telling the truth and protected by his offer to undergo the water test and thereby spare him any adverse repercussions, thought of how to proceed with this accusation.

If Philippe was telling the truth then obviously this Jew was guilty, but what of the others, the rest of the town?

Henri envisioned a far larger crime, a more sinister collaboration.

Surely the Jew at the river could not have killed the child on his own. What need could one Jew have for so much blood? The murder must have been committed by all the Jews of Blois!!

Thus ensued the thought process of a mind filled with hatred and dominated by that hatred.

Henri saw all Jews as accomplices to the crime, helping each other murder the youth and then drain the blood for their Passover rituals! The Jew at the river had merely been given the task of discarding the child. Guilty, of course, but no more so than the rest of the town! It was quite obvious that the machinations, the strategies and the extent of that town's evil were far grander than Philippe had the insight to understand. Who knew how many other Christian children had been murdered throughout France?

Yes, all the Jews of Blois were equally guilty, not just one. Subjecting one Jew to justice and punishment would not solve anything. The crimes would continue because the criminals would still be free to commit them!

Henri reasoned the only way to insure the safety of honest and decent Christians throughout France was to destroy the criminals, all the criminals. The ideal way to accomplish that goal would be to place the entire Jewish community on trial, make all of them answer for the heinous crime they undoubtedly committed, pronounce them all guilty and then burn them all at the stake! Henri immediately realized there were some obstacles to this plan. How would he explain the involvement of the Jewish women and children? What of the infants?

That could prove a difficult dilemma indeed, but Henri was determined to pursue justice against all the Jews, not just Yitzchak. He would have to invent some pretext, conjure up some reason to include even the women and young children in any punishment that would be meted out against the town. Surely everyone in the town, even the suckling babe, benefited from the blood of Christian children.

Henri quickly understood that he could never succed in this undertaking without help. There would be too much opposition from the local populace and he lacked the manpower and the weapons to secure the Jews if they chose to fight back. He needed Count Theobold's help, his men and his influence. With Theobold at his side, nothing could prevent him from succeeding. He decided he would travel to Theobold and confer with him about his plan. Theobold, no lover of Jews, would probe into the matter and arrive at the only logical and apparent conclusion, that the entire town had participated in this outrage. Theobold had the ability to inflame the passions of the local populace; they revered their ruler and trusted his beliefs. Theobold would also provide the soldiers necessary to keep the Jews restrained while a council conducted its work. But most importantly Henri would be rewarded for his eager and thorough determination to insure the honor and security of Frenchmen everywhere. He could almost feel the prestige and authority that would be bestowed upon him for his efforts.

"There is no time to lose, Philippe. We must travel to Theobold and tell him at once what you have seen. He will guarantee that vengeance is exacted against those criminals."

Philippe did not like Count Theobold, the ruler of the region that included Blois. He had worked for him in his youth and found him harsh and insufferable. He hoped never to see him again and for a moment thought of asking Henri to choose another servant as an escort. But Philippe wanted to be there, despite his memories of Theobold's harshness, to personally relate what he had seen at the river. Philippe knew that his story would have a greater impact on Theobold if he heard it directly rather than from a third person. He wanted Theobold to be as angry and agitated as Henri and to spur him into swift and decisive action. Henri told Philippe to prepare the horses; they would leave in the morning.

The journey to Theobold's palace in Chartres, just north of Blois, did not take long. The superior quality of Henri's horses expedited the travel and they arrive shortly before noon. Henri informed Theobold's servants who he was and stressed the urgency of his visit. He was immediately led to the room where Theobold met visitors.

The room was richly decorated with linens of various colors that hung near the ceiling. Large crosses were fixed above two windows and prayers carved in stones inlaid with rubies adorned the front wall. The floor was covered with an imported wine colored rug, which enhanced the aura of the room and added a touch of elegance. Theobold sat on a large chair made of solid wood trimmed in gold. He was grossly overweight and when he moved, the chair creaked and its legs tottered and appeared as if they might snap. He had a large head with small shifty eyes, which made him look like a weasel.

Theobold was not fit to rule. He was callous and vain, but had two invaluable assets, which made his reign as protector of the region inevitable. He was a direct descendant of Charlemagne the Great and he was married to the king's daughter.

He cared mostly about riches and wealth and hid his inadequacies as a leader behind lavish decoration and ceremony, and by pleasing his subjects to the point that they overlooked his flaws.

Theobold slowly stood up to welcome Henri as he and Philippe entered the room. "I am surprised you have arrived unexpectedly, Henri. You are aware that you will never advance in position if you fail to follow rules of proper respect and etiquette! Tell me, what matter impelled you here so impatiently?"

Henri knew he should have sent word of his impending arrival, that his conduct was a breach of protocol. He believed, though, once Theobold heard Philippe's startling story, he would understand his zeal and quickly forget his impropriety. "I am sorry, Theobold, for visiting without notifying you in advance. However, my servant, Philippe, has observed a most heinous crime which I wanted to bring to your attention personally. I did not wish to delay, even to afford you notice of my arrival, because I felt the serious nature of my servant's observation necessitated immediate attention."

Theobold looked intrigued as Henri motioned for Philippe to come forward and recount what he had seen. Theobold did not recognize his former servant and likewise motioned for Philippe to rise. Philippe eagerly complied and related the tale of Yitzchak the Jew and all that had transpired at the River Loire the previous day. He repeated almost verbatim the conversation that had taken place between him and Yitzchak, including Yitzchak's protestations of innocence, which Philippe admitted he found unavailing. Philippe finished, then resumed his position at the far end of the room.

Theobold was quiet for a few moments, processing the slave's accusation. He had no doubt that it could be true, those Jews were murderers and scoundrels. He also believed other Jews in the town were most likely involved. Theobold knew that Henri had come seeking his assistance, his guards and his influence, without which he could never muster the resources to pursue justice and vengeance against that Jew and perhaps others as well. Theobold correctly understood that Henri arrived so hastily because Henri saw this episode as an excellent opportunity to ingratiate himself with the populace and position himself for greater power. While Theobold cared little for the Jews, he did not want them killed for their crimes, since it would remove for all time the one saving grace, that one prize which made their existence worthwhile. Money. Theobold realized the slave's story could provide an ideal opportunity to extract a huge ransom from the Jews, allow them to remain alive despite the crime by forcing them to pay for it. Theobold envisioned levying a sort of tax on their souls, to purge them for the murder of a Christian youth! Theobold knew he could demand outrageous sums, far more than the Jews could afford, and wait for them to beg or sink into debt to redeem their very lives. With any luck the Jews of Blois would spiral into bankruptcy and despair and depart Blois dejected and humiliated. That would be far more satisfying than demanding their lives at the stake. Who would benefit from that?

Theobold knew Henri would not agree to that: He wanted revenge, he wanted justice and he wanted the king to know that the Jewish criminals were vanquished by him and his efforts. Theobold, though, was adamant. The more he thought of the financial possibilities, the less inclined he was to aid Henri in condemning the Jews. Theobold knew that he could not openly refuse Henri, he could not withhold his assistance in solving a gruesome murder. He would have to appear to agree with Henri, lead him to believe he would help him in punishing the Jews and restoring French honor. He would play his part, rally the local populace, dispatch soldiers and minimally harass the Jews. Then at the last moment, he would snatch the victory from Henri, negotiate a deal with the Jews and reap untold financial gain. Theobold understood that Henri would have to believe he was his ally all along or he might turn to other lords for assistance, possibly even to the king himself. Theobold could not give Henri any reason to believe he did not wholeheartedly agree with his plans for the Jews of Blois. Theobold decided he would rouse Henri into a frenzy of hatred and disgust. He would plot with Henri and scheme at punishing the Jews of Blois. He would evoke images of the Jews as evil men and rally Henri to the only sensible conclusion.

Theobold was pleased with his plot and could not think of any reason it would not succeed. He dreamed of the wealth this matter would bring him and remembered that Henri was waiting for a response. Theobold did not want to disappoint him.

His ploy was about to begin.

Theobold rose and then launched into what sounded like a tirade. "Yes, I have heard that a Christian family nearby recently went into mourning over their young son who had been missing and was presumed dead. The boy's disappearance raised concerns wild animals were once again threatening the area. Now the mystery is solved. The boy was not attacked by animals. He was abducted and killed by Jews! This Jewish menace has now far exceeded any tolerance we must have for them. We will not suffer this criminal activity!!" Theobold shouted as he raised his fist in the air. While waving his hand back and forth, he continued, "I heard about an incident that happened in Norwich, England about thirty years ago, when the Jews there used the blood of a Christian boy. It seems that these vile practices have now spread to this part of Europe! I do not want Jews anywhere to ever think they can murder our children and use their blood in their rituals. I will deal swiftly and cruelly with all Jews who are found to have acted in this fashion! Make no mistake, make no mistake, the Jews will suffer for this unspeakable offense."

Theobold was certain that his harangue would satisfy Henri, and for a moment he even believed it himself. He was aware that knowledge of the venom and rancor he just displayed would surely reach the Jewish community and could ultimately translate into an even larger ransom.

So far his plan was working.

Henri readily agreed with Theobold's conclusions and requested permission to be an integral part of any procedure which condemned the Jews.

Theobold answered in the affirmative, bade Henri farewell and told him that the matter would be dealt with as soon as Easter concluded. He ended the meeting by informing Henri that he and his servant had done a great service to the Christians of France.

While returning home Henri reflected on the endeavor he would soon be undertaking. He thought of Yitzchak and the rest of the Jews. True, Philippe swore he saw the dead child, but what purpose would be served by drinking a child's blood or mixing it with other foods? He heard that the Jews were bloodthirsty but what did that mean? He recalled the story he was taught as a youth about a Greek man who was fattened at the Temple in Jerusalem in preparation for human sacrifice. Antiochus, the Greek ruler, became aware of that and investigated thoroughly. Henri forgot what Antiochus concluded, but that story was so old and probably false, and in any event had no relevance to the Jews of France in 1171. Surely not even heathens like Jews could find blood delectable or even drinkable. Perhaps Philippe was mistaken.

Henri entertained considerable doubts.

There was a chance, thought Henri, notwithstanding his servant's assurances to the contrary, that what fell from the cloak was not a dead child, but hides, as the Jew insisted. After all, what kind of person would carry a dead child close to the bosom where the pungent odor would make traveling so uncomfortable? And carrying hides there to protect them from bandits was logical, it made perfect sense.

Surely there were enough holes in the story that would force anyone honestly investigating the matter to conclude that the Jew at the river and the rest of the Jews were innocent. Henri knew that would be disastrous to his future. No doubt he would never gain the power and authority he desperately craved and he would likely be stripped of his present sphere of influence. He would always be remembered for his cruel and vicious unfounded attack on the Jews. Henri suddenly realized he had to put a stop to this ludicrous escapade, retain his stature in the eyes of the public.

No, he could not allow this quest to continue. He would have to prevent Philippe from testifying about what he witnessed. Without his testimony there could be no determination of guilt. Henri concluded that he would contrive a reason to have Philippe sent to Rome, on some urgent matter where he would be gone for at least two years. His absence would ensure that any interest in this matter would die down and Henri could retain his honorable reputation and his continuous pursuit of greater patronage and honor.

Philippe, who had been walking quietly behind his master, was likewise deep in thought. "Master, I have been wondering, do you suppose that the evil Jews who murder children and use their blood find it tasty? Their evil intentions cannot be denied, but perhaps they are merely fulfilling devilish urges which compel them to act in this corrupt way?"

Henri nodded his head and shrugged his shoulder in doubt. Philippe said he would ask the local priest in the morning.

Henri was bothered by Philippe's question. What was the nature of the Jew? Was he constrained to act this way by unknown forces or did he enjoy it? His mind started to race.

The Jew is different and cannot be judged by conventional behavior, his urges are peculiar, his lusts irregular.

Of course the Jew murdered the child! There can be no question, as Philippe correctly noted, of a Jew's evil.

Philippe's question started to dispel Henri's doubts.

The story made little sense but it further reinforced the strangeness of the Jew, which only supported his guilt!

That any good Christian would never drink blood merely highlighted the Jew's very disturbing actions.

Yes, the Jew had committed this crime. The holes in the story which he previously entertained were all part of the Jew's deception, and he had almost fallen prey to his cunning! Henri saw the situation clearly now and inwardly thanked Philippe for clarifying his earlier indecision.

Henri told Philippe that he was not sure about the true nature of the Jew and would accompany him to the priest. The guilt of the Jew, Yitzchak, concluded Henri, could not be denied.

As master and slave continued on, Henri resolved to pursue this case with increased determination.

Indeed, master and slave were reflections of one another.

4

The couple walked in silence. They hurried through the dark streets, on their way to Rabbi Shimon. They passed Gedaliah's home and Yitzchak promised himself that if by some miracle he could survive the ordeal he would enter into a partnership with him.

They reached Rabbi Shimon's house and Yitzchak knocked softly.

No response.

Their knocking grew louder and louder until finally the rabbi's son, Gavriel, awoke. Members of the community had visited at night, but not recently. Who was there? Gavriel left his bed, ran to the door and opened it.

It was Yitzchak and his wife, Tamar. What problem did they have that could not wait until the morning?

Gavriel stood at the entrance, reluctant to invite them inside. He was hoping they would sense his hesitation and postpone the visit until morning. Tamar stood back from the doorway while Yitzchak, oblivious to Gavriel's hesitation, asked him to wake his father. Gavriel was upset by the request. He did not want to disturb his father's much needed rest unless it was absolutely necessary and he doubted whether their concerns were that important.

Gavriel responded, "I am sure you are aware that he has not been feeling well lately and waking him now will only further delay his recovery, but if it is an emergency and the matter must be dealt with immediately then I will wake him."

Yitzchak nodded. "Thank you," he whispered.

Gavriel showed them in, lit a wick in his father's study and asked them to wait. By now, Rabbi Shimon had heard the commotion, so he dressed and entered the study. He thanked Gavriel for attending to their midnight guests. Rabbi Shimon bade Gavriel return to sleep and Gavriel readily agreed. As Gavriel left the study, Rabbi Shimon closed the door behind him.

"Greetings, Yitzchak and Tamar," said Rabbi Shimon, half asleep. What brings you to my study at this hour of the night?"

Rabbi Shimon hobbled to his table, moved the stack of the books he had used on the Sabbath and sat down. He motioned for Yitzchak to begin. "I am not very good at telling stories, Rabbi Shimon, but a terrible thing happened earlier today at the River Loire. While on my way home I stopped to rest there and water my horse. I led the horse to the brook and as I bent over to drink, some hides I was carrying in my cloak fell out and floated away."

Rabbi Shimon interrupted, "Why were you carrying hides in your cloak?"

"Because travelers are often robbed on the way home. The thieves are usually in a hurry so they just grab whatever bags are attached to the saddle and run off. I therefore carried the most expensive materials as well as money inside my cloak."

The rabbi nodded and Yitzchak continued, "A Christian slave was also watering his horse nearby and the splash of the hides as they fell into the river startled the horses. The slave's horse shied away from the riverbank, which piqued the interest of the slave. He looked up and saw the hides floating downriver. He stood motionless for a few moments, then he accused me of discarding the body of a dead Christian child, which he claimed I had drained of its blood. I initially believed that he was mocking me but I then realized his accusation was serious. I insisted that what fell in the river was nothing more than hides I recently purchased in Paris but he refused to believe me. He kept repeating that I had murdered a Christian child. He told me that he would inform his master, Prince Henri, about my crime and his master would see to it that I am punished appropriately. Rabbi, you must help me!"

Yitzchak lost his composure and started to cry.

Rabbi Shimon sat in disbelief, absorbing the horrid tale Yitzchak had just related. There were so many questions that needed answering. Was the slave serious? Would a person of power and authority such as Prince Henri expend time and energy investigating the ludicrous accusation of an illiterate slave? And could anything be done to help Yitzchak?

Rabbi Shimon sat quite still, gripped by a sense of helplessness and dread as he watched the terrified couple seek to comfort themselves as they waited for him to respond.

Gavriel stood trembling on the other side of the study door. He had heard every word of the story.

Gavriel had always known there were Jew-haters in the world, everyone knew that, but he never fathomed the depths to which that hatred descended. He now understood that the slave's hatred was so venal, so irrational, that there was nothing Yitzchak could have said, no proof he could have produced which would have made the slave acknowledge he was mistaken. Gavriel perceived that the slave's mere accusation was sufficient evidence to judge Yitzchak guilty and that if the slave carried out his plans as promised, Yitzchak was in deep trouble. The tale opened Gavriel's youthful eyes and mind to a world full of scheming and loathing that he would spend a lifetime desperately trying to escape.

He returned to his bed trembling, suddenly aware of the horrors of the world that surrounded him.

Rabbi Shimon remained quiet. He knew Prince Henri and knew he was gullible enough to be swayed by this nonsense and lured by thoughts of prestige. He also knew there was one thing that could spare Yitzchak's life, one way for Yitzchak to escape harm.

Money.

If Yitzchak could raise enough money he could probably pay off Prince Henri, subdue his lusts with gold and riches. But where would Yitzchak, a simple garment merchant, find the enormous sums that would be needed to buy his freedom? Rabbi Shimon wondered whether the entire town could raise the funds needed to save Yitzchak.

Rabbi Shimon looked up, rose from his chair and moved toward the couple.

"The man at the river was a slave of Prince Henri, a local lord and notorious Jew-hater. He will undoubtedly welcome his slave's accusation but he is too cowardly and afraid to act without the approval of the regional authorities. I am certain that he will talk to Count Theobold and request his assistance and guidance in bringing you to justice. If there is any chance at all to save you from the wrath of Prince Henri you must intercede with Theobold; he wields the true power in this region."

"Rabbi Shimon, will you help me?"

Rabbi Shimon heard the fear in Yitzchak's voice and saw the couple before him devoid of hope or answers. He lowered his head in silence.

This was the most important problem anybody from the community had ever presented to him. This was not something as trivial as Leah's complaint, which he knew he could resolve with a heartfelt sermon coupled with strategic glances at various members of the synagogue, or other petty problems, which he had easily handled over the years. This was not even on par with the case of Reuven the dye merchant. This far exceeded his skill and capability as a rabbi. Perhaps years ago, when he was more vigorous and dynamic, he could have done something to help a congregant with a similar problem. But now he was tired and weak and lacked the mental and physical stamina that he knew successful intervention required. This problem needed an inordinate amount of talent and courage, both of which he no longer possessed. He would fail if he tried.

How could he tell this to them?

How could he let them down?

But if he did not help, who would? He was Yitzchak's only chance for survival. How could he turn his back on them just because he was weak?

No! He would muster his last remaining strength, prepare himself this one last time to try and save his poor unfortunate children. He had to. In resuming his authority as the leader of the community just the other day, he had invoked Moses, the greatest of all Jewish leaders. He would emulate him, act like him, never tiring and never conceding defeat. He would pray for an audience with Theobold and convince him that Yitzchak was innocent. He would review the evidence with him, point to the slave's ignorance and hatred and highlight the sheer absurdity of the accusation. Rabbi Shimon would insist the slave was mistaken and would resolutely remain there until Theobold would concur. It would not be easy. Theobold was powerful and determined, and would have to be bribed, but Rabbi Shimon committed himself to the cause of Yitzchak. He lifted his head.

"Yes, Yitzchak and Tamar, I will help you. I will try to arrange a meeting with Theobold, but I must warn you that Theobold will never entertain assisting you without receiving a very substantial bribe. Do not misunderstand me, Theobold is no lover of Jews but he is more pragmatic than Henri and for the right price will allow this entire matter to be forgotten. I am aware you do not have nearly enough money to satisfy Theobold's greed, but that is the key to your survival. Do you know of any way the money could be raised?"

The couple nodded in unison. Yitzchak had a long-time friend, Rabbi Baruch, who was considerably wealthy. In fact, he would be arriving the next day for the Passover holiday.

"Is he the renowned Baruch the book collector? I have heard of him and his efforts to replace the many books lost during the Crusades. He is a saintly and caring man. Very well then. If he would be willing to pay the bribe to Theobold then I am confident you will suffer no harm. I also think you should not mention any of this to him. I think Rabbi Baruch would be more willing to help you if I presented the problem to him as a communal leader, and stressed the urgency of his support," said Rabbi Shimon with a glimmer of hope. "I will find an opportune moment to raise this matter with him, sometime immediately after Passover. In the meanwhile, there is nothing more we can do at this time. Why don't you return home, try to get some sleep and pray earnestly for a favorable resolution. I will visit you in the morning."

Tamar and Yitzchak approached the rabbi, thanked him for his help and quietly went home.

They could not sleep for the remainder of the night, too worried about the menace that loomed over them. They passed the time in the dark, preparing for Passover, waiting for the sun to rise and with it, some better news. Rabbi Baruch was a kind and generous man, and a dear friend. Surely he would bribe Theobold and end this horrible situation.

Rabbi Shimon too could not sleep. He had promised to help and by doing so dedicated himself to their cause no matter the consequences.

He returned to his seat behind his desk and reviewed Yitzchak's options. The best that he could hope for was for his wealthy friend to agree to expend enormous sums of money to bribe Theobold and deliver Yitzchak from the wrath of Henri. That venture would surely financially ruin Rabbi Baruch, but Yitzchak's life would be spared. Even this would prove difficult to accomplish: Theobold would maintain a firm stance in favor of the slave's accusation and Rabbi Shimon would have to engage in much cajoling and negotiations to persuade Theobold to accept the bribe. But Rabbi Shimon was confident that if the amount offered was truly significant then ultimately Theobold would agree to the bribe and this whole unfortunate incident would quickly disappear.

Rabbi Shimon knew there was a chance Theobold would reject any bribe no matter how high the offer, that he would stand by the slave's accusation and assist in Henri's pursuit of justice and revenge. If that were to happen then there was virtually no hope for Yitzchak. He would be burned at the stake.

A horrific thought.

Rabbi Shimon shuddered for a moment. Was that the worst that was in store for the Jews of Blois?

In Norwich, England, many Jews were placed on trial and lost their lives following a similar accusation leveled against one Jew.

Could the same thing happen here? Could Theobold put all the townspeople on trial for the crime charged against Yitzchak?

Would Theobold and Henri dare test the limits of their power in so brazen a fashion? Could their hatred and contempt for the Jews allow them to carry out such an outlandish plot? Were they so cruel? Rabbi Shimon dreaded to think the situation could ever descend to such unsavory depths and remained awake, praying and hoping.

But thoughts of Norwich never strayed too far from his heart.

Gavriel lay awake, replaying the hate-filled story he had overheard. Gavriel was no longer a child, no longer filled with that brimming optimism, that belief that anything is possible, that unbridled passion to conquer the world. He lay in bed exposed to the world's cruelty, aware for the first time that he was despised and degraded and that his very survival depended on the whim and caprice of those who hated him. Gavriel wondered how he could alleviate the suffering of his brothers, how he could lessen the pain, soften the blows that he knew were destined to fall. He realized then that like his father, he would serve his people, guide them, teach them and try as best he could to protect them. He was still unsure what role of leadership he would undertake, but he was determined to rise above the crowd, impart meaning and encouragement to them and provide inspiration to the Yitzchaks of the future. He would dedicate his life to helping his people, who often seemed so helpless.

He swore he would do it.

His life had changed.

The next afternoon Rabbi Baruch arrived. The appearance of his old and dear friend lifted Yitzchak's spirits and he went outside to welcome him. Rabbi Baruch was a tall, distinguished man dressed in finely tailored clothes. His coach, which was drawn by four horses, was piled with many books, more than most of the townspeople had seen in their entire lives.

Rabbi Baruch descended and was pleased to see Yitzchak already waiting for him. "Welcome, Rabbi Baruch," said Yitzchak cheerily. "We have been looking forward to your arrival since Hanukkah, when you wrote that you would be spending Passover here. How was your journey? You must be tired. Please, allow me to show you to your room where you may rest awhile."

"I am feeling fine," answered Rabbi Baruch, happy to be out of the wagon. " It is good to see you, Yitzchak. I have been looking forward to this for quite some time. Is there any way I can be of assistance before I take a rest?"

"No, Rabbi Baruch, Tamar and I would never allow our guests to help around the house. Rest and recover from the journey. If you like I will introduce you to our rabbi, Rabbi Shimon. I am sure you and he would find much to talk about."

"I would be delighted to meet with him, but first I would like to rest awhile, refresh myself and then make his acquaintance."

"All right, let me show you to your room." Yitzchak motioned for Rabbi Baruch to follow him, which he did obligingly.

The room was modestly decorated, and Rabbi Baruch immediately felt at home. He was glad to be with friends. Rabbi Baruch had no family and instantly regretted not visiting sooner. He did have many students and apprentices but he had never forged a warm relationship with any of them and never felt comfortable in their homes. He removed his shoes and laid down anticipating a pleasant and relaxing holiday. He quickly fell asleep.

Yitzchak and Tamar remained in the kitchen preparing for the holiday. Yitzchak grew increasingly anxious knowing he would have to wait until after the holiday to discover whether Rabbi Baruch had the means and the desire to help him. He did not believe he could wait that long. "Tamar, do you think Rabbi Shimon will confide in Rabbi Baruch anytime soon? I cannot stand all the waiting and doubt! I feel my future depends on the generosity of our dear friend. He is the next room and I cannot even speak to him!" Yitzchak began pacing.

"Yitzchak, Rabbi Shimon already told us that he will not say any-thing to Rabbi Baruch until Passover has ended, and I agree with him. Why should Rabbi Baruch be burdened during this most joyous holi-day when no action will be taken anyway? Why cloud his mind and burden his conscience just to calm your own spirits? I know it is weighing heavily on your mind. It concerns me greatly as well, and I too did not sleep last night. But we must keep our pain to ourselves and confide in each other to maintain our spirits. We still have an obligation to enjoy the holiday with our family and more importantly to try and make the children understand the significance of Passover. I know it is difficult but we can do it together. Together."

Yitzchak realized she was right, he had a commitment to his family which could not be ignored. He also understood that it was selfish of him to impose his needs on Rabbi Baruch before Passover was over. He promised himself he would maintain his composure, conceal his tor-ment and treat Rabbi Baruch with the honor and dignity he deserved.

Yitzchak, though, returned once again to the events at the river. He began to view the entire episode as a test, to examine his resolve, to probe and to prove his faith and dedication to G-d. At the river, Yitzchak had wondered why he had been chosen, what wrongs he had committed to deserve this terrible challenge. He had questioned G-d's wisdom and the seeming unfairness of his predicament. Yet the very desperation of the situation had helped him come to the realiza-tion that he needed to place his fate in G-d's hands, to trust G-d's mercy and to hope that the matter would be concluded favorably. He did not want to fail this test and remain mired in the frailty of his own inadequacies. He refused to admit that he feared defeat by exhibiting anger or indifference toward the Almighty. He knew that he must re-main committed to his faith despite this challenge he now faced. It would not be easy, his future seemed very grim indeed, but he was certain that was the key to his survival. Yitzchak was optimistic that disaster could be diverted.

He waited for Rabbi Baruch.

5

"**I**t is an honor to meet you," said Rabbi Shimon as he extended his hand. "I have heard so much about you, especially about your collection of books. Here in Blois we have very few books: some volumes of the Talmud, a few copies of the Prophets and several Bibles," proclaimed Rabbi Shimon sadly. "You undoubtedly have more books in your coach than we have here in the entire town!"

"It is a pleasure to meet you as well," answered Rabbi Baruch, returning the handshake. "And yes, I do own many books; I have been collecting them most of my life. I began as soon as I was old enough to understand the damage that had been wrought during the Crusades, not just to Jewish life but to Jewish heritage as well. The Crusaders marauded through towns, pillaging and burning at will, destroying Torahs, books and other religious items. I met countless Jews starved for knowledge, but they had no books from which to learn. I feared that if the situation was not rectified all could be lost! I then began my life-long pursuit, hunting for existing books and even writing as many as I and my apprentices could copy, to try to restore some of the damage."

"That is very admirable," answered Rabbi Shimon.

Rabbi Baruch continued, "But I realized a few years ago that I had been spending so much of my time and energy collecting and copying books that I had been ignoring the writing of Torah scrolls! I decided it was time to stop copying the books and to spend the next few years training young men in the art of writing scrolls. My students and I have written numerous Torahs but we still have not been able to replace all that have been destroyed. We have also written mezuzahs, tefillin and Scrolls of Esther. This shall be my legacy, Torah scrolls, books, mezuzahs and tefillin for the coming generations to utilize and treasure." Then Rabbi Baruch asked, "I am always looking for young men interested in being apprenticed to me. Do you know anyone who would be a good candidate to become a scribe?"

Rabbi Shimon immediately thought of his son. He had never really given much consideration to Gavriel's future; he had assumed he would also become a rabbi. But Rabbi Baruch's proposal intrigued him. It could provide a way for Gavriel to serve his people without the accompanying burdens and hardships that leaders always faced and, as Rabbi Baruch had noted, it could help insure Jewish survival.

"Well, I do have a fifteen-year-old son," answered Rabbi Baruch. "He might be interested in learning that trade."

"I would very much like to meet him and speak with him about it personally."

Rabbi Shimon continued to converse with Rabbi Baruch, to learn more about this fascinating man and to try to gauge whether he would assist Yitzchak.

Yitzchak had been standing beside the men and waited patiently as they talked. He had promised himself to try and maintain feelings of happiness and optimism during the holiday but wished that Rabbi Shimon would mention his problem and immediately ascertain whether Rabbi Baruch would help him. Yitzchak even considered informing Rabbi Baruch himself. He knew, though, that Tamar was correct and it would be improper to burden Rabbi Baruch during the holiday simply to placate his own unease, and he restrained himself. He reminded himself that his ordeal was designed to prove his dedication to the Almighty and that the Almighty would protect him.

Rabbi Shimon discovered that Rabbi Baruch was a kind and generous man and was convinced he would assist Yitzchak. He too considered bringing up the topic now, assured of Rabbi Baruch's response, but understood that prudence and courtesy demanded waiting until after Passover.

Rabbi Shimon sensed it was time to end the conversation and allow Yitzchak and Rabbi Baruch to return home. "I am sure that you and Yitzchak have much to do before the holiday," remarked Rabbi Shimon. "Why don't you and Yitzchak go back home where I am certain Tamar is waiting with a long list of last minute preparations! We shall talk more over the holiday and I shall introduce you to my son, Gavriel."

"Very well, Rabbi Shimon. It was wonderful meeting with you and I am very anxious to meet Gavriel. Until then, good day, and if I do not see you until tomorrow, enjoy the Passover!"

Yitzchak, too, wished the rabbi well and walked back to the house with Rabbi Baruch, who said, "Rabbi Shimon seems knowledgeable and kind. You are fortunate he is the leader of this town."

"We are very lucky, Rabbi Baruch, he is the most caring man I know."

Rabbi Baruch sensed that Yitzchak was apprehensive and agitated but attributed it to the holiday preparations.

Passover.

The one night when all Jews, rich and poor alike, play the roles of kings and beggars. Identifying with exile, reliving the freedom of the past, longing for the freedom of the future. Eating unusual foods to recall suffering and liberty. Dual rites of poverty and bounty commemorating the ebb and flow of the Jewish people. A holiday shrouded in ritual, sacred meaning and custom. Above all, yearning to return to the holy land of Israel in the service of G-d and to rekindle the flame of autonomy and sovereignty extinguished so long ago.

Passover.

Everyone in Blois was exhausted but eager to enjoy the special night. The townspeople had been looking forward to this night for an entire year. Waiting until their children were just old enough to understand its significance and importance. Waiting to look into the wide eyes of their curious and innocent children and relate to them the story of Passover, the story that stretches far across the annals of time and memory.

Yitzchak's children were particularly delighted. Their favorite "uncle," Rabbi Baruch, would be joining them. Rabbi Baruch had never spent a significant amount of time with Yitzchak and the family and this first occasion was truly a treat for the children. Devorah, sporting her new green scarf, sat in a corner reviewing the "Four Questions" she would later ask her father. The boys were busy helping Tamar with the last minute preparations. Yitzchak quickly assisted the boys and in a short while the home was ready for the holiday.

Night soon fell and the men went to the synagogue for evening services. Following the prayers, the congregants rushed home to begin the *seder*. Rabbi Shimon moved toward Yitzchak, took his hand, held it to his heart and whispered, "I am praying for you."

"Thank you, Rabbi Shimon. Your caring and concern mean a great deal to me."

Rabbi Baruch, standing behind Yitzchak, found this exchange puzzling but said nothing. He greeted the Rabbi, then walked home with Yitzchak in silence.

Gavriel and his father also walked home quietly, both thinking about Yitzchak.

As much as Yitzchak tried to fulfill the pledge he made to himself and Tamar, he found himself sinking deeper and deeper into despair. Yitzchak was very subdued, almost lifeless, and though the children were too caught up in the excitement to notice, Rabbi Baruch observed Tamar gaze at her husband sorrowfully and sigh softly, and he knew something was wrong.

The hours passed and the *seder* progressed. Yitzchak remained still while he pondered the meaning of many of the customs he had performed his entire life without ever truly thinking about them. He drank wine to emulate royalty but saw his life dangling from the rope of a French nobleman charging him with mixing blood with this very wine. He reclined in the manner of kings but felt more like a slave than Philippe, his accuser. He sang of redemption and G-d's endless bounty but felt frightened and in exile. He displayed his finest tableware and dressed in his best clothes, but perceived himself as a man already sentenced.

How did the Jews of Norwich, the communities during the Crusades or other persecuted Jews find the courage to act like royalty, behave with dignity and self respect, when death and despair encircled and engulfed them? How were they able to praise G-d in song and prayer when all they experienced was misery and persecution? How could Yitzchak zealously pretend he was of royal stock, even for one night, when he was being treated like a common criminal?

True, righteous men find the ability to worship and trust G-d in all circumstances but were all the Jews killed at Norwich or during the Crusades so righteous? How did the ordinary and common Jew, like Yitzchak, muster the strength to withstand hate's terrible storm with song and praise?

Is any Jew truly ordinary?

Or does every Jewish soul share that spark of sacrifice, that innate ability to endure the wrath of the enemy, to rise above depression and death and to sing and glorify G-d in the most dire of situations?

Yitzchak wondered.

He had no answers.

The *seder* proceeded uneventfully and quickly. There were no stories to stimulate the children, no legends of grandeur to marvel at with renewed faith and love. The only time Yitzchak even raised his voice was when he recited, "Pour out thy wrath upon the nations," which he uttered in a shrill, loud tone, practically in tears. Rabbi Baruch instinctively knew something had happened to Yitzchak, problems with finances, no doubt. He did not say anything as long as the children were awake.

The *seder* concluded and after much cajoling the children were sent off to bed. After the table had been cleared Rabbi Baruch looked at

Yitzchak. "What is the matter, Yitzchak? You have been acting very unusual today. Is everything all right?"

Yitzchak pondered whether he should just tell Rabbi Baruch now, disregard Rabbi Shimon and Tamar and finally confront Rabbi Baruch with his gnawing dilemma. He stole a glance and noticed that Tamar looked equally confused. He knew he had undertaken not to indulge in self-pity or sorrow or regret, but staring into the eyes of the only man who could rescue him caused his fears to resurface.

Yitzchak realized that he would never be able to sustain the facade throughout the entire holiday and lamented that he lacked the faith to do so. He also apologized to Rabbi Baruch for placing such a monumental burden on him during the most festive time of the year.

Yitzchak told Rabbi Baruch everything that transpired at the river only a few days ago. Rabbi Baruch sat listening to his friend's bitter tale. When Yitzchak finished, the two men embraced. Rabbi Baruch looked at Yitzchak and remarked, "I think Rabbi Shimon is correct with regard to the slave and his master, Prince Henri, and also concerning Theobold. He wields the real power in this region and it is to him we must turn!"

"Will you help me, Rabbi Baruch?" cried Yitzchak.

Rabbi Baruch now understood that Rabbi Shimon was aware of the situation and had afforded Yitzchak some encouragement following the prayer services. He also knew that he was Yitzchak's only hope. "Yes, Yitzchak, of course I will help you."

"Thank you, Rabbi Baruch. Oh, how I thank you; you have given me hope."

"Here is the way I view the situation," continued Rabbi Baruch. "I am certain that Theobold is aware the accusation is entirely unfounded. But he is shrewd and clever and will never admit the charges are baseless. He will portray you as a guilty and evil man, and will probably initiate some sort of tribunal to question you and pass judgment upon you. But do not worry, it will all be a ruse, a trick to make others believe you deserve to be killed. At some point, somehow, he will make us aware that he will accept a ransom, a payment for your life. When that moment arrives, I shall be there and I shall offer him enough money to secure your freedom. Trust me, Yitzchak, I have dealt with him in the past. Theobold craves money and waits for these very situations, where he can exploit people like you and watch as he forces them into debt and a life of squalor to pay for their existence. Theobold knows me and although he hates me, he will trust that any amount of money I offer will be forthcoming. If he becomes aware of my presence here in Blois, I am sure the ransom amount will be truly high indeed, but I will be ready for him. Do not worry, Yitzchak, he will most likely frighten you and intimidate you and threaten you with all forms of tortures and interrogations, but he only craves money, not your Jewish blood." He then ended in an uplifting tone, "I understand that you are terrified by what transpired and that you believe you are in very grave danger, but I really do not think there is much to be concerned about. I believe that we should all enjoy the holiday and not pay any mind to Theobold or Henri or the slave at the river. Forget about them and concentrate on enjoying this wonderful holiday! In all likelihood this crisis will be resolved quickly and painlessly."

Yitzchak felt relieved, now that he knew that Rabbi Baruch would help him. He was also comforted by the fact that Rabbi Shimon and Rabbi Baruch had both assessed the situation and reached the same conclusion. He was grateful to Rabbi Baruch and was overjoyed that the news did not seem to dampen his spirits at all.

"When do you think Henri and Theobold will begin this tribunal you mentioned?" asked Yitzchak.

"They probably will wait until after Easter has passed, and as I said before, we can enjoy Passover without fear or worry."

Rabbi Baruch's assurances sounded very convincing and almost led Yitzchak to expect an easy solution to his dilemma. But something was still nagging him, still tormenting him. Rabbi Baruch sounded too optimistic, too sure that he could so easily bribe Theobold and

Henri to forget the crime Yitzchak was accused of committing. Yitzchak recalled the slave's burning hatred and was not convinced that his survival would be as easy and effortless as Rabbi Baruch predicted. Something kept telling him that it would be far more complicated and tenuous, if he could be saved at all.

Yitzchak went to sleep and did something he had never done before. Although it was Passover night, he recited the nightly prayers of protection and locked the door.

6

Theobold looked out the window and watched Prince Henri and Philippe walk down the long path which led away from the castle as they headed home. Theobold liked Henri, a good Christian and a fine nobleman. But Henri was a simple man, too caught up in revenge and vindication. Where would that get him? He failed to recognize that this was a perfect opportunity to reap untold fortune, to financially ruin all the Jews of Blois and thereby force them to abandon their homes and flee. Never before had Theobold had the good fortune to demand the ransom of an entire town and amass so much wealth so quickly! The prospect was so tantalizing that Theobold felt happy, almost giddy. He wondered whether Henri would ever develop the appreciation for wealth and luxury, and he scorned Henri's desperate strivings for prestige as petty and juvenile.

Theobold could no longer distinguish their shapes and moved from the window. He had been biding his time, waiting many years for this. With so much wealth he could begin commissioning his own army and successfully position himself to become the next king of France! He would let nothing stand in his way, certainly not Henri's crusade to exact punishment on the Jews.

Theobold paused.

Perhaps Henri was correct, perhaps the magnitude of this crime demanded a different sort of solution, one that would demand the death of any Jews found guilty of murdering the child.

Theobold conceded that Christian honor and French pride were surely more important than his selfish desires for financial gain. Theobold had just been informed of an unspeakable crime committed by a Jew and no doubt other Jews as well. Did this crime not demand the punishments sought by Henri? This time the Jews had brazenly engaged in bizarre religious rituals using the blood of that unfortunate murdered child. They committed an unthinkable sacrilege upon all the Christians of France. Could Theobold treat that lightly and demand nothing more than a ransom? True, Theobold had accepted ransoms many times before for all sorts of petty and meaningless offenses, but this was not meaningless. This was a fight for the very soul of France! A fight Theobold did not wish to lose! Theobold found himself confused. He knew he would never encounter an opportunity to seize this much wealth but felt ashamed he was compromising the honor of France. Theobold wished the king had already expelled the Jews, thus sparing him his dilemma. But where could they have gone where they would be treated any differently?

Theobold laughed.

Theobold's wife, Alix, entered. Like Theobold she was overly plump and had small, shifty eyes. She spent her days roaming the palace hallways hoping to greet petitioners, foreign officials and Church dignitaries. Her father, King Louis VII of France, had arranged her marriage to Theobold when they were both young and she never let Theobold forget it. Over the years she grew jealous of Theobold as his rise in authority diminished her importance as the king's daughter. She continued to grasp at the reins of power by constantly reminding him that she was born of royal stock and would always support her father the king, even at Theobold's expense. Theobold despised her shallow attempts at dignity and found her desperate references to her father immature and of no consequence.

About the only thing they had in common was their lust for money and possessions.

What did she want now?

"Why didn't you inform me that Henri was here? You know how I adore entertaining guests!" said Alix, genuinely upset that she had missed Henri's company.

Theobold had purposely not summoned Alix, otherwise Henri's visit would have lasted all day. "Henri did not come for a social visit. He came to inform me of a grave crime which his servant testified was committed by a Jew," he answered curtly.

Alix's eyes lit with curiosity, "What crime?"

"His servant was at the River Loire and observed a Jew from Blois throw a dead Christian child into the river. The child was white, pale, almost ghostly, drained of its blood. He confronted the Jew about it and of course the Jew denied it."

Alix motioned for Theobold to continue. Her interest in the story seemed exaggerated. What was her concern? Theobold related the rest of the story, then added, "I told Henri that I would convene a tribunal and punish any of the Jews found guilty of this crime. You are aware that this is an opportunity to force a ransom on the Jews by making them pay for their actions," reasoned Theobold.

"Yes, I am aware, and I am excited by how much wealth we can demand from the Jews. But Theobold, if the slave's story is accurate then we are dealing with a gruesome murder, typical anti-Christian Jewish behavior. I wonder whether we should forfeit any ransoms and wealth and rather ally ourselves with Henri to punish those villains?" Theobold had still not resolved the dilemma that Alix now raised once again. But the more Theobold considered it, the more tempted he was to seek the ransom.

"I am aware of the seriousness of the accusation, and I believe that will only increase the amount we can demand from them. Imagine, Alix, how this one episode will enhance our lives forever! I feel for our French brethren but this ransom is too tempting to ignore."

Alix was intrigued but firm. "I am also very tempted to force a ransom upon them, but when I consider the nature of this crime something tells me it is selfish and petty. When I contemplate the loss of that poor innocent child I cannot satisfy my conscience with a ransom, no matter how great! No, Theobold, not this time."

Theobold ignored Alix's appeal and remained convinced he too would be vouchsafing the honor of all French Christians. "I also want to avenge the death of that child, Alix, and forcing the Jews to become beggars and paupers because of what they have done to that child is sufficient punishment for me!"

Alix nodded and walked off. It was an interesting problem, she thought. Was Theobold serious? Was reducing the Jews to poverty a satisfactory punishment for murder? Or did Theobold simply crave money more than justice and pride?

Did she?

Alix could not resolve the dilemma.

At the door she quickly turned and headed back toward Theobold. "How do you plan to initiate an exchange with the Jews?"

That was an odd question, what did she have in mind?

"Well," responded Theobold, "I have not given it that much thought, but I will probably first throw the entire town into prison for a while, frighten them and lead them to believe they are in very grave danger. That always helps to raise the stakes. After a few weeks I will send one of the Jews from here, probably Abraham, with instructions about how much ransom will be required for their freedom."

Alix nodded. She understood, but one thing still bothered her. "What about Pulcelina?"

Theobold turned white. So that was the point of all these questions.

Pulcelina was an aristocratic Jewish woman who lived in Blois. Theobold first met her many years earlier when her husband, Aaron, petitioned Theobold for permission to engage in money lending. Of course permission was not needed but Aaron sensed it would be best if he first consulted with Theobold, to make him feel important and in charge. Theobold was not very powerful then and the respect

Aaron displayed toward him impressed him greatly. Theobold would have reduced his usual twenty percent fee to ten percent but waived it entirely for Pulcelina's sake. Theobold and Aaron forged an important relationship, one that greatly benefited the Jewish community, since Aaron's influence convinced Theobold not to meddle in their affairs. Theobold was truly affected by Aaron's death a few years later.

Since that first meeting between Theobold and Aaron, Theobold had treated Pulcelina with esteem and it aggravated Alix terribly. When Aaron died, Alix went so far as to follow Theobold when she suspected he was up to no good. Of course nothing improper ever happened. Pulcelina ignored Theobold entirely. Yet Theobold continued to extend her privileges. He ordered all tax collectors to bypass her home and demanded that the local lords, including Henri, refrain from harassing or intimidating her. This caused friction between Henri, who grew to despise Pulcelina, and Theobold. Theobold did not care, although Pulcelina was completely inattentive to his favoritism. Theobold was too conceited to notice. Time and again Theobold showered Pulcelina with all manner of special gifts. Pulcelina consistently dismissed him and he disregarded her disdain.

Alix's hatred for her only increased over time. Alix had considered murdering Pulcelina but her insane jealousy so clouded her sense of reality that she believed Theobold would kill her in return! Alix had been waiting many years to ruin Pulcelina. She pressed him again. "Will you be treating Pulcelina differently?"

Theobold paused. He admired Pulcelina but despised the rest of the Jews. He was convinced her townspeople were murderers and wished to intimidate them, punish them, but felt she was different, unique, special.

Theobold perceived a dilemma often faced by men who harbor ill will toward the Jews. Once a connection is made with one, it serves to undermine the unfounded hatred. On rare occasions, this causes the hatred to dissipate. Would Pulcelina be made to suffer along with the rest of Blois? Lock her up and treat her like a criminal? Or, perhaps spare the town for her sake. Perhaps her gratitude would result in a change of attitude. Forget about Henri, the dead child and the Jew at the Loire, and put up with more of Alix's jealousy. Should he elevate a Jew over his own wife and country?

And what of Alix's argument that it was wrong to covet the wealth of the Jews without demanding more? Theobold was not sure what to do and he concluded that he would retain his original plan, at least for now.

Theobold then turned to his wife, "Do not worry, Alix, there will be no favoritism shown to anyone." Theobold moved to the door.

"Good," replied Alix condescendingly. "I would hate for the king to learn that you were careless in dealing with Jews!"

Theobold nodded and walked off. He hated when Alix threatened him with mention of her father. He found it irritating and an indication of weakness. It bothered him that he was married to a woman who drew strength from the power and domination of others. But her father was the most powerful man in the country, and he knew he would not have achieved his present stature without the king's support, which made it all worthwhile.

In a few days Easter would be over and he would introduce his plan. He would imprison all of the Jews, but not Pulcelina, and then initiate ransom negotiations.

Theobold thought of other aspects of his plan. He knew the local residents did not particularly care for the Jews but he did not want them to think he was cruel and unjust and was mistreating the Jews for no reason.

Theobold knew he would have to convince the local populace, make them realize the Jews were being treated this way to protect them and their offspring.

He remembered the family in that nearby region that had recently lost a child. He would send several of his guards to that family, to witness their suffering and misery firsthand and convince them the boy had been kidnapped by the Jews, who killed the child, drained the body of its blood and tossed it into the river. That family was the key. If they could believe the tale then so would everyone else.

Theobold walked toward the forest as his thoughts returned to a ransom. Would it end there? Wouldn't the Jews continue in their evil practices as long as they were allowed to live? Was bankrupting them a sufficient way of teaching them that their evil would never be tolerated? Again, he was not sure.

Theobold was confident that he would resolve these inner conflicts.

In due time.

7

Two days after Passover, just as Rabbi Shimon was about to journey to Chartres to plead with Theobold, Theobold's guards entered the town of Blois and imprisoned all of its Jewish inhabitants. Except for Pulcelina. Theobold specifically ordered the guards to spare her the inconvenience and to place her under house arrest instead. Theobold had not changed his mind about her. He had never intended to imprison her, and had told Alix otherwise merely to placate her. Sensing Theobold's weakness for Pulcelina, Alix had invoked her father's name when she warned the guards not to allow Pulcelina to see Theobold when he arrived. Pulcelina remained in her home and watched as the townspeople were pushed, shoved and whipped until they were all ensconced in jail.

The jail was located at the edge of the town, near the forest. The structure was not designed as a prison: it was originally built as an assembly hall for soldiers enlisted in the Crusades. It was a large stone building consisting of one enormous room. Over the years the building had fallen into disrepair. It was quickly converted into a jail, complete with chains bolted to the walls. Straw, which served as bedding, was scattered about in haphazard fashion. No candles or torches were provided and sunlight entered the building through small windows near the ceiling. The building had no rooms or doors and provided no privacy. Escape was not a possibility, but they could move about, although each person had one foot chained. Theobold had stationed guards outside the building.

Nobody inside knew why they had been gathered to this place. Some had even forgotten the building even existed. Everyone temporarily put aside their questions and curiosity to tend to Rabbi Shimon.

Rabbi Shimon had been struck by a guard for walking too slowly, and he was visibly in pain. He told everyone that he was all right. The pain of the blow would soon pass, he reassured them, and requested some space where he could muster his composure. He knew the people were looking to him, looking up to him, anticipating that he would protect them from further harm. He could not let them see he was suffering.

After Rabbi Shimon sufficiently recovered he stood up and called everyone to gather around him.

"I want all of you to know why we have been incarcerated here. A few days before Passover, a terrible thing happened to our dear friend Yitzchak. He was watering his horse at the Loire when he dropped some hides in the water. A slave standing nearby accused him of murdering a Christian child, using its blood and discarding the body in the river."

"That's ridiculous," shouted somebody.

"Absurd," asserted another.

"There is no doubt about that, we all know the accusation is simply preposterous. It seems that the local rulers of the region have used this accusation to imprison us all," responded Rabbi Shimon calmly.

Yaakov now understood the reason for his parents' midnight trek to Rabbi Shimon's home. He wondered why his father had not confided in him.

"Why are *we all* here?" asked Nachum the baker, caressing his two-week-old baby.

Rabbi Shimon was not sure. He had conferred with Rabbi Baruch the other day and believed that only he and Yitzchak would be im-

A Promise Fulfilled / 63

prisoned. But Rabbi Shimon knew that his appearance as a strong and confident leader would be the most effective way of lifting the spirits of his confused and scared flock. He had to be ready to respond to any of their concerns and he hoped they would believe him. "I suspected they would treat all of us in this shocking and violent manner, to frighten us and to intimidate us. But no harm will come to us and we should be released in a few days." Rabbi Shimon did not directly answer the question but he effectively assuaged Nachum's fears.

Rabbi Baruch then motioned that he wished to address the townspeople. Rabbi Shimon urged Rabbi Baruch to stand by his side. "You all know Rabbi Baruch, a friend of Yitzchak and Tamar. He has been here in Blois since this whole ordeal began and he has conducted many dealings with the leaders of this region in the past. He can better explain what will be transpiring in the next few days."

Rabbi Baruch turned to the crowd, "I have been here since the day before Passover and have known about this for some time. I apologize on behalf of Rabbi Shimon and myself for not informing everyone this might happen: We did not want to alarm anyone unnecessarily. We did anticipate that we would all be brought to some kind of prison to intimidate us, and make us feel fearful and helpless. Besides the initial feeling of powerlessness and the inconvenience of this place, no further harm should come to us. Do not let this dampen your spirits. I know how Theobold operates. In a few days all of us will be released, except for Yitzchak. Shortly after that, Theobold or his representative will arrive and initiate ransom negotiations for Yitzchak. Theobold craves money and all of the mistreatment toward us is nothing more than a way for him to demonstrate that Yitzchak's release will be costly indeed. Do not worry about that, I will offer him enough to secure Yitzchak's release and safe return. I am confident that this whole matter will be over in a few weeks and that everything will conclude favorably. Our most difficult challenge is enduring being locked up in this despicable place."

"What if you are wrong, Rabbi Baruch? What if Theobold is not interested in money? What will happen to Yitzchak? To us?" asked Gedaliah, who still had doubts even in the face of Rabbi Baruch's certainty.

"Obviously there are no guarantees that everything will unfold as I have predicted. I have dealt with Theobold in the past and if those dealings are any indication of his way of thinking then I believe we have every reason to be optimistic. Theobold is no fool. He understands that a ransom will advance his pursuit of the crown far more than a dubious accusation against a small town of Jews."

Gedaliah persisted, "But Yitzchak is being accused of a murder!"

"Yes, that is true, but it is only an accusation, one that I am sure Theobold does not truly believe. He is far too educated to accept the ravings of an illiterate slave without the slightest proof to support them. He will never reveal what he really thinks and he will undoubtedly make us think that a serious crime was committed here. But that is all part of his ploy, his scheme to drive up the ransom price. Theobold is very predictable; you will all see how this unfolds!"

A few of the townspeople were put at ease by what Rabbi Baruch and Rabbi Shimon said. Others were not pacified by the confident assurances of Rabbi Baruch.

Yitzchak had been listening quietly, huddled together with his family. No one thought for a moment that he was guilty and Yitzchak knew that. He was embarrassed in any case because of the discomfort he caused. He stood and asked for everyone's attention. He moved toward Rabbi Shimon and addressed the crowd.

"I am fully aware that you are all here because of me. Maybe I was careless in the way I acted at the river, I don't know. Perhaps I should have been more willing to engage the slave and convince him of my innocence" — Yitzchak shrugged his shoulders — "but I cannot believe the manner in which this has escalated. You are all suffering on my account and I want to apologize to all of you. I am truly sorry and after we have successfully defeated this enemy I will host a feast on Sabbath afternoon for the entire town. Until then, let us pray and have trust in the wisdom and skill of Rabbi Shimon and Rabbi Baruch."

Yitzchak resumed his seat. All the townspeople quickly assured him that he was not to blame and should not feel obligated to apologize for anything.

Devorah asked Yitzchak, "Father, what were you talking about?"

"Nothing, little Devorah, are you all right?"

"Yes, I am wearing the green scarf you bought me. The guard who came to the house told me we will be visiting a special place so I am wearing my special scarf."

Yitzchak kissed her, grateful that she was still too young to be discomforted by these conditions.

Rabbi Shimon suggested that everyone remain with their families, try to keep the children entertained and continue to fervently pray for a favorable outcome.

Gavriel remained quiet, almost oblivious to the chains on his foot and the darkness and dust surrounding him. He was deep in thought, contemplating the future.

Would there be a future?

Would he survive?

Would anyone?

He was not sure. He so desperately wanted to believe Rabbi Baruch that money was the solution that could save the town. But he remembered Yitzchak's story and the brutality of the slave, and he could not imagine how the slave could be placated by anything other than Jewish blood.

How much blood?

One man?

Yitzchak?

Others?

Was this the reason for jailing the entire town? Would everyone in the town be killed? Gavriel was uncertain. He looked at his father, who was coughing and wheezing. This place was not good for him. Gavriel felt sorry for him. His greatest challenge as leader was at hand and he was physically incapable of providing adequate encouragement and support.

But Gavriel understood that there was nothing his father or anyone could do and that without G-d's help and intervention their schemes would prove futile. They were genuinely helpless.

If money would not free them then nothing could. Petition the king? Hardly. His son-in-law was allied with the accuser. He surely would not entertain a petition from a helpless band of Jews when to do so would embarrass and humiliate Theobold.

Escape? Impossible.

Fight? How?

Gavriel realized that Rabbi Baruch and his father were fostering false hopes. They were in no position to demand anything from Theobold and if he refused their ransom there were no other means to secure freedom, no other way to avoid disaster, to remain alive, except to pray to G-d to somehow spare them all.

Without fervent and heartfelt prayers, the survival of the town rested with the simple choice that would be placed in front of Theobold.

Money or death.

How much money?

How many deaths?

There was no answer.

Rabbi Baruch, too, was deep in thought. He was very apprehensive but was hiding it well. Nobody suspected that he was utterly shocked by Theobold's brazen display of force and intimidation. He could not believe that Theobold had imprisoned all the Jews in the entire town. He had expected one or two of the town's elders, Rabbi Shimon perhaps, to be jailed, to pressure the town into offering a significant ransom for Yitzchak's release. But Rabbi Baruch could not comprehend what Theobold sought to gain, what benefit he could reap by imprisoning all the inhabitants. It was highly unusual, virtually unheard of, for a French nobleman to imprison innocent people unless he could issue some kind of accusation. Unless, Heaven Forbid, the whole town was accused!

Rabbi Baruch shuddered. That was the only explanation. How else to perceive Theobold's bold and outrageous conduct? The whole town was under suspicion for murdering the boy, not just Yitzchak!

Somehow, Theobold and Henri had twisted the slave's allegation, and had concluded that the entire town was at fault! Indeed, the situation was infinitely more serious than he first imagined. Would Theobold still accept a ransom for Yitzchak to remain alive? What about the rest of the townspeople? Would he have to ransom all of them as well? He could not know for certain but considered that perhaps the town would be pillaged but nobody would be executed.

Rabbi Baruch had been confident a bribe for Yitzchak's freedom would be successful. However, Rabbi Baruch was now beset by doubt, unsure whether money, or any bribe, could save not just Yitzchak but the rest of the town. Rabbi Baruch looked at Rabbi Shimon and sensed he was already aware of this danger.

Forty Jews, women and children included, simple and common people, prayed that G-d would thwart the greedy schemes of the despotic Theobold.

8

Hatred impedes truth. It confuses the mind and creates a false reality, which feeds on itself, grows stronger and more venal, impervious to common sense. Hatred creates absolutes, which transcend reason and debate. The truth becomes arbitrary and meaningless. A mind filled with hate is a mind that is not rational.

Theobold sat in his parlor, contemplating the best way to initiate ransom negotiations and maximize his share. He looked pensive and ignored the buckling sound the chair seemed to make each time he moved his body forward. He admitted he was excited by the prospect of such a potentially large windfall and had all but forgotten any feelings of honor and justice for the poor unfortunate dead child and the Christians of France. He had sent several of his more trusted guards to the bereaved family. The guards found the family so ignorant and superstitious that they could never be relied upon to help rally the populace. He remained quiet, reviewing his options. A servant then entered the room to inform Theobold that Father Charbrand had unexpectedly arrived and was waiting in the sitting room. Theobold rose quickly and in so doing cracked one of the legs of the chair.

He admonished the servant. "Father Charbrand is here? Have you made him as comfortable as possible? Please, bring him my choicest wine and order the chef to prepare his finest delicacy. Then inform Father Charbrand that I will join him shortly. Hurry! Hurry!"

The servant bowed and rapidly left the room. He had never met Father Charbrand before but correctly assumed Theobold held him in high regard. It was the first time he had heard Theobold utter the word "please."

Indeed, Father Charbrand was Theobold's mentor. In Theobold's youth Father Charbrand had taught Theobold the ways of a Christian, and a deep and lasting friendship developed between them. They had not seen each other in quite a few years but their relationship was one that was not easily diminished by either time or distance. They kept up a frequent and meaningful correspondence and it was from Father Charbrand that Theobold sought advice concerning his most difficult and pressing concerns. Theobold respected Father Charbrand more than any other man. Father Charbrand, too, loved Theobold like a son and it was to Theobold that he turned whenever he needed local assistance with any affairs of the king or nobles.

Why had he come?

Theobold sensed it had something to do with the Jews of Blois but Father Charbrand was an interesting man, and the visit could be about almost anything. Theobold washed himself and then changed into his finest clothes. He knew that Father Charbrand would enjoy seeing his protégé dressed in the wealth and opulence of royalty.

Theobold hurried to the sitting room and was surprised, almost shocked, to find Father Charbrand caressing a candelabra such as he had seen Jews using. He knew Father Charbrand was up to something but he dare not question him.

"Hello, Father. Welcome to my home," said Theobold excitedly. Theobold approached Father Charbrand, who had placed the candelabra on a nearby table. Theobold kissed his hand. Father Charbrand acknowledged Theobold's welcome.

Father Charbrand was a tall, slender man, almost the exact opposite of Theobold. His hair had turned gray and it lent him an appearance of dignity and superiority. He always walked slowly, never rushed or frazzled. He looked at Theobold with admiration.

"It is wonderful to see you, Theobold. You appear even more dignified than when we last met. I am sure you are wondering why I have come here without notifying you first, and why I brought along that Jewish relic." He pointed to the candelabra.

"I was surprised and excited to hear that you were waiting for me, and yes, I was a bit disturbed when I saw you holding that thing in an endearing fashion. Tell me, Father, why did you come and bring that candelabra with you?"

"Well, Theobold, I brought it to teach you a lesson. You will then understand why I am here. Tell me, when you saw me caressing it, what was your initial reaction, the first thought which entered your mind?"

Father Charbrand was driving at something, but what?

"To be honest, Father, I was immediately repulsed by the sight and watching you hold it in a loving fashion made me feel betrayed," responded Theobold.

"That is exactly how I wanted and expected you to feel. Would your betrayal have been minimized if I told you that I stole this from Jews and therefore did not pay for it?"

Theobold looked puzzled. "It would not matter because you would still be demonstrating affection for our enemy!"

Theobold instinctively realized that Alix was correct and his lust for the Jewish wealth of Blois was improper. He now understood why Father Charbrand visited but waited for the priest to explain.

"That is correct, Theobold. Now please tell me, what will happen to the Jews of Blois? Will you caress their money in front of all of France and allow their hated ways to spread like a disease? Or, will you do what is necessary to show the world that such actions cannot be ransomed, no matter how spectacular the offer?!! Do you not see, Theobold, that if you let the Jews escape this time you will be condoning their crimes, looking the other way, accepting bribes and ransoms when death is the proper remedy! You were repulsed when I held one Jewish relic. Do you not realize that their money is their religion and all

A Promise Fulfilled / 71

the more repulsive! No, Theobold, you cannot embrace their wealth, you cannot welcome it and allow it to wash away their sins and cleanse their souls! You cannot turn a blind eye to their evil in this hour of need. I am pleading with you to reject any ideas you might have about a ransom and join with Henri and myself in convening a tribunal and placing that entire miserable town on trial for the vicious murder of a Christian child!" Father Charbrand then sat down.

Theobold knew he would have a difficult time resisting Father Charbrand's wishes, and saw his ransom slipping away. He needed to convince Father Charbrand that the success of any tribunal was not readily attainable. "But the entire tribunal will rest on the testimony of an unreliable peasant slave," protested Theobold. "It will be difficult to pass judgment on the basis of such questionable evidence."

Father Charbrand sensed Theobold's hesitation. "Do not worry about that, Theobold. I have been informed the slave has agreed to a truth verification test and I shall see to it that the slave passes that test! Moreover, the tribunal will question each member of the town, providing ample evidence and testimony. And anyone wishing to confess his or her crime will receive a slight reprieve, thereby soothing your fears the tribunal will be viewed as bloodthirsty."

Father Charbrand stood up, drew toward Theobold and urged him to move away from the table and the menorah. Father Charbrand led Theobold to the front of the castle, where a huge cross hung over the entrance. Here, thought Father Charbrand, there will be no distractions. He turned to Theobold. "Please, Theobold, you must help maintain French honor and Christian pride. We have been disgraced too many times to allow this provocative and blasphemous incident to go unpunished!" Theobold understood that there would be no ransom this time. He looked at Father Charbrand and knew that he was righteous. He himself had considered joining Henri as Alix insisted, but he allowed his greed and lust for wealth to overpower his sense of reason and justice. But Father Charbrand once again taught him the truth and very gracefully exposed his error. This outrage could not be overlooked in exchange for Jewish wealth; it required more, much more. Theobold studied Father Charbrand

and saw a man he could not refuse, a man he could not disappoint, a man he would not disappoint.

"Father, as always, you are correct. I cannot accept a ransom for the unspeakable acts those Jews have committed. I will join you and Henri, listen to the testimony of the slave eyewitness and anyone else who wishes to be heard. We will then pronounce judgment on that band of filthy Jews! You can rest assured that I will arrange for the tribunal to gather in a matter of weeks and that the judgment shall be swift and cruel." Theobold embraced Father Charbrand and the two men walked to the dining room, where a magnificent repast awaited them.

Theobold's servants had prepared a lavish feast for Theobold and Father Charbrand, with enough wine and many dishes of meat and pheasant to satisfy half the region. They laughed together and ate and drank well into the night.

Father Charbrand had removed the last hope the Jews still retained. It appeared that any chance for freedom and survival was lost.

9

Pulcelina awoke to an unnatural silence that frightened her. There were no men studying Talmud, no women softly gossiping and no children running about. It was strange staring at empty streets, almost surreal. A void that was shocking and terrifying.

Pulcelina was afraid.

She never felt so isolated before. She immediately thought of her townspeople. They were together yet infinitely more alone.

Why had this happened?

She sensed Theobold was behind it and was certain she was spared because of him.

What would Theobold do next?

How could she know? She was not aware of anything that had been done to precipitate such cruel treatment. Her immediate reaction was to try and help.

Where to go?

Run to Theobold? She could not. She first had to find out what had transpired. There was only one thing she could do. Surreptitiously leave her home and speak with Rabbi Shimon. Remind him of her freedom and that she could intercede with Theobold. Leaving her home would be dangerous, she could be killed if caught, but her only alternative was to sit and wait. Like so many ordinary Jews who muster great courage and daring in times of distress, Pulcelina knew that idleness spelled disaster.

She spent the entire day planning when she would escape her home, how she would travel to the jail, and how best to remain undetected. She rehearsed what she would say to Rabbi Shimon, she would be quick and concise. There would not be time for extended conversation.

Darkness fell and Pulcelina was ready.

She waited for the guards patrolling her home to disperse, probably to eat something, refresh themselves and prepare for the long night ahead. As soon as they were gone, she climbed out of the far window of her home and raced for the jail. While walking, she happened upon three guards and froze in silence less than half a street length from where they were standing. She knew that if they saw her they would kill her. She had not anticipated some guards leisurely strolling during the night and was gripped with terror. As she waited, she noticed the moon and wondered whether its light had cast her shadow on the ground behind her. She dared not turn around for fear of exposure and stood motionless and silent. A few moments passed and the guards moved out of sight. She was safe, for now. Should she turn back? Let fear overtake duty? She quickly dismissed such thoughts. But she proceeded with great caution.

None of the townspeople locked in the jail realized that Pulcelina was free. No one had bothered to check if any were missing and since Pulcelina had no family in Blois, her absence had gone unnoticed. When some of the men sitting in the far corner of the room heard a faint whisper emanating through a crack in the wall, they were startled. The whisper grew louder, "Rabbi Shimon, I must speak with you, Rabbi Shimon, what shall I do?" Nachum the baker, soothing his fretful infant, approached Rabbi Shimon and told him he heard what sounded like a woman's voice calling him.

Was this some kind of trick? A ploy by Theobold to taunt them further?

Uncertain, Rabbi Shimon cautiously approached the crack.

The whisper was now clearly audible to all, "It is me, Pulcelina. I was not taken with the rest of you and I wish to help. Rabbi Shimon, can you hear me?"

"Pulcelina? I did not realize you were not here. Is anyone else still left in the town?" asked Rabbi Shimon, surprised.

"Yes, it is me, Pulcelina, and I am sorry to inform you that I was the only Jew not taken. I watched in horror as you were all dragged here. Please, Rabbi Shimon, what can I do to help?"

Rabbi Shimon placed his mouth near the crack in the wall so he could speak softly and not arouse the curiosity of the guards. "Pulcelina, what you are doing is very dangerous. You should turn back and go home immediately. You will be caught by the guards. Then you will surely be in danger along with the rest of us."

Pulcelina was defiant. "I will not turn back! Not when I am still capable of helping." She continued, "Do not worry about the guards, I found this crack at the back of the building where the guards do not patrol. We have a few moments where we can talk in peace. Rabbi Shimon, you of all people are aware of the manner in which Theobold regards me. That is surely the reason he left me in my home. I want to plead with Theobold, intervene with him and convince him to free you all."

Rabbi Shimon was apprehensive. "Pulcelina, I know you mean well but do you know why we are here? It is because Yitzchak has been accused of murdering a Christian child and using his blood and then casting away the body. We believe Theobold has imprisoned us all to frighten and intimidate us but we are still in danger and Yitzchak is in very grave danger. Please, Theobold will not forgo whatever plans he might have simply because you ask him. I am not even sure that any appeal you make to Theobold at this time will prove productive. He may remember all the times you rejected him and reject you in turn. We really do not know what Theobold wants and therefore, we do not know how best to approach him. No decision we make can be done hastily. We must proceed carefully. I could be harming Yitzchak as well as the rest of us by rushing a decision which further reflection would prove unwise. Do not misunderstand me, Pulcelina, your freedom could turn out to be the miracle we are all praying for, but right now we must proceed with caution. That is why I am advising you to return home and wait until we can better evaluate the situation."

"But valuable time may be lost in the interim," countered Pulcelina.

"That may be true, but I cannot condone a meeting with Theobold which might hurt our chances for survival."

Pulcelina conceded that Rabbi Shimon had expressed some valid concerns and promised him she would not do anything hasty or rash. She ended by noting that should Theobold visit her, and she was certain that he would, then she would try to engage him in a way where she could discern his true intentions and then act accordingly.

Rabbi Shimon warned her that he was sly and cunning and might purposely mislead her. Pulcelina responded that she would be careful. She then hurried home under the protective darkness of the night.

Inside the prison, Rabbi Shimon told Rabbi Baruch what had just transpired. Rabbi Baruch agreed that Pulcelina's freedom could prove valuable to them eventually. He concurred with Rabbi Shimon that her impulsiveness could jeopardize and perhaps hurt their chances for freedom. Rabbi Baruch had not confided to Rabbi Shimon that he thought all the townspeople were in terrible danger. He was reluctant to, as he still hoped he was wrong.

Rabbi Shimon sat down near the crack where he had spoken to Pulcelina. He began to examine the crack, the thin line that split one stone in two. Once this was a mighty building, an imposing structure carefully constructed with the finest materials of its time. Now it was starting to age and decay. The eroding stones were cracking, coming apart. Soon the building would become unsafe and would, in time, be torn down. Would anyone remember what took place here? That the Jews of Blois were herded here like cattle and locked up for days without much food or water for a baseless reason?

Would anyone care?

Rabbi Shimon felt the warmth of someone's hand caress his shoulder. "Father, how are you feeling?" It was Gavriel. "I am concerned about you, Father. This place cannot be good for you."

"I know, Gavriel. The dust is bothering me, but to be fair, that is not my primary concern at the moment."

Gavriel looked worried.

"I am aware, Father, but you must tend to your health," insisted Gavriel. "I have been thinking that there is really nothing you or Rabbi Baruch can do. Either Theobold will accept a ransom and we will be freed, or he will accept a partial ransom and some of us will be freed or he will not accept it at all and a terrible fate will befall us. But I don't think you should ignore your health because your participation, your input now is pointless. I do not mean to sound hopeless, but you must agree. Notwithstanding everything Rabbi Baruch has told us, your ability to control our release or to demand anything from Theobold is simply illusory."

"You are mistaken, Gavriel. We shall be released in a matter of days."

"I am sorry, but you cannot be certain of that. We shall only be released if that is Theobold's wish. I know you are trying to remain confident but you cannot expect Theobold to call off his plans simply because you will offer him some gold!"

Rabbi Shimon was stunned.

He was fully aware that he was in no position to demand anything from Theobold but listening to Gavriel awakened him to the futility of their plans. Until that moment he still believed that somehow he could manipulate Theobold, steer him toward a ransom and away from harm and destruction. Rabbi Shimon now understood that there was nothing he could do or say to change Theobold's mind. He had surely already decided what would become of them. Rabbi Baruch could not surprise Theobold with an offer to purchase their freedom, Theobold had long concluded whether or not that would happen. The more Rabbi Shimon reviewed his newfound appreciation of Theobold's cunning, the more he realized that in all likelihood Theobold would not accept a ransom and a terrible tragedy would befall his people. Rabbi Shimon grew angry with himself. He was called upon to serve the townspeople, he advised Pulcelina, he spoke of optimism and assured everyone of a favorable conclusion, but he had been unable to perceive the terrifying climax to this unfortunate episode. Of course he knew there was a Divine plan and only with G-d's mercy could the town be spared. He knew he had to seize upon the efficacy of prayer, the submission of man's feebleness to G-d's mastery. With the voice of the whole town crying and praying in unison, with sincere devotion, they might be saved. He called everyone together to recite Psalms and pray for a favorable outcome with all the feeling and intensity they could muster.

Rabbi Shimon returned to the corner of the jail and wondered whether Rabbi Baruch had already reached the same conclusion and had spoken with such encouragement and assurance only to inspire an otherwise demoralized group. But Rabbi Shimon was amazed that his son so keenly analyzed their predicament. He was sharp and perceptive and demonstrated an unnatural ability to look beyond emotion and tension and study the situation slowly, calmly. He took a long look at his son. He was proud of Gavriel. Yes, Gavriel would make a fine rabbi.

Rabbi Shimon knew he would have to confer with Rabbi Baruch, and possibly adopt a different course of action. But what would that accomplish? What else could be done? Like Gavriel, he came to see that their survival lay only with Theobold. Their future clearly rested in the hands of an evil man.

Rabbi Shimon sat down, closed his eyes and waited for that man to make his appearance.

The moment Father Charbrand left the castle, Theobold knew he would not let him down. Yet, he was still drawn to the allure of a ransom and could not bring himself to destroy the town without first placating his curiosity, without first learning how much he could demand from the Jews. Moreover, Theobold wanted to mislead the Jews, give them every reason to think they would be given an opportunity to ransom themselves, foster their false hopes. Then, just when they would be ready to taste their freedom, he would begin the tribunal and watch them cower in anguish and dread. Theobold knew he could never succeed in deluding the Jews without the assistance of another Jew and summoned Abraham, from Chartres. Abraham was well known throughout the Jewish community as an industrious and callous individual who would do just about anything to please Theobold and the Christians of France. His dealings with the nobles of France enhanced his prestige. Although he was asked numerous times, he did very little to help Jews who were being exploited.

Abraham arrived shortly before noon and was immediately led to Theobold's chamber, the one used to greet lesser dignitaries. The chamber was a simple, sparsely furnished room. It had one wooden bench with two small tables at each end and a large table in the center of the room surrounded by eight plain chairs.

Abraham walked with a slight hunchback, which made him ungainly and slow. His infirmities made him look oafish and ignorant, and for a moment, Theobold thought he had chosen the wrong man. Abraham did not know why he had been summoned. He had received a message from Theobold and responded immediately. While waiting in the parlor he noticed a menorah, the same one Father Charbrand had left behind, which had inadvertently been placed there by one of Theobold's servants. Abraham wondered why Theobold possessed a Jewish relic. It was a plain menorah, not very decorative or ornate, and Abraham speculated as to how it had come into Theobold's possession. The obvious answer, that it was stolen, made little sense. What use could Theobold have for a menorah?

A few moments later, Theobold entered the room. His huge presence scared Abraham, who retreated in awe of the large man. Theobold did not wish to appear unapproachable and took Abraham's reverence as an opportunity to inject some levity. "There is no reason to be afraid of me. Only criminals need fear me. Tell me, are you a criminal?" Theobold laughed and moved toward Abraham.

Abraham immediately rose and bowed before Theobold. "No, my lord, I am not a criminal. I am here because you have summoned me and I wish to be of service to you."

"Good," replied Theobold. "Now please sit down so we can discuss why I have invited you here." They moved to the large table. "I have a mission for you, Abraham. It is an important mission and I have chosen you because I feel you will succeed and you shall be rewarded when you do succeed. The mission is not a dangerous one. You will not face pirates or robbers, but you will face scoundrels of a different sort. Are you prepared to accept?"

Abraham thought Theobold wanted him to deliver a message, to the king perhaps. He was excited that Theobold had chosen him. "Yes, my lord, what is your wish?" answered Abraham unhesitantly.

"I need you to travel to Blois, to the Jewish quarter. You have not yet heard but the Jews of Blois have committed a horrific act, an unspeakable crime. I cannot at this time disclose the nature of the act, but suffice it to say, the entire town has been incarcerated as a precaution. There is a possibility that I might be inclined to accept a ransom, a payment for their lives, and I will consider such payment as a sufficient punishment for their misdeed. I want you, Abraham, to determine from the Jews how much money they will offer for their lives. You must be firm with them. Insist that I will only be swayed to accept a ransom in lieu of some other punishment if the amount tendered is truly significant. Do not accept their initial offer. On the contrary, whatever amount they propose, reply that I will be expecting at least double! The negotiations should not take very long. The more firmly you deal with them, the more quickly they will realize you are bound by the limits I have given you and they will meet the demands imposed on them. Do you understand this mission? Do you have any questions?"

Abraham was surprised by Theobold's assignment and was too shocked to protest or question his mission further. "I understand, my lord, I will not disappoint you." Abraham answered.

"Then go now, Abraham, go to Blois."

What could the Jews of Blois have done? Nothing that serious, concluded Abraham, since Theobold was willing to accept a ransom, however high the amount, instead of torture or death.

"Good, you will be rewarded for this, Abraham. To increase your incentive to deal harshly with them, I will base your payment for this mission on the amount you extract from them. The more they are willing to pay, the greater your reward. I am glad that you understand."

Theobold continued instructing Abraham how best to negotiate with the Jews while Abraham remained silent. The more Theobold spoke, the more Abraham fathomed Theobold's ruthlessness, which was truly thorough and stern. Abraham had spent years trying to flatter Theobold and his cohorts so as to be considered their equal. Now, for the first time, he was exposed to his scheming and hatred and utter disgust for the Jews.

Abraham was repulsed by Theobold. He had spent a great deal of time currying favor with him, basking in his good graces and doing his bidding. Now he had been called upon to pressure and coerce his brethren. He did not like it and he felt ashamed. But there was nothing he could do about it. He could not abandon the mission; that would mean certain death.

Abraham nodded, kissed Theobold's hand and left the room. On his way out of the castle, he once again passed the menorah on the table, sighed, and continued walking, dejected and confused.

10

Man is troubled by injustice. Why do some claim the right to oppress and persecute others? Why are some villains oftentimes revered as saints and showered with undue affection and praise? Why are the righteous rejected and ridiculed and sometimes killed? These are serious challenges, which can only be properly addressed by the faithful.

Yitzchak had been pondering these very questions and continued to probe his own subconscious. True, he had flaws but did they warrant this outcome? He dared not question the judgments of Heaven and surely would not disagree with them. This led Yitzchak the Jew, an ordinary man from a small town in provincial France during the twelfth century, to a startling yet far from original conclusion. The decrees of Heaven must be met with joy and enthusiasm no matter how they might be perceived by Man. If his fate would be to die then he would accept it with the selfsame ardor and zeal as he would all the world's riches. Yitzchak searched deep within himself and discovered that as a Jew he must remain faithful and trusting even in sorrow, even in death. Yes, he did not desire it and would beg and plead to remain alive, but he now accepted his fate with a serene joy that comes with the knowledge of supreme fulfillment. He had recognized, like so many Jews before him and tragically like so many still, the ultimate culmination of life, which ends in martyrdom. At the river, Yitzchak felt betrayed, abandoned by events he thought unfair. But Yitzchak had changed. He no longer shunned or doubted the justness of his destiny. Yitzchak had absorbed the lessons of the past few weeks and by doing so perpetuated an essential characteristic of the Jew. The Jew does not question injustice, the Jew accepts it, lives with it and waits for the Eternal Day when all wrongs will be righted.

Yitzchak too had begun to realize what Rabbi Shimon, Rabbi Baruch and Gavriel had already discovered, that any chance of survival appeared very unlikely. Indeed, Rabbi Shimon sensed the rest of the town beginning to come to the same understanding. It was therefore surprising to just about everyone when the door to the jail opened and Abraham entered. Only Rabbi Baruch knew who this man was. But the appearance of another person, a Jew, from the outside world instantly brightened everyone's spirits.

Rabbi Baruch immediately approached him. "Abraham? Is that you? Do you remember me? What brings you to this awful place? Are we to be released?"

Abraham did remember Rabbi Baruch, who had displayed unusual kindness toward him and had given him money to pay off his creditors many years earlier. Rabbi Baruch did not know Abraham then, but when he heard a fellow Jew was in trouble he immediately offered his assistance. Abraham felt guilty. He could not behave in a ruthless manner to a man so kind and gentle. He had not been informed that Rabbi Baruch was one of the imprisoned Jews and could not believe he was guilty of anything improper. He would have refused the mission had he known he would be forced to confront Rabbi Baruch. But he could not turn back. "Yes, Rabbi Baruch, of course I remember you, I could never forget all that you did for me," Abraham answered, then tried to change the topic. "I do not want to waste any time. I am here on a mission from the lord and protector of this region, Theobold the Good."

Abraham continued talking about the mission and how he could not decline Theobold's orders, but to Rabbi Baruch it was all a blur. Theobold had finally done what everyone had been waiting for, initiate ransom negotiations. Rabbi Baruch had all but ruled out that such negotiations would ever take place, and staring at Abraham reawakened within him the need to negotiate tactfully and artfully. Rabbi Baruch now believed that following these intense negotiations they would probably be freed. He was still unsure of Yitzchak's fate but Yitzchak's situation was always more precarious than everybody else's. He would of course try to ransom him as well, at least now there was hope! Rabbi Baruch was excited.

Rabbi Shimon and Gavriel were also marveling at the arrival of this Jew and began dismissing all of the terrible consequences they initially feared. Rabbi Shimon even stopped coughing.

Abraham was still talking. He was humbly explaining why he had been chosen by Theobold and kept apologizing for what he believed would be grueling and sensitive negotiations. He was attempting to ease the tensions he was sure would soon follow. When he finished, Rabbi Shimon declared to anyone who had not yet heard that Abraham was an emissary of Theobold and had come to discuss a ransom.

The crowd began to murmur. Before anyone had a chance to say anything, Rabbi Baruch drew near Abraham. This was the moment he had been waiting for. Rabbi Baruch requested silence from the crowd and then announced, "Tell Theobold I will pay him forty pounds of gold if he will release us. That amounts to one pound per person. Forty pounds is more money than most people have seen in their lives! I believe it is a fair offer, one that Theobold will accept!"

Everyone hushed in amazement.

Fair? thought Abraham, that number was astronomical! Abraham doubted if even the King had that much. Abraham surely had never seen an amount that large.

Could Rabbi Baruch deliver that much? He knew Rabbi Baruch and believed the staggering offer was indeed sincere. The group too was shocked by the amount offered by Rabbi Baruch. They were convinced Theobold would grab the offer, possibly even free Yitzchak and allow everyone to return home. Rabbi Baruch, though, knew the offer would be rejected, all initial offers are, and he would be forced to increase the amount by approximately ten to fifteen pounds. There would be further bargaining and a final amount would be reached somewhere in the vicinity of sixty pounds. That amount comprised almost all of Rabbi Baruch's entire fortune, but Rabbi Baruch never thought of that, he just hoped it would be enough.

Abraham was confused. He knew that forty pounds would more than satisfy Theobold's greed and nearly bankrupt Rabbi Baruch in the process. But he remembered Theobold's command that any amount offered by the Jews had to be rejected for an amount double the original number. Eighty pounds.

Eighty pounds?

Surely Rabbi Baruch did not have eighty pounds. Abraham was embarrassed to even counter the offer with such a ridiculous and unfair response. How could he reject such a generous amount by demanding double, from the man who once saved him from financial ruin? It would make him appear vicious and greedy and ungrateful. Rabbi Baruch would not believe he was only following Theobold's request. Nobody could believe Theobold was so avaricious and would reject this magnanimous offer in so brazen a fashion. No, he would be blamed for Theobold's greed and the man who once salvaged him would look upon him with contempt. Should he just turn and run away? Forget his mission and Theobold? Maintain his dignity among his brethren? Live the rest of his life as a fugitive? Or perhaps accept the offer and then lie to Theobold?

What to do?

Abraham did not have the courage nor the moral stamina to remain wanted all his life or to become tangled in the lies which would surely one day catch up with him. No, Abraham had to remain sensible and reject such possibilities. He also knew he had to complete this mission and report back to Theobold. For now he would press on. He noticed Rabbi Baruch was pleased with the offer he had just tendered and was waiting for a response.

Abraham reluctantly replied, "I do not know how to say this but I am sorry to inform you, my brothers, that I have been specifically instructed by Theobold to reject the first amount offered and demand from you no less than double your original offer. Therefore there will be no further negotiations unless you agree to pay eighty pounds of gold. I am sorry that I must deal with you in this irrational manner but I cannot violate the instructions of Theobold. Please forgive me." Abraham turned to leave in shame and disgrace.

Eighty pounds. Half the room could not even imagine such wealth. Rabbi Baruch felt dejected. He knew that Abraham was acting at the behest of Theobold and realized he was merely an innocent messenger without any evil or harmful motives. Rabbi Baruch accurately assessed that Theobold was the real monster. Rabbi Baruch also realized something more sinister still. He drew close to Rabbi Shimon.

"Rabbi Shimon, I must talk with you privately. It is very urgent."

Rabbi Shimon was a little surprised by Rabbi Baruch's sudden need for privacy and suggested that it wait until later. Rabbi Baruch insisted it could not wait, excused himself and walked to the far corner of the room. Rabbi Shimon quickly followed as the townspeople looked on. Abraham too was surprised by this obvious display of rudeness but was too embarrassed to object.

When they were alone Rabbi Baruch whispered, "Why would Theobold direct Abraham to immediately reject our offer and demand double? That is not Theobold's style. His style, like that of all clever negotiators, is to try to squeeze a bit more than initially offered. I surmised that if I started my offer at forty pounds, then the actual ransom would be somewhere in the range of sixty pounds. I assumed that forty pounds would be summarily rejected, then there would be a counteroffer of sixty or sixty-five pounds. Then, there would be the customary back and forth of all negotiations and an agreement would have been reached somewhere between fifty-five and sixty pounds. But eighty pounds? Demanding such a large sum makes no sense. It defies all conventional negotiating tactics and it runs the risk of ruining otherwise productive negotiations. I strongly believe that this entire negotiation is nothing more than a ruse, for what purpose I am not entirely sure. If Theobold were truly serious about accepting a ransom then he would have directed Abraham to negotiate in a sincere manner. I have had many dealings with Theobold in the past and I have never known him to act in this fashion. Since I have grave doubts whether this ransom will ever set us free, I feel we should agree to pay the eighty pounds and wait for Theobold's next move."

Rabbi Shimon agreed with Rabbi Baruch but was still concerned about one detail. "Do you have eighty pounds, Rabbi Baruch?"

"No, I do not. I could probably manage to collect about sixty-five, but that is all. If we needed more I suppose I could borrow it or sell my books."

Rabbi Shimon did not want to see that happen and had one more question, "Do you realize, Rabbi Baruch, that if an offer of eighty pounds is accepted by Theobold, the town will never be able to repay you? You will become a broken and bankrupt man."

"And Rabbi Shimon, don't you wish that the Jews in Norwich during that blood accusation, or the Jews in Worms, Mainz and countless other towns during the Crusades would have had money to buy their lives? I certainly do. Please, do not worry yourself with these petty concerns, we have much greater issues that need to be dealt with and my financial future should not be among them."

Rabbi Shimon nodded, "Well, then I agree we should accept the counteroffer of eighty pounds."

The two returned to Abraham, told him they understood the negotiating demands were Theobold's alone. They urged Abraham to tell Theobold that the Jewish community of Blois would pay eighty pounds for their freedom.

The town was astonished by the offer. They knew it was far too exhorbitant but would not object to the graciousness and generosity of Rabbi Baruch; they were eager to return to their normal everyday lives. They remained silent as Rabbi Shimon related the offer.

Abraham, though, was too humiliated to respond. He merely nodded, approached the door, was led out by a guard and traveled back to Theobold with the news of a possible agreement.

Inside the jail, the townspeople were curious. They all heard that the offer had been accepted but why the secrecy between Rabbi

Shimon and Rabbi Baruch? Wasn't everyone entitled to know what was transpiring? Someone approached Rabbi Shimon and Rabbi Baruch and asked them why they so rudely left Abraham's presence and huddled together in the back of the room. The two rabbis looked at each other and knew they could no longer keep the truth, or their perception of the truth, from them. Rabbi Shimon told everyone that he had come to believe that they would never be able to even offer a ransom and he was expecting a horrible conclusion to this unfortunate episode. He continued that he became very excited by Abraham's arrival and the possibility that he was wrong about Theobold and a ransom. But Rabbi Baruch pointed out that Theobold's demand was ludicrous, almost insulting, it defied all conventional negotiating strategies, and therefore, he had serious doubts about Abraham's mission. Rabbi Shimon explained that he spoke with Rabbi Baruch privately to review their options. Rabbi Baruch confessed that he did not have eighty pounds but since he doubted the sincerity of the offer, felt it should be tendered in any event. Rabbi Shimon concluded by stating that they had nothing to lose by agreeing to the offer and could be in no worse a position because of it.

Someone shouted, "If the negotiations were not serious then why were they undertaken by Theobold?"

"We are not entirely sure," answered Rabbi Shimon. "Possibly to taunt us, or perhaps degrade us by demonstrating that he can negotiate in this outlandish manner and still get his price."

Gedaliah spoke up, "If Theobold will not accept the offer, what will happen to us?"

The room turned silent. That was the question on everyone's mind but until now no one dared ask it for fear of hearing the answer. Gedaliah too was afraid of how Rabbi Shimon might respond but was more afraid to remain in the dark, terrified of the unknown.

Everyone was fully aware that the answer to the question was something very terrible indeed. Either death or torture or destruction of their homes or a sinister combination of all three. Rabbi Shimon did not wish to antagonize the people any further and told Gedaliah and everyone else that it would be premature to consider a rejection of the offer. That did not satisfy anyone, and everyone knew Rabbi Shimon intentionally evaded answering the question but no one pressed him any further. The possibilities were too terrible to contemplate, too much to bear.

They waited and prayed that somehow disaster could be averted.

Yitzchak had come to the conclusion that if any members of the town were to be spared, he would surely not be among them. He did not harbor any ill will toward Rabbi Shimon and Rabbi Baruch. On the contrary, their determination and hope proved very inspiring. But he heard as well as anyone the ridiculous demands dictated by Theobold, and, like Rabbi Baruch, doubted Theobold's sincerity in freeing the town. He now knew that whatever would happen to the rest of the town, his fate was sealed.

He accepted that he would be killed.

He readied himself for that noble cause.

11

Henri was growing impatient. Easter had already passed, it had been over two weeks since Philippe first reported the incident at the river, and still no action had been taken. Yes, the Jews had been imprisoned, but that bothered Henri for two reasons. It created a sense of complacency, which led him to believe the momentum had stagnated. Pulcelina, that woman always granted special treatment, had been spared prison. Henri hated Pulcelina, she was a thorn in his greedy and exploitive nature. Her special status was a constant reminder that he had bounds from which he could not escape. He resented being reminded of his own inadequacies and bore a visceral contempt toward her. Henri knew Theobold favored her, therefore her special treatment in this regard and the sluggish momentum of the whole affair caused Henri to question Theobold's total commitment and dedication to ruining the Jews of Blois.

He did not wish to visit Theobold again, remembering Theobold's lukewarm reception when he had arrived unannounced, and decided to write a letter instead.

Henri detailed the slow progress this pursuit seemed to be taking. He also boldly demanded that all the Jews should have been treated with equal scorn. Henri further reminded Theobold that unnecessary delay would only work to benefit the Jews: The longer they remained jailed the greater the possibility that other Jews would hear of their plight and seek to bribe the king. He concluded the letter by stating he was growing impatient while waiting to fulfill this holy and important mission. Henri dispatched Philippe to deliver the letter.

Theobold received the letter later that day and understood Henri's concerns. This had dragged on long enough. Theobold, though, took exception to Henri's subtle objection to his treatment of Pulcelina and dismissed it as the rumblings of impatience and zeal.

Theobold agreed that further delay would not be prudent. The time had come to visit the Jews of Blois, investigate the claims of Henri's slave and pass unrelenting and swift punishment.

But not until Abraham returned from his mission. Theobold could not act without first knowing the riches he would be forgoing.

Later that afternoon, Abraham returned, discouraged and disgusted with himself. He was immediately led to Theobold's smaller chamber. Abraham did not see the menorah and took that as a bad omen.

After a brief wait, Theobold entered and Abraham related the exorbitant price that Rabbi Baruch had accepted on behalf of the Jews. Theobold was understandably astounded. Eighty pounds! That was more than he could ever amass in his whole lifetime. He immediately had second thoughts. He wished he could just accept the money and forget the nonsense of ritual murder. If they were offering eighty, he could surely realize ninety or perhaps ninety-five! With that much wealth he would stand unchallenged to become the next King of France! He would never rebel, of course, against the present king, his father-in-law, but he could assemble an army, and have the funds to sustain them, to simply wait for the king to pass on and then succeed him, undisputed. These thoughts enticed Theobold.

But Theobold remembered Father Charbrand. How could he betray his mentor, his teacher and his spiritual protector? And what would he say to Alix or Henri or the king perhaps, when asked why he failed to safeguard French honor? No, he could not back down now. Too many people had their eyes on him, watching his every move.

But Theobold would not give up. There had to be a way. There had to be something he could do and still reap the reward he so craved.

But how?

He could do it, *if* the Jews were also punished in the process!

Therein lie the answer to Theobold's dilemma. Keep the huge financial reward and condemn the Jews at the same time!

Have the best of both worlds!

But how to get the Jews to pay that huge sum if they were to be killed?

The only way Theobold could envision this would involve letting one or two of the Jews remain alive. He was sure he could convince Alix that sparing two, or three Jews at most, was surely worth eighty pounds. Virtually the entire town would be killed. That would far overshadow the measly few who would be permitted to live, and the financial windfall would be well worth it. He was also sufficiently confident that Father Charbrand would not object to two or three remaining alive when Theobold would remind him that with this wealth his protégé would emerge as the heir apparent!

Henri, though, would prove more difficult. He had already written expressing his objection to the way he handled Pulcelina. He might not consent to allow a few Jews to remain alive without some benefit to himself. Theobold, though, did not wish to share any of the wealth with Henri and concluded it would be better not to inform him at all. Theobold would have to mislead him, and hope he would never discover the truth.

The more he thought about it, the more it pleased him. Death and destruction of almost every Jew in Blois and untold wealth.

He would have to convince Alix about the importance of keeping Henri in the dark. How could Alix object?

Theobold understood that Pulcelina would suffer the same fate as the rest of the town. If some Jews were to be spared, Alix would surely never allow one of them to be Pulcelina. He knew it would be difficult enough persuading Alix to allow some Jews to live and she would never consent to Pulcelina being among them. He would not even try to save Pulcelina; it was a battle he would never win. At one point he had considered freeing the town for her sake. Those were distant memories now. Theobold suddenly felt isolated from Pulcelina, removed and detached from her concerns and he wondered why he ever favored her. He now regarded her as a common Jew not worthy of any special treatment. Her fate was sealed.

Who would be spared?

Theobold knew one of them would be Rabbi Baruch. He was very resourceful and could supply Theobold with valuable services or money in the future. And who else? Theobold did not know. He decided he would make up his mind after visiting the town first hand.

Now that Abraham had returned, he was ready to visit Blois.

The moment had arrived.

The following morning Count Theobold, Prince Henri and Philippe traveled to Blois. Father Charbrand had already notified Theobold that he would be arriving in the afternoon with a number of priests who would comprise the members of the tribunal. Father Charbrand trusted that Theobold would not surrender to his greedy urges, and Theobold promised he would not yield to them, but the priest correctly sensed some weakness in Theobold's assertions and wished to provide support in case the temptation became too great for Theobold withstand. Father Charbrand also decided that the tribunal about to take place would carry more validity and authority if presided over by a number of priests. Father Charbrand knew that their presence would insure that none of the locals would question the propriety of Theobold's quest or the justice of the verdict.

The local populace was notified that Theobold and Father Charbrand were visiting Blois and many came to greet them.

Theobold and Henri arrived together in the same coach, and the noise of the horses startled the Jews held in the prison. Rabbi Baruch and Rabbi Shimon were informed that Theobold had just arrived and that soon the entire ordeal would be over. Several of the townsfolk were able to peer through cracks in the wall and make out the figures of Henri and Theobold both richly attired, each wearing silk embroidered with gold. As the wagon reached the jail, Theobold ordered the driver to stop. Theobold descended first, followed by several retainers, then Henri and Philippe. Theobold ignored the locals waiting to kiss his hand, walked toward the jail and ordered a guard to open the door. The guard complied and as the stream of light filtered through the dim room the people inside stood quickly and waited. As the Jewish leader of the town, Rabbi Shimon immediately hurried to the door to greet Theobold.

Rabbi Shimon barely had a chance to get close to him when a guard placed a lance in front of Theobold and announced that the leader and protector of the region had come to the town of Blois. Theobold brushed the lance aside and stood face to face with Rabbi Shimon.

"Where is Yitzchak the Jew?" roared Theobold, intentionally slighting Rabbi Shimon.

Yitzchak heard his name being called and was startled. Tamar and Rabbi Baruch had quietly emphasized the importance of maintaining a courageous and fearless facade.

Yitzchak was not afraid. He had been waiting for this moment, waiting to accept his fate with joy and serenity, whatever the outcome. He rose, brushed off the dust and made his way to the entrance. "I am Yitzchak the Jew, I am the man you are looking for," he said with a boldness which even startled himself.

He looked like a very simple and humble man, hardly a murderer. But Theobold remembered Father Charbrand's warning that the Jews were very deceptive. "So you are the Jew accused of murdering the child. You can be sure that you will receive a fair and just trial. I have visited the family of the boy you are accused of killing and I can assure you that your alleged deed has caused them untold suffering." Theobold appeared angry. Yitzchak responded, "My lord, I wish to tell you —" Yitzchak had barely begun when he was summarily interrupted by Theobold, "You will have plenty of opportunity to speak when the counsel interrogates you. Now I would like to speak with the leader of this town. Where is he?"

Rabbi Shimon had been standing beside Yitzchak. "I am the leader," declared Rabbi Shimon humbly.

"You!" laughed Theobold. "You don't look like someone who could lead a congregation."

"True, my physical prowess has diminished but I am emotionally capable of providing inspiration to them," returned Rabbi Shimon quickly.

"They will need more than inspiration," Theobold muttered.

Theobold had planned to allow the Jews to return to their homes. There was no longer any reason for keeping them imprisoned. He was in the town now, things were under his direct control, nothing could go wrong by allowing them to return to their homes. In a few short weeks the matter would be concluded and the Jewish presence in Blois would cease to exist. Permitting them this small comfort for the last remaining weeks could do no harm to his mission.

Theobold turned to the guards, "Unchain the Jews and release them from this jail. They may all return to their homes, except Yitzchak the Jew. He shall remain locked up while my colleagues and I question various members of the town." Theobold moved for the door.

The people was overjoyed when they heard they could return home. They wished to thank Theobold for his kindness and generosity but were unsure how best to accomplish that. Rabbi Baruch suggested that as they exit they should bow to him and softly express their thanks.

Everyone prepared to exit and was busy gathering belongings when Theobold announced that no one would be permitted to leave the town on pain of death until the questioning had been completed, and that the questioning would begin as soon as Father Charbrand arrived. Everyone nodded.

Rabbi Shimon feared that a vital opportunity for clemency was slipping away. He approached Theobold and pleaded with him. "Is there any way, my lord, that this matter can be resolved amicably?"

Theobold looked indignant. He had been waiting for that question. "How would you react if one of your sons was murdered and sucked of his blood? Would you request a friendly resolution?"

Rabbi Shimon was taken aback by Theobold's response. It appeared Theobold had already made up his mind! Rabbi Shimon pressed on. "With all due respect, my lord, Yitzchak has done nothing wrong."

Theobold expected the leader to immediately claim innocence. It was the way all guilty parties act. Theobold wished to preempt any notions of leniency or mercy. He raised his arm, pointed at Rabbi Shimon and warned, "Do not arrive at conclusions concerning this matter before I have completed the investigation! I will not allow this holy mission to become a laughingstock. You will each have a chance to speak when you are brought to me for questioning, and you may never criticize my methods." Theobold turned and left the prison.

Rabbi Shimon felt doomed. Rabbi Baruch had been on target. There would be no ransom. Each member of the town would be questioned and undoubtedly punished. Why else would Theobold find it necessary to interrogate the entire town? For what purpose? Rabbi Shimon surmised that Theobold would question them all and then pronounce everyone guilty.

Their chances for survival appeared slim indeed.

Rabbi Shimon had known this moment would come and was prepared. He asked to be taken to a corner where he could talk with Gavriel in private. Chana wanted to come too but Dina, the childless woman, held her back.

Gavriel and Rabbi Shimon retreated to the back of the room.

"Gavriel, now that we are alone, I must tell you that I fear terrible things are in store for us. I know that we have spoken about this before and everyone became excited when Abraham arrived. But I looked into Theobold's eyes and I did not see a man of reason. He acts as if he has made up his mind and if that is true then all the money in the world will not help." Rabbi Shimon held Gavriel's hand.

"I am sick now, Gavriel, and growing worse. I do not know how much more my body can withstand. I do not want to sound discouraging, but I have made arrangements with Dina, the woman who always sits with Chana in the synagogue. She will care for you and Chana should anything happen to me."

Gavriel looked upset, but he had suspected as much. He had seen his father speak with Dina and her husband, Shalom, the day after Passover and concluded it was about Chana and their future. He felt compassion for his father. A reluctant and tired rabbi faced with an impossible crisis and two motherless children.

Could it get any worse?

Gavriel tried to lift his father's spirits. "Do not say that, Father. You will recover and hopefully, somehow, we will survive this ordeal and lead normal lives again."

"I hope you are right, Gavriel, I hope you are right."

From the corner of his eye Rabbi Shimon saw the door open once again and heard chains rattling. The room was filled with confusion until one of the guards spoke. "You are aware that Theobold has decreed that you may all return to your homes. I am reminding you that you may not leave the town on pain of death. You must stay in your homes until you are called upon for questioning. Yitzchak, however, must remain here."

The townspeople heeded the warning and quickly began exiting the building. They were happy to be out of that cramped and uncomfortable room. Soon the only people remaining were Yitzchak, Tamar and their children.

Among their children only Yaakov truly understood what was happening and he approached his father, gazed deeply into his father's soul and with that special bond between father and son, let him know that he would always love him. He then gave his father a hug and kiss, said nothing and left the prison. The other children quickly followed.

Tamar and Yitzchak were alone. Tamar could hardly speak. She had been trying to hold back her tears but could not do so any longer and burst out crying. Yitzchak consoled her. He told her that he had already made peace with his fate and would confront the future with understanding and joy. He wished it could be different, he told her, but he learned to welcome it. Yitzchak promised he would remain strong and never appear crushed or defeated.

Tamar turned to Yitzchak and thought of their life together. He always made her very happy and she was disheartened that she would lose the chance to grow old with him and watch their children mature into fine and honorable Jews. But Tamar also perceived a higher purpose, a more demanding and exacting role for the Jew, which led her to the same conclusions as Yitzchak.

"I too have accepted that whatever my fate, I will embrace it with happiness and contentment. To do otherwise would be unthinkable. Being in here has led me to realize that those who hate us will never defeat us. They might set us back every now and again but we shall always rise because we trust in the truth and that truth has been promised to us. I wish I would have the chance to see grandchildren one day, but if my lot is otherwise then so be it. Yitzchak, I shall sing praises to the Lord as I am led to my death if that is His will."

There was nothing more for Yitzchak to say. When they were wed they had created a new union built on mutual trust and respect. Now they would take the bonds they had forged over the years, together in death if that was their fortune. He wondered whether the others, Gedaliah, Nachum, Dina, Shalom and the rest of the town, had also come to terms with their destinies, whether they would accept their fates with the same understanding and serenity.

He would soon find out.

12

Father Charbrand arrived later that day with an entourage of accompanying priests and quickly ordered the guards to prepare the prison, converting it into an area suitable for conducting a tribunal. The chains were taken away and windows were chiseled out of the walls to provide ample light. A long table was brought in as well as chairs and a few small tables. Yitzchak was forced to remain in the far corner of the room, still chained, but the airiness and illumination of the changed environment helped make conditions more tolerable. He stood watching while the guards transformed a decrepit and gloomy building into a makeshift courtroom where his fate and the fate of his friends would be decided.

He waited.

Nothing more happened that day. The next day, however, Father Charbrand, Theobold, Henri, Philippe and four priests entered the building and seated themselves at the long table. They all wore long, black robes. Yitzchak realized they had taken upon themselves the role of judges and were dressed to fit the part. They stood for a few moments with their heads bowed while Father Charbrand offered a short prayer. Father Charbrand then sat down, followed by Theobold, Henri and Philippe. A few moments later Leah was led in by one of the guards and was directed to one of the small tables. She had been randomly selected to be the first member of the town to be questioned.

She sat down.

What did they want with her?

Leah sat quietly, visibly terrified. She was shaking and found it hard to remain poised. No one sitting at the long table calmed her or eased her fears. They sat and stared.

Finally Father Charbrand spoke. He was harsh yet calm and questioned her respectfully. "My name is Father Charbrand and I am told that your name is Leah, is that correct?" Father Charbrand waited as Leah nodded in agreement. Father Charbrand continued. "Leah, we would like to ask you some questions concerning a young Christian boy who was reported missing by his family. He lived here in Blois and was no more than two years old. Do you know the boy I am speaking about?" Father Charbrand was very reserved and waited patiently as Leah thought how best to respond. She noticed Henri moving about in his seat and sensed that the moment she answered, he would lash out at her and condemn her response as a lie. He terrified her. Of course Leah knew nothing about the boy or his family. She hardly spoke to the Christians in Blois and except for a few shopkeepers, knew none of them by name. She had heard that some of them had on occasion sought Rabbi Shimon's help but could not identify them and definitely did not know any of the children. She understood that she was being questioned about the boy Yitzchak was accused of murdering, but could not comprehend what they sought to accomplish by interrogating her. She concluded that her best course of action would be to simply tell the truth. She collected her thoughts and responded.

"Father Charbrand, I am not familiar with any Christians in Blois and I surely do not know any children. I am sorry to state that I did not know that child or anything that might have happened to him," Leah sounded afraid yet firm. She hoped she would not be questioned further. She glanced at Theobold, waiting for his response, but he sat quietly, almost motionless. Surprisingly, Henri and the other priests also remained at ease.

Father Charbrand responded, "We suspected that you would deny any knowledge about that poor boy. Are you aware that you and the rest of the town are accused of murdering that boy, using his blood for your rituals and then appointing Yitzchak with the task of getting rid of the body? Do you still insist you do not know the boy? Do you not remember the evils that were done to that boy and to Christian honor? Will you still deny the truth?" Again, Father Charbrand was calm, he did not raise his voice or speak excitedly.

Leah was shocked by the accusation and the extent of its reach. Her denials were meaningless: Father Charbrand had obviously concluded that she and everyone else in Blois were guilty! She nevertheless felt she must answer those ridiculous charges, try to inject a glimmer of doubt in Theobold or Henri or some of those priests, perhaps force them to concede that the accusation was baseless. She observed Theobold acting so placidly and wondered whether he disagreed with the priest's conclusions and that perhaps her denial might further widen any rift developing between Theobold and Father Charbrand. She believed that was unlikely but worth the effort. More importantly, though, she needed to answer them, maintain her own honor, her own dignity as a Jew. She asserted herself and answered Father Charbrand.

"I would like the tribunal to be aware of the fact that it is forbidden for Jews to eat blood. I myself have spent hundreds or perhaps thousands of hours removing any traces of blood from any meat or fowl that I cook for my family. If you do not believe me then I suggest you accompany me to the home of any Jew and observe how meat is prepared. You will find that the meticulousness and precision of the blood removal goes far beyond any concerns for health or disease, rather it is in allegiance to our laws. Not just here in Blois but all over the world Jews practice in this fashion. Your accusation can easily be refuted by the daily practices of Jews everywhere. I understand that this accusation is based on some witness or other evidence, but I assure you that your evidence is seriously flawed."

Leah had defended herself and her people. Her arguments were simple yet incisive. They would be repeated countless times to countless villains over the long exile and each time would fall on deaf ears.

Leah tried to read their expressions and determine whether her explanation was well received but everyone sat quietly, almost lifeless. She wondered whether anyone had been paying attention at all. Father Charbrand told Leah she could return to her home, the tribunal had finished questioning her. Leah stood, bowed before them, and left. Theobold was intrigued by Leah's explanations and knew they were probably true. But he continued to believe that a crime had been committed and that she was guilty along with everyone else, notwithstanding her assertions to the contrary. He needed Father Charbrand, though, to explain her excuse. Father Charbrand sensed that Leah's explanation made Theobold a little uneasy and knew he should address those concerns.

As soon as Leah departed and the tribunal was alone Father Charbrand stood and turned to Theobold, Henri and Philippe. "We have all just heard what the first witness has stated. I want to emphasize that it sounded convincing, even plausible, but remember the Jews are notorious at devising elaborate and fanciful tales. Do not believe any of it, it is all nonsense. If you wish, I can prove, based on their own writings, their affection and fascination with the blood of Christians, especially young boys. Do not be swayed by the arguments of that woman or any other Jew. They will devise other so-called proofs to lure you away from the truth, but withstand their temptations! Remain firm in your convictions and France shall be avenged!"

Father Charbrand resumed his seat and waited for the next Jew to be brought in. He never felt the need to repeat himself.

One by one the townspeople were brought before the robed men sitting behind the long table. Each person was questioned about the dead child and each person gave roughly the same responses as Leah. None of the townspeople ever appeared afraid or nervous and the questioning proceeded without much excitement. Henri and Philippe remained silent almost the entire time. Father Charbrand did virtually all of the questioning. There was an occasional remark from Theobold or the other priests, but nothing vicious or confrontational, simply questions clarifying the situation.

The questioning dragged on. Yitzchak was the only person permitted to remain in the room while the interrogation was progressing. He remained in the far corner, chained, and watched as his friends and townspeople all answered the tribunal in the same respectful yet defiant manner. Everyone denied any knowledge of the dead Christian boy, some even expressed sorrow for the boy's family, but they all insisted the idea of utilizing blood was totally preposterous.

Yitzchak had never spent so much time with the members of the town. Although he was forbidden to talk to them, he learned a great deal about them, even in this distant manner. He was always too caught up in his own life like most people, that he never gave his neighbors much thought. Now he had an opportunity to observe them, see them confronted with a life and death crisis, and he realized they were a lot like him. Hard-working people dedicated to their families, struggling to survive in a cold and hateful world. He admired them. This dilemma was far greater than anything they had ever experienced before and they seemed to accept it unconditionally. They demonstrated courage and determination that he never knew existed in them. He expected some of them to buckle under the pressure of the questioning and beg for mercy or clemency. None of them did so. He knew that some of them were still clinging to the belief that everything would be all right, but he somehow instinctively knew that they would join him in triumph and fulfillment if they all met the same end. He again thought about Jews all over the world. He recalled the Crusades, and the persecutions, which stretched far back across the annals of time. He had once wondered how Jews could cope and survive with the specter of hatred breathing down their necks. He watched as each man and woman in Blois renewed their dedication to the Torah and rejected the accusations and the world that bred them. He came to view Jews as heroes, giants among men with a fierce loyalty to G-d, which enabled them to champion the worst that history had in store. He now felt as if the entire town were kindred spirits, each growing and maturing on the strengths of each other.

He loved them all.

The festival of Shavuos was only a few days away. It had been six weeks since Passover had ended and still the ordeal was not yet finished. Nobody had thought it would take this long.

Seven weeks.

Usually the time between Passover and Shavuos is marked by a gradual awareness of man's purpose in the world and a commitment to fulfilling G-d's Torah. This year the townspeople understood that the difficulties they were experiencing were the greatest opportunity to proclaim their unwavering devotion to the Torah. Of course, they would have wished for a more common and mundane way to demonstrate their reverence and faithfulness to G-d, such as intense prayer or Torah study. But they had come to the same realization as Yitzchak had, and no longer saw themselves as objects of pity. They had come to understand that they were embarking on the greatest journey a Jew could undertake and accepted it wholeheartedly.

The arrival of the holiday reminded everyone that this episode was still ongoing and nobody could predict when it would end.

Tamar had approached Rabbi Shimon and inquired whether there was a possibility that Yitzchak could be released, just for the two-day holiday of Shavuos. Rabbi Shimon was reluctant to petition Theobold and Father Charbrand for additional favors, but Rabbi Baruch accurately noted that things could really not get that much worse and there would be no harm in merely making the request. Rabbi Shimon was surprised when the request was immediately granted. Theobold warned Rabbi Shimon that if Yitzchak were to escape there would be terrible punishments unleashed against the town. Rabbi Shimon assured Theobold that Yitzchak would not engage in such reckless behavior and would not even leave his home except to go to synagogue. Theobold likewise informed Rabbi Shimon that this gesture did not mean the tribunal was growing soft toward Yitzchak. Rabbi Shimon nodded and returned to Tamar with a small sense of victory.

Tamar was delighted. She had not seen Yitzchak since she had been called into the courtroom for questioning almost three weeks earlier. The children too were excited that their father would be coming home. The happiness, though, was bittersweet: Yitzchak, Tamar and Yaakov knew it would be their last holiday together.

Theobold's guards escorted Yitzchak home shortly before sundown on the day before Shavuos. Yitzchak quickly washed himself and prepared for the holiday. He was happy to be home. He enjoyed the warmth and the sights and sounds of the home he spent so many years building. Yes, it would be his last holiday, of that he was certain, and he was determined to make it special.

Later that night after Shmuel, Shalom and Devorah were asleep Yitzchak entered the kitchen and noticed Yaakov studying by the light of a flickering oil lamp that would extinguish at any moment. As Yitzchak entered, Yaakov looked up from his book.

"What are you doing, Yaakov?"

"I am studying Torah," answered Yaakov.

"Yaakov," Yitzchak moved toward his son. "I am very proud of you. Your dedication to Torah study is admirable. But I want to discuss something with you. Surely you are aware that after the holiday terrible things will undoubtedly happen here in Blois. You know that the town is being questioned for the murder of a Christian boy which started with an accusation made against me."

"Yes, father, I am aware. I knew something was wrong the moment you went to visit Rabbi Shimon in the middle of the night. I wondered why you did not tell me, trust me and share your worries with me." Yaakov looked hurt. He continued, "Do not worry, Father, I have forgiven you. I cannot harbor any ill feelings now. I am sorry for even telling you about this."

"Do not apologize, Yaakov, I wanted to confide in you, you are so strong and sure of yourself, but you must realize that I was so scared that day I did not know what to do. My failure to confide in you was due to the confusion of coping with what had happened to me, not a lack of trust in you. In fact there is something very important I must tell you. You are my oldest son and you are old enough to become the head of this household. I want you to protect Mother and the children, make sure they are cared for and that the children find proper marriage partners. I know that I am asking much of a fourteen-year-old, but I believe you are mature enough to contend with all of the problems you will face. Be strong Yaakov, be strong for the children. They will need your strength. You do not know, Yaakov, how much the children will need you. I am so sorry that this has happened to you."

Yitzchak drew close and embraced his son. Yaakov promised to fill his father's shoes as best he could. Yaakov did not really believe he and the family would survive but he kept that to himself and promised his father he would not let him down. The wick finally burned out but they remained in each other's arms for a long time.

Rabbi Shimon and Gavriel were also discussing the future.

They had a different relationship than Yitzchak and Yaakov and they made no pretenses about their own survival. They both wondered about Chana and whether the children would be spared. But even if Chana were to be left alive who would care for her? Rabbi Shimon had no answer. Gavriel suggested sending her to another town, where other Jews could raise her. Rabbi Shimon strongly doubted that Theobold would permit such elaborate machinations. Gavriel agreed that he did not know what would become of her and was consoled by the fact that she was still too young to fully comprehend how ominous the situation truly was.

Rabbi Shimon usually spent the first night of Shavuos in the synagogue but could not tear himself from the few remaining days and nights he had left with his family. He studied all night at home, together with Gavriel.

Rabbi Shimon began to feel tired and he realized he needed to refresh himself. He went outside for some air and Gavriel joined him.

Outside, Gavriel spoke. "Father, I must confess, the night Yitzchak and Tamar first came to visit you, I stood behind the door and I heard the entire conversation. I know I shouldn't have but curiosity got the best of me. I heard the fear in Yitzchak's voice and I sensed his helplessness and sorrow. At that moment I decided that I wanted to become someone who could somehow help our people. Ever since that night I have been torn by my desire to serve my People, and the knowledge that

I won't have that opportunity. That led me to realize all of the hopes and dreams of the people here will become consumed by the fires of injustice. I am sure you are aware that a body has never even been recovered, yet these accusations persist! How I wish I could stop it. Really, I do."

"Son, you have a good heart and if time would have allowed you would have matured into a caring and wonderful rabbi. But G-d has other plans and we cannot question them. You have made me very proud, Gavriel, and I do wish we could have had more time to grow together! Come, Gavriel, let us return to our studies and continue to pray with all our might that disaster may yet be averted."

Suddenly Gavriel felt something strange, something unnatural yet comforting. He was overtaken by a feeling, a premonition, that somehow he would live through the tribunal's evil justice unharmed. He tried to shake it but could not. He knew then what lay in store for him. He drew close to his father and whispered to him that he sensed he would survive. He then followed him into the house.

Throughout the town all the Jewish families were acting as if this was the last time they would have an opportunity to speak with each other and everyone felt a closeness, a special bond, and knew they had to seize the moment. Husbands apologized for flaring tempers, wives regretted missed opportunities, and children, those who were old enough to comprehend, bemoaned the inability to prove themselves to the world.

It was a sad and quiet holiday.

Only Pulcelina had no one with whom to commiserate. Her husband was deceased and she was childless. Her thoughts turned to Theobold. Why did he not come to visit her? What was he waiting for?

She had delayed approaching him, unwilling to appear desperate, and was certain he would eventually arrive but he still did not come. Pulcelina knew that time was running out. She could no longer wait. It was now time to place practicality ahead of pride.

She waited until the night after Shavuos ended and when it was very late, almost midnight, she made another nighttime trek through the town, to Theobold's temporary housing to beg for the lives of her people. She recalled the courage and persistence of Queen Esther who long ago placed her life in jeopardy and pleaded with the King of Persia to save her people. Pulcelina was determined to emulate Queen Esther's resolve and beseech another loathsome ruler in a different time and place to spare innocent Jews. She knew she was the only person in the town who had a chance to succeed and she cautiously approached his home. She was sure Theobold would be sleeping but would admit her once he awoke.

Theobold's temporary abode was located near the edge of the town in a vacant house that had been cleaned and readied prior to Theobold's arrival. He brought many of his own possessions with him to provide a distinctly regal ambiance.

Pulcelina hoped there would be no guards at the door. They would not allow her to speak with Theobold at this late hour and she was pleased to find no one protecting the house. Pulcelina approached cautiously and knocked on his door a number of times, applying greater force with each knock until she saw the light of a lamp ignite inside the home.

"Who is there?" roared Theobold.

Pulcelina announced, "It is me, Pulcelina."

"Are you aware it is the middle of the night? What brings you to my home at this late hour?" Theobold sounded sarcastic, he knew why she had come. Pulcelina did not respond and after a few moments of silence he opened the door.

Theobold had known that Pulcelina would arrive. He had been waiting for her, waiting to tell her that he no longer felt any obligation to favor her. The debt to her husband, Aaron, had long since been paid back and he owed her nothing.

"Ah, Pulcelina," mused Theobold, "once you were beautiful, but time and sorrow have marred your allure. Tell me, Pulcelina, did you think you could come here and beg for mercy after what has been done in this town? Did you think I would so quickly forget the crimes committed here? You know I could have you killed for trying to influence me."

Pulcelina realized she would have no influence over Theobold. He had changed. She was not sure if Father Charbrand or Alix had inspired him to reject her so quickly, or perhaps Rabbi Shimon was right, all her rejections of Theobold's favors had finally left an impression. His very demeanor was different, no longer willing to engage in discussion, and she knew the future was grim indeed. But she had ventured forth in the hopes of emulating a righteous queen who had succeeded in reversing an evil decree and she had to try, just one last time. Maybe he would be willing to entertain some ransom, some deal to release several of the townsfolk. She would question him about it, she had nothing to lose. She approached Theobold, bowed to his feet and cried to him.

"Theobold, you know why I am here. You know I am not here to bribe you, and if you wanted to kill me you could think of a better reason than that. I am here to discuss the possibility of a ransom. You are surely aware that Rabbi Baruch is a very wealthy man and has offered Abraham the astronomical sum of eighty pounds. You must know that the sum is far more than the measly lives of a few Jews is worth. I know that you possess kindness, you once displayed it for my husband. Please, Theobold, I beg you, have mercy on us. Accept the ransom and allow the tribunal to leave Blois without ever arriving at a decision!"

Pulcelina remained on the ground, with her head down. She had purposely invoked her husband, she thought his memory could still possibly sway Theobold. She slowly raised her head and saw Theobold standing almost lifeless, deep in thought. He then motioned for her to rise.

"What you say, Pulcelina, is very convincing and I admit that I was inclined to treat this as I have other crimes in the past. However, after much thought I concluded that I could not accept a ransom in this case. The crimes perpetrated by your friends in the town were crimes committed against all the Christians of France! I cannot allow the pride and honor of so many people to be disregarded for a mere ransom. It is the seriousness of the crime which necessitates my harsh conduct. You view me as a cruel man unwilling to negotiate for the release of your friends. You view this as a petty, insignificant matter and even wonder what I am doing here. But you are wrong, Pulcelina, the crimes committed here are so much bigger and more important than anything you can imagine. I am unwilling to ransom Jews because their guilt will not permit me to do so. Yes, Pulcelina, your begging and crying will not help you now, your fate has already been sealed. I display kindness to people like your husband who are deserving of such treatment, not murderers and bloodthirsty criminals. There will be no mercy this time. You should have thought of that before you murdered a helpless little boy!"

"But you know those accusations are false, Theobold."

"Pulcelina, are you questioning the conclusions of a holy tribunal? That is a terrible sin, it is blasphemy. Do you know the punishment for such disrespect?"

Pulcelina understood with regret that Theobold would never help her. "What does it matter Theobold? How many times can I be killed?"

Theobold escorted Pulcelina to the door, and with his hand ready to close it, managed to inject, "But tell Rabbi Baruch to come visit me tomorrow night, alone. There are a few matters I wish to discuss with him. That is all, Pulcelina, I suggest that you now return home." Theobold motioned for Pulcelina to move away from the door, which he quickly closed.

Pulcelina walked home mentally replaying her meeting with Theobold. She had never imagined that Theobold was uninterested in a ransom but he was treating this as a crime against France and the church, something above money and compromise. Yet, he informed her that the town had already been judged guilty, which seemed to make any further questioning unnecessary. Yitzchak, the only person with any link to the crime at all, and Philippe, the only witness, had yet to be questioned. As she walked home she reminded herself that she, like Queen Esther, had maintained her dignity and had not demeaned herself in the manner she was sure Theobold was expecting. At least she could be proud of that much, or that little.

What about Rabbi Baruch? What did Theobold want with him? To steal his money and then bind him to the stake along with the rest of the town?

She realized she had yet to fathom the depths of Theobold's cunning.

She planned to visit Rabbi Baruch in the morning.

13

It was the day after Shavuos and everybody in the town had been questioned except for Yitzchak, Rabbi Shimon and Rabbi Baruch. Theobold purposely saved them for last. He felt that would better suit his plans to ransom a few of the Jews. Father Charbrand also agreed that the last Jews to be questioned should be Yitzchak and the important personages in the town, but his reasons concerned the integrity of the proceeding. Rabbi Baruch was the first of the leaders to be called for questioning. Everyone now knew the end was soon approaching, Theobold had said so, and while that knowledge was frightening at least the town glimpsed closure to the ordeal that had dragged on for so long. Rabbi Shimon suspected he and Rabbi Baruch would be questioned last and discussed the questioning with almost everyone Father Charbrand had interrogated.

Rabbi Baruch had already spoken with Pulcelina and sensed Theobold wished to discuss a ransom, at least for some of the Jews. That provided him with a little optimism and he knew that the questioning which was about to take place was quite meaningless. He answered Father Charbrand's questions in a nonchalant, almost bored manner. Theobold detected Rabbi Baruch's casualness and lack of interest and correctly assessed that Rabbi Baruch had spoken with Pulcelina and was anxiously awaiting a discussion with him. Theobold dared not mention it in front of Henri, Father Charbrand or the other priests, and he remained silent as Father Charbrand continued his oft-repeated accusation of murder and barbarism. Rabbi Baruch was indeed anxious to meet with Theobold and was concentrating on that while answering Father Charbrand. The questioning concluded routinely and Rabbi Baruch made the usual bow of respect and left the room.

Father Charbrand wondered why Rabbi Baruch, one of the leaders of the town, barely put up a defense and practically conceded defeat. He concluded that Rabbi Baruch as well as all the rest of the Jews probably recognized the futility of such efforts and had resigned themselves to the fate of the tribunal.

Father Charbrand was pleased. Only two more Jewish witnesses and then Philippe the slave, and the Blois region would be free of Jews.

Rabbi Baruch did not tell anyone that he was meeting with Theobold. It would only complicate matters, give some of the people false hopes, lead them into thinking they might be spared. Rabbi Baruch did not want to think about choosing whom to rescue should Theobold accept a ransom for a few of the Jews. He concluded that he would not make that impossible choice, even if a ransom hinged on it.

Rabbi Baruch arrived in front of Theobold's home and through the window noticed a lamp already lit. As soon as Rabbi Baruch drew near to the house, the door opened and Theobold stood at the entrance with an outstretched arm and a warm smile.

Rabbi Baruch was repulsed by Theobold's shallowness but remained silent. To save lives he would play the part just as well. Rabbi Baruch took Theobold's hand and held it in a manner pleasing to Theobold. Theobold sensed the awkwardness of the moment, withdrew his hand and motioned for Rabbi Baruch to follow.

Once inside Theobold did not waste any time. He offered Rabbi Baruch a seat and stood in front of him. Rabbi Baruch finally heard the words he had hoped he would hear since finding out what had happened, after the *seder* over seven weeks ago.

"Rabbi Baruch, I am sure you understand why I have asked you here. As predicted, the evidence against the Jews of Blois is very strong and I am sorry to say that mercy or clemency is simply out of the question." Rabbi Baruch did not flinch. This much he already knew. Theobold continued, "However, I am inclined to ransom a few of you, two or three perhaps, if the price is right. I know that Abraham accepted your offer of eighty pounds, and obviously that must be rejected. After interviewing virtually each member of the town and determining the level of deceit and harm committed by them, I cannot accept that meager sum as an adequate ransom. The price is now one hundred pounds of gold, as well as the cancellation of another one hundred pounds of debt owed to Jews throughout this region by various French nobles! If you cannot meet my demands, then you, Rabbi Baruch, shall suffer the same fate as the rest of your friends!"

That was not quite what Rabbi Baruch had been expecting. True, he was now given an opportunity to save a few Jews, but at a price he simply could not afford. Even if he were to sell all his books and possessions he could not guarantee the cancellation of that much debt, virtually all of which was owed to other Jews. He felt that Theobold's new demands were unfair and that the amount of money requested was so excessive that it was impossible to meet. He never thought he would have to concede that he could not rescue a Jew's soul, and he lowered his head in shame. All the planning, thinking and hoping that he had undertaken with Rabbi Shimon had now come to a head and he lacked the necessary means.

Should he admit failure and lose the few Jews that could otherwise be saved?

Was he permitted to fail? He knew he had to somehow raise the money and save whomever he could. He would need some time, ten months or perhaps a year. He was certain that if he had the time he could raise the money and save a few Jews, begin with them anew in another, friendlier place, if such a place even existed. Yes, if he had time he could meet the demands. Rabbi Baruch was instantly filled with feelings of rage and disgust which were totally out of character for him. Granted, the town would be killed out, and maybe some Jews spared, but it bothered him that Theobold would become wealthy in the process. Rabbi Baruch resented that someone so cruel would be rewarded in such a glorious fashion. He knew that it was wrong to question the unjustified flourishing of evil but the thoughts persisted. He promised revenge.

Theobold was waiting for an answer.

Rabbi Baruch turned to him, "Well, Theobold, I will agree to pay you one hundred pounds within the next week and arrange for the cancellation of eighty pounds of debt over the course of the next year." Rabbi Baruch thought he could lower the outstanding number by twenty pounds, a considerable sum in its own right. Theobold did not even notice the difference, he was too caught up in the completion of the deal. Rabbi Baruch continued, "In return, I am seeking the ransom of five Jews from Blois."

Theobold's jubilation suddenly turned nasty. He suspected Rabbi Baruch would try to deceive him. "You Jews are all the same, always squeezing for more and more. I told you, Rabbi Baruch, that the arrangement would be for two, possibly three Jews and now you demand five! I should call off the deal right now!!"

Rabbi Baruch knew that Theobold would never abandon such a huge windfall. He also knew that Theobold would never agree to five, he only said it to secure four. Rabbi Baruch knew Theobold would react this way and was ready for him.

"Theobold, I was surprised by the increase of your demands, yet I met them without complaint. I am merely exhibiting the same negotiating tactics that you employ so well. If you do not agree with my terms then I will request four Jews."

Theobold knew he could reject that as well but understood that he might need Rabbi Baruch again in the future and reluctantly agreed. After all, what was one more Jew?

Rabbi Baruch was pleased that he could save at least one more Jew, a bittersweet victory indeed.

They shook hands and each gave his word that the agreement would not be broken. Rabbi Baruch was reluctant to remain any longer. They did not discuss which Jews would be permitted to live.

Rabbi Baruch was well aware that no one's blood was thicker than anyone else's and would not make the determination. His fears were quickly eased when Theobold informed him that he was one of the four souls that would be ransomed and that he, Theobold, would determine the other three. Theobold bade Rabbi Baruch farewell and he walked home.

Once outside Rabbi Baruch felt that he had been successful. He had managed to save himself and three other Jews. True, he would be bankrupt but that did not concern him. He was also happy that he would not be forced into making impossible choices of life and death. But whoever would be chosen could join him and search out a new home in an area of peace and tranquility.

He believed he had done the right thing.

Rabbi Baruch passed the home of Nachum the baker and saw him pacing and caressing a sleepless child. Surely the quiet of the night would give Nachum time to reflect on recent events. What would Nachum think of Rabbi Baruch's performance tonight? Would he agree the meeting with Theobold was a success?

Maybe.

He heard Nachum call out to him and moved toward him. "How are you, Rabbi Baruch? Sleepless like my little Moshe, eh?"

Rabbi Baruch looked at Moshe. He could not have been more than two-and-a-half-months old. So young and fragile. So full of future and promise. What will become of him? Of Nachum, his father? Of Yitzchak's daughter, Devorah, and the other children in Blois?

No, he had not succeeded with Theobold. There could not be success with so much destruction, so much loss. Rabbi Baruch had negotiated for a surviving remnant, a pathetic fragment of a once vibrant and thriving town, which was failure indeed. Rabbi Baruch could not face Nachum, he could not face any of the townspeople or even himself. He kissed the infant and walked away feeling helpless and ashamed.

Rabbi Shimon was called for questioning the next day and, like Rabbi Baruch, found the whole affair tedious more than anything else.

Rabbi Shimon knew the tribunal had already concluded they were guilty and wished a final judgment would be rendered. Again, Father Charbrand was courteous yet firm and when the questioning was finished, Rabbi Shimon was escorted home.

Yitzchak was then released from the bonds restraining him since the day after Shavuos and was brought before the table where each of the witnesses had been questioned. He was seated, but this time Father Charbrand was not pleasant. He was abrasive and loud. He started by informing Yitzchak that he would not be questioned, there was no reason to do so since Philippe had witnessed his participation in the crime. In harsh tones he began lecturing Yitzchak, saying that his actions represented a terrible stain on France, which he had been sent by the church to rectify. Father Charbrand spoke for an hour about the evils of the Jews and the crimes they perpetrated against the humble Christians of France. He noted that it was impossible for him or other church leaders to uncover every misdeed committed by the Jews, but that Philippe was fortunate enough to have witnessed at least this one. He concluded by promising revenge and swift justice.

Unlike the other witnesses, Yitzchak was not permitted to speak. Father Charbrand did not doubt the truth of Philippe's account; however, he was concerned that if Yitzchak were given a chance to defend himself he would manipulate and twist the words of the illiterate slave. Besides, Yitzchak could say nothing that would change his mind.

After listening to all this, Yitzchak was told to stand up and Father Charbrand ordered that he be taken outside. One of the guards standing at the far end of the room approached Yitzchak and led him near the door. No one was sure why he was being led outside, but no one questioned it either. Yitzchak was quite happy. The door opened and Yitzchak took a deep breath and held it for a while. He did not know how long this would last and he savored every moment. The guard permitted him to walk to a nearby tree and as Yitzchak felt the cool, soft breezes caress his face, he treasured the feeling most others take for granted.

Yitzchak appeared to possess an inner contentment, like someone who has come to terms with an overzealous creditor, and he walked calmly and happily. He was thrilled to be outside and was busy relishing the simple pleasures of life.

Inside the building, Father Charbrand directed some guards to fill a huge basin of water, large enough to hold at least one person. Now that all the Jews were questioned, Father Charbrand was preparing the truth verification method, which Philippe had volunteered to undergo. No one was certain whether Father Charbrand truly believed that Philippe would defy nature and float in the water, and Theobold was particularly anxious to see his mentor perform a miracle.

The guards quickly brought a tub, which Father Charbrand had prepared just for this occasion. He had done this once before, about fifteen years earlier, when a landowner from Orleans accused his slave of stealing his money. The slave denied it and his owner agreed to undergo the water test. Rumors spread that Father Charbrand employed the test and that the owner had floated for fifteen minutes, proving his claims that the slave was a thief. Most people believed Father Charbrand a miracle worker and an able servant of the church, but questions about the details of the test led some to suspect Father Charbrand's methods. Some accused him of fabricating the miracle. Father Charbrand did not wish to make the same mistake and concluded the most effective way to do that would be to conduct the test in private. That way he and Philippe, the illiterate slave, would be the only ones who could comment on what took place.

When the tub had been filled Father Charbrand waited an hour or so for the water to warm up. He then sent everyone out of the building, except for Philippe. Theobold and Henri wanted to remain but Father Charbrand would not permit it. Although he trusted Theobold and had nothing to fear from Henri, he could not afford rumors about something this serious. Father Charbrand assured Theobold and Henri that he was confident Philippe would pass the test.

Theobold, Henri, the priests and the remaining guards all exited the building, leaving Father Charbrand alone with Philippe and the large tub of water. Father Charbrand warned Philippe that he was about to undergo a holy and important task and that he should not be afraid of the consequences. Philippe nodded and began to undress.

Some time later, Father Charbrand opened the door of the building and, with an imposing smile, informed the rest of the tribunal that Philippe had in fact floated and told the truth! He explained that Philippe remained afloat for the better part of an hour and surely dispelled any doubts among those who refused to believe him!

Father Charbrand was not questioned about any of the details of the test and its methods were never examined. The tribunal could now move to the next stage. Father Charbrand immediately suggested a short prayer, and was joined by the priests, Theobold, Henri and Philippe.

Forty Jews had been accused of a vicious act. Forty Jews would now suffer.

This episode began at the waters of the Loire and concluded with the water of Father Charbrand's test. It seemed as if the entire ordeal was as slippery and elusive as the liquid itself.

Perhaps history would remember that the fires of hatred could not easily be quenched.

14

Wednesday, the twentieth day of the month of Sivan in the year 1171, began with an intense heat unusual for late May. Ever since Passover and the unseasonably warm weather, everyone knew this would be an unseasonably hot summer. But the intensity of the sun this early was particularly strange. The townspeople of Blois were woken to the shrills and screams of guards commanding everyone to report to the center square located near the synagogue. Everyone at once knew the end was at hand.

The townspeople had been waiting for this day for a long time and yet when it arrived many of them were truly shocked. Some had thought disaster would be diverted somehow, others had refused to believe the day would ever really come. Everyone moved slowly to the town square.

The first to arrive there was Rabbi Shimon. The moment he was woken by the guards, he rushed there to greet his forty children and try to provide them with some comfort and solace. Theobold, Henri and Father Charbrand were already standing there, clad in long black robes. Behind them stood the other tribunal priests. Father Charbrand greeted Rabbi Shimon and then turned away. Theobold informed Father Charbrand that four Jews would be freed. Father Charbrand was not in favor of releasing even that many but when he heard the amount of money secured by Theobold, he relented.

Rabbi Shimon stood and gazed at Father Charbrand and Theobold, who were busy talking. There was nothing he could say anymore and he remained standing in silence. One by one the townspeople arrived, and while they tried to appear resilient and optimistic, they found it increasingly difficult to shake thoughts of impending disaster. Every Jewish member of the town eventually arrived.

Without any further orders from Father Charbrand, everyone was led back to the building which had first served as their prison, and they were all directed to go inside. There were many large wooden poles stuck into the ground. The guards led the townsfolk to the stakes and began binding their hands to them. Rabbi Baruch was told not to enter the building and he remained outside. As the members of the town were being led in, Theobold stopped Gavriel and likewise ordered him to remain outside. Theobold vowed to honor the pledge he had made to Rabbi Baruch and selected Gavriel randomly, or so he thought. Gavriel had been holding hands with Chana and their father. Theobold's directive caught the three of them by surprise. Theobold forcibly separated Gavriel from his father and sister and provided no explanation to any of them. Rabbi Shimon was confused. He moved back and forth, craning his neck in all directions, wondering where Gavriel had been taken. He instinctively reached for Gavriel, who by now was too far away. Gavriel watched as Chana stretched out her small arm and wiggled her delicate fingers in an effort to reconnect with her brother. Rabbi Shimon was still confused, but as he moved forward, he managed to see Gavriel standing outside next to Theobold with tears rolling down his cheeks. Rabbi Shimon smiled, squeezed Chana's hand and proceeded into the building.

Gavriel stood there watching them until they were out of sight. He never forgot that smile and he never saw them again.

Theobold also stopped two other men, Nathan the teacher and David the wine merchant. The two of them were half crazed with confusion, and when they saw their families being led into the building they both panicked and ran away. Theobold made no effort to stop them. He had fulfilled his part of the bargain.

As Pulcelina approached the entrance she saw Henri smiling with delight. Yes, he had hated her for so very long, for receiving special treatment, always just beyond his reach, and now he was gleefully watching her suffer her greatest defeat. Pulcelina knew why Henri was so delighted and refused to give him any satisfaction, even now. She held her head high and with the aristocracy and elegance for which she was noted walked proudly into the building.

As Yitzchak approached the entrance, Father Charbrand braced himself for wild accusations or possible pleas of mercy. But Yitzchak walked into the building with an eagerness and excitement that greatly surprised Father Charbrand as well as Theobold. Yitzchak entered with his wife and children beside him and took his place among his townspeople and took his place in history.

When the entire town was securely inside, the guards closed the door. The clang of stone meeting metal made a loud noise, which seemed to seal their fate.

A few moments later the door opened and Father Charbrand entered. He had his own agenda, which he had not shared with anyone. He stood near the entrance and asked for everyone's attention. "You all know why you are here. You all know what will be happening shortly. I am here to tell you that all of you may be freed instantly. You may all return to your homes, free men and women. All that you must do is embrace the Cross and accept baptism. If any one of you converts to our wonderful and glorious religion, you will receive immediate freedom and eternal redemption!"

Father Charbrand waited.

Yitzchak looked around the room. This was all his fault. Would anyone succumb to the pressure, spurn Yitzchak and G-d and seek salvation elsewhere? The offer was very easy to accept. Was everyone's faith and dedication as strong as his own? He waited, too.

Nobody in the room moved; no one approached Father Charbrand. Father Charbrand was visibly angry and repeated his offer. Again, no one moved.

Yitzchak finally understood that he was not special or particularly devout, but that he was a Jew and along with his friends and loved ones would willingly sacrifice for their beliefs, even with their lives.

Yitzchak hoped this would never be forgotten.

The silence in the room was as annoying to Father Charbrand as the rejection it represented. He had thought that at least half the room would have the sense to grab such an offer. He concluded that the Jews were a stubborn people indeed.

Father Charbrand then proceeded to leave. On his way out, he threw in a fiery torch and the building was soon ablaze.

Rabbi Baruch and Gavriel watched in horror as the fires took hold and raged on and on. After a few moments Rabbi Baruch heard faint singing coming from within the building. He looked at Gavriel and saw that he heard it too.

Were they mad?

The singing grew louder until they could hear the words that accompanied the melody. Rabbi Baruch recognized them immediately. They were the words of *Aleinu*, the prayer sung during the High Holy Days and at the conclusion of every prayer service. Gavriel also identified the words and immediately knew they were not mad, just faithful. They were praising and singing to G-d, even now, even in pain and sorrow. Gavriel wondered whether he would have been able to muster the same energy and dedication if he were there with them. Gavriel heard the town sing in unison, "We bend our knees, bow and acknowledge our thanks before the King Who reigns over kings," and ran to Rabbi Baruch for comfort.

The singing lasted for quite awhile, much to the dismay of Father Charbrand and Theobold. As time wore on and the intensity of the fires grew to strengths no human could endure, the singing stopped. Gavriel watched as the smoke rose above the roof toward the heavens, taking the cries of the people with it. He knew life was crumbling inside and felt his own life crumble as well. As their singing stopped so did the singing in his soul, the will to live on, the desire to meet and conquer the challenges of life. He had wanted to help his people, lead them, make their lives better, but now could think of nothing but Father Charbrand and Theobold. He was disgusted with them and all they represented and wanted nothing to do with them or their successors.

Yet, as he stood looking into the emptiness that lay ahead, he was somehow supported and sustained by the faith and perseverance of his brethren. Their courage and plain beliefs gave Gavriel the understanding that he could not give up on life, he could never give up on something so hallowed, and would simply have to take any pitfalls or setbacks in stride. The moment he stopped caring and admitted defeat was the moment Theobold could truly be called the victor. Gavriel promised he would never let that happen. In those few moments, Gavriel learned and absorbed the greatest lesson of all. He would remember it forever.

Yes, he would survive, and he would miss his father, sister and the rest of the town terribly. But Gavriel was prepared to shoulder the burden of the memories of his townspeople for the rest of his life. As the fire raged, so did Gavriel's soul. He rejected his thoughts of defeat and isolation. Somehow he would infuse his future with meaning and determination.

Somehow.

Rabbi Baruch stood silently, transfixed by the dedication and allegiance that forty ordinary Jews displayed at a time of extreme helplessness. He admired them, was proud of them and would spend the rest of his life honoring them.

He already had an idea in mind.

Rabbi Baruch was so hypnotized by the sacrifices of his friends inside the building that he scarcely realized that Gavriel was still clutching his hands in fear and anguish. Rabbi Baruch then belatedly understood that this was not something to which a young boy should be exposed. He took Gavriel and, with only the clothes on their backs, left the town. They left behind their dead relatives and friends and never returned. Rabbi Baruch would visit Theobold later in the month with further payment and would continue paying him for a year and a half, but Jewish life in Blois had ended, never to be restored.

While leaving, Gavriel's mind was now clear. He harbored an intense hatred toward Theobold and Father Charbrand. And yet he knew that the town had accepted upon themselves this evil decree with enthusiasm and joy, which would provide inspiration and motivation to countless Jews everywhere. He was more determined than ever to impart his experiences to as many Jews as possible and knew he would surely try to become a rabbi.

On the outskirts of the town they stopped at the Loire to rest. This is where it had all started.

At the river.

The trauma had so drained Gavriel that he lay down under some bushes near the bank and fell asleep. Rabbi Baruch sat down to rest, still replaying the events in his mind, trying to make sense out of them.

Gavriel awoke and was alone with Rabbi Baruch. Rabbi Baruch could say nothing to console Gavriel; that would take time. Nor could Rabbi Baruch try to explain it to Gavriel; he would have to work things out alone, question what happened, reconcile his feeble understanding of justice with G-d's. It would not be easy but Rabbi Baruch knew that in time Gavriel would come to terms with what had transpired. But Rabbi Baruch did want to talk with Gavriel, he had something urgent to tell him and it could not wait. The destruction of the town had been weighing on Rabbi Baruch and he was wondering how he could create an everlasting tribute to the brave and holy souls who had perished. He thought he had found a way but wanted Gavriel to be the one to actualize it. After all, Gavriel lived there all his life and Gavriel's father was their leader. Rabbi Baruch knew that it would be most fitting if Gavriel would undertake to fulfill what Rabbi Baruch had in mind.

Gavriel was sitting near the river staring into the water, the source of all the misfortune. Rabbi Baruch hesitated to strike up a conversation with him but did not want to forfeit this opportunity. He approached Gavriel cautiously.

"Gavriel, are you all right?"

Gavriel barely nodded as Rabbi Baruch sat down beside him. Gavriel did not look well. Rabbi Baruch thought that it might be better to wait until later. Gavriel then turned to Rabbi Baruch. "I have been thinking, Rabbi Baruch, what can I do for my father and sister and the rest of the town? How can I commemorate and make enduring the memory of the townspeople? I want to do something special, something important to honor and glorify everyone who died in Blois. I want to erect a monument for the entire world to see. No, Rabbi Baruch, I do not care about the rest of the world anymore, they do not warrant my emotions. I only care about our people. I want Jews everywhere to see my monument and have it serve as a memorial to honor our dead. I have decided to become a rabbi and help people whenever I can, but tell me, Rabbi Baruch, what do you suggest I do to honor the martyrs of Blois?"

Rabbi Baruch was amazed at the boy's intelligence and sensitivity. Gavriel had raised the very issue that Rabbi Baruch desperately wished to discuss with him. He knew the time was right. He drew closer to Gavriel.

"As you know Gavriel, I am a scribe, I write Torah scrolls, mezuzahs and even books. I write them because there are not enough of them in the world. There have been so many Torahs that have been destroyed over the years. Gavriel, I think you should learn to be a scribe and dedicate your life to writing Torahs. You can never bring back the townspeople of Blois but you can perpetuate what they stood for! Your Torahs will serve as an everlasting reminder, the monument that you spoke of to honor and glorify the people of Blois. I will train you, Gavriel. I will work with you, teach you and guide you as you mature into a professional and expert scribe."

Rabbi Baruch continued, "Gavriel, you can start a legacy which could span hundreds of years. Of course I expect you to marry and raise children and be a dedicated and caring rabbi, but I am speaking of a different sort of legacy. One that touches the mind of each Jew, affects each Jew in a most intimate and personal way. By writing Torahs dedicated to the tragedy of Blois, you will not merely pass through history, you will become history. I am sure you are aware that a well-written Torah, one where the finest ink and parchment is used, can last for many generations. For the next one thousand years whenever one of your Torahs is read, it will stir the souls of our people and forever remind them of the courage we just witnessed. Gavriel, I can think of no better memorial than this."

Gavriel absorbed every word of Rabbi Baruch's suggestion. Gavriel knew that Rabbi Baruch was correct: it would be a perfect testimonial, a proper monument to his father and the town. But something was missing. He felt Rabbi Baruch's idea needed to be a bit more personalized. Gavriel thought a few moments and instinctively knew the answer.

Yes, he would become a scribe and make a significant contribution to Jews everywhere. He would learn the trade and write many Torahs. But there would be one Torah, a special Torah that he would write to specifically commemorate the downfall in Blois. He would spend a lifetime writing it. It would be beautiful, nay, the most beautiful scroll imaginable. Each letter would be individually crafted, written again and again, until perfection would be achieved. The parchment would be the most expensive, the ink the finest. Quills would be imported from the world over, and anyone who looked at the Torah would marvel at its detail. The meticulousness, the distinction of each letter, the craftsmanship would surely result in the most eye-catching and striking Torah anyone would ever behold. And most of all, the beauty of the Torah's message, of its enduring and inspiring teachings, would draw people close to it, to cherish it and the larger spirit of the Jewish People which flows from it. Gavriel would spend a lifetime on this project, writing others in the meanwhile, but always returning and refining and reviewing that one Torah scroll.

And that would be the memorial to his father, his sister and the rest of the martyrs of Blois.

Gavriel told Rabbi Baruch about his plan and Rabbi Baruch agreed wholeheartedly. Gavriel pledged to Rabbi Baruch that he would do it.

They began walking toward a new home and a new life.

Rabbi Gavriel looked up with a tear in his eye. It had been so many years and yet the memories were still sharp and focused. He recalled that when the great Tosafist, Rabbeinu Tam, had heard what had happened to the Jews of Blois he proclaimed the infamous day, the twentieth of Sivan, a day of prayer and fasting, and compared the calamity to the assassination of Gedaliah the son of Achikam shortly before the First Temple was destroyed in Jerusalem.

Rabbi Gavriel always fasted on that day and instructed his children to do likewise. In recent years, though, Rabbi Gavriel no-

ticed that fewer and fewer people undertook the observance of the fast day.

Would the tragedy become forgotten?

Rabbi Gavriel already had a difficult time recalling the names of everyone who had lived in Blois. Wouldn't the passage of time further dull the memory and meaning of what had happened?

Rabbi Gavriel drew close to the Torah. It truly was a masterpiece, far more beautiful than Rabbi Baruch would ever have imagined.

The Torah was finally finished, his promise to Rabbi Baruch fulfilled.

Shortly before the Torah was dedicated in the synagogue that Rabbi Gavriel had helped build, he summoned his youngest granddaughter, Rachel, who was married to Rabbi Yisrael the town scribe. He instructed her to weave a cover for the Torah, made of the finest silk she could find. Rabbi Gavriel further instructed her to embroider onto the front of the cover a brief inscription; that this Torah was written to commemorate the tragedy which took place in Blois in 1171 and to record the year 1239, the year the Torah was completed. Rachel readily complied. She knew her grandfather's story well and felt honored to be able to participate in this important and meaningful endeavor. Following an elaborate ceremony, the Torah, wearing its beautiful cover, was placed in the synagogue where it remained for many years.

Rabbi Gavriel had undertaken this project to commemorate and perpetuate the honor of those massacred at Blois, to remember the heroes and prove to the world that Theobold and Father Charbrand had been utter failures in their evil quest. They could massacre Jews, but the spirit of the Jews could never be extinguished. The Torah's beauty would always endure, calling Jews to it, to study it and marvel at its uniqueness and special role in the world and thereby continue to perpetuate the legacy.

Would he succeed?

Only time would tell.

Huesca, Spain 1465

Sir, state your wishes now in the presence of these Jews, for, truth to tell, you are placing all of us and yourself in great jeopardy. Make certain that you are not impelled by excitement or by any other motive other than reverence for the Law of Moses.

— Rabbi Abraham Bibago to Juan de Ciudad

15

Juan de Ciudad wanted to go to the secret meeting but could not excuse himself when the church beckoned. Juan made every attempt to attend all the meetings held by the secret Jews in Plasencia, but Father Pedro had summoned him to the church. He knew that if he refused, he would invoke Father Pedro's immediate suspicion. Juan feared that Father Pedro already suspected that he was a secret Jew and did not want to do anything to reinforce those suspicions.

Juan hated when he missed a meeting. Even after all these years, although there was little more for him to learn, he found the atmosphere comforting and reassuring. At this meeting, Alfonso Cabrerro, the spiritual leader of the secret Jews, was scheduled to speak about the Sabbath, a topic particularly dear to Juan. But he could not attend this time, it was simply too risky, and he wondered how long this could go on. As he walked to the church, Juan knew something had to change, and soon.

Juan de Ciudad was not much different than the other secret Jews in Plasencia except that he seemed to be more troubled by the double lives they lived. His background was so typical of a secret Jew in Spain in 1465 that many of his friends wondered where he acquired the drive, the determination and the will to break from a routine everyone else seemed to accept blindly. Occasionally, Juan himself wondered the same.

It surely did not come from his parents. They were compliant and simple people, not the type to ever question or challenge their lot in life. Juan's parents were born Jews, but they converted to Christianity during the terrible wave of violence which swept through Castile and the rest of Spain in 1391. Juan's father, Miguel, had converted along with his family after succumbing to the pressures of an angry mob that offered them either conversion or death. Miguel was only eleven years old at the time but embraced his new religion enthusiastically. He never again entered a synagogue and no longer observed the Sabbath or the holidays. Juan's mother, Elienor, also eleven at the time, converted along with her family after a local priest threatened to destroy the family farm.

Like all conversos, recent converts to Christianity, Miguel had been forced to attend the "great" debate held in the Catalonian town of Tortosa in 1413 and 1414. The Church had sponsored the debate in an effort to prove the truth and supremacy of Christianity and to humiliate and demean the rabbis, who were not permitted to adequately defend their faith. Miguel had forgotten almost all he had known about Judaism, but nonetheless recognized the unfairness and imbalance of the proceedings. It was in Tortosa that Miguel met Elienor, who had likewise been forced to attend.

Miguel and Elienor married soon after the debates, and Juan was born the following year.

The couple moved to Plasencia in Western Castile, not far from the border shared with Portugal. Miguel began apprenticing as a silversmith and soon became very wealthy by crafting religious symbols. By the time Juan was of age to enter the business it was the most successful shop in Plasencia, employing three additional artisans.

Miguel and Elienor attended church regularly and participated in all the Christian rituals. Juan was raised as a Christian: He was baptized soon after birth and had not been circumcised.

Juan and his parents were no different in practice or worship than other Christians in Plasencia.

No, his parents had done virtually nothing to inspire Juan to return to Judaism. About the only thing he could remember was his mother's instruction that he marry someone Jewish. Juan did not understand why that mattered, but he complied with her demand anyway and married Margarita, the daughter of converted Jews.

Yes, Juan clearly remembered what drove him to the secret Jews.

It was his neighbor, Diego Nasso.

Juan and Diego were close friends. They were both actively involved in the church. Diego was a merchant of religious relics and bought almost all his wares from Juan. They were both men of means and often talked of going into partnership. Margarita and Diego's wife, Luisa, were also very close and both were active in many of the church charities and community events. Three years after they were wed, Margarita conceived. Luisa cared for her and helped around the house, especially in the later months when Margarita was often tired and confined to bed. Luisa and Diego were childless, and as Margarita's due date approached, Luisa seemed as excited as the young couple.

On an unusually warm late summer evening in 1445, Diego came to visit. He looked shaken and scared, as if something terrible had happened. Juan immediately led him into his home and offered a drink but Diego refused. Diego murmured that he needed to speak with Juan, privately. Margarita, who had been cooling herself with wet towels, slowly rose and left the room.

The two men were alone.

The home was richly decorated, mostly with silver relics crafted by Juan's artisans. There were numerous small figurines depicting different Christian figures and saints as well as crosses of various sizes hung throughout the room. Near the window was a small wood table where some decanters and goblets were placed.

It was very hot and Diego was sweating profusely. He looked awful.

What was the matter?

Diego wiped his face with a handkerchief to remove the perspiration. He still appeared distraught. He retreated to a chair while Juan poured himself a drink and sat down next to him. "What is the matter, Diego, is everything all right?" asked Juan, "You look a little flustered."

"I am feeling a little better now, Juan, thank you. But something terrible has happened to me and Luisa; that is why I am here."

Juan looked startled. What could have happened?

Diego composed himself and turned to Juan. "I do not know how to tell you this, Juan, but after tonight I do not think you will ever see me again," he said calmly.

Diego had been waiting for this moment for three years. Ever since he had learned of Juan's Jewish roots, he wanted to tell him the truth. Diego always envisioned telling Juan under happier circumstances, however, not in haste and secrecy. He took a deep breath and continued. "You see, Luisa and I are secret Jews, known as marranos. We are dedicated to the Torah and try as best we can to fulfill the commandments. We are part of a growing number of Christians who were born as Jews and who have returned to a Jewish way of life. We practice Judaism in private and in secrecy. Most of us were raised as Christians and lack even some of the most elementary knowledge of Judaism. We initially attempted receiving religious instruction from some of the rabbis here in Plasencia, but associating with those who are obviously Jews was and still is very dangerous. We could not risk being caught socializing with Jews, so we stopped the instruction and have not had any significant contact with the rabbis in years. I am sure you are aware that true Jews, those who remained Jewish throughout all the turmoil of the past fifty years, do not have to hide and pray and worship in secret."

The church had concluded that all Jews who converted to Christianity, and their children, were full-fledged Christians, just like any natural born Spaniard or Frenchman. They were not troubled by the fact that many of the baptisms, which took place in 1391 and again in 1414, were done simply to avoid death and were not sincere. The church cares little for the motivation behind a conversion, especially that of a Jew. Once the church secured all those conversions they were not willing to reverse them.

"We cannot practice in public because a Christian is forbidden to practice Judaism. It is heresy, which is punishable by death. That is the reason we cannot simply return to Judaism. In the church's view, we are Christians and will always remain Christians. Therefore, we cannot even associate with Jews; we could be accused of heresy. It has happened numerous times already. But those Jews who survived the mobs and riots of those years and refused to convert are protected by the edicts of kings and Popes. They conduct themselves as if the church does not have jurisdiction over them and cannot intrude in their religious practices. Of course the church seeks to convert them as well, and pursues that objective relentlessly, but for now they are free to openly practice Judaism. Since the secret Jews cannot unite with the practicing Jews, the secret Jews are left without proper guidance. It is very difficult indeed. We have tried our best with smuggled books of Talmud and Maimonides and whatever else we could acquire, but believe me, Juan, it has not been easy."

Juan sat in amazement. He had known Diego for about three years. They had met soon after he and Margarita were wed. He always considered Diego a bit eccentric, taking many late night walks, especially on Fridays, but had attributed it mostly to Plasencia's unbearable weather. He recalled that Diego rarely worked on Saturdays but assumed it was because he was tired after a busy workweek. He never for a moment considered that his friend, his soon to be business partner who sang glorious hymns in church, was risking his life for something about which he knew so little.

What drove Diego to compromise his successful business and relatively carefree life in exchange for secret meetings, danger and constant fear?

Juan already knew much of what Diego had said. He knew there were secret Jews in Plasencia and all over Spain. He had heard the endless sermons preached by Father Pedro that secret Jews were deemed by the church to be full fledged Christians and that if one knew the whereabouts of any secret Jews they were required by Christian law to reveal their identities. He even remembered when Ernesto, the church caretaker, was accused of being a secret Jew. The church investigated the matter and after believing the accusers, killed poor Ernesto. But that episode never touched Juan because he barely knew Ernesto.

But this was different. Diego was his best friend.

Why hadn't Diego confided in him before? And what happened to prompt Diego to suddenly turn to him now?

Juan returned to the same nagging question that would soon explode into a burning and unquenchable desire that would change his life: Why would Diego risk it all?

Juan knew that he was Jewish since both his parents were born Jewish, something which baptism could never alter. But he hardly ever gave it any thought. Other than his marriage to another child of converted Jews there was nothing Jewish about him. He knew almost nothing of Jewish ritual and law and most of what he did know had been taught to him disparagingly by Father Pedro and the church. Juan considered himself a Christian in all respects. He attended church regularly and had formed a close, warm and personal relationship with Father Pedro. He had no Jewish friends and barely spoke to Jews at all.

He knew secret Jews existed but thought they were too few in number to be taken seriously and believed the church's attacks on them a little overdone. Juan was no different really, than any other Christian in Plasencia.

Yet Diego's story captivated him, moved him.

Those few moments, hearing of Diego's struggles to maintain and preserve that which he held so dear, touched Juan, awakened within him the spark that his parents chose to extinguish in 1391 when they opted for baptism over martyrdom. Juan never thought much about religion, any religion. He accepted blindly, like most people, the rituals he had performed since his youth and barely thought to attach to them any meaning or significance. But staring at Diego, and imagining the ferocity and care with which he guarded his secret religion and the extent he would go to perpetuate those secrets, excited Juan. He wanted something that special, something that important to be passionate about. He wanted to find out what it was about those secret meetings and about Judaism that made Diego so dedicated, so willing to risk his very life.

He had to know.

He was determined to find out and he was willing to risk his life, like poor Ernesto.

That night Juan took his first steps on a journey, a continuing journey, one he was still traveling twenty years later as he hurried to Father Pedro while lamenting that he would be forced to miss another secret meeting. It is a journey embarked on by those people who in the core of their being know that they lacked meaning and purpose in their lives and decided to do something about it. It is a journey of growth, of understanding and of faith. As Juan stared into the eyes of his friend, he saw a world where sacrifice was important, where each ritual was a matter of life and death, where teachings were revered and studied and hopefully passed on from father to son. Juan saw a world in which he suddenly wanted a share.

Diego saw the confused look on Juan's face and thought he made a mistake, that perhaps Juan did not understand him. But he could not stop now. He still had more he needed Juan to hear, and Diego continued his story.

"Last night a circle of secret Jews was exposed. We still do not know how Father Pedro found them, but Father Pedro and several church guards entered the home during evening prayer and caught them in the act of practicing Judaism. Many of my friends were killed on the spot, even though they did not resist. The rest will undoubtedly forfeit their lives after lengthy trials held publicly to humiliate them and frighten other secret Jews. Luisa and I were not there last night so we were spared. But we will surely be arrested soon, when our friends reveal our names under torture. There is no way we can prevent it. Do not worry about Luisa, she escaped earlier this morning. She is safe now. She wishes you well and will always remember your kindness. I, however, could not leave with her. I know that the authorities will be coming for me at any moment."

Juan interrupted, "Why now, Diego, why are you telling me now?"

Diego had been waiting for that question and had a response ready. "I am sorry for not telling you about our secret sooner. I did not know how you would react and I was not sure I could trust you. Luisa and I always planned on telling you and Margarita one day, and encouraging you to join us at the meetings. We just needed more time. We knew that eventually you would embrace our cause and desire to learn all you could about Judaism. You are a caring and passionate man and would be drawn to the teachings of the Torah. We were anxious to confide in you, to share our secret with you. We just needed to be absolutely certain that we could trust you. Just last week we decided that the time had come to reveal our secret. But things are different now. Luisa has already left and I won't be around much longer." Diego held back tears as he drew closer to Juan. "I would like to invite you to the next meeting which the secret Jews of Plasencia will be conducting on Friday night. The time has come for you to return to your past, to return to your heritage. You will be given the details shortly. It will not be easy, there will be many obstacles along the way and you will consider abandoning it many times. Please be strong, Juan, do not let anything stand in your way, it is where you belong."

Diego motioned that he still had more to say but Juan interrupted him. "I have heard everything that you have said, Diego. I have watched you these past few moments and I am humbled by the loyalty and sacrifice you have toward Judaism. I do not share that attitude toward Christianity. I never have and I never will. I have decided, Diego, that I will go to the secret meeting on Friday night. I want to feel committed. I want to share the passion and zeal and love you feel so intensely. I want to — at least, I think I want to, return to my heritage. I doubt if I can retun to the church after hearing what you said."

The journey had begun.

Diego approached Juan and embraced him. He then whispered the name of Alfonso Cabrerro, a secret Jew who would assist Juan on his journey.

There was so much Juan wanted to ask Diego, so many things that were racing through his mind as he tried to absorb it all. What had inspired Diego to lead this life? How did he come to be involved with secret Jews? How long had he been a secret Jew? How many secret Jews were there?

Juan was determined but confused. He was already thirty years old and settled in his comfortable life. Would he have the perseverance to carry through with all these changes? And Margarita? Could he convince her? And what of their unborn child? Would it be fair to raise the child surrounded by underground prayer meetings, secret rituals and incomplete knowledge of the laws and customs? These questions troubled Juan.

He understood he would have to resolve them, over time.

Juan knew Alfonso Cabrerro, who held a relatively high position at the church. Juan never realized that such distinguished people were also secret Jews. Juan wondered who else might be a secret Jew. He began to perceive that the church was not possessed after all. The secret Jews had managed to infiltrate the church, the very institution they spurned, and yet they remained undetected! Juan wondered whether one day the church would simply surrender as the secret Jews, the conversos, spread their message until their numbers were large enough and they were strong enough to simply abandon the church altogether without any opposition. But Juan confirmed that he would visit Alfonso Cabrerro and renew the heritage abandoned by his parents over fifty years ago. He wished Diego could be there with him, to watch with pride as his slow and steady evolution took place.

Juan continued to stare into the eyes of his friend, to peer into his soul, perhaps, and learn what he could in their few remaining moments together. Juan beheld a truth he had not known before, inspiration he thought was reserved for clerics or mystics. Juan saw a holiness he would spend the rest of his life trying to emulate.

He wished Diego could stay. He did not know why Diego had not fled with Luisa and thought it might be because of him. Maybe Diego could not escape, not without first confessing and revealing to him a different option, an option for a more precious life. Maybe Diego did not run away with Luisa so that Juan's life would be infused with meaning and purpose.

Maybe.

The two men sat motionless, and each felt a bond, a connection that their friendship had never experienced before. It was a moment Juan would never forget.

Diego smiled, stood up and moved away. He knew that he had succeeded: Juan would become a secret Jew.

Suddenly, Margarita hobbled into the room. She was quite surprised by the stillness and solemnity which was palpable between the two men.

"I am sorry to interrupt, Juan, but I hear some of the church's soldiers in the street and they are headed for Diego's house." She then turned to Diego. "Is everything all right, Diego?"

Diego looked serene, as if a weight had been lifted. "Things could not be better, Margarita."

Margarita noticed that Diego, who had entered the house apprehensive and worried, now appeared buoyant, almost happy.

Then they all heard the cries coming from outside, in gruff and harsh voices, "Diego Nasso! Diego Nasso! You are wanted for the crime of heresy. Surrender yourself this instant!!"

The cries grew louder and louder.

Juan suggested that he stay and hide and then escape to Luisa when the streets were safer, but Diego refused.

"I already told you, Juan, I could not escape with Luisa. I must face the consequences. Remember everything I have said, Juan, and remember the hidden treasure."

He slipped out the back door and made his way through the shadows until he was out of sight. The soldiers, experienced in their evil work, heard his footsteps and set off after him. There was the sound of a scuffle and then silence.

Juan never saw him again.

Juan did not know what his friend, Diego, meant by the hidden treasure. It was the first time he ever heard that phrase.

One day, he would find out.

Juan closed the door and returned to where Margarita was sitting, stunned. She knew Diego would never return. She moved toward Juan, who tried to comfort her without success. He told her everything Diego said, and the two wept bitter tears. Juan did not yet know how Margarita felt about becoming a secret Jew and could not ask her. She was traumatized by what she had seen. Her time had come.

The birth was difficult and her recovery slow and sporadic, and he could not leave her side. Margarita gave birth to a boy *and eight days later Juan failed to have him circumcised. He had yet to understand its significance. He missed the secret meeting. In truth, Juan did not even know that circumcisions were still practiced by Jews.*

Once Margarita was sufficiently recovered they named their son Diego.

As Juan made his way to the church he wiped away a tear as he remembered his old friend.

16

Juan almost reached the church steps and again wondered whether he could somehow excuse himself without arousing the suspicion of Father Pedro. He could feign illness but he knew that would not fool anyone.

Juan truly hated missing the meetings, especially those that revolved around discussions of the Sabbath. Juan treasured the Sabbath, more so than the other secret Jews, primarily because his first secret meeting had taken place on the Sabbath. His initial exposure to Judaism on that special day left him with such a strong appreciation for it, which only grew deeper as the years passed. He felt especially upset if he missed an opportunity to review its meaning and significance almost as much as he missed Diego Nasso. Juan credited the Sabbath itself for his transformation.

Juan remembered his first secret meeting twenty years ago. It was shortly after Diego was apprehended. He had heard that Diego had been executed the following week while in prison but that rumor was never confirmed.

His first secret meeting was on a Friday night, a few weeks before Rosh Hashanah, the Jewish New Year. Juan had already confided to Margarita his intentions of attending secret meetings and of becoming a secret Jew. He had missed the meeting Diego told him about due to the birth of their child. Margarita also realized there was no longer anything for them at the church and she readily understood his newfound interest in Judaism. The terror she had witnessed the night Diego was taken awakened her soul as well, and she even expressed a hope to join him on some occasions, when Diego grew a little older. She urged Juan to be careful and watched as he walked down the street until he was no longer in view.

What if he were caught? What if it was a trap? What if tonight's meeting meant the end of the circle of secret Jews?

Margarita was nervous. She believed he was doing the right thing and she wanted to join him on their newfound quest, but it was fraught with so much danger. Each time they left the house, who knew whether they would return! She understood the enormous risks they were taking and hoped that as they became more comfortable with leading a double life, the dangers could be taken in stride. But as Margarita watched her husband leave for the meeting, she was seized with a sudden sense of fear and dread and she felt faint.

For the first time in her life, she prayed for his safe return.

The meeting was held at the home of Alfonso Cabrerro, one of the most devout secret Jews in Plasencia and a member of the choir at the church. There were nearly thirty men in the room, many of whom Juan recognized from church. Virtually every aspect of the meeting was arranged in a way to avoid detection from neighbors and pedestrians. They were instructed to arrive and depart at ten-minute intervals, to forestall the appearance of a gathering. Juan, who was unaware of that requirement, arrived at the same time as Carlos, another secret Jew. Each secret Jew brought along an article of clothing, a basket of food or a Bible, so that if they were challenged by a guard or a priest they could justify their late night walk by explaining they were visiting a sick or needy friend. The actual meeting was conducted in total darkness. The presence of even a few candles would enable a suspicious neighbor to trace the images of far too many shadows together in one home. Two people never spoke at the same time, to aviod a heated discussion that could grow too noisy and waken a restless neighbor. Juan found the atmosphere eerie, yet mystical. He could hardly wait for the meeting to begin.

Juan's presence caught no one by surprise; they were expecting him.

Juan found a seat on the floor of Alfonso's back room and joined the circle formed by the other guests. The meeting would begin in fifteen minutes.

Juan waited in silence. He wondered whether he would feel comfortable with Alfonso and the other secret Jews. He knew many of them, and hoped they did not harbor contempt toward him for not coming sooner. He hoped they were understanding.

Juan imagined that the meeting which had led to Diego Nasso's capture was very similar to this one. Would he be caught tonight, at his first meeting? His thoughts of danger began to gnaw at him. After Diego had spoken with him, he felt bold, almost defiant. Now the possibility of being caught terrified him. Juan did not want those fears to distract him, and he returned to the anticipation of learning about his new and exciting religion.

He continued to wait.

The room was pitch dark and Juan could not distinguish any of the surroundings. He knew that Alfonso was wealthy, he was a tax collector, but Juan could not discern whether the home of a secret Jew was different that his. He then recalled the interior of Diego's home and for the first time realized that Diego did not display any crosses or figurines, only pictures of nature, fruit, horses and boats. Juan knew that many aspects of his life would have to change.

About fifteen minutes later, Alfonso stood up and moved to the center of the circle. It was time for the meeting to begin. Alfonso spoke in soft tones, almost a whisper, as he addressed the crowd.

"Before we start tonight, I would like to welcome Juan de Ciudad." Alfonso waived his hand in Juan's direction.

"I am sure that many of you already know him from church and from the years his family has resided in Plasencia. Diego Nasso, may his memory be blessed, spoke of him often and longed for the day when Juan would join our circle. We are excited that he is here." Alfonso then addressed Juan directly. "Señor de Ciudad, welcome to our circle and welcome to my home. We are all very happy that you are here and we hope that you will grow with us and in time become a regular member of our small yet determined circle. I know that right now things are strange and unfamiliar. That is normal and it will pass with time. You should not feel intimidated by any of us or by these unusual surroundings. We all remember the initial surprise each of us felt at our first meeting and we want to make you feel as comfortable as possible. We are a loving and caring family and we will try to make your transition pleasant and smooth. If there is anything any of us can do for you, please let us know. Is there anything you wish to say before we begin?"

Juan did not know how to respond. He now felt confident they harbored no ill will toward him and they were happy he joined the circle. But he sensed that he did not belong there and that he never would. Everyone else seemed so confident, so aware of the dangers and so willing to disregard them. He questioned whether he possessed the nerves and the temperament to lurk in shadows and attend secret underground meetings, practicing a religion he hardly knew. But Juan had to say something, at least to acknowledge the welcome he received.

"Thank you, Alfonso, for that very caring and warm greeting. I had planned on attending ever since Diego was captured but could not leave my wife until recently. She was recovering from the birth of our son and needed constant care and attention. She is better now and I was able to steal a few hours to be here tonight. I do not want to delay the meeting any further, and again, thank you for making me feel welcome here."

Alfonso spoke again in a low yet forceful voice. "Since you are here for the first time, Juan, I think it would be prudent to review some of the rules which we must adhere to at all times in order to maintain our secrecy. I know that many of you have heard this numerous times already, but the importance of what I am about to say cannot be reiterated often enough. All of you, especially Juan, must try to attend church at all times. You should not miss any services unless absolutely necessary. The best way to deceive Father Pedro and the other Christians is to make them think we are sincere observers of their faith. Many of the secret Jews who were discovered over the past few years had stopped attending church. They could not bring themselves to attend, they found it too foreign and repulsive. While I understand those sentiments, we must realize that their continued absence roused imminent suspicions among the church clergy. Those secret Jews were then followed and watched very closely until they were caught practicing Judaism, practicing heresy. They failed to realize how important it is to act Christian at all times, how vital it is to our survival. As repugnant as that might seem to some of us, it is the only way to insure the continued practice of Judaism. I, for one, have not missed a Sunday morning service in over twenty years. I am very close with Father Pedro and volunteer to help him whenever I can. I despise everything that he stands for but I do it to maintain my secrecy. It is imperative that we do not draw any attention and suspicion."

Juan was surprised to hear Alfonso refer to the church in such negative terms but realized that he would be hearing a lot of that from now on. Juan was very confused. He tried to maintain the passion and inspiration that Diego imparted to him but was suddenly preoccupied by the risks and dangers which Alfonso's instructions only seemed to reinforce. Juan was torn between the truth he knew existed in Judaism and the risks a commitment entailed. He had hoped the meeting would placate these fears, but the aura and mood of the meeting so far only increased and intensified them. He felt he should not have come. True, the church would never again be his home, but he could not cope with the deceit, the lies, the pitfalls and hazards of life as a secret Jew. Juan concluded this would be his last meeting.

He lowered his head in shame.

He had failed Diego Nasso.

Alfonso, unaware of Juan's changing attitude, continued his in-structions to the gathering. He then reminded everyone that they could never reveal the identities of any secret Jews to any church officials, even under torture. Alfonso knew this demand sounded hollow since Diego Nasso had been captured because some of their friends had not withstood the torture. But Alfonso said it any-way, if only to stress the importance of maintaining absolute secrecy. There were other instructions of lesser importance which Alfonso communicated to everyone in the room, mostly for Juan's sake. When he finished, he began lecturing about Judaism.

Alfonso decided that since Juan was present he would review some of the basic beliefs and rituals, which had already been dis-cussed at previous meetings. Nobody minded, though; they could all benefit from extensive review.

Juan sat quietly, uninterested and bored. This was not for him.

Alfonso began by informing everyone that as Jews they were required to obey the Torah, the sacred Book that Moses wrote af-ter receiving instruction from G-d. Alfonso stressed that despite the church's teachings to the contrary, the Torah was alive and vi-brant and relevant to each and every Jew. He explained that the Torah contained numerous commandments, and that their obser-vance brought one closer to G-d. He admitted that, due to his lack of learning, he had no knowledge of many of the commandments and regretted that he would focus on the same handful he always mentioned. He spoke about honoring parents, even those parents who practiced Christianity, circumcision, and observing the holi-days and the Sabbath. Alfonso only possessed a very elementary understanding of these practices but he still knew more than any-one else. He taught with a passion and fervor which no one else could equal. He continued to speak for a long time.

Juan's initial indifference soon wore off, as Alfonso's lecture grew more and more interesting. After a short while, Juan found himself listening very intently, and found it very moving. He saw in Alfonso the same determination and love and sacrifice he had seen in Diego. Alfonso reminded him of Diego and as he watched Alfonso speak, he became Diego, with that look of perseverance and truth that Juan had never forgotten. Juan closed his eyes and remembered staring into Diego's eyes and feeling secure and comfortable. It would not be easy, Juan knew that, but he could not let the fears, the risks and the danger to life cloud his purpose and frustrate his potential. Juan decided that he was not quite ready to quit. There was a heritage he needed to acquire, a new religion to learn and understand. He resolved to try once again. Alfonso rekindled in Juan the same interest Diego had first sparked.

Juan felt more confident when he considered that he was in the company of ordinary men, simple townsfolk. Somehow, they managed to surmount the extraordinary challenges of which he was so afraid. Surely everyone in the room avoided detection and struggled to maintain the secret. Diego, Alfonso and everybody else there taught him that he needed to engage and confront his fears and conquer them the way they had conquered theirs. He was no different really, an ordinary townsman in an ordinary city. This led Juan de Ciudad to ask the same question raised by another Jew in another country almost three hundred years earlier: Was any Jew truly ordinary?

Juan looked around the room and wondered where everyone had acquired the same dedication, that same unyielding conviction to perpetuate the religion and maintain the heritage? Juan did not know but he recalled that he never heard Father Pedro speak or act with such fervor! It was Juan's first exposure to the Jewish religion and what impressed him more than the beauty of the commandments, which he did not yet fully understand, was the zeal and devotion that was so evident, first in Diego and now in Alfonso. Juan knew that adjusting to the religion would take time, the dearth of his knowledge was vast and the dangers were many. He would have to proceed slowly and cautiously. But he felt humbled by Diego and Alfonso. They were ordinary citizens of Plasencia, raised as Christians in a Christian country. Where did they develop this sensitivity to Judaism? How did they cultivate an appreciation for Jewish rituals and customs amidst all the pressures of Christian life? How were they able to rise above the dogmas of the church and cling to the ideals of Judaism? From where did they derive such motivation?

Juan was determined to find out.

Alfonso continued his discourse and spent a great deal of time explaining the meaning and significance of the Sabbath, the day of rest. Juan listened intently as he tried to make sense of it all. Juan started to feel more comfortable at the meeting and saw his commitment to this cause begin to solidify. He was still fearful with regard to maintaining a double persona but at least he was willing to attend other meetings and give it more of a chance. He enjoyed the material, it was refreshing and beautiful. It did not have any of the rigid approaches so common in the church that he always found stifling and contrite. True, the Jewish laws he heard so far were more complex but they were concise and sharp and refreshing in a way he found very appealing.

He was still afraid, but much more at ease. He knew that the more often he attended the meetings, the more quickly he would appreciate the calm and discipline of the commandments and feel less threatened by the dangers of exposure. They would always be there but they would lose their intimidating effect as he became increasingly bound and connected with the life of a secret Jew.

He looked forward to the challenge.

Alfonso continued discussing the Sabbath and Juan accurately assessed that the Sabbath was one of the most intricate and complicated commandments of Judaism, and yet he seemed to be drawn to it in a way he could not explain. He incorrectly believed it was the warmth and enchantment of the Sabbath day itself that fascinated him. Juan would later recognize that he would feel this way about all the commandments, not just the

Sabbath. Each was unique in its own way and each possessed depths which he could not fathom, but this was the first, and it held a singular place in his heart.

As the meeting was drawing to a close, Juan had come full circle: He was forever committed to the cause of the secret Jew.

A short while later, Alfonso finished, thanked everyone for attending and reminded them that they would be notified about the next meeting. A few people remained and were talking quietly; the rest went home. Juan had been told when to leave, to avoid too many people exiting at the same time, and he obliged. Before he exited, Alfonso approached him. "Juan, I would like to express my happiness that you have decided to attend one of our meetings. As I said before, we have been waiting for you for a long time. I did not want to mention this in front of the others, but Diego once told me he could not wait for you to join. He believed you were an integral part of our survival, that you could insure the perpetuation of our cause. He even told me that he would risk his life for you. Anyway, Father Pedro has asked me to travel to Seville, on church business. It will be a short trip, no longer than two weeks. He always insists that I travel with an escort. The roads can be very dangerous at times. I hope you can accompany me. It would give us an opportunity to become better acquainted and discuss at great length many questions which I am certain are puzzling you."

Juan nodded his head in agreement, but was lost in thoughts of Diego. Alfonso just confirmed it: Diego had stayed behind for his sake! Diego did not escape with Luisa and had surrendered his own future, to insure that Juan's would have purpose! Juan could not understand why Diego felt he was so important. He surely lacked that sharp discipline which made some of the others such as Alfonso so remarkable. He theorized that perhaps since Diego had no children, he regarded Juan as his legacy, his adopted heir. Juan did not know the reasons, but he could not dwell on this any longer. This newfound knowledge imbued Juan with an even greater purpose, a higher sense of commitment, an *appreciation for the lengths to which the secret Jews would go to insure they remained vibrant and devoted to the Torah. Juan understood that by accepting this new life he was more than a renegade Christian, a marrano, risking his life practicing a hidden religion. He saw himself as a crucial link in the continuing chain of Jews that stretched back so many generations. While he did not possess enough knowledge to lead the circle of secret Jews, he came to believe that he would mature and develop into an indispensable part of the group and that they in turn would be dependent on him for inspiration, comfort and survival.*

He would not let them down.

Juan walked home quietly, serenely. He reviewed the evening's events in his mind, from his initial reluctance to remain, to his awareness of Diego's love for him. He was still amazed and would never cease to be amazed by the sacrifice and danger that everyone in the room was willing to embrace in order to learn and to congregate with other Jews.

Juan continued home, preoccupied by these thoughts.

He did not realize it at the time, but he had celebrated his first Sabbath.

Juan returned home to a relieved Margarita. He told her everything that had taken place at the meeting, including his upcoming trip with Alfonso, and they discussed it until late into the night.

Juan lay in bed and could not sleep. He was too excited, repeating in his mind the words of inspiration Alfonso had spoken at the meeting. He got out of his bed and approached his son. He drew closer to the sleeping babe and whispered in his ear something he had learned that night. He whispered to Diego that it was the Sabbath day, and he would remember it and keep it holy.

17

Juan finally reached the steps of the church after vividly recalling his first encounter with the circle of secret Jews. It had been twenty years of secret meetings and as he climbed the church steps he regretted again that he could not attend today's meeting. What bothered him even more than missing the meeting itself was the knowledge that this could not continue. He could longer remain a secret Jew. He knew he had to leave Plasencia with his family and journey to where they could practice Judaism openly, with proper instruction and teachers. Not that he faulted Alfonso in any way, he revered his commitment and wisdom, but there was virtually nothing left for Juan to learn: He had absorbed everything Alfonso knew. After twenty years of reviewing and repeating the same handful of rituals, Juan realized the meetings were no longer fulfilling. He saw himself stagnating with no chance for further growth. He needed more. Juan only attended the meetings to review what he already knew and to stay connected with the cause he cherished so dearly. He could not learn from the rabbis though, associating with Jews was more dangerous than ever. Juan was now ready for a deeper understanding, a more heightened awareness of the customs and rituals, but, locally there was nowhere for him to receive that instruction. In addition, neither Juan nor Diego had been circumcised. They knew it was required of them but there was no one in Plasencia who could perform the ceremony. Juan was fifty years old, and as he looked back on his life, it was his greatest regret.

Juan had considered leaving many times in the past but two things prevented him from doing so. The first was Margarita. She did not want to leave, she was happy in Plasencia. She too, had become a secret Jew but her participation in any dangerous activity was marginal, almost inconsequential. She did not face many of the pressures Juan dealt with on a daily basis and she failed to understand how desperately Juan longed for more knowledge. She sensed Juan was ready for a more involved and engrossing dialogue but she was reluctant to press the issue. She enjoyed the town, her friends and her comforts. Juan knew she wanted to stay and would not aggrevate her by insisting that they leave. Secondly, and perhaps more importantly, Juan could not bring himself to leave. Ever since his first meeting, and the trip to Seville which had solidified his dedication to the secret Jews, Juan felt compelled to remain in Plasencia. He viewed himself as an integral part of the secret Jewish community and had come to believe he was needed for its survival. He never forgot what Alfonso had told him that Friday night twenty years ago, and felt that his absence might precipitate the downfall of the circle. As much as he desired to leave, he could not do it.

But lately the situation had changed. Father Pedro had become extremely intolerant, almost obsessed with the secret Jews in Plasencia. He spoke against them at virtually every sermon and had increased all efforts to discover the meeting places of the secret Jews. He looked the other way when angry mobs attacked secret Jews and other Jews who were accused of helping them.

It was always dangerous attending the meetings, but Father Pedro's recent crusade against them made attendance virtually impossible. In the past month, ten secret Jews had been killed, numbers unheard of in recent years, and five or six others were beaten by those angry mobs. In fact, since Diego and his circle were captured twenty years ago, Juan could not think of more than two secret Jews who had met with a similar fate. These pressures turned away many secret Jews and forced the truly dedicated to limit their participation.

Juan wondered whether the entire underground network was slowly falling apart. He had suggested to Alfonso and the group that they all leave together, and Margarita was amenable to that solution, thereby solving both of his dilemmas, but the community was reluctant to agree. They maintained that while life was difficult, it was predictable and stable and they were convinced that the situation would surely improve. But Juan had seen the situation grow worse, not better, and he saw it deteriorating still further. Like Jews of all ages, they were unwilling to accept that the future might not be as optimistic as they would like and they should prepare for unpleasant possibilities. Juan recalled that at a meeting a few weeks ago, he had heard that Don Isaac Abarbanel, a prominent Jewish leader in Spain, had predicted 1465 to be a very unpleasant year for the Jews.

Is this what Don Isaac meant?

The end of the secret Jews?

Juan neared the church and admitted that he had grown to despise Father Pedro. He had once thought him to be respectable and honorable, and even as Juan became more attached to the secret Jews, he had always considered the priest a decent man. True, he punished secret Jews and spoke against them but he never seemed to act passionately or aggressively. It appeared he was simply doing his job, a job which Father Pedro did not seem to do with exceptional fervor. But Father Pedro's recent preoccupation with the secret Jews had made him angry and cruel. Juan avoided him lately, partly to salvage the respect he once had toward him, but primarily to be spared the rancor and venom of his tongue. Juan believed he was being summoned by Father Pedro to reconcile their differences, to bridge the gap that had recently spread between them. Juan was afraid he would lash out against Father Pedro and inadvertently reveal his secret.

Juan knew he had to restrain himself as he reached the church entrance.

Juan stood at the entrance and watched as the large center door slowly opened. Father Pedro was standing in the vestibule and motioned for Juan to enter. Juan reluctantly followed him.

Father Pedro was a tall, dark-skinned man, almost seventy years old. He had been born in Valencia, Spain but spent most of his life elsewhere. Soon after he had entered the priesthood he left Spain to preach Christianity abroad, mostly in North Africa. He had earned a reputation as a kind and gentle man and was well respected in Plasencia, where he had been the priest for the past thirty years.

"I am glad that you were able to come, Juan. There are some important matters I want to discuss with you," said Father Pedro flatly, as he greeted Juan.

"I would not miss an opportunity to be of assistance to you, Father. Tell me, how can I help you today?" Juan always addressed Father Pedro respectfully, swathing an inner contempt with blandishments.

"Come inside, Juan, what I want to discuss with you is quite urgent." Again, Father Pedro spoke listlessly.

Juan followed Father Pedro as they walked into the Church and proceeded to the far end of the building, where there were several cubicles usually occupied by parishioners reading or studying. Father Pedro found an empty room and entered. They both sat at a small reading table. Father Pedro remained stiff, almost inanimate.

This meeting would not be about reconciliation, of that Juan was now fairly certain. Father Pedro was rigid and static, not the sort of behavior he would have expected from a man eager to bond with a wayward congregant. Father Pedro did not smile when he greeted him, nor did he even offer his hand for Juan to kiss. He exhibited none of the warmth and gentleness he had often displayed in the past.

No, this meeting would have a dire outcome.

He knows the truth! thought Juan.

He has discovered my secret and he has brought me here to taunt me, to play tricks with me, and then arrest me and force me to face trial for heresy!

Juan wanted to get up and run away, but he could not. He knew there were guards stationed outside and he would never make it past the hall. He stared at the insipid and staid priest and was filled with rage and disappointment.

But Father Pedro remained silent, sitting quietly.

Say it already!

Accuse me now!

What are you waiting for?

Juan was growing impatient. He did not know how much more of this procrastinating he could endure.

After several moments, Father Pedro spoke. Juan sat nervously, tense and afraid.

"Juan, I have asked you here because there are grave issues which I must discuss with you. It concerns the *marranos*." Father Pedro addressed him in the same monotonous tone he had used till this point.

Juan hated the word *marrano*. It meant "swine" and it was the name the church and the rest of Christian Spain used to refer to those *conversos* who were secret Jews. A few years ago he would have been surprised that someone as respectful as Father Pedro would use such a derogatory word so freely. It did not surprise him anymore.

Father Pedro continued, "For the past seventy-five years, the church has been plagued by the *marranos*. They act like Christians in public but practice Judaism in secret. The church's position regarding them is clear. Since they were baptized, they are full-fledged Christians and their practice of Judaism is heresy, which is punishable by death. But for too long the church has allowed them to flourish and prosper. This is due in part because the church simply does not know who they are. They maintain positions of prominence in all areas of Spanish government and some have even risen to prominence in the church! This must stop. They can no longer be permitted to practice Judaism." Father Pedro finally sounded a bit enthusiastic.

Juan was puzzled. Why was Father Pedro providing him with a history lesson? Why was Father Pedro delaying the charge, procrastinating the inevitable? It was uncharacteristic of his swift style, his terse manner. No, Father Pedro did not suspect him of heresy, of practicing Judaism. If he did, he would already be in jail awaiting trial. Father Pedro was being cold and distant, yet companionable. No, Father Pedro did not suspect him at all. He was engaging Juan, spending time with him, talking about history and Church policies, as colleagues often do, but why? If Juan was not being accused, then why was he summoned there?

A sudden shudder overtook Juan.

Margarita!

Father Pedro had discovered Margarita!

That was why Father Pedro had called for him, to explain the church's actions concerning her.

Father Pedro was acting amicable, he was trying to soften the blow.

And what about Diego? Was he safe?

Juan could barely restrain himself. He could not stand the waiting. Was he correct? What was he doing there? When would Father Pedro break the news?

Juan knew he had to remain calm. He sat in his chair, barely able to remain poised.

Father Pedro continued, "Juan, I know that your parents were *conversos* and you might have been tempted to slip back to your old faith along with those other *marranos*. But I have been watching you for a long time I am confident that your allegiance is firmly with the church. However, I regret to tell you that your wife does not share your obedience to Christianity. A few days ago she was seen practicing Judaism, lighting candles on a Friday night. The witnesses organized a mob and earlier today they stormed your house and — and attacked your wife."

Juan stood up, pale and trembling.

"No! Not Margarita, no! It can't be."

Father Pedro hesitated, then continued. "I know this is hard for you, Juan, but it is true. I saw her myself. The mob threw her body on the church steps. I think the mob was expressing their displeasure with me, blaming me for failing to discover these heresies sooner. Two of the priests quickly ran to your wife but I am sorry to tell you that she was no longer alive." Juan suppressed a scream but a whimper escaped. Father Pedro tried to comfort Juan and placed his hand on

Juan's shoulder. Juan squirmed and Father Pedro quickly withdrew. It was too early to offer solace, or so he thought.

"Juan, I am sorry that I have to be the one to relate this unfortunate news. I am certain that you loved her dearly, but she was accused of being a heretic and some of our more zealous citizens will not tolerate heretics here in Plasencia. I regret that this all happened so suddenly. I myself sometimes have a difficult time controlling their outbursts. Do not worry about your son, Diego; he is safe. He has not been seen doing anything improper — neither have you, for that matter — and these mobs have enough sense and restraint not to harm anyone without any specific suspicion. Juan, my son, your wife is dead. You will never see her again. I am truly sorry."

Father Pedro rose to leave, visibly shaken by the news he just imparted. He had always liked Juan and although he was secretly pleased that an unruly mob had taken care of otherwise sensitive church business, he felt sorry for him. He would come to Juan's house later, to pay his condolences, after the initial shock wore off and Juan was more receptive to sympathy. He started out of the room.

Juan was devastated. He had had an intuition that something terrible was brewing when he initially observed Father Pedro's somber and serious demeanor. And yet the moment Father Pedro uttered the words, Juan was elsewhere. He was a young boy promising his mother, Elienor, that he would never marry a girl who was not born Jewish. He was the father of a baby, named for a man who died so his life could have meaning. He was a wealthy businessman who managed to secretly divert some of his profits to help repair the synagogue he was never able to visit. He was a secret Jew, spending the last twenty years in underground, clandestine, dark and silent meetings, huddled together with other dedicated souls sharing torn pages of books written in a language they barely knew how to read. He was a soloist in the church choir, singing Christian hymns, which brought the priests to tears. He was a man who loved the Sabbath and rarely worked on that holy day.

And in that one moment, the moment he learned his wife was gone, it all came crashing down. The double life, the dangers, the risks, the scurrying about at midnight, the crosses, the statues, the church, the lack of fulfillment in either religion, the confusion and the knowledge that now he was alone.

It was all over.

It had lasted a long time, longer than he initially had thought possible. But now it had come to a horrific end. Juan felt so alone, so lost without his wife, the woman who had encouraged him and supported him for the past twenty-three years. He felt like falling down and sobbing uncontrollably but he could not, not in front of Father Pedro, it would have to wait until later. Juan knew he could not stay in Plasencia any longer. He could not remain in a church and sing hymns and participate in observances along with Margarita's murderers. He also knew he would probably soon be caught as well. He regretted that the secret Jews would have a difficult time without him, but there was nothing for him in Plasencia anymore. He once believed he could never leave. Now he knew he could not stay.

But first he had to be certain about Margarita, he had to find out what really had happened to her. He knew Father Pedro had guilt feelings regarding this ordeal and might be vulnerable to granting any request. He called to the priest who was almost out of the room and asked sheepishly, "Father Pedro, do you think I can see Margarita one last time?"

Father Pedro was a little startled by the request but did not want to refuse Juan in his time of sorrow. He turned and started toward Juan. "Your request is a bit unorthodox, Juan, but I see no reason not to grant it," Father Pedro paused, took a breath, then continued, "but her body is in a horrid state."

Juan withheld his tears and then asked if he could see her anyway. He needed closure, finality, to his many years in this dreaded town.

Father Pedro reluctantly granted Juan's request and he led Juan to a dungeon. Located in underground passages of the church, Juan had never known of its existance. There he saw his wife's lifeless form.

Juan could no longer contain himself and burst out crying. He then told Father Pedro he needed to be alone and hurried home to plan his escape.

On his way home, Juan knew he would have to act quickly. He would not even have time to properly mourn his wife. He could not delay any longer. It was only a matter of time before he and Diego were also discovered, and those mobs were everywhere. He thought of Margarita. He recalled her spirit, her love of the Sabbath that equaled his own. He remembered that she always lit the Sabbath lights on Fridays at dusk, no matter the danger. She understood that the light brought joy and happiness to their home which was otherwise filled with so much darkness, so much deceit. For a few moments before sundown, Margarita allowed the family to bask in the light of those Sabbath candles, which meant so much more than oil and wick. In those fleeting moments, each week, the de Ciudads were able to break from the depths of their deception and observe a sacred rite like all other Jews. It usually did not last for more than a few moments, neighbors were very suspicious, but to the family it offered hope that one day they could worship their religion in radiance and openness. She had been found out while performing that ritual, she sacrificed her life while tempting fate to provide her family with a brighter and more forthright future.

Juan would make sure all her hopes, all that longing and anticipation, would be realized.

He would leave Plasencia.

But where to go?

He reached home and saw Diego crying as he entered. He must know, thought Juan. Diego ran to him, sobbing.

"Have you heard what they have done with Mother? They came early this morning, shortly after you left. They said they were going to kill her. I tried to stop them but there was no possibility I could overpower them all! What shall we do now, Father? We cannot remain here, we shall be next!" Diego placed his head on Juan's shoulder and continued weeping. Afraid that he would break down, Juan remained silent. There was nothing for him to say.

Juan understood that Father Pedro was partly to blame for Margarita's death, because he did nothing to stop the terrors of the mobs. But Juan also knew that Father Pedro had shown kindness in Juan's hour of despair. While he acknowledged Father Pedro's compassion, he would never forgive him. Like Diego, Juan realized that there was nothing he could have done to prevent this from happening. He could no longer hold back and began to weep.

Juan knew they were pressed for time and that he and Diego had to compose themselves and prepare the horses and wagon. Juan stressed that they needed to leave immediately, that night if possible. Diego readily agreed and started equipping the horses.

Diego suggested they travel to Huesca, a city to the northeast. Diego heard that in Huesca conditions were less harsh. There were rabbis there who trained secret Jews and educated them to relinquish the hiding and secrecy to which they were so accustomed, to blend in as open Jews. Juan knew of no other town to which to run and agreed they would travel to Huesca. Whatever was in store for them there could not be worse than Plasencia.

Father and son busily spent the next few hours packing their belongings for the journey. Juan knew no one would come to offer condolences so soon after the tragedy. He knew they would be alone and undetected while they readied themselves. Juan instructed Diego to take only what was necessary, as they would need to maximize the space on the wagon.

While rummaging through his belongings, Juan stumbled upon a large old box that lay deep within his closet. For a moment, Juan could not remember what it contained. Then he reminded himself that it held personal items that belonged to his parents, mostly family heirlooms and some worn linens. Juan's parents cherished these items greatly and urged Juan to keep them safe within the box, which also carried great personal meaning for his parents. Juan could not imagine why these things were so important to his parents but it was one of the few requests they had asked of him, and he had never parted with the box or its contents. He recalled that he had not seen it in nearly thirty years and had practically forgotten he still possessed it.

Juan quickly opened it and saw the dank and faded linens. He considered leaving the worthless stuff behind, mere relics of the past, but remembered how much they meant to his parents. Diego helped him load the box onto the wagon. Juan and Diego finished collecting their belongings, packed it all on the wagon and then quickly reentered the house to be certain they had not forgotten anything important.

Before they were ready to leave, Juan informed Diego that he needed to visit Alfonso and he would only be gone a few moments. Juan felt he owed it to Alfonso to tell him he was leaving and that he was sorry for any problems that might cause, but he could not stay. He was sure Alfonso would understand.

Juan approached Alfonso's home and as he drew close, he heard Alfonso's son Hernando, wailing uncontrollably.

Juan drew a little closer and saw Alfonso's wife, Sarafina, run into the street weeping.

He knew what that meant.

Alfonso had been discovered.

Indeed, things were falling apart.

Juan hurried back to his house, sad and heartbroken.

Juan returned to the wagon and found Diego and the horses ready. They climbed into the wagon and quietly left town.

As they traveled, Juan thought of what he was leaving behind. How much he already missed Margarita! Maybe it would be easier in new surroundings, where he would not encounter memories at every turn. He would miss the circle of secret Jews, men and women with whom he had become very close over the years. He then thought of his fortune, his business, his home, the church and Father Pedro and all the memories of his loathsome and difficult life. He would miss none of it. He could not wait to get away from it all, to start life afresh, in a town free from the secrets he had come to find intolerable.

He grabbed the reins from Diego and prodded the horses to move faster.

18

Rabbi Abraham Ben Shem Tov Bibago put down his quill and threw up his hands in exasperation. His brother, Rabbi Isaac, had asked him to address several newcomers, to greet them and welcome them, but Rabbi Abraham could think of nothing to say. He was not that adept at delivering a lecture, especially to secret Jews adjusting to new lives of open worship. Rabbi Abraham was more of a scholar. He felt at home in the library, poring through books and writing new and interesting commentaries and observations. In fact, his recent book, "The Way of Faith," revealed his talents, explaining the philosophical elements of Judaism in a clear and original manner. But in front of an audience, he was stiff, tongue-tied and not charismatic. He had been trying for the past two days to organize his thoughts, some words of encouragement for the beginners embarking on the difficult process of shedding their secret ways and their often incorrect understandings of the religion. He wanted to make a good impression on them but found this so frustrating. He decided to take a break for a while and try again later.

Rabbi Isaac, on the other hand, was the true lecturer in the family, a gregarious, outgoing and witty teacher. He connected with the secret Jews the way Rabbi Abraham identified with books. He was electrifying and animated, enabling his listeners to learn and enjoy themselves at the same time. The larger the crowd, the more alive he became. He seemed to thrive on greater numbers. He had helped over one thousand secret Jews adjust to new lives.

Rabbi Isaac knew that his brother was not that vivacious in front of a group and that he preferred not to speak at all, but Rabbi Isaac had no choice. New secret Jews were scheduled to arrive and he could not be there. He had been summoned by Ronaldo Pallo, Huesca's most powerful and wealthiest citizen, to diagnose and treat Ronaldo's infant daughter, Maria, who had developed a raging fever. Everyone knew that Rabbi Isaac was the best doctor in Huesca and probably all of Aragon. He was frequently called upon by the nobles and elite citizens of Huesca and the neighboring towns for his medical expertise. Rabbi Isaac tried his best to accommodate these nobles. He was well aware that one day he might need something in return.

His profession often took him away from what he considered his primary occupation, teaching secret Jews. For the past twenty years, roughly the same time Diego Nasso had been captured halfway across Spain, he had been training secret Jews to cast off their inhibitions and faulty understandings and practice Judaism properly. Rabbi Isaac began this undertaking with one woman who mysteriously appeared in Huesca. She claimed she was a secret Jew but refused to reveal anything about her past. Rabbi Isaac questioned her about Judaism and while she seemed very dedicated and committed, she knew very little law and custom, and most of what she did know was inaccurate. Rabbi Isaac could not have expected her to know more, she never had received proper instruction. Rabbi Isaac was aware of the difficulties the secret Jews faced throughout Spain and saw this woman as the product of those difficulties. He endeavored to change that as much as he could. He instructed her and imparted to her the knowledge she was lacking. More importantly, he taught her how to practice Judaism openly, something she had never done. She found it very difficult to shake the fear, the deception and the underground surroundings to which she was so accustomed. But Rabbi Isaac persevered and she proved a quick and sharp student. Twenty years later she still lived in Huesca and came to help Rabbi Isaac from time to time, usually when new people arrived. A few months after his success with her, more secret Jews came and before Rabbi Isaac knew it, he was running a makeshift school for secret Jews.

Rabbi Isaac loved it. He found it meaningful and important. He cherished his role as religious provider and sought new and interesting ways to reach his students. Rabbi Abraham also participated along with Rabbi Isaac but he developed a more subdued and subtle approach. He mostly helped those secret Jews having difficulties with various philosophical concepts. He was able to communicate with them. He resolved many of the doctrines they found complicated and confusing, as long as he met with them on an individual basis. He just could not relate to large audiences. Rabbi Isaac and Rabbi Abraham both achieved success with their own unique methods and styles. Almost all of the secret Jews throughout Spain had heard of the Bibago brothers, the work they were doing and the impact they had on their pupils.

The fortunate ones were able to find their way to them.

Rabbi Isaac arrived at the home of Ronaldo Pallo and was immediately led to Maria's room. The journey to the home, which was situated in the hills surrounding Huesca, had taken most of the day. Rabbi Isaac had been there many times before and each time he marveled at its beauty. In truth it was not really a house, it looked more like a castle. It was a large fortress-like building with imposing towers at each end. It was constructed of large stones, of a size he had never seen anywhere else. There were always guards stationed outside. Inside, the home was truly regal. There were large statues strategically positioned throughout each room, mostly of Biblical and Christian figures. There were silks draped around the windows of each room and marble and alabaster columns defined alternating alcoves. Rabbi Isaac thought the garden the most elegant part of the home. There he saw the most unusual flowers, planted in rows that formed circles that turned larger and larger. In the center of the circle lay a small pool of water that rippled pleasantly in the breeze. It was truly beautiful.

Maria's room was at the back of the home, near the garden. Rabbi Isaac followed a servant, until they made their way to the child's room. Ronaldo did not permit anyone to enter the room, for fear of disease, and Rabbi Isaac went in alone.

The child was asleep. Rabbi Isaac examined her, diagnosed the problem and provided Ronaldo with the remedy. It was a common childhood disease, nothing life threatening. He was confident she would recover in a few days and urged Ronaldo to notify him if she took a sudden turn for the worse. "Thank you, Rabbi Isaac, for coming this quickly. I was so nervous about my little Maria, I panicked and summoned you right away!" Ronaldo sounded relieved.

Rabbi Isaac was not upset by the visit, even though it was not truly urgent. He enjoyed helping the nobles of Huesca whenever he could. He just felt sorry for Rabbi Abraham, who he imagined was completely disheartened by now!

Rabbi Isaac turned to leave.

"Please, Rabbi Isaac, do not leave so soon! Come join me in the garden."

Rabbi Isaac had never been invited to the garden before. He was delighted to see it, but why was Ronaldo being so friendly?

Ronaldo led Rabbi Isaac to a remote corner of the garden where they sat down on a bench near several rose vines. "I am very thankful that you are always available to treat my children. I know I am most probably over-protective, but I love them dearly and I only want the best care for them. You must be aware that you are the best doctor in Huesca?"

Rabbi Isaac flushed.

"There is no need to be humble, it is the truth. All my friends agree, whenever someone is sick, they ask for no other doctor, only Rabbi Isaac Bibago!"

Again, Rabbi Isaac turned red.

Suddenly, Ronaldo became serious. "Rabbi Isaac, I summoned you here for another reason, unrelated to my child. Please listen carefully to what I am about to say and heed my warning. I am aware that you help *marranos* adjust to their new lives as Jews and have established a school for that purpose. It is no secret that you have been doing it for the past twenty years. Frankly, neither my friends nor I really care. We believe that if those people do not want to be Christians anymore and were not sincere Christians all along, then there is no place for them in the church. We understand that our view is contrary to the church's, and that the church tries to dissuade people like you. I am sure you have wondered why the church has overlooked your activities all these years. I must take the credit for that, along with my friends, other wealthy landowners from the neighboring towns. We have persuaded the church not to interfere with your efforts and to allow your school to flourish. We have done this because you are special, you are different. You are the most intelligent and perceptive physician in all of Aragon and your absence would be a terrible loss. We convinced the church of your unique medical talents and for all these years the church has listened to our influential opinions. Begrudgingly, the church has looked the other way, even when it hears reports of your successes. The church is not happy but tolerates it."

Rabbi Isaac listened respectfully. He already knew most of what Ronaldo was saying. He was well aware that he was permitted to teach and inspire secret Jews without fear of the church because he offered medical services that no other doctor could equal. He wondered why Ronaldo was telling him this. And what was the warning of which Ronaldo spoke?

Ronaldo continued, "I have not invited you here to boast about my kindness toward you, I am certain you knew all that already." Ronaldo placed his hand on Rabbi Isaac's shoulder. "Rabbi Isaac, I want to warn you. It has come to my attention that the church will no longer turn a blind eye and condone the existence of your school and your activities as graciously as they have until now. In fact, I believe the church wishes to close down the school entirely but understands it cannot do that. Instead the church will try to curtail your influence. This change was precipitated by the recent struggles and battles for power and control of the country. New kings rule now and they heed their advisors who manifest an obsession with the *conversos*. Their advisors and notables have installed new priests throughout Spain, including Father Ramon here in Huesca. He is particularly aggravated by the extent and breadth of your operation, which he believes has grown too large. He wants to limit your success and curtail your influence. This change is part of the larger trend I spoke of which has spread throughout all of Spain —

Seville, Toledo, Madrid, Plasencia and Barcelona. I have even heard the dreaded Inquisition has been invited to some cities in Castile. These younger priests like Father Ramon are fanatical and dangerous. They will ruin Spain! I will tell you now, Rabbi Isaac, the Inquisition will never be welcomed in Huesca, not as long as I have a say in the matter. The Inquisition is a cruel and vile institution. It breeds fear, mistrust and pain. It is secretive and does not allow criticism, and it fosters deceit and hatred. I do not believe the religious arm of the church should wield so much power and cause so much suffering. Are you aware that the Inquisition prosecutes people and tears families apart on the flimsiest of proof? I want none of that here in Huesca!"

Ronaldo was excited, his face was red and flushed with anger. Ronaldo realized he had said too much. He knew it was improper to denounce his own religion in front of a Jew, but just could not contain himself. He took a deep breath, exhaled slowly and then continued.

"I am sorry I digressed for a moment, I did not mean to imply that I have any complaints with church policies. I do not. I just believe that in their enthusiasm to spread the true word of Christianity and to maintain the purity of our religion, some priests have gone too far. Father Ramon is waiting for a reason to repudiate me and my influence. That is all and again I apologize. Please, allow me to return to the topic at hand. I believe that you face no actual danger, as long as you do not take on any additional recruits. The larger you grow, the more you will spark the fires of Father Ramon's wrath."

Rabbi Isaac knew this day might come. His attempts had been permitted to flourish for quite some time without interruption. Keeping a low profile for a while did not seem unreasonable. "I understand, Ronaldo. Thank you for that advice. I will instruct my brother to minimize our activities a bit and hopefully that will satisfy Father Ramon."

Ronaldo nodded, "But it is a little more dangerous than that. I heard that Father Ramon will be sending spies seeking to infiltrate your school. They will claim that they are secret Jews, seeking guidance and instruction. They will appear helpless and lost, yearning for you to train them as you have done for so many others. Please, do not let them fool you. You must be very selective and careful. If one of these spies manages to get close to you, I fear terrible consequences will follow. Once in your inner circle, these spies will report that all sorts of blasphemies and heresies are taking place, that you are luring secret Jews away from Christianity. They will disclose that you are slandering and belittling Christianity in an effort to sway secret Jews away from their adopted faith. Whether or not those charges are true, it will be the excuse Father Ramon is looking for to demand that you face charges for inciting and persuading others to commit heresy. He will close down your school and persecute you and your brother. They will demand that you suffer the same fate as every other individual who promotes heresy, despite your medical talents. Rabbi Isaac, I am telling you all this because I respect your integrity and I do not want anything to happen to you. The next time Maria is sickly, I want to know you will be available!"

Ronaldo bade Rabbi Isaac farewell and Rabbi Isaac began the journey home.

Could everything Ronaldo said have been true?

Would Father Ramon be so devious?

Rabbi Isaac did not like Father Ramon. He had been in Huesca only a few months and was already causing broad-based unease. At every opportunity he spoke out against Jews who associated with secret Jews and warned any Christian who would abandon his or her faith. Through his talents as a doctor, Rabbi Isaac had formed an intimate bond with many of the town's inhabitants, regardless of religion. His relationship with everyone was friendly and cordial. But many Jews and Christians saw Father Ramon's provocative behavior as destructive to a tenuous and delicate friendship. Father Ramon was a prototype of this new priest to which Ronaldo had referred: a young zealous Spanish cleric consumed by and preoccupied with the undermining of Spanish culture, which he blamed on the *marranos*. Rabbi Isaac believed Father Ramon would only increase his troublemaking as he became more comfortable in the city. Would he actually send spies to check out the school?

Rabbi Isaac saw no reason not to believe Ronaldo. It made sense. If Father Ramon lacked the political means to override Ronaldo and his friends openly then he would have to resort to other means, deceptive means. He would need to discover or create some strong and overriding argument for ridding Huesca of the school, something of such magnitude that not even Ronaldo could object. Proving that the school taught and promoted blatant heresies would surely convince even the most indifferent Christian that it could not continue to exist. The spies would provide first hand evidence of the crimes, removing once and for all any speculation people had that Ronaldo's claims were accurate. The spies would effectively eliminate any protection Rabbi Isaac enjoyed, paving the way for Father Ramon to put a stop to the learning forever. Rabbi Isaac understood that if spies managed to infiltrate the school and become close to him, it could be very dangerous indeed. It would mean the end of hope and inspiration for so many who had nowhere else to turn. And Rabbi Isaac and Rabbi Abraham would be in mortal danger!

He was convinced that Ronaldo had given him good advice. If Ronaldo believed that Father Ramon would send spies then it was probably true. Ronaldo knew many things. Rabbi Isaac concluded that he would have to heed Ronaldo's warning and severely curtail the number of secret Jews allowed into his circle. He was not happy about it: He knew it would force so many secret Jews to be denied the teaching they so desperately needed. But it suddenly became very risky. Now lives were at stake, not only his own and his brother's but every secret Jew presently under their instruction. He could not expand his current circle of disciples and risk endangering all the gains that had been realized until this point.

The end of his dream was in sight. All secret Jews would be turned away, each candidate could be a spy, sent to ruin him. There was nothing Rabbi Isaac could do to prevent this. He found consolation in the fact that he had been able to carry on for this long.

Rabbi Isaac then focused on Ronaldo's tirade against the church. He had never heard a Christian speak so critically of the church before. Ronaldo had explained that he was merely upset with the zeal and ardor of some of the younger priests, but that was not how he came across when he attacked the Inquisition. For the first time Rabbi Isaac became aware that decent and ordinary Christians likewise despised an institution that degraded, tortured and even executed innocent people. Rabbi Isaac wondered whether the Jews and moral and decent Christians like Ronaldo could ever join together and rid Spain of this terrible scourge. The Inquisition was just beginning to make its presence felt throughout Aragon and it already had earned this most terrible and despicable reputation. Rabbi Isaac knew there had to be others: Ronaldo could not be the lone Spaniard to feel such indignation toward this new trend. Rabbi Isaac hoped that as more and more Spaniards came to agree with Ronaldo, an opposing coalition of Christian and Jew would emerge powerful enough that the Inquisition would be forced to cease its work. Rabbi Isaac predicted that within a short while the Inquisition would vanish under the resistance and intolerance to its reach.

Rabbi Isaac was to be proven very wrong indeed.

Rabbi Isaac returned home and was immediately greeted by his brother, Rabbi Abraham. Rabbi Isaac was tired and wanted to rest but he knew he could not; he first had to find out the outcome of Rabbi Abraham's speech.

Rabbi Abraham was beaming, "It went very well, dear Isaac, really it did. I only stammered about three or four times!"

Rabbi Isaac was relieved. He knew that if Rabbi Abraham would allow himself the time and energy to prepare, these speeches would become second nature to him. He thanked his brother for filling in for him and told him about Ronaldo's warning.

"Now that you have mentioned it, I did notice several particularly strange looking men. I thought maybe they had stolen their clothes and did not have an opportunity to bathe properly before coming here. Maybe they are spies?" Rabbi Abraham sounded concerned.

"I do not think so, " answered Rabbi Isaac. "Father Ramon would not be foolish enough to send odd and strange looking characters. No, the spies that he sends will look so much like the typical *converso* that it will be extremely difficult to discern who they are. It is those people we must watch closely."

"But if that is so, how can we continue to welcome these people into our circle? We will be inviting danger, welcoming the enemy!" Rabbi Abraham was confused.

"That is correct," responded Rabbi Isaac. "You have pinpointed the problem. We shall no longer permit newly arrived secret Jews to become part of our circle. The risks are simply too great. It is an unfortunate situation but we can no longer allow strangers to become associated with us. We shall have to turn people away, send them back from whence they came."

"But what will happen to those secret Jews who know so little and will be lost without us? Where will they go to receive the tradition, the heritage? Where can they go?" Rabbi Abraham was troubled.

"I do not know, my brother, I do not know. This is a most difficult situation. I do believe that it is the only option that we have, the only solution to insure that our current circle of pupils remains safe and can continue their spiritual growth. If we continue to accept new secret Jews and some of Father Ramon's spies are among them, the results will be disastrous. I am sorry, but we shall no longer receive any more secret Jews."

Rabbi Abraham understood.

For the first time the Bibago brothers perceived and experienced the fear and isolation they had spent twenty years teaching others to overcome.

19

Juan and Diego de Ciudad traveled throughout the night and the entire next day. They wanted to cover as much distance as possible before anyone in Plasencia, especially Father Pedro, realized they had escaped. They were exhausted. It was almost nightfall and Juan suggested they soon stop for the night. Diego readily agreed.

They pulled the wagon off to the side of the road, fed the horses, made place in the wagon in which to sleep and lay down. It was decidedly uncomfortable, the space they allotted was small and cramped, but it was better than sleeping in an upright position. There were so many questions that plagued Juan, so much he wanted to sort out, but he was too tired and did not have the energy to make sense of all the sudden changes in his life. He looked over at Diego, who was already asleep. In a few moments Juan drifted off as well.

The next morning they awoke to the warmth and illumination of the sun's rays, which seemed to herald a brighter and more radiant future. After washing up at a nearby stream, Juan motioned for Diego to grab his cloak and they proceeded to walk deeper into the forest.

Diego was puzzled, "Where are we going, Father?"

Juan looked surprised, "We are going into the forest where no one will see us. We cannot pray this close to the road!"

Diego persisted, "But why are we going there, Father?"

Juan thought that perhaps Diego was disoriented from a poor night of sleep and was not aware he was repeating himself.

"I told you already, Diego, we cannot pray where someone might see us. Come now, we have much to do!"

Diego realized his father did not understand what he was saying. He turned to him and uttered the words Juan had been waiting twenty years to hear. "Father, we are no longer secret Jews, we do not have to fear the church or Father Pedro or any man for that matter. Now we can act like all other Jews. We may worship anywhere and at any time of day! We shall pray here for all the world to see!"

Juan thought about it for a moment. Of course it was true. In this new place, it was no longer dangerous to practice Judaism in public, especially since no one knew who they were! Juan felt as if a burden had been lifted, as if a rumor which had tainted his reputation was proven false and he could once again walk in public with pride and confidence. Juan had been preoccupied with getting as far away from Plasencia as possible that he had scarcely given any thought to what it was that he was running from. But Diego reminded him, helped him appreciate that he was free! No longer bound to deception and dishonesty. No longer restricted to the darkness, the shadows, the endless moonlit gloom and the dreaded obscurity of the night. All the waiting, the hoping, the secret candle lightings and the clandestine meetings had finally come to an end.

Juan smiled and reached for his cloak.

Juan finished praying and waited for Diego. Juan's prayer this time had been different, unencumbered. He still found himself peering over his shoulder every few moments and automatically ceased praying a number of times when he heard the slightest noise made by an animal or by the wind. He knew that his reactions were rooted in twenty years of fear and erroneous understandings, and anticipated more than ever a gradual distancing from those tendencies. But for the moment he prayed the prayer of a free man, with unlimited possibility and potential. He cherished the moment.

They mounted the wagon and proceeded to Huesca. They traveled at a more moderate pace; now that they no longer perceived themselves in danger they saw no need to hurry and needlessly tire the horses. They knew Father Pedro would send guards to search for them but were reassured by the commanding lead they already had, as well as the fact that no one knew that they had left or where they were going. They were confident they would not be found.

They journeyed in a slow, almost lazy manner. Juan took a long look at his son. He was so proud of him. For as long as Juan could remember, Diego had shouldered the burden of living a dual life with responsibility and caution. Even as a young boy, Diego had expressed an inordinate interest in the oft misinterpreted rituals of the secret Jews. By the time he reached the pivotal age of thirteen he was responsible for instructing many of the children in the ways of the Torah. He was now a young man of twenty, strong and robust. For the first time Juan thought of his son's future. Soon he would be seeking a wife. Would the community in Huesca accept them and offer Diego a suitable bride? Juan then thought of Margarita, his own wife. She had been gone only a few days but the quick escape, the constant traveling and his new approach to Judaism made Margarita seem far away, as if they had been separated for a lifetime. Juan now had a few moments to contemplate his loss. He truly missed her. He wished she could have experienced the same freedom, the same unrestrained worship that he was now permitted to engage in. He imagined that if she were still alive, she would brandish her newfound privilege and light the Sabbath candles with all the meaning and concentration she could muster. She would have the luxury of time, that great gift which the secret Jews were consistently denied, as they hastily performed each ritual under the shadow and specter of exposure. She would watch the candles burn late into the night, patiently and slowly, savoring their illumination. She would draw strength from the brilliance and glow of those holy flames, providing her with the inspiration to triumph over the pitfalls of the coming week. As the candles flickered and finally extinguished themselves she would retreat to her bed with a sublime satisfaction, anticipating the challenges she knew she had the strength to master. Yes, he wished she were with him and once again he bemoaned his loss.

Father and son proceeded toward Huesca. They traveled in silence, thinking about the future, and the past. After a few hours they again stopped to rest and feed the horses. Juan turned to his son, "Diego, what made you suggest we travel to Huesca? It is not a large or famous town. What have you heard about that place?"

"I am surprised, Father, that you have not heard of the famous Bibago brothers," answered Diego. "I do not know their first names, but they are renowned for their efforts in helping people like us, secret Jews like us. Those brothers have assisted hundreds if not thousands of secret Jews in understanding Judaism properly and have further helped them overcome many of the obstacles and inhibitions the secret Jews face. I have heard they are wonderful people."

"I do not understand. Why does the church in Huesca allow secret Jews to associate and study with regular Jews? We could not do that in Plasencia!"

"I do not know. Perhaps they are more tolerant of secret Jews in Huesca, or perhaps the Bibago brothers are very influential and their work is overlooked by the church." Diego shrugged his shoulders. "Whatever the reason, I only hope we can have the opportunity to learn from them and grow from their instruction."

"You are right, Diego, it is not important to question the church's reasoning. I sincerely wish these two brothers are as helpful as you claim!"

Juan and Diego arrived in Huesca almost two weeks later. Neither of them had ever been there before and like all newcomers, they headed directly to the local inn. The inn was situated at the edge of the town and was run by a Spaniard named Fernando. He was about sixty years old, small and slightly overweight, and had been a widower for several years. He dressed in an informal, almost disrespectful manner and strolled the streets as if he had not a care in the world. He spoke many languages and seemed to know the business of every citizen in Huesca. He referred to everyone as "señor." He particularly enjoyed overcharging innocent and naive customers.

He often boasted that he once charged an unassuming young man four times the going rate for a single night's lodging!

Fernando knew all about Rabbi Isaac and Rabbi Abraham and the work they were doing in Huesca, and found it very good for business. Their efforts brought so many people to an otherwise obscure town, each needing a place to stay. Most of the secret Jews generally stayed at the inn for about two weeks, until Rabbi Isaac managed to find homes for them among the Jews in Huesca, but the flurry of secret Jews always passing through made Fernando busy and rich. Like Ronaldo Pallo, Fernando was worried about Father Ramon's new and terrifying campaign against Rabbi Isaac and Rabbi Abraham. He cared little about religious matters but feared that Father Ramon's oppressive tactics would prevent additional secret Jews from traveling to Huesca, and that would impact negatively on his fortunes. Fernando recalled that over the past month or two the steady flow of people had diminished somewhat and wondered whether Father Ramon's new regulations had contributed in any way. Fernando understood that if Father Ramon succeeded he would undoubtedly have to close the inn.

Fernando's musings were interrupted by the sound of a horse drawn wagon approaching the inn. The wagon, atop which two men were seated, pulled up in front of Fernando and abruptly stopped. Juan descended and drew near.

Fernando observed Juan closely. No doubt he was a secret Jew, why else would anyone come to Huesca, and yet there were subtle differences. He seemed more dignified, almost elegant. Wearing long robes of silk and a turban with rich colors, he was almost regal in appearance. His beard was trimmed and he carried himself with an air of confidence, something he usually did not see among the other secret Jews. He exuded an aura of wealth, which greatly pleased Fernando. Fernando observed Diego and correctly concluded he was Juan's son. He resembled him in appearance, manner and dress and was respectfully waiting for his father to speak first.

"Greetings, fine sir," said Juan genially. "Are you the keeper of the inn? We are seeking lodgings and something to eat."

Fernando saw an opportunity to ask at least twice the usual rate. "Yes, I am the innkeeper, and my name is Fernando. You are in luck, my friend, I do have a room available. The price is but twenty crowns a night. Shall I help you with your belongings?"

"Twenty crowns!" responded Juan, surprised. "I believe twenty crowns is rather high for one night's lodging."

Fernando was expecting Juan to respond this way and retorted, "You are correct, señor. I see that you are a very astute businessman, but I shall serve you a feast that would make the king himself envious!"

Juan thought it was still too high but was famished and did not wish to argue any further. He accepted and waited while Fernando unloaded their belongings.

Fernando was busily emptying the wagon and called down to Juan. "What is in this box, señor? This box cannot fit in your room. It is too big! What shall I do with it?"

The box.

Juan did not want to leave it on the wagon. He did not want anything to happen to his family's heirlooms. "Is there anywhere you can store that for me during my stay? I will pay you an extra two crowns a week."

Fernando laughed and realized this man was very free with his money. He could have asked for thirty crowns a night!

"Yes, señor. I will store it in a room that is currently not being used at the far end of the inn. If you need it, that is where it will be."

"Thank you, Fernando, and please, allow me to introduce myself. I am Juan de Ciudad and this is my son, Diego."

Fernando climbed off the wagon and shook Juan's hand. "It is good to meet you, señor, " Fernando said. He turned to Diego, "You too, señor."

"Tell me, Fernando, I am looking for two brothers, their name is Bibago. Have you heard of them?"

"Of course. Rabbi Isaac and Rabbi Abraham."

"Do you know where they live? My son and I wish to see them, we have important matters we must discuss with them." Juan did not wish to disclose the reason he sought the brothers.

"Everyone knows where they live, señor. You do not have to speak mysteriously about them. I know why you wish to see them. It is obvious that you and your son are secret Jews!"

"I beg you, Fernando, do not report us to the church. We have traveled so far and have waited so long for this!" answered Juan nervously.

"Relax, señor. Do you think that I would risk losing twenty crowns a night plus two more each week for the box because of a religious dispute which has nothing to do with me?! I do not have the patience for that! Do not worry, if you pay the fee as you promised, your secret is safe with me."

Fernando then told Juan where the brothers lived and the fastest route to their home.

"*Gracias* Fernando."

Fernando nodded and walked off. Diego reminded his father that he had chosen Huesca specifically because secret Jews could openly associate with Jews without fear of the church. Juan had been suspicious of that but now saw that indeed things were different here.

It was getting late; in a short while it would be dark. Juan and Diego opted for their first decent meal and a good night's sleep in two weeks and would then proceed to the Bibago brothers in the morning.

Juan turned to enter the inn and saw two men arguing bitterly as they walked down the road. As they reached the inn he heard them furtively whispering to each other.

"It is your fault," said one. "If you would have remained silent he would have accepted us!"

"That is not true," retorted the other. "Rabbi Isaac explicitly stated that it was too dangerous to teach us and it was nothing personal! He told you three times that he harbored no ill will toward either of us!"

Juan turned white. Could they be talking about Rabbi Isaac Bibago? Was he refusing to accept secret Jews? Juan had to find out. He approached them. "I am sorry to interrupt, but I could not help overhearing your discussion. Are you talking about Rabbi Isaac Bibago?"

The two men suddenly turned quiet. Should they answer him? What if he was a Christian? They stood in silence, not knowing what to do.

Juan pleaded, "Please, you have nothing to fear from me, I must know. Were you talking about Rabbi Isaac Bibago?"

The two men saw the sincerity and passion of Juan. They concluded he was a secret Jew and answered him.

"Yes, we were talking about Rabbi Isaac. We are secret Jews and came from Toledo just the other day. We went to see Rabbi Isaac earlier and he told us that he was very sorry but that he could not help us. He said that the church has recently expressed much dissatisfaction with his efforts and would not allow them to continue. He told us he is no longer accepting new students into his inner circle. My friend here thinks he did not want us because of something I said, but it had nothing to do with that."

"Yes, it did," the man persisted. "You are to blame for this!"

The men walked off, still arguing.

Juan and Diego stood silently. Was it true? Would they be turned away? Would the church again frustrate his desires, deny him his heritage?

Juan had no reason not to believe those two men. If Rabbi Isaac had refused them why would he and Diego be treated differently? If the church finally managed to do in Huesca what it accomplished in Plasencia, then they were wasting their time, they would gain nothing by remaining here. Juan wondered whether they should leave immediately. Why prolong this fruitless venture? Diego pointed out that it was almost dark and they would have to stop traveling in a few hours in any event. He suggested they stay the night and then leave in the morning. He apologized to his father but reiterated that he had heard things were different in Huesca. Juan of course did not blame Diego for their misfortune and conceded that it was too late to continue on their way. Juan resolved to stay the night and then leave in the morning.

Where could they go?

Certainly not back to Plasencia, that would be courting disaster. Juan decided they could not travel anywhere in Castile, it was simply too dangerous for them to reside in close proximity to their hometown.

Juan was convinced he would hear of another friendly town, one that treated Jews better than the rest. But he would hurry there only to discover that those benevolent policies had changed and life as a Jew was as uncomfortable there as anywhere else. Then he would wander to another Christian city, where rumor told of the fair treatment of Jews. But Juan would learn that that city would also one day conform to the protocols of every other city. He would wander hither and thither seeking that one place, that lone town that would accept him and treat him with the respect and dignity he deserved.

Would it ever end?

20

Diego could not sleep. He wondered how to convince his father not to leave Huesca. Diego heard those two men report that Rabbi Isaac would not want to teach them, but felt his father should not give up so hastily. They had traveled this far and really had nothing to lose by meeting with Rabbi Isaac. If Rabbi Isaac refused to accept them, they could leave at that point. Diego believed that his father had a better chance of winning Rabbi Isaac's approval than the two men arguing at the inn. Juan was considerably older than they and carried himself with a certain presence that was impressive and dignified. Moreover, Juan and Diego would meet Rabbi Isaac as father and son, infused with a unique importance and vitality, representative of the ongoing connection to their illustrious heritage. He hoped Rabbi Isaac would be reluctant to abandon them. Diego resolved to urge his father to reconsider in the morning.

There was another reason, a more personal reason Diego did not wish to leave. He felt it was time he married. He knew he first needed to have a circumcision, for which he had been mentally preparing for as long as he could remember. But, he believed it was time he found a spouse and established his own home, free of the duality and dishonesty of his childhood. He fully understood that those evils were necessary to preserve the heritage but he had had enough of it and could not wait to escape its reach. Diego did not even have a desire to remain in Spain. He wanted to leave it behind. For now, though, Diego believed he would find a suitable bride in Huesca, one who shared his desires and his goals. He understood his father's indifference. Without the Bibago brothers Huesca was a most unattractive town, but it offered him opportunities he might not find elsewhere. It was a tolerant place. Even if Rabbi Isaac could not teach him, he could at least try to cultivate a proper understanding of Judaism without fear of danger. And Huesca had many Jews, presumably with eligible daughters. Surely one would be suitable for him.

Diego did not want to resume traveling, spending months or years searching for a place where his father would feel comfortable. They would be branded transients, a guest in every town, at home in none. Diego was convinced that constantly relocating, never being able to plant roots in any one place, would further frustrate his chances of finding an appropriate wife. He would explain this to his father and hope it would change his mind.

Juan too had been wondering whether his decision to leave was rash and impetuous. Like Diego he realized there was nothing to lose by simply visiting Rabbi Isaac. In fact, the more Juan thought about it, the more he wanted to meet Rabbi Isaac and persuade him to accept him and his son. He understood from the men at the inn that the church no longer looked the other way regarding Rabbi Isaac and his school. But he refused to believe that the danger Rabbi Isaac would be placing himself in would be so much greater if he admitted two more pupils. Surely there could be some way for Rabbi Isaac to deceive the church, to mislead them into thinking he was a strict adherent of the church's new policies while continuing his important work unabated. He and Diego had been doing that for the past twenty years! Juan was determined to press that point to Rabbi Isaac in the morning.

Juan arose early, about two hours before sunrise, and awakened Diego. Juan informed Diego about his change of heart and Diego nodded in agreement. Diego said nothing about remaining in Huesca even if Rabbi Isaac were to reject them, and purposely neglected to mention anything about his plans for marriage. He felt his father was preoccupied and would not give it due consideration.

After daybreak, they walked silently to Rabbi Isaac's home, following the route Fernando mapped out for them. While walking, Juan observed that Huesca greatly resembled Plasencia. They were both small towns, with simple homes and narrow paths. Like Plasencia, Huesca boasted a large and imposing church, which seemed visible from virtually every street. And both towns still featured some of the Muslim architecture which had once filled the markets and bazaars of Spain.

They reached Rabbi Isaac's home, a large and neat looking house in the Jewish quarter. Juan noticed a small rolled piece of parchment affixed to the doorpost. He did not know what it was. He showed it to Diego, who likewise could not identify it. Juan knocked and waited a few moments. A tall, middle-aged woman opened the door and invited Juan and Diego inside.

"My name is Abigail. I am the wife of Rabbi Isaac Bibago. Are you here to see my husband?"

She spoke softly, in a warm and comforting tone.

"Yes, we are."

"I do not believe you have an appointment. He did not tell me he was expecting anyone at this early hour. Is that correct?"

"Yes."

"All right. I shall tell him you are here and he will be with you shortly."

Juan was surprised he and Diego were admitted so readily. She did not question their motives or their purpose for visiting.

She led them through the house, to the far back room. She told them to wait there and left. The room was quite large, with about forty chairs neatly lined in rows and a table near the front. Juan and Diego concluded it was a classroom. There were many Hebrew phrases affixed to the walls; virtually none of which Juan nor Diego could read. In the back stood a shelf laden with books. Juan opened one, recognized the Hebrew writing and quickly closed it.

This was the room where thousands of secret Jews came to shed their inhibitions, their faulty and misconceived customs and rituals. This was the place where so many dedicated Jews came to confront their pasts, improve themselves and to continue the long journey they embarked upon the moment they accepted a life of secrecy and deception. For Juan, this was the culmination of twenty years of waiting, waiting which began the night his friend Diego Nasso, for whom his son was named, was taken. This was the realization of endless longing and hoping, countless lies which after time eroded his sense of integrity. Finally, after twenty years of dual allegiances, clandestine meetings, cryptic observances and the death of his beloved wife, he too had arrived.

Yet, his future hung in doubt. He did not know whether Rabbi Isaac would welcome him. Diego too was contemplating what this room represented and waited anxiously.

An austere looking man quickly entered, holding a quill in his hand. He appeared very serious, almost sad. He had deep, penetrating eyes, a graying beard and very large hands. He headed directly toward the pile of books, noticed Juan and Diego and stopped to greet them.

"Welcome."

"It is good to meet you, Rabbi Isaac."

The man smiled, "I am not Rabbi Isaac, I am Rabbi Abraham, his older brother." Rabbi Abraham immediately grew wary. Could these two men be spies? Rabbi Abraham thought it was very clever of this man to mistake him for his brother, it added a touch of innocence, a certain credibility that sounded endearing and honest. Rabbi Abraham thought that if this man was a spy he was quite skilled and crafty and he decided to engage him further.

"And what is your name?"

"I am Juan de Ciudad. This is my son, Diego."

Rabbi Abraham nodded to Diego.

"Where are you from, Juan?"

"Plasencia."

"That is in Castile, near Portugal?"

"Correct."

They continued speaking about Plasencia, Juan's story and that of his son, Diego.

Rabbi Abraham was confused. On the one hand Juan sounded genuine, he could almost hear the longing in his voice. But Rabbi Abraham was concerned. Juan came from a town too distant to allow for proper verification. And he came with his son, that continual link, that everlasting and perpetual bond no Jew ever wants broken. The presence of Diego troubled him, made him skeptical: Perhaps the church had sent a man with a son merely to garner sympathy and approval.

Rabbi Abraham pressed on.

"Tell me, Juan, what brings you to Huesca?"

"Well, my wife was recently found lighting candles on Friday night. She paid the ultimate price at the hands of an angry mob. My son and I knew it was only a matter of time before we were caught as well so we escaped and came here. My son had heard that in Huesca you and your brother help secret Jews like us. Please help us, Rabbi Abraham, we need your guidance!"

Again, Juan sounded honest and innocent, a trusting soul. But his story seemed to be scripted by the church itself! In addition to a father and son, a likeable and compelling pair, he had a wife who had been killed for practicing Judaism. Juan's story was so heartfelt, so touching and moving it almost seemed cruel to turn him away and deny him the new life he so desperately desired. This was precisely Rabbi Abraham's dilemma. Juan's story seemed too contrived, too perfect, as if every aspect of his life had been scripted for the specific purpose of appealing to his emotions and those of his brother, Rabbi Isaac's. True, there had been men and women who came to them over the years with stories even more pitiful and depressing. But that was just it. Juan's story was sad, yet not too distressing or unduly outrageous. It was perfectly blended with enough sorrow to engender sympathy, yet enough strength and moral courage to foster respect and admiration. Juan had not said very much but the force of his words and the passion in his voice lent his few words great distinction.

Was he a spy? Was the church that inventive and shrewd? Rabbi Abraham did not know but he respected his brother's decision to no longer accept new students into their circle. The mere fact that he was uncertain about this man demonstrated the level of awareness and caution they had to take to insure they would not be ruined by the church. His brother had made a wise decision indeed. Rabbi Abraham looked at Juan. He was an interesting man and although they had spoken for only a moment or two, he was intrigued by him. If Ronaldo Pallo had not warned his brother, this man would have been welcomed with open arms. Rabbi Abraham continued to wonder about Juan and finally realized that it did not matter, he would be dismissed. In a few moments Rabbi Isaac would arrive and turn them away. Then he would never see Juan and his son again. If they were the spies, he and his brother would succeed in thwarting the church's plans. If Juan was telling the truth, then rejecting him was an unfortunate consequence of the precautions necessary to protect their work and themselves. Rabbi Abraham felt remorse about that but knew there was no alternative.

Juan had been standing near the stacks of books and saw a woman out of the corner of his eye. It was the same woman who had been Rabbi Isaac's first pupil and was a frequent guest at his home. Juan only glimpsed her for a moment. She quickly darted past the entrance of the room and was no longer in sight.

Did he know her?

He believed he did. The instant he saw her he realized he had seen her before.

But where?

Juan tried to recall her image and search his memory for this mysterious woman. He was interrupted moments later. Rabbi Isaac had entered the room.

Rabbi Isaac looked much like Rabbi Abraham but more youthful and vibrant. He too was tall and imposing. His beard was not as gray as his brother's and his eyes looked softer, calmer.

"Good morning, dear brother," said Rabbi Abraham, relieved that his brother would be the one to turn away Juan and his son. Rabbi Abraham recently discovered that the only thing he detested more than lecturing to large crowds was informing the secret Jews that they could not stay. Rabbi Isaac did not like it any more that his brother but accepted that as leader and teacher of the community, it was his responsibility. Rabbi Abraham sensed that this time it would be particularly uncomfortable and quietly slipped out of the room.

Rabbi Isaac immediately approached Juan, then Diego, and introduced himself. He asked Juan and Diego to take seats at the front of the room. Rabbi Isaac sat down near them and briefly inquired about their backgrounds. Rabbi Isaac was as captivated and confused as Rabbi Abraham. Juan was an extraordinary man, but quite possibly a Christian spy. Rabbi Isaac had decided that he would make no mention of spies to any of the secret Jews he would reject. He did not want Father Ramon to know that he was privy to his schemes. Rabbi Isaac resolved to blame his inability to accept new pupils squarely on the church and stress the risks and dangers such acceptance would pose. Rabbi Isaac always apologized profusely when sending the secret Jews away, a gesture he knew meant very little as he saw the faces of those despondent and dejected souls wander aimlessly and hopelessly away from his home. Juan was interesting indeed, which made Rabbi Isaac all the more reluctant to accept him.

Rabbi Isaac never liked to prolong greeting and getting to know the new secret Jews, it only made it more difficult to send them away. Rabbi Isaac had been conversing with Juan and Diego for several moments and knew the time had come. Rabbi Isaac composed himself and turned to Juan.

"I am sorry, Señor de Ciudad, but it is with great sorrow that I must ask you and your son to leave, I cannot accept either of you. It is nothing personal to be sure, but the church has me under close scrutiny and they frown upon my continued accomplishments and achievements. I have been told that I must watch myself very carefully and I cannot allow my work to grow or flourish in any way. I am permitted to retain the students I already have but I can no longer guide and instruct new ones. I hope you understand. We live in a Christian land and the church has spoken."

Diego was surprised. He thought his father's impressive manner and his own presence would sway Rabbi Isaac enough to make an exception that he had been willing to make for others. Diego believed that Rabbi Isaac's fears were genuine and that perhaps in a year or two he might be inclined to reverse this policy. He understood Rabbi Isaac's decision and began rehearsing the arguments he would use to persuade his father to remain despite the rejection.

Juan, on the other hand, was shocked. He had heard the men at the inn describe almost word for word Rabbi Isaac's rejection. And yet, the moment he heard it directly from Rabbi Isaac he could not believe it. He could not imagine that Rabbi Isaac would so quickly cower in panic and fear from some Christian edicts and concede defeat during the hour of need of so many secret Jews.

He had been evading the church, risking his life right under its very watchful eye, for the past twenty years. He could not even read Hebrew and surely did not know the Torah as proficiently as Rabbi Isaac. His understanding of Judaism was so incomplete that he often wondered if he was more Christian that Jewish, and he still was not circumcised. Yet, he felt that he exhibited much more sacrifice, much more risk and determination than Rabbi Isaac.

Why was Rabbi Isaac so reluctant, so afraid to accept the ultimate challenge of Judaism, to perpetuate the heritage in the face of danger and death?

Was he too comfortable, too used to an easy and carefree life to endure the daunting demands of Judaism?

Was that the reason his parents, Miguel and Elienor, and their parents, had been willing to embrace the Cross and abandon a thousand long suffering years of Jewish courage and heroism?

Juan took a long look at Rabbi Isaac. He had fond feelings for him, a decent man, a respected leader and teacher. He had helped countless Jews, an important undertaking which cannot be negated. But Rabbi Isaac disappointed him, the way his parents and grandparents and a generation of Spanish Jews disappointed him when they forsook the heritage that had been forged in history. Although Rabbi Isaac dedicated his life to restoring that heritage, he was afraid to take the next step, too frightened by the threats and the consequences. Juan could not fault Rabbi Isaac. It was a decision too complex and too personal to question. But Juan wanted to remind Rabbi Isaac, awaken his soul to a higher purpose, to that special spark which flickers within each Jew and evokes a heightened sensitivity to the legacy that is Judaism. Juan wished to infuse Rabbi Isaac with the understanding that by perpetuating the legacy in spite of the danger, in the face of death, he was fulfilling the most majestic and time-honored tradition of the Jew.

How could he get Rabbi Isaac to understand all that? How to convince him, explain it all to him?

Juan did not know but he wanted to return to the inn and to figure it out. He quickly thanked Rabbi Isaac for his time and patience, beckoned to Diego and left.

Rabbi Isaac apologized and believed it was the last time he would ever see them.

On the way back to the inn, Juan told Diego they were not leaving yet. He would try to think of different ways to touch and influence Rabbi Isaac. Diego did not object. For the time being they would remain in Huesca.

As they proceeded back to the inn, the church loomed in the distance. Juan wondered whether he could ever escape its presence.

At the inn, Juan was anxious. He had been rejected but he would not give up. He was determined to change Rabbi Isaac, make him realize that his work must continue despite the church's threats. Juan's mind was racing as he tried to formulate the best way to present his argument to Rabbi Isaac.

There was a knock at his door. "Señor! Please open the door, I must speak with you."

It was Fernando. Juan immediately allowed him entry.

"I am sorry, señor, but I no longer have room for that box of yours. A cousin of mine from Seville has unexpectedly arrived for a few days and he has nowhere else to stay. Again, I apologize but I need the space!"

Juan had all but forgotten the box. He did not have time for this now, he was busy reclaiming his heritage. He knew, however, that he could not argue with his host.

"All right, Fernando, my son and I will remove it in a few moments."

"But señor, where will you put it?" Fernando appeared impatient.

"I am not sure. I suppose I will leave it on my wagon." Juan wanted to avoid that. It could be stolen or ruined, but he had no other option.

"Very well, señor, I shall meet you and your son at that room, shortly."

Fernando left and Juan and Diego proceeded to the room that housed the box. Juan wanted to act quickly, move the box and resume planning a course of action aimed at reaching Rabbi Isaac, while the passion and determination still burned within him. Fernando opened the door and Juan and Diego carried the box to their room. Diego, who sat bored while his father plotted, asked if he could open it and rummage through the things which had belonged to his grandparents and perhaps his great-grandparents. Juan quickly consented; with Diego occupied he would be free to think and plan.

Juan and Diego placed the box on a long table in their room. Diego was excited, but Juan merely wished to help Diego open it quickly and return to his overpowering obsession of influencing Rabbi Isaac. Juan quickly returned to the far corner, deep in thought.

Diego carefully opened the box.

Inside, Diego saw neatly folded clothes and sheets. They were quite ordinary. Not the sort of things one would expect to save for generations. Diego began removing the items hoping to discover something unique, something special, something which might shed light on the personalities of his ancestors. But a few moments later the box was empty and Diego had not recovered anything particularly important.

"There is nothing in this box, Father, just some old clothes."

"Please, Diego," returned Juan, "I am not interested in that right now." Diego once again peered into the empty box, to make sure he had

192 / *A Promise Fulfilled*

not inadvertently left anything inside. The box was indeed empty, but now Diego observed that the bottom plank of the box had a slight bulge. He stood back a few paces and carefully gauged the slight slope of the bulge protruding from the bottom of the box and realized the plank was not the bottom of the box at all. He quickly called his father. "Come, Father, you must see this."

Juan looked up, annoyed that he had been disturbed once again but he saw the look of amazement on Diego's face and approached him. "What is it, Diego?"

Diego showed his father the bulge and Juan confirmed that the plank indeed was not the bottom of the box. "There must be another compartment, another section to this box. I never noticed this before. I was completely unaware this box contained additional space. Diego, help me remove this false bottom so that we may see what is underneath."

As father and son stood in front of the box with a hidden compartment, Juan was suddenly seized with an overwhelming sense of destiny.

Juan pulled at the sides of the box trying to ascertain whether any planks were loose and could be removed easily. He motioned for Diego to pull on one side while he pulled on the other. After a few moments both ends of the box cracked off and the false bottom fell off the table.

Inside the secret compartment lay a Torah scroll.

The scroll was covered with a beautifully designed cover with words sewn onto the front that neither he nor Diego could read. The scroll was ensconced within rags and old clothes to prevent it from shifting. Carefully, Juan lifted it from the box, waited for Diego to move the broken pieces of the box on the floor and then placed the Torah on the table.

Juan removed the cover and unrolled it. It was the most beautiful and remarkable thing he had ever seen. Juan could not read it but marveled at the boldness of the lettering, the starkness and finesse and singularity of each letter. The scroll was so perfectly written with so much attention to detail and such precision that Juan just stood, astonished and humbled. Juan could not draw himself away and continued to gaze at it. He felt the beauty and charm of the symbols on the parchment call to him, beckon him to learn its words and meaning and grow old trying to understand its essence. He sensed a warmth and holiness he never experienced before and as he became lost in the endless streams of exquisite words and letters, he glimpsed for a moment all that he was missing. He knew at that instant how empty and unfulfilled he had been, how utterly lost he was without the teachings which lay within this scroll. Juan lowered his head, kissed the Torah and began to weep.

Unlike Juan, who had seen a Torah scroll once before, Diego had never seen one. Diego, though, was also able to discern the patience and care the scribe had taken while writing it and likewise could not tear himself away. The graceful and enchanting curves of each letter also beckoned him to understand their meaning. Following his father, Diego too kissed the scroll.

Juan did not know how this scroll found its way to his home and felt guilty that it had been treated with disrespect for so many years. He wondered if the words on the cover would provide the answer. He caressed it and placed it back in the box. The two stood in silence marveling at it, almost mesmerized by its mystery. Juan saw in the scroll the answer he was seeking.

Juan estimated the scroll was quite old, but he could not guess when it had been written. The core beauty of the scroll, however, the elegantly crafted letters which formed the words he could not read, remained untarnished, unsullied by either time or distance.

"Father, were you aware that this Torah scroll was hidden in our house all these years?"

"Of course not, Diego," answered Juan abruptly. "I did not know about that secret compartment and I would never have stored something this exquisite in so irreverent a fashion."

"It is a true find, Father, a genuine treasure!"

A treasure.

Juan had not heard that word since Diego Nasso mysteriously whispered it to him that fateful night twenty years earlier. He had all but forgotten it, and now Diego reminded him.

The hidden treasure.

It was Diego Nasso's message, his legacy and final warning, not to forget the hidden treasure. Gazing upon the scroll, Juan finally understood what he meant. Diego Nasso was long dead but his lesson lived on, his final words ultimately realized by another Diego.

Juan was now determined to go back and convince Rabbi Isaac that closing the door on him and other secret Jews was as shameful as neglecting the holy Torah itself.

To prove his point Juan would bring along the scroll he just discovered.

He covered it, returned it to the broken box, loaded it onto the wagon and sped toward Rabbi Isaac's home.

21

Juan had entered the Jewish quarter and was nearly at Rabbi Isaac's doorstep. Juan recalled that he needed to make a sharp right turn. As he did so he came face to face with a priest and five armed guards.

Juan was forced to stop his wagon. The men blocked its path. "Step down from the wagon," demanded the priest. Juan immediately froze. Could Father Pedro have gotten word that he was in Huesca? There was nowhere for Juan to turn so he obeyed the priest's command.

"I am Father Ramon. What is your name?"

"Juan de Ciudad."

Father Ramon was tall and uncharacteristically light skinned.

"And what brings you to Huesca, Señor de Ciudad?" Juan was unsure how to respond. He knew he could not say he was there seeking guidance from Rabbi Isaac and Rabbi Abraham, that would surely further jeopardize their lives. But he would not lie and say he was a Christian. He was through with that sort of deception. He quickly thought of a plausible answer.

"I am merely passing through with my son on my way to France."

Father Ramon pressed on, "Then where are you going now?"

"For a ride."

"In such haste?"

This confrontation was not going well. How would he explain the speed of his wagon? How would this end?

"Well," stumbled Juan, "I was merely testing the swiftness of these horses. I paid very handsomely for them and I wanted to make sure I was not cheated. The seller swore to me these were the fastest steeds in all of Spain!" Juan doubted Father Ramon believed him but it was the only response he could invent.

Father Ramon appeared uninterested in Juan's answer. He allowed him to finish and replied, "Then why were you seen at the home of Rabbi Isaac Bibago? Was he the man who sold you these horses?"

Juan immediately understood from Father Ramon's sarcasm that he did not believe him at all. Father Ramon was merely playing with him, waiting for the right moment to emerge victorious, having exposed his lies. Juan did not know how to answer Father Ramon's charge about Rabbi Isaac. He knew this could not continue. He just stood in front of him and remained silent.

Father Ramon continued, "I see you cannot answer me. Is it not true that you and another man, presumably your son, were seen leaving the home of Rabbi Isaac Bibago? Tell me, what business did you have there?"

Again Juan remained silent, afraid to answer the accusation he saw coming. Father Ramon approached Juan.

"There is no need to answer, Señor de Ciudad. It is obvious that you are a *marrano* and have come here seeking guidance from Rabbi Isaac. As a baptized Christian, I am sure you are fully aware that instruction from a Jew is strictly forbidden by church doctrine. You have committed a terrible sin, drinking water from the well of others. You must be punished for your crimes." Father Ramon then motioned to his guards, "Take him away."

The guards immediately surrounded him and placed him in chains. He did not care about that. His sole concern was what would happen to the Torah. He did not want to bring it to Father Ramon's attention, who might realize its value and destroy it. Juan kept a watchful eye on the wagon as the guards quickly proceeded to the church. He saw Father Ramon push the wagon to the side of the road and heard him tell one of the guards he would meet them at the church. He then saw Father Ramon leave the wagon intact and walk in the opposite direction.

The Torah was safe, at least for now.

Juan was brought to the towering church that seemed to loom menacingly over the town. Once inside he was led to a dungeon and thrown in a cell holding a sleeping man. The rattling of the chains woke the man, who grunted upon being shaken from his slumber.

The cell was actually one of several cells, but the others seemed to be empty. All the cells faced a central door that was unusually large, made of black iron, which led out of the dungeon and back through underground passages to the main floor of the church.

The man smelled and Juan reckoned that he had not bathed in a month. What was his crime? The man sat up on the thatch of straw that served as his bed and introduced himself as Peter. He told Juan he had been there for three months. He had been caught stealing chickens, had confessed and was sentenced to four years in the dungeon. He explained that he did not mind. He had food to eat and a bed to sleep on, what else could a man need?

"And why are you here, señor?" Peter was still half asleep.

"It is a long story, one I cannot elaborate on at this time."

Peter hardly seemed to care. He grunted, lay down once again, turned away from Juan and fell back asleep.

Juan sat in the cell planning his next move. He had to insure that the Torah was safe. He had to get out of here, but how? His only hope lay with Diego. It would be hours before he realized something was the matter, and by then it could be too late! And even if Diego discovered he was missing, he would never find him. He would run to Rabbi Isaac, who could be of no assistance. Fernando would also prove ineffective. No, Diego could not help him. The only person who could rescue him, oddly enough, was Father Ramon. He would visit Juan shortly, of that he was certain. He would offer him a chance to repent his evil ways and if Juan accepted he would be freed immediately.

But Juan would not repent. Meeting with Rabbi Isaac was neither a crime nor a sin in his eyes. He swore that he would never again practice Christianity and would refuse to atone for visiting the sage. It was tempting, though, merely uttering a few meaningless words of regret in exchange for freedom. But Juan would not seek solace and absolution from Father Ramon.

Juan conceded that this unfortunate turn of events was very dreadful indeed. The moment he would reject Father Ramon's offer of repentance, he would be summarily repudiated, and like poor Peter, the chicken thief, his life would be reduced to one of emptiness and solitude. He had been so close, he had stood in the very room and touched the very books for which he had been yearning for so long. He had even met the man he believed would be his final teacher, the one that would help him conclude the journey he began first with Diego Nasso and then Alfonso Cabrerro. Only a few hours ago his life was so different, so promising. Now he was in an obscure, secret dungeon with no means of escape. And what about the Torah, that special and beautiful Torah, what would become of it?

And Diego? How would he learn the truth about his father's disappearance?

Juan felt overwhelmed by his helplessness and frailty. Was this the end? Was this the finale to so much anticipation and heartache?

Juan could not accept that he would remain here.

There had to be a way out.

There just had to be.

Over two hours later, the huge iron door to the dungeon swung open and Father Ramon entered and cast Diego inside. Father Ramon told them they would be visited again in the coming week, at which time they would be given a chance to repent their wayward deeds and once again embrace the Cross and everything for which it stood.

As soon as Father Ramon was gone Diego protested, "I will not do it, Father, I will not kiss the Cross. I am done with lying and deceiving myself. I will no longer practice Christianity!"

"I must admit, Diego, that I feel the same. It has taken me twenty years, but I have finally learned that I can no longer lead two lives and practice two religions. I have chosen Judaism and with Judaism I shall remain."

Diego drew close to his father and held his hand, "You are aware, Father, that we will die here."

"Yes, Son, I know."

They embraced and comforted themselves with the knowledge that at least they were together.

"Diego, do you know what happened to the wagon and the Torah? I was stopped on my way to Rabbi Isaac and Father Ramon left it on the side of the road. Was it recovered?"

"I do not know, Father. I was taken from the inn shortly after you departed. I have not seen the wagon since."

Peter awoke and, noticing an additional person, immediately began staking his territory within the small cell. He insisted that the straw belonged to him and that only he had the right to sleep on it. He also maintained that when the guards brought the meals, he would eat first and Juan and Diego would have to wait and satisfy themselves with whatever he left over. Neither Juan nor Diego objected. They had other concerns on their minds and were barely paying him any attention.

A week passed with no sign of Father Ramon. In a strange way, Juan was content. It gave him the time and energy to prepare for the harangue he knew would follow when he spurned Father Ramon's plea for repentance. Diego was likewise pleased with the delay. The routine to which he quickly adapted seemed more reassuring and definite than the unknown that awaited him and his father. But they both mourned that the Torah, that hidden treasure they had been so lucky to find, was gone forever.

One week became two, then three. Would Father Ramon ever come? Had he just forgotten about them and chosen to leave them to rot along with Peter, the chicken thief? Juan had to admit that the dungeon was bearable, even tolerable. They had enough to eat, even if it was Peter's leftovers, and additional straw had been brought in for him and Diego. But was there any way for them to escape?

Juan was frustrated. What bothered him more than being jailed was the uncertainty and doubt which hung over them.

They waited.

A few days later, while Peter was devouring his meal, one of the guards opened the cell and ordered Juan and Diego to follow him. They did not know where they were going but readily submitted. Juan wished Peter farewell but he was too busy eating to respond.

The guard led them through the dungeon, not speaking to them. He led them to a room in the back of the church and then through the church to the main entrance. The guard opened the door and told them to step outside. Juan and Diego complied and as soon as they were outside, the guard quickly closed the door. They stood on the church steps breathing in the fresh air they had been denied for almost a month.

This was all so puzzling. Who had rescued them? Where was Father Ramon?

Juan's first thought was to race back to that street where he was taken and see if the Torah was still there. Perhaps someone had taken the horses but had left the wagon. Juan conceded that was extremely unlikely but worth a look anyway. They started walking down the stairs of the church, eager to distance themselves from those horrible memories. As they reached the bottom of the staircase they were met by a woman, that same mysterious woman Juan had fleetingly seen at Rabbi Isaac's home.

"Hello, Juan," said the woman. "Don't you remember me?"

Juan finally had a chance to study her appearance. He did remember her!

Luisa!

Juan had rarely given her much thought over the years and seldom wondered whether she was still alive. Now, seeing her after so many years brought back the memories of the town he desperately wanted to forget.

"Luisa, is that you?"

"Yes, Juan, it has been a long time."

"Twenty years, Luisa."

"When I left, Margarita was expecting. Is this your son?" She pointed to Diego.

"This is Diego. He is named after your husband."

Luisa shed a tear as the memories she had suppressed for so long surfaced. "He looks a lot like you, Juan."

"Thank you."

"Please, you must come with me and I will explain everything. It is dangerous for you to remain here for too long."

"Before we go, I must know one thing. What became of my wagon and the box that was inside it?" asked Juan nervously.

"Do not worry, all those things are in my possession now."

The Torah was safe.

Juan and Diego followed her home.

They arrived at Luisa's house, not far from Rabbi Isaac's. It was a modest home, plainly furnished. Luisa provided wet cloths so they could wash themselves and remove the stench of the dungeon. When Juan and Diego were refreshed, Luisa called them to the dining room where she had prepared a modest meal for them.

Juan studied his surroundings. Luisa was little changed. She had aged somewhat but still evidenced the kindness and caring that had made her such a dear friend in the past. Juan and Diego sat on a small bench while Luisa made herself comfortable on a sewing chair, which she positioned facing the bench. Diego remained quiet while Luisa and Juan drifted back to their memories and their pain.

Luisa told them that she knew for certain that Diego her husband had been murdered. She explained that she did not leave Plasencia the day Diego was taken. She remained in hiding, till rumors of his death were confirmed by a fellow secret Jew. She finally left Plasencia and never returned. She wandered the countryside, drifting aimlessly — with no husband and no future — until she found her way to Huesca. She never knew what drew her to Huesca but she decided to remain, alone and afraid. Eventually she became more comfortable; she visited the synagogue and for the first time practiced Judaism in an open and carefree environment, the way she and Diego had desired for so long. But the services and rituals she saw there were so different, so foreign from the customs she was used to that she finally understood how barren and empty the worship of the secret Jews really was. She now had the opportunity to reverse so many years of incorrect teaching and understanding. She met with Rabbi Isaac and persisted in convincing him to instruct her and guide her in the ways of Judaism. Indeed, she was his first pupil. She related that she frequently came to Rabbi Isaac's home to help with whatever chores were necessary and to find if anyone from her old hometown Plasencia had arrived.

Juan then related that after Diego was taken he had joined the circle of secret Jews and had been with them ever since. He told her what happened to Margarita and their recent escape from Father Pedro and the mobs.

Both Juan and Luisa understood that their reunion was not an accident, nothing ever was. There was some deeper purpose to their meeting again after so many years. Perhaps Luisa could recommend someone suitable for Diego to marry. Surely Luisa would vouch for his family's integrity and lineage.

Luisa believed that seeing Juan again confirmed her husband's idea that the way to attract *conversos* back to their heritage was to confront them directly, to allow the beauty and eloquence of the rituals and customs speak for themselves and thereby lure those lost souls ever closer to the truth and meaning of the Torah. It had worked with Juan de Ciudad. It reminded Luisa that her husband, Diego, had been so wise, courageous and understanding. She confessed that she missed him so much and was still crushed by his death.

"When I saw you at Rabbi Isaac's home last month, I could not believe my eyes! I knew it was you, Juan, the moment I saw you. Before I even had a chance to approach, you were already gone! I know you think that Rabbi Isaac is dispassionate and uninterested in perpetuating the heritage, but believe me, his fears are justified. He possesses reliable information that Father Ramon plans on planting spies posing as secret Jews! Father Ramon's scheme is to have those spies learn all they can about Rabbi Isaac's teachings and then close down the entire school for promoting heresy. Rabbi Isaac has to reject any new secret Jews that come to him seeking instruction, they could be spies! You could be a spy, Juan!"

"Do you really think I am a spy, Luisa?"

"Of course not, but Rabbi Isaac does not know who you are. He could not risk accepting you. You have met Father Ramon. You have experienced his cruelty and ruthlessness. Rabbi Isaac can no longer accept any new secret Jews. It is simply too dangerous."

Juan was disappointed and waited for Luisa to continue.

"The day after you left, I spoke with Rabbi Isaac and I told him I knew you. He warned me not to meet with you, and that under no circumstances would he accept you. He explained that Father Ramon was watching him very closely and even if he were certain you were not a spy, by accepting you he would be in deeper danger by expanding the number of students. I needed to see you and I decided to ignore Rabbi Isaac's warning. A few hours later, I left his house with the intention of visiting you at Fernando's inn, where I was certain you were lodging. I had walked three blocks when I saw Father Ramon approach and arrest you. When Father Ramon and the guards were safely out of sight, I quickly took your horses and wagon and brought them to my house. I then spent the next month arranging for a bribe to free you both. Rabbi Isaac knows none of this. As far as he is concerned you are long gone and forgotten. I begged the help of a wealthy Christian man who owes Rabbi Isaac many favors. I finally convinced him to intercede on my behalf and yesterday he informed me that you would be released today. Juan, you must travel to him and thank him personally!"

Juan was impressed with the ingenuity and persistence of Luisa. Twenty years earlier she had been a quiet, unassuming albeit warm woman. She had matured into a cunning and resourceful advocate. But he could not understand how Rabbi Isaac and Luisa were so ready to succumb to the pressures of Father Ramon. Had Luisa so easily forgotten all the sacrifice and risk she had undertaken to preserve the heritage and perpetuate the legacy? What had happened to her?

Juan and Diego thanked Luisa for all her efforts and agreed to thank the man for rescuing him and Diego. However, one thing still troubled him. "Where is the box that was on the wagon?"

"It is in my yard at the rear of my home. I have not opened it. Would you like to see it?"

"Please."

Luisa and Juan walked to the yard. Juan opened the box, saw the Torah safe and secure, breathed a sigh of relief and went into the house.

"Is everything all right, Father?"

"Yes, Diego, it is safe."

Luisa was intrigued by Juan and Diego's fixation, almost obsession with that box. "What is inside it, Juan?"

"You will know soon enough, Luisa. Right now, I must show it to Rabbi Isaac."

22

Juan headed to Rabbi Isaac, traveling a different route hoping to avoid once again encountering Father Ramon. He arrived a short while later, anxious to present the Torah to Rabbi Isaac and Rabbi Abraham. Juan knocked and waited for Abigail, Rabbi Isaac's wife, to answer and allow him entry. He was surprised when Rabbi Isaac himself slowly opened the door.

"Hello, Rabbi Isaac. I don't know if you remember me. I am Juan de Ciudad. My son, Diego, and I came here nearly one month ago."

Rabbi Isaac seemed frightened, and hurriedly responded, "I remember, why have you returned?"

"There is something that I must show you, something on my wagon that I believe you should see." Isaac pointed to the wagon.

Rabbi Isaac hastily peered over Juan's shoulder and saw the box on the wagon. What could be inside? Rabbi Isaac admitted he was curious but could not allow Juan entry. Over the past month, life in Huesca had grown unbearable, intolerable. Secret Jews, pupils of Rabbi Isaac, were routinely attacked and arrested, some had disappeared and were killed. Many other Jews were also harassed by Father Ramon, accused of harboring and associating with secret Jews and were likewise tortured and jailed. Rabbi Isaac had all but virtually closed down his school. In fact, Juan was the first visitor in over a week. No one had come since Father Ramon had killed a secret Jew from Madrid who Rabbi Isaac had refused. The man had lingered in Huesca, like many rejected secret Jews contemplating where next to travel. He was spotted by Father Ramon, interrogated, placed on trial and then killed. Rabbi Isaac felt partly responsible for his death and understood that he could soon meet a similar fate. He even considered leaving Huesca but Ronaldo Pallo, the wealthy landowner, convinced him to stay and assured him he faced no actual danger. Reluctantly, Rabbi Isaac consented, but he knew that the days when he could train secret Jews without fear or interruption had long passed. No, he could not welcome Juan. That would surely precipitate Juan's death and possibly his own. He hoped he would not even be seen conversing with him.

Rabbi Isaac looked at Juan. Who was this man, risking his life over the contents of a box? Did he not understand that this visit could provoke dire consequences? Rabbi Isaac pitied him and thought that perhaps he lacked his full mental faculties and was unaware of any danger. He answered him softly, yet forcefully.

"I am sure that the contents of your box are fascinating indeed but I have no interest in seeing them. I have already told you that it is quite dangerous for me and for you to enter my home. I am sorry but I am not in the position to change that. In fact, last week a man very much like yourself was killed when he remained in town after being told I could not accept him. Please, act wisely and leave this town right away. Today if possible, it is the best course of action for you and your son!"

Juan was unaware of the recent terror the Jews in Huesca had been facing while he had been in jail, and did not care, nor was Juan deterred by Rabbi Isaac's warning. He had to show Rabbi Isaac the Torah, to have the Torah speak for him and the countless other secret Jews who had been abandoned due to fear, neglected by the lack of will to challenge adversity.

He had to.

Juan knew he had to say something that would make Rabbi Isaac change his mind and admit him entry, at least to open the box.

Something that would appeal to Rabbi Isaac, reach out to him, stir his soul and his conscience and compel him to invite him inside.

Rabbi Isaac turned to close the door, but Juan thrust his hand over the threshold and held it ajar.

"Please, Rabbi Isaac, do not speak to me of danger! For twenty years I have lived in constant fear, practicing Judaism in secret and in darkness. If I had been caught I would have been killed! I accepted those risks because it was the only way for me to sustain my heritage, the heritage tragically abandoned by my parents." Juan paused then continued.

"A few months ago my wife was caught lighting candles one Friday night and she was killed. My son and I could no longer remain in our town. Our affiliation with the secret Jews would have surely been revealed and we would have met with a similar fate! We escaped here to you and your brother seeking the instruction and guidance we have been denied for so long. I must admit I was devastated when you rejected us and I disagreed with your reasoning. I promised myself I would return and convince you of your mistake and I tried to do so later that day. I never quite reached your home, though; I was arrested by Father Ramon and sent to the dungeon where I remained until today." Juan observed that Rabbi Isaac was visibly moved by the story.

"I have braved so many dangers over the past twenty years, I will surely not be deterred by the threats and intimidation of Father Ramon. I have sacrificed so much to preserve the faith. Will you not do the same?" Juan withdrew his hand, looked at Rabbi Isaac and indicated he was waiting for a response.

Rabbi Isaac was speechless. He heard many daring stories of secret Jews before and knew their dedication and willingness to accept the risks far exceeded his own. But Juan was so headstrong, so serious and persuasive, so unrelenting that Rabbi Isaac felt ashamed. True, he had done much to help the cause of the secret Jews over the years, but he never took any risks. He never sacrificed anything for them, for their cause, for the Torah. He conveniently hid behind the political influence of Ronaldo Pallo and his friends, secure and out of harm's reach. He did not have the time to fully sort out these confusing new feelings which suddenly swept over him, that would happen later. But he knew he could no longer deny Juan the legacy he had suffered so much to reclaim. Rabbi Isaac decided he would invite Juan inside, speak with him awhile and view the contents of the box that was so mysterious, so alluring.

But one thing still troubled him.

"I am touched by your story Juan, yet I must know: How did you manage to secure freedom from the dungeon in so short a time?"

"A friend bribed the priests for me."

"You know people here in Huesca?"

"Yes, many years ago I was a neighbor and friend of Luisa your first student."

"You are the man of whom Luisa spoke?"

"Yes, Rabbi Isaac."

Rabbi Isaac felt comforted that Juan and Luisa were old friends and scarcely remembered that she had disobeyed him, putting their lives in jeopardy. He could not explain it, but he believed she had made the right decision.

"I have listened very carefully to you, Juan. I am truly moved by your story, your heroism and your perseverance. I am sorry that your wife could not live to join you. I am certain she was a special and holy person. I will allow you and your son into my home and I will view the contents of that box of yours. But not now, not during the day, it is too dangerous. Leave the box here, it will be safe. Return later, after midnight, and make sure you are not followed. Until then, please be careful."

"Thank you, Rabbi Isaac, you will not be disappointed."

"Very well, Juan, goodbye."

"Goodbye."

Juan quickly headed for Luisa's house and waited for nightfall. He walked cautiously through the streets of Huesca. Juan knew he only needed to wait a few more hours and all his yearning would finally be over.

Juan was very excited and barely noticed the church in the distance.

Rabbi Isaac had taken the first step in defying Father Ramon. There was no turning back.

Juan and Diego returned later that night, disappointed that they once again had to resort to midnight meetings and clandestine rendezvous. Juan had sworn he was through with that sort of deception but admitted this was different since he was no longer practicing Christianity. Juan also knew he would make an exception for the venerable Rabbi Isaac. He hoped that if Rabbi Isaac accepted them then future late night meetings would be a thing of the past. Juan knocked softly and the door immediately opened.

"Come in, Juan, come in, Diego," whispered Rabbi Isaac.

"Were you followed?"

"I do not think so. I was very cautious, very attentive," answered Juan.

"Good, now please follow me."

Rabbi Isaac escorted Juan and Diego to the classroom, the same room they had briefly visited a month earlier. The hallways of the home were lit with candles, yet there were not enough of them to provide ample light. Juan knew that too much light was an invitation to disaster and was accustomed to dimly lit passages. In the classroom Juan noticed that nothing had changed. The box lay on the table near the front of the room.

Rabbi Isaac stared at the box, anxious with curiosity. "You may open it now."

Juan and Diego opened the box, carefully removed the Torah, and then gently placed it on the table in front of Rabbi Isaac. The rabbi's eyes opened wide and he gasped. He saw the Hebrew words on the Torah's cover. "This is quite remarkable. Never have I seen anything the likes of this: A Torah cover embroidered with a detailed description of its history." Aware that Juan and Diego could not read Hebrew, he translated for them.

"It says this Torah scroll was completed in the year 1239 to commemorate the massacre which took place in Blois, France in 1171. I have heard of the incident. It was truly an overwhelming tragedy," commented Rabbi Isaac. "The writing continues that a woman named Rachel, the granddaughter of the scribe of this scroll, Rabbi Gavriel, gave the scroll to her son, Gavriel, who left France and settled in Plasencia in 1306. The narrative continues, but the stitching which comprises the woven letters is now different, the colors are more vibrant, newer. Obviously this was added at some later date. It says that Gavriel's son, Moshe, gave the Torah to his son, Rabbi Chasdai, who entrusted the Torah to Andreas de Ciudad in 1391. The narrative concludes that Rabbi Chasdai could no longer keep the Torah. His family had been killed during the riots and he was planning a hazardous escape."

Rabbi Isaac looked up. "Is that everything it says?" asked Juan excitedly.

"Yes, Juan, that is all. Are you familiar with any of the names I read?"

"Of course, Rabbi Isaac, that man Andreas was my grandfather. But I do not understand something. He accepted the Cross and was baptized along with my father in 1391, during the same year in which Rabbi Chasdai hopefully escaped to safety. Why would my grandfather keep this holy Torah at the same moment that he rejected what the Torah stands for? Why would he accept it from Rabbi Chasdai and then hide it away and embrace another religion? I am very confused!"

Rabbi Isaac agreed that Andreas de Ciudad's actions were strange indeed. Rabbi Isaac gazed intently at Juan, the product of the tragedy which befell so many Jews back in 1391. After a few moments he realized that Andreas de Ciudad's actions were not strange after all.

"I believe I understand what happened," offered Rabbi Isaac. "Your grandfather was faced with an enormous pressure to convert, pressure which unfortunately he could not withstand. He most assuredly knew he was making a tragic mistake and could not bear to fully sever all ties with Judaism. He obtained this Torah and nestled it hidden in a box as a constant reminder of where the truth could one day be found."

Juan stared at the words woven on the cover, which he could not read. He realized that Rabbi Isaac's theory was accurate and that now this Torah was infused with even greater purpose. He slowly moved his fingers across the woven letters of the cover and wept while recalling the sequence of events recorded there. He quickly wiped away his tears and knew the time was right. He turned to Rabbi Isaac.

"Please, Rabbi Isaac, let us remove the cover and look at what is underneath."

Juan then pulled off the cover and unrolled the Torah.

Rabbi Isaac moved toward the table to examine it more closely. He stood motionless, mesmerized by its beauty and workmanship. It was the most remarkable scroll he had ever seen. He did not know much about the art of writing scrolls but was able to discern that this was truly a masterpiece.

Rabbi Isaac continued to stare at it and could not tear himself away. His thoughts drifted back to earlier in the day when Juan had confronted him regarding his own inadequacies as a leader, for his failure to defy Father Ramon and continue the instruction despite the risks and threat of death. Rabbi Isaac had been troubled by Juan's harangue for the remainder of the day. The more Rabbi Isaac thought about it, the more he concluded that Juan was correct. He had failed so many unfortunate secret Jews. But Rabbi Isaac conceded that he lacked the strength, the courage to resist the pressures and authority of the church. He admitted that he did not possess that fortitude, that unabashed perseverance, that sense of destiny that made people like Juan so unique. Rabbi Isaac agreed that he had failed. He was weak and afraid and could not think of a way to overcome it. He had spent the rest of the day regretting these shortcomings.

Yet, staring into the scroll now, delving into the depths of the carefully crafted shape of each letter, changed Rabbi Isaac. He saw in that scroll the patience, the unremitting determination that one Jew exhibited for the Torah. He understood finally that there could be no Torah without discipline, without sacrifice. The magnificence of the scroll made it feasible for him to recall so many of the tragic heroes of Jewish history. The martyrs of the Crusades, of Blois and the countless secret Jews who were groping aimlessly through Spain, sinking and dying in the abyss of Spanish life. Juan's question haunted him still: When would he accept the sacrifices and risks borne by his brethren? Rabbi Isaac took one more look at the scroll and knew the answer. He lowered his head, kissed the scroll and began to weep. He then turned to Juan, placed his hands on Juan's shoulders and embraced him. He urged Juan and Diego to remain and study the sacred and holy Torah with him. Juan readily accepted and he and Diego also wept.

Rabbi Isaac quickly moved toward the door, "Please wait here, I shall return shortly."

Rabbi Isaac rushed from the room and returned a few moments later with Rabbi Abraham. Rabbi Abraham approached the scroll, looked at its beauty and splendor and he too was filled with feelings of duty, sacrifice and regret. Rabbi Abraham had trained as a scribe in his youth but had not practiced in a very long time. He estimated the scroll was at least two hundred years old and although he was not certain, believed it was written in the French style. It was the most beautiful scroll he had ever seen.

Who was this Rabbi Gavriel?

Had he written other Torah Scrolls?

How had this treasure managed to remain hidden for so long?

Rabbi Abraham conferred with Rabbi Isaac and agreed that Juan would be welcomed. Any risks they would face were the consequences of their renewed dedication and faith. They were still afraid, they could not shake that fear, and maintained that Juan and Diego's instruction could only take place at night, when their activities would be least noticeable. Juan agreed. He no longer objected to the nocturnal visits. He finally knew where his journey would end.

The four men remained in the room and placed the Torah back in the box.

There was a knock on the door.

Father Ramon?

Could he have discovered what had just taken place? Was he aware they had defied his authority?

Rabbi Isaac began to shake, "It is Father Ramon. If he has uncovered our plan, he will surely have us killed! Nothing can save us!" He began to panic.

"Let me answer the door, Isaac," said Rabbi Abraham, calmly. "Perhaps one of the townspeople has taken ill."

Rabbi Abraham carefully opened the door and saw Ronaldo Pallo. His face was pale, almost ghostly. He was sorry to see Ronaldo in such poor health but was relieved it was not Father Ramon. "Ronaldo, you look ill. Please come in and allow my brother to examine you."

"Thank you, Rabbi Abraham, but there is nothing physically wrong with me. I am fine but I need to speak with you and your brother," gasped Ronaldo. "It is important."

Ronaldo entered and immediately sat down. Juan and Diego waited in the classroom, assured by Rabbi Isaac that they had nothing to fear from this man.

Ronaldo appeared impatient, restless. The moment the two rabbis entered the room he wasted no time.

"I am here to say goodbye, Rabbi Isaac. You have been a wonderful friend and a most trustworthy doctor, but I am leaving Huesca. I have discovered that within a matter of days I shall be arrested! Imagine that, the richest man in town thrown in a dungeon to rot!"

"But why, Ronaldo, what have you done?"

"Father Ramon claims to have evidence that I have assisted some *conversos* and have encouraged them to return to Judaism. Of course those accusations are ridiculous, but I will not be able to defend myself. The moment the accusation is made, I will be arrested and imprisoned. If Father Ramon wants me to remain in a dungeon then all the money in the world will not help me. I will not spend the rest of my life in a dungeon, Rabbi Isaac, I will not. My family has already gone. I sent them to relatives in Italy. I will be gone by morning."

Rabbi Isaac remembered Ronaldo's contempt for these very policies that were forcing him to escape. He tried to appeal to those sensitivities. "But why not stay here and fight the terrible power that Father Ramon wields? Surely there are other decent citizens that would join you, and rid Huesca of this terrible scourge."

"Rabbi Isaac, you are quite naive. This wave of violence and terror that Father Ramon and others like him have initiated is so powerful, so potent that it cannot be stopped, not unless the Pope himself intervenes. A few of my friends and business partners would be crushed within a matter of days if we ever sought to challenge Father Ramon. Trust me, Rabbi Isaac, that would be a fruitless and devastating venture!"

Ronaldo stood up and drew close to Rabbi Isaac. "I can no longer protect you, I can barely protect myself. I do not know what will happen to you. I have heard that Father Ramon is unsure of how to treat you. He has learned of your medical ability and for now will most likely keep you alive as long as that serves his needs. I am sure that if he ever discovers you have done anything improper he will have you killed. Please be careful, Rabbi Isaac, and remember, you are always welcome in Italy. I will be living in Milan with my family! Farewell, my friend, goodbye, Rabbi Abraham."

Ronaldo embraced both brothers then quietly slipped out the front.

Rabbi Abraham looked serious. "You are aware Isaac that by accepting Juan and his son, we are subjecting ourselves to constant fear and dread? I do not know how long we will be able to avoid Father Ramon and his watchful eye. We are undertaking a most dangerous mission!"

"I am aware of that Abraham, but after seeing that Torah and all it stands for, I readily accept the challenge."

"As do I."

The brothers returned to the classroom and, although it was well past two in the morning, urged Juan and Diego to sit down. Rabbi Abraham asked Juan if the Torah could remain in their home. He wished to show it to some of the town elders. Juan readily consented.

He knew the Torah scroll would be safe and well cared for in the Bibago home. Rabbi Isaac approached Juan and Diego and welcomed them to his school. He informed them that he would deliver most of the lectures and that Rabbi Abraham was available for individual sessions should the need arise. He quipped that his brother was not that fond of large groups but when given the chance had proved an adept and skilled lecturer.

Rabbi Isaac spent the next hour questioning Juan and Diego, in an effort to determine how much they knew and where to begin their studies. When he finished, Rabbi Isaac bade them farewell, reminded them to proceed with caution and told them he would see them tomorrow at midnight.

Juan and Diego left satisfied with the knowledge that their journey was over, and another one was just beginning.

23

Diego and Juan proceeded quietly, they did not speak for fear of being overheard. That suited both of them, they were each deep in thought. Diego saw his life finally coalescing, all the doubt and fear that once clouded his future was now crystallizing in a way that went beyond his greatest expectation. Only a few weeks ago he feared he would become a vagabond, a wanderer, moving through Europe with his father as a bitter, unfulfilled man. But how things had changed! Now he was given an opportunity to learn the ways of the Torah with proper instruction and meaning! Diego knew the instruction would be lengthy and difficult and he would become aware of customs and rituals that he had never known existed. He could already envision how he wished to conduct his life. Diego knew it was time to marry and forge his newfound ideals together with a wife and family. He was hopeful that Luisa could recommend him to a family in Huesca with an eligible daughter. Without her influence surely no family would want a man of unknown lineage. Diego decided he would mention it to his father as soon as they arrived at Luisa's home.

Juan, too, was thinking about his future. Could he stay in Huesca and spend his life lurking in the darkness and the shadows of late night silence and repose? Would he ever have the opportunity to practice Judaism freely? Juan also realized that over time he would come to appreciate the laws and customs and participate in observances with the proper understanding. But where would it end? How long could this deception, this concealment go on? Juan knew that Diego would soon marry and start a family elsewhere. Conditions here were not fitting to raise a family. Juan also knew that he could never remain in Huesca alone. He could not manage all the late night maneuverings on his own. Juan realized he would have to leave. Where could he go? Surely he could not stay in Spain. There were no towns in Castile, Aragon, Navarre or even Granada where Jews were treated with dignity and respect.

No. There was only one place he could go.

They quietly returned to Luisa's house. It was late and Juan started for bed. Diego motioned he wished to speak with him, and although Juan was tired he followed Diego. Juan sat down, barely able to stay awake. Diego, though, was quite animated. He approached his father and calmly yet forcefully told him that he believed it was time he married. Juan was not surprised by Diego's sudden declaration and instantly found himself alert and no longer ready for sleep. He had been expecting it and agreed the time was right for Diego to find a wife. He rose, moved toward Diego and embraced him. Juan told Diego that he was certain Luisa would help find a suitable bride. But Juan mentioned nothing about his decision to leave Huesca. He wished to see Diego wed and he was hoping that the new couple would ultimately join him.

Juan could not sleep. He wondered how long he would have to wait for Diego to marry, even with Luisa's help. The more Juan thought about it, the more he realized that he no longer belonged in Huesca. Other than the Bibago brothers, the town was beginning to resemble Plasencia in a great many ways.

The next morning Juan entered the kitchen as Luisa was preparing breakfast. Although Juan had assured Diego that Luisa would help them, he wondered if she would genuinely and convincingly praise Diego to any prospective families in Huesca. Juan hoped she appreciated the magnitude of her influence.

Juan's entrance startled Luisa. "Good morning, Juan, you are up quite early. Did you sleep well last night?"

"Good morning, Luisa. Unfortunately I barely slept at all."

"Is anything the matter?"

"It is Diego. Last night he informed me that he wishes to marry. I readily embraced the idea, but where shall I find him a suitable bride? I do not know anyone in Huesca and you are the only person who can verify Diego's lineage and character. Will you help us, Luisa? Will you help Diego find a wife?" Juan was certain she would help but wished to stress the importance of her participation.

Luisa was shocked by Juan's plea. "Is that why you couldn't sleep? Did you entertain doubts whether I would help you? Have you forgotten how I tended to Margarita when she had a difficult time? I waited so patiently to see that baby, caress it and care for it with tenderness and affection. That baby needs my help! Do you think I will fail him now? Do not worry, Juan. I will do what I can to find a wife for Diego. In fact, I am in the midst of arranging a meeting between Diego and Sarah. Two days ago I was approached by Rabbi Abraham Almosnino, one of the town elders, regarding Sarah. She is a seventeen-year-old orphan who lives in his home. Rabbi Almosnino was interested in proposing a match between Sarah and Diego and inquired about Diego's character and background. Rabbi Almosnino is a kind and caring man. Although I do not know Sarah, I am told she is a girl of impeccable character. I am meeting her tomorrow and I will tell her all about Diego!"

"Thank you, Luisa, we owe you so much!"

"No, thank you, Juan, I have been waiting for you for quite some time."

Juan rushed to tell Diego about Rabbi Almosnino's proposal. They were excited by the suggestion and could barely wait for Luisa to return.

Juan then told Luisa all that had taken place the previous night. She was genuinely happy for Juan and Diego, yet surprised that Rabbi Isaac and Rabbi Abraham changed their minds. What could have led them to disregard Father Ramon and his terror tactics? Was Juan so persuasive, so influential that he could change the attitudes of two very inflexible leaders?

"It is wonderful to hear this, Juan, but the situation here has deteriorated to the point where Rabbi Isaac and Rabbi Abraham considered leaving Huesca. How did you convince them to stay and accept you?"

"It was not I who convinced them, it was the box. The box has saved me and my son," said Juan, relieved.

"What is in that box that you guard so carefully, and where is it now?"

"That box contains the greatest treasure you could imagine! The next time you visit Rabbi Abraham, ask him if you could see it. I have left it there for safekeeping. It is truly wondrous to behold!"

Diego was very anxious to meet Sarah. Luisa had been introduced to her and raved about her beauty and character. Yet, there was one thing that prevented him from meeting her, one obstacle which first had to be overcome. Diego wondered if his father could have forgotten or perhaps he had banished thoughts of it deep within the recesses of his mind. There was no escaping it, what had to be done next could not be avoided. A few nights later, after Juan and Diego had returned to Luisa's house, Diego turned to Juan, "Father, there is something missing in our lives."

"What do you mean, Diego?" Juan was perplexed. "Our studies are progressing wonderfully and soon you shall be meeting a prospective bride!"

"That is true, Father, we have much to be excited about but we still are uncircumcised," whispered Diego.

Juan turned his head in embarrassment. Of course he had not forgotten. It permeated his thoughts every waking moment. Yet he had been so involved, first with Rabbi Isaac and Rabbi Abraham and now with making arrangements for a meeting between Sarah and Diego, that he lacked the time and the mental stamina to do something about it. But Diego was correct. This imperfection had been present far too long.

Who would perform the ritual? Rabbi Isaac? Rabbi Abraham? Rabbi Almosnino, perhaps? Juan did not know if they were capable, or if they would venture to take such a major and obviously dangerous risk under Father Ramon's watchful eye. They might urge them to travel elsewhere, possibly to Jerusalem, where the circumcision could be performed in a more tolerant and safe environment. But Juan wanted the procedure performed in Spain. It was there his heritage had been denied him and it was there he wished to complete his return to the faith, before journeying elsewhere. Juan was certain that the procedure would require medical attention and while Rabbi Isaac was a capable physician, the entire effort might prove more dangerous than the brothers were willing to undertake. But he would ask them and anticipate a favorable response. Juan reassured Diego that he would not neglect such an important and holy commandment and that he would ask Rabbi Isaac tomorrow. They continued to the house in silence.

The following night Rabbi Isaac missed the session. A medical emergency required his attention. Juan would have preferred discussing the matter with Rabbi Isaac but did not want to delay any further and approached Rabbi Abraham. He was embarrassed to admit he was still not circumcised but was more embarrassed to allow the problem to remain unresolved. Rabbi Abraham was occupied returning books to shelves at the back of the room. He saw Juan walking toward him.

"Hello, Juan, did you understand tonight's lecture? Do you have any questions about the commandment prohibiting wearing linen and wool in one garment? Do you wish to review it again?"

"No, Rabbi Abraham, thank you, I fully understood the lecture. Rabbi Isaac was quite correct, you are an interesting and engaging lecturer!"

"Thank you, Juan. Now tell me, is anything the matter?"

Juan grimaced and slowly responded. "Yes I do not know how to quite tell you this. Neither I nor my son are circumcised. Back in Plasencia there was no one who could...."

Rabbi Abraham had heard this many times over the past twenty years, stories about secret Jews who were still uncircumcised. Rabbi

Abraham could not fault them. The procedure was difficult to perform, requiring an exacting degree of training and expertise. He knew that the skill had been neglected and ultimately forgotten by the secret Jews. Rabbi Abraham had performed many circumcisions over the years and had initiated many secret Jews into the covenant of the Torah. He quickly wanted to reassure Juan not to feel ashamed or unduly guilty. "Please, Juan, there is no need to explain this shortcoming," interrupted Rabbi Abraham. "These are very difficult times and we cannot pass judgment. I am glad you have brought this to my attention. We must rectify it immediately!"

"But, Rabbi Abraham, who shall perform the ceremony for me and Diego?" cried Juan.

"Do not worry, Juan. I have performed many circumcisions in the past. I am skilled in this task and I shall perform the circumcision for both of you."

"What about Father Ramon? Surely if you are caught, we shall all be killed! Are you no longer afraid?"

Rabbi Abraham conceded that he was afraid; it was a natural reaction to all of Father Ramon's pressures. But Rabbi Abraham understood that his fears could no longer control his duty, his destiny. They could no longer suppress his responsibility to his people. He would perform the ceremony and suffer any of Father Ramon's consequences. If he were caught he would walk to the gallows with an inner contentment, a sense of allegiance to his faith and the Torah. He would not regret it.

"Yes, Juan, I am afraid. But some things are more important than fear."

Juan was a little surprised that Rabbi Abraham had demonstrated his appreciation of his plight and so quickly reversed his attitude. Juan knew the Torah he brought precipitated Rabbi Abraham's new sensitivity and understanding, and he wanted those sentiments to endure. "Rabbi Abraham, I have decided that the Torah should remain with you and Rabbi Isaac. Of course I now know that it is a cherished family treasure but after witnessing the impact it has had on you and your brother I know that this is where it belongs. The Torah will have a greater opportunity to influence needy souls if it remains in your possession. Diego and I have already been inspired by its beauty and essence and I long for other Jews to be similarly moved and touched by it. Your school is the only place where this scroll can continue to inspire others the way it has inspired us. I have explained my decision to Diego and he has readily agreed."

Rabbi Abraham stood in awe of the man who interrupted discussing his greatest challenge to bequeath his most cherished possession.

"I am honored by your decision, Juan, and I pledge to care for it and utilize it as you have suggested."

Juan was happy he had mentioned the Torah. It momentarily diverted his attention from the circumcision. Now he knew he would have to confront the last issue still troubling him, that one aspect that prevented so many other secret Jews from seeking circumcisions. It bothered Juan terribly and he could not undergo the procedure without first knowing the answer. "Will the pain be bearable?"

Rabbi Abraham placed his hand on Juan's shoulder. He did not want to frighten Juan but he would not lie to him. "Please understand, it can be a painful procedure, especially for an adult. But Rabbi Isaac is a fine doctor. He will oversee the procedure, insure that you are healthy and recover in due time. I do not anticipate any complications. Juan, do not concentrate on the pain. It shall pass, but the change you will undergo will endure forever. "

"Rabbi Abraham, I know."

"Very well. I think that Diego's circumcision should take place one week after yours. That should provide you with sufficient time to heal and be strong enough to provide inspiration and encouragement to your son. Is that satisfactory?"

"Yes, Rabbi Abraham, thank you."

Rabbi Abraham became solemn. He had almost forgotten the most important element of the entire procedure. "Before you go, Juan, there is something I want to share with you. The circumcision is more than a ceremony, a religious rite. It will signify your total and complete disavowal of the church and everything for which it stands. It will represent your unswerving commitment to a Jewish way of life. It will be your rebirth, your reawakening, your conversion. Do not be offended, Juan, I do not mean to imply that you are not Jewish and require an official conversion. I am fully aware of your geneology. Luisa informed me of your background. I speak to all secret Jews seeking a circumcision in the same manner. All the years you spent in the church, participating in their rituals and sacraments necessitates these rules. Your hair will be shaven, you will be given a Jewish name and you will immerse in the ritual bath. I will administer further instructions to you in the presence of a quorum of ten men, all in accordance with Jewish law. Then I shall perform the circumcision and you shall enter into the congregation of the Jewish people. Go home, Juan, and prepare yourself. The ceremony will take place the day after tomorrow!"

Juan nodded and quickly exited the room. Rabbi Abraham turned to the table and resumed returning books to the shelves.

Juan hurried to Luisa's home to relate the news to Diego.

24

Rabbi Isaac informed about thirty Jews that a circumcision would be taking place. He only notified those Jews he trusted, those who would never reveal he was engaging in heresy. All thirty Jews braved the dangers and made sure they were present to witness another Jew enter the covenant. All the town elders were there including Rabbi Almosnino, Rabbi Moses Arrondi, Rabbi Isaac and Rabbi Abraham. The ceremony was scheduled to take place in the classroom. It was decorated with streamers of ribbon of varied colors. In the front of the room stood two chairs next to a table on which was placed the ritual knife. One of the chairs was very ordinary, it was made of plain wood, without any carvings or engravings. The other one was beautifully ornamental: The edges were trimmed with gold and there were three Hebrew words of gold carved into the back of the chair. Although Juan could not read it, he correctly concluded it read "Chair of Elijah," the ancient prophet who according to legend is present at every Jewish circumcision. The women were directed to the kitchen until the completion of the ceremony.

Juan and Diego arrived shortly after dawn and they were escorted to the classroom. Juan insisted he was ready and he appeared calm and subdued. He had been anticipating this moment for twenty years and saw no reason to be nervous or afraid.

The moment Juan entered the classroom Rabbi Abraham stood up and welcomed him. Rabbi Abraham was dressed in white and looked very solemn and serene. He approached Juan and addressed him loudly enough for the whole room to hear, "Welcome, Juan de Ciudad. Do you wish to enter the covenant?"

Juan was a little embarrassed by Rabbi Abraham's welcome but he understood that it was necessary. "Yes, Rabbi Abraham," answered Juan excitedly, "I do wish to enter the covenant!"

Rabbi Abraham knew that Juan was sincere and was motivated by the noblest of intentions, yet he would adhere to tradition and ask Juan the same question that was asked of every convert, regardless of background. Rabbi Abraham also wished to remind everyone in the room, since they were abetting Juan's heresy, that their presence at this holy gathering was life threatening and they should take great care to conceal their knowledge of the circumcision.

Rabbi Abraham urged Juan to move to the front of the room and stand near the two chairs and Juan obliged immediately. Juan realized he now faced the entire room and he and Rabbi Abraham were alone near the front. Rabbi Abraham turned to Juan. "Sir, state your wishes now in the presence of these Jews, for, truth to tell, you are placing all of us and yourself in great jeopardy. Make certain that you are not impelled by excitement or by any motive other than reverence for the Law of Moses."

Juan stood poised and ready. He had been ready since he had discovered the significance of this rite over twenty years ago. He had survived the deaths of his dear friend, Diego; his mentor, Alfonso Cabrerro; and his beloved wife, Margarita. He dwelled in the magnificent pews of the great church of Plasencia and the dark and clandestine back rooms of secret Jews. He had braved so much, sacrificed so much, waited so long, all for this. For this one rite, the rite that would finally and irrevocably separate him from the Christian past from which he could not wait to escape. Juan turned to the room full of Jews.

"There is only one reason that I wish to be circumcised and that is to rekindle my heritage, return to my religion and my people. I wish to become a Jew! I wish to become a Jew!" Juan repeated the phrase several times and burst into tears. Rabbi Abraham quickly ran to him and realized that they were tears of joy. He was satisfied with Juan's response, but he could not proceed as yet. There were still a few more questions that needed to be asked.

Rabbi Abraham looked at Juan, "What reason have you for desiring to become a convert? Do you not know that Israel at the present time is persecuted and oppressed, despised, harassed and overcome by afflictions? Are you aware that the Jewish religion demands adherence to six hundred and thirteen commandments and thirteen principles of faith?"

Juan looked around the room and noticed everyone was waiting for him to respond. Of course it was true, being a Jew meant oppression, mistreatment, persecution, anguish and sorrow. It meant a perpetual longing for tranquility and peace that was denied them so often. And yet, Juan never thought of those distractions. He concentrated on the lofty ideals that Judaism epitomized. He knew the reasons to run to Father Ramon and embrace the church and all of its external superiority. But he was also aware of the reasons to stay, surrounded by the warmth and wisdom and perseverance of Rabbi Abraham and Rabbi Isaac and Maimonides and Rabbi Gavriel — the scribe who had penned that scroll — and Rashi, Rav Saadia Gaon, Abaye, Rava, Rabbi Akiva, Rabbi Yochanan Ben Zakkai, King David, Joshua and Moses. Juan understood that he was the next link, the perpetuation of a tradition that stretched so far back in time. He would fulfill his role with duty, honor and trust.

"I am aware, Rabbi Abraham, of the predicament of our People, but this is where I belong! I accept all the commandments, all the principles of faith, with promise and enthusiasm. I am not deterred by the volume of Law I must master, I am eager for my training to begin! Nor am I distracted by the sorry lot of our People. I am ready, Rabbi Abraham, I am ready!" Juan turned around and started walking to the plain chair. Rabbi Abraham saw Juan's sincerity and determination and knew the time had come.

Rabbi Abraham moved toward the table and reached for the knife. When he finished, Rabbi Abraham recited the blessings and Juan's new Hebrew name. He would be called Yaakov, after the Patriarch who taught all Jews how to cope with life in exile.

The circumcision went better than Juan expected. The pain lasted for less than two days. As soon as Juan was able to walk, his hair was shaved and he immersed in the ritual bath. Diego's circumcision took place the following week in a more subdued and quiet ceremony. Diego too received a new name. He would be known as Yehudah, the son of Yaakov.

Father Ramon heard that some religious rituals had taken place and he was so obsessed with finding out what they were, that he left the town alone while he plotted a course of action. That afforded everyone present at either ceremony with sufficient time to fabricate a story as to their whereabouts on those days and completely frustrate Father Ramon's plans.

Juan was content that he and Diego finally reached this important personal milestone, and Juan looked forward to fulfilling his pledge to learn the laws and customs of Judaism, but not in Huesca. Juan decidede to leave Huesca as soon as Diego married and was waiting to see if a match between Diego and Sarah was forthcoming.

One week after his circumcision, Diego was introduced to Sarah in the home of Rabbi Abraham Almosnino and a few weeks later a wedding date was set. While preparing for the wedding, Juan and Diego spent the next few months receiving intense instruction from Rabbi Isaac and Rabbi Abraham. They were not the only ones. Others heard that the Bibago brothers had once again renewed their efforts to teach secret Jews and many of them returned, yet the sessions were held in strict secrecy. Rabbi Abraham and Rabbi Isaac were pleased they could still provide instruction to so many needy souls but lamented the fact that their reach and influence had shrunk to this pitiful degree.

To Juan, the knowledge and understanding was everything he had hoped for. He was very quick and sharp and was able to grasp subtle nuances which the other students failed to comprehend. Juan quickly learned Hebrew and memorized sections of the Torah in a matter of weeks. Diego too, felt enriched and accomplished in ways he only used to dream about. Their studies continued unabated with the solemnity and dedication they knew it warranted.

The day of Diego and Sarah's wedding was rapidly approaching. One evening Juan escorted Diego to Rabbi Almosnino's home. Sarah was waiting for them outside and as Juan and Diego approached she joined them as they all continued down the street. Juan was proud that Sarah, a bright and caring girl, was to be his daughter-in-law. He was happy Diego had found such a worthy bride. They passed Rabbi Isaac's home and the three of them continued walking. It was too early in the evening to be seen there. A few blocks away Juan stopped and turned to the young couple. "I want to tell you that after the wedding I shall be leaving Huesca. I did not come here to continue the nocturnal meetings and the constant hiding and lurking. Yes, I have learned so much but I need more than knowledge — I need freedom, the unrestrained ability to worship as I please, without pressure and danger. I cannot stay here; it has become as dangerous as Plasencia. I have decided to leave Spain and go to that one place, that one land where we can truly feel at home. After your wedding I am going to Jerusalem. There I can worship freely and consider proper penance for my many years of Christian fealty." Juan stopped and tried to discern whether they seemed captivated by the idea. He was hoping they would join him.

Diego and Sarah glanced at each other with an understanding that needed no words. "Father, we had been considering your very proposal! We decided recently that we could not stay here for the same reasons you just mentioned and we hoped we could convince you to join us! How wonderful, Father. We shall start new lives together in Jerusalem!" beamed Diego.

Juan was pleased the couple would be joining him. It would help ease the transition to a new life and to a new country. But what about everyone else? What about all the Jews and secret Jews scattered throughout Spain who did not have the sense or the ability to leave?

What would become of them?

Diego and Sarah were married in a modest yet tasteful ceremony. The following week Juan told Luisa that they were leaving for Jerusalem. Luisa was not surprised; she had suspected Juan would not remain. She fully realized that almost overnight Huesca had turned into a violent and dangerous town. She had likewise considered leaving but she could not bring herself to abandon the life to which she was so accustomed and she hoped the situation in Huesca would improve. "I am happy for you, Juan. It has been good to see you again after so many years. I shall truly miss you." Luisa tried to hold back tears, but could not and began crying.

Juan tried to comfort her. He told her he would always remember her kindness and all the help that she had provided for him and his son. "Do not cry, Luisa, I never forgot all that you did for us twenty years ago and I will never forget what you have done for us these past few months. Today we have the luxury of wishing each other farewell without haste or the dread of imminent capture. Twenty years ago we were not so lucky. May our next meeting be even happier still!"

Juan expressed his sincerest gratitude for her warmth and caring. He bade her a final farewell.

Juan proceeded to Rabbi Isaac's home where Diego and Sarah were waiting for him. They had said their farewells to Luisa earlier and Sarah spent the rest of the day visiting her friends throughout the town. Diego and Sarah approached Rabbi Isaac and Rabbi Abraham, and Diego thanked them for all their training and teaching. "Remember, Diego," warned Rabbi Isaac, "you have not yet mastered all of Jewish learning. You must continue your studies in Jerusalem."

"Of course, Rabbi Isaac, I understand."

Diego and Sarah bade farewell to the two brothers and waited outside the house. Juan and Rabbi Abraham and Rabbi Isaac were alone.

"The warning I gave to Diego applies to you as well, Juan. Do not forsake the learning!"

"Yes, Rabbi Isaac, I will continue my studies when I reach Jerusalem."

Rabbi Isaac and Rabbi Abraham understood that Juan had revitalized their desire, their duty and their commitment to help the secret Jews. Without his persistence, his unwavering drive, they would have reduced themselves to insignificant town leaders. They owed him so much. "We must thank you, Juan de Ciudad. You helped us see so much light amidst all this darkness," beamed Rabbi Isaac.

"No, dear Rabbi Isaac, it is to you and Rabbi Abraham that I owe my life. Without the two of you I would still be groping in the dark, searching for meaning and purpose," retorted Juan.

"Then perhaps we shall always be indebted to each other, Juan!" teased Rabbi Isaac.

Rabbi Abraham and Rabbi Isaac wished him farewell and watched as he exited their home. He joined Diego and Sarah as they began the long trek toward Jerusalem.

But the Torah, Rabbi Gavriel's Torah, remained in Huesca.

Krasnystaw, Poland 1666

Yet, I persist in my opinion. I do not believe that the Messiah will come in this way. According to our tradition, this is not the way. I shall oppose them publicly, but the convictions in my heart have not changed.

– *Rabbi Chaim Abulafia of Hebron, 1665*

25

Velvel and Hershel woke at exactly the same moment. They had been rising early for about three weeks, ever since they had heard the news. They were very quiet about it, they did not want to wake anyone in the house, especially their father, Reb Zundel. Reb Zundel refused to believe the news and they were certain he would scold them harshly if he discovered what they were doing. It was unusually cold, surely the coldest night of the winter, yet the brothers quickly dressed in silence. There was about two hours left until sunrise, just enough time to make it to the clearing, meet with the others and return home. They insulated themselves with their coats and caps and left the house, thrilled that another pre-dawn escape had gone smoothly. They walked down the road toward the forest, and the clearing beyond it, as snow fell heavily, smothering the town with a new and bitter layer. They knew many townspeople were already there and many more would arrive after them, and they looked forward to sharing their experiences with others. The brothers trudged toward the forest, amidst the gusts of wind and torrents of snow.

The walk took nearly half an hour. Velvel recalled that when they were younger they could run to the clearing in fifteen minutes, but now he was seventeen and Hershel was fifteen, and they had outgrown that boundless spurt of energy they had possessed as children.

The brothers battled the huge mounds of existing snow and the on-going storm, which further slowed their pace. They continued in total darkness, guided only by the shadowy reflection of the moon and their boyhood memories of the place they would escape to with friends. But tonight there would be no games, no innocent fun with schoolmates. There was important and holy work to be done.

"Why do you think Father is opposed to the news?" asked Hershel, trying to break the monotony of the trek.

"Because he does not want to believe, he does not allow himself to believe. But do not worry, Hershel, he will change his mind soon, in a short while it will be impossible to deny! But until then we cannot di-vulge what we are doing, the preparations we are undergoing. It will greatly anger Father and we will suffer the blows of his wrath!"

"I am aware, Velvel, that he speaks so disparagingly of Reb Berish. I would never let Father know we meet with him every night," agreed Hershel.

"Good, Hershel. Let us hurry, at this pace we shall arrive there at noon!"

The brothers quickened their stride and soon reached the edge of the forest. They began the hike up a short hill, which led to a huge clearing beyond which lay the continuing forest. It was an ideal place for large crowds to gather. Halfway up the hill, Hershel started to feel the snowy winds pierce his three layers of clothing and found himself shivering uncontrollably. He could not go on, it was simply too cold. He knew what was expected of him once he reached the clearing and he was petrified he would freeze to death. He positioned his feet securely on the small slope a few hundred feet from the top and sat down.

"Get up, Hershel!!" yelled Velvel. "We are almost there!"

"I cannot make it, Velvel, it is too cold," shouted Hershel, trem-bling. He then continued, "And even if I reach the top, I feel I will not be able to withstand the afflictions tonight. You go ahead, Velvel, I will wait for you here."

Velvel, who was a few feet ahead of Hershel, turned around and started back toward him. Velvel was surprised that his younger brother had suddenly refused to endure the extreme sacrifices they experienced each evening. While a few people became ill from these nocturnal escapades – one elderly man even died as a result — Reb Berish repeatedly insisted that a pure heart and proper concentration would protect anyone from harm, and that whoever suffered illness from the cold did not truly believe in the cause and was being punished for his betrayal. Velvel knew that Hershel was still a dedicated and fervent follower of Reb Berish and their cause. He concluded Hershel was merely experiencing temporary feelings of indecision, no doubt brought on by the unusually cold weather. Hershel needed some reassurance, some motivation and encouragement to inspire him to continue on this bitter frosty night.

"Please, Hershel," pleaded Velvel, "do not give up now, we are almost there! I know it is very cold but we must remain dedicated, we must continue our penance. We cannot allow the weather or any other obstacle to frustrate our resolve. We are preparing for *his* arrival, which will bring peace and salvation to our People and ourselves, and we must overcome any hindrance, whether it is a blizzard, a raging river or even this steep hill, with courage and patience. Come, Hershel, I shall help you the rest of the way."

Velvel graciously held out his hand, which Hershel eagerly grabbed. Velvel jerked Hershel's hand forward and slowly pulled him into an upright position. Hershel knew that his brother was right. Although he was still shivering he would continue the journey, he could not let anything stand in his way. He would forge ahead.

Near the top, Hershel suddenly stopped. Velvel turned to him. "What is the matter now, Hershel? Are you still reluctant to proceed tonight?" Velvel was slightly annoyed that Hershel halted again.

"Nothing is the matter, Velvel, I just wanted to give you a fair chance," retorted Hershel.

"For what?"

"To see if you could reach the top before me!" Hershel immediately darted for the peak followed close behind by Velvel, hurrying to overtake his brother.

They raced to the top, momentarily reliving their youthful antics while the snow continued to fall.

Hershel reached the top moments before Velvel. "One day, Hershel, I will reach this summit before you!" The brothers turned around, looked out into the clearing and were startled by the number of people already there. Three weeks ago less than ten men had come, but more had joined them every night until now there were close to one hundred!

The brothers immediately searched for Reb Berish. He could never be found in one spot. He was always moving about, assisting those who needed his help. It was still dark and the brothers were unable to distinguish between one face and another. They walked aimlessly, circulating within the clearing until Hershel bumped into someone. Hershel looked up and at this close distance identified Reb Anshel, the cheesemaker. "Excuse me, Reb Anshel, have you seen Reb Berish?" inquired Hershel politely.

"Yes, Hershel, he is over by the large tree trying to light a fire that will be protected from the snow. But on a night like this I do not think he will have any luck!" Reb Anshel pointed toward the tree and displayed his hand, which the brothers noticed was bloodied and bruised. They thanked him and rushed to the tree.

In front of the tree stood Reb Berish, desperately trying to light a fire. The snow was falling too furiously for any spark to catch and Reb Berish looked exasperated. He had removed his coat to allow himself easier maneuverability to ignite a fire, and snow had settled under the folds of his shirtsleeves. Reb Berish was of average height, slightly overweight, with a short, trimmed, graying beard. He perspired profusely and always looked tired. He was the caretaker of the synagogue and was respected and liked by everyone. He was a very knowledgeable and learned man and assisted the rabbi with many of the lectures and study classes given to the townspeople. On the ground near Reb Berish lay several bundles of thorns neatly tied with thin strips of rope. "Ahh!" exclaimed Reb Berish, "I have finally done it!" The brothers observed a small spark burst into a strong flame and Reb Berish quickly shielded the fire with a makeshift overlay made of thick branches specifically designed to protect the flame from the continuosly falling blizzard. The brothers drew closer to warm themselves. Reb Berish turned to Velvel. "Welcome, Velvel, are you and Hershel ready?" Reb Berish now appeared excited and pleased. Velvel looked at Hershel who nodded quickly, signaling that he was no longer constrained by his earlier hesitancy. The brothers enthusiastically answered in unison, "Yes, Reb Berish."

"Good," beamed Reb Berish, "then grab a bundle of thorns and proceed to your usual spot at the rear of the clearing. You know what to do once you get there. I will follow you shortly."

Velvel and Hershel thanked Reb Berish and turned to leave the warmth and glow of the fire and engage in their practices at the edge of the clearing. Reb Berish continued to fuel the fire, making sure it remained lit. Suddenly Reb Anshel approached panting and out of breath, "Come quick, Reb Berish. Something terrible has happened to Betzalel, the orphan who works for Hindl the seamstress!"

Velvel and Hershel remained motionless as Reb Berish dropped the twigs he held and followed Reb Anshel toward the center of the clearing. On the ground lay Betzalel, a youth of fourteen, wrapped in blankets, surrounded by about two-dozen curious onlookers. "What is the matter with him?" asked Reb Berish. "Why is he lying on the ground?"

Reb Anshel bent down and removed some of the blankets, exposing the boy's left leg. Betzalel screamed in obvious pain, "Please, Reb Anshel!" Betzalel's arms were flailing as he desperately tried to cover his leg. Reb Anshel caught Betzalel's arms and held them firmly in place. Reb Berish observed the leg tangled in thorns, bleeding profusely. He lowered himself, reached for the stem and tried to remove them. He instantly cut his hand but would not let go: The boy would surely die if the thorns were not removed! Betzalel shrieked uncontrollably as the force of Reb Berish's pressure caused the thorns to sink deeper into his skin. Reb Berish realized he could never dislodge them this way and released them. He quickly stood up. "We need a knife, Reb Anshel, quickly, does anyone have a knife?!" Reb Anshel nodded and told Reb Berish he recalled seeing Wolf the tailor carrying his bag which no doubt contained a knife or scissors or some other utensil. Reb Anshel immediately left and returned a few moments later with a sturdy pair of scissors. Reb Berish grabbed them and cut the thorns loose. Reb Berish then wrapped the leg with the blankets and stopped the bleeding. "Are you all right, Betzalel? I always urge everyone to use extreme caution when using the thorns, they can cause much damage when handled improperly. What happened?"

"My hand slipped and I quickly became enmeshed in the thorns and could not break loose. I am feeling better now, thank you. I know that it was dangerous and I shall not attempt it again but my sacrifice did not go unnoticed!"

"Yes, Betzalel," said Reb Berish curtly. Reb Berish waited for several men to take Betzalel back to his home. As soon as Betzalel had been taken away Reb Berish walked toward Velvel and Hershel and many other men waiting for him.

Betzalel's mangled leg haunted him. Such maltreatment, such injury was destructive, it was unnatural. How could this activity be worthy of Heaven's approval and blessing? Reb Berish understood these acts were necessary. They facilitated repentance at this important juncture in history, but to this horrific extent? Could such damage be so productive? Reb Berish did not have time to sort out this dilemma. He reached the edge of the clearing and was immediately approached by Velvel. "Is Betzalel alright? We heard something happened to him," asked Velvel.

"He is better now, Velvel. He had a slight accident with his bundle of thorns and he cut his leg. He is being taken back to his home and I am sure he will recover. Please be extra careful tonight, one mishap is more than enough!"

Reb Berish escorted Velvel and Hershel to a quiet area at the far end of the clearing near the forest edge. The snow slowed to a soft flurry and the very first rays of sunlight could be seen filtering through the trees. "Hurry boys, it will be daylight soon!" shouted Reb Berish. The two brothers walked with Reb Berish and they passed many of the townspeople along the way. Everyone seemed excited and enthusiastic. Velvel stopped near the edge of the clearing, and stood within a few feet of the continuing forest, and proclaimed, "This is our usual spot."

"Are you ready, boys? Then hurry and return to me when you have finished, I wish to speak to you and everyone else before the night has ended!" Reb Berish left the brothers and turned to see if any one else needed his assistance or guidance.

Velvel and Hershel undressed and stood shivering in their long woolen underwear. Hershel looked down at the cold, fresh snow. He recalled his earlier hesitation and Velvel's encouraging words of support. He did not wish to delay any longer, permit his doubts to resurface and dull the importance of the moment. He knew he was about to engage in bizarre yet mystical and sublime rituals, actions that would help to hasten an already long delayed-promise. He was suddenly seized with a warm feeling of enthusiasm and zeal. He grabbed Velvel's hand and together the two of them plunged into the snow. They dropped to their knees then spread their bodies on the ground and proceeded to twist and turn in the snow. For Hershel it was always the same, the initial contact was exhilarating, almost refreshing. He did not sense the coldness of the snow immediately and could tolerate the first few moments. But then the icy touch of each flake seemed to gnaw at him and his body began to writhe from the extreme temperature. He could not stay in the snow for more that two or three minutes. Velvel, though, had conditioned himself to ignore the winds and the freezing ground and he could remain there for longer periods of time. On several nights, especially the warmer ones of the past few weeks, his mind was so preoccupied with sanctifying his soul by defying the limits of nature that he had remained on the ground for nearly half an hour.

After three minutes Hershel stood up and, while shivering, proceeded to the bundle of thorns, which he loosened. He placed it on the ground and waited for Velvel. When Velvel was ready the two brothers made use of the thorns, then raced to the fire to warm themselves.

Velvel joined Hershel fifteen minutes later with the bloodied bundle of thorns. He threw the bundle into the fire, whose blaze had increased as the snowfall calmed to a weak, almost pleasant flurry.

The fire made a distinct crackling noise as it scorched the thorns, which for Velvel signified the end of another momentous night. Velvel stared into the fire and appeared ecstatic, almost in rapture. He was certain the acts he endured burned his sins as thoroughly as the fire consumed those thorns. Others who had engaged in the same rites joined the brothers.

The sun's rays began to filter through the forest, casting an eerie glow on the sacred, secure and dark clearing, which they had sanctified during the night. Soon it would be morning and many of the townspeople started back to their homes. Reb Berish called everyone to remain still for a moment, there was something he wished to say before they returned to town.

"We have all participated in wondrous and holy work tonight," exclaimed Reb Berish. "We have all participated in unique acts, intended to repent for the evils we have committed. Now is the time for atonement, remorse and repentance. We must continue to undergo these severe rites and to increase our observance of the Torah; to enhance our concentration during prayer and while we recite the Psalms; to purge the evil from our hearts and minds; to insure that we are found worthy; to secure our place in the new kingdom. We do not wish to be left behind, to languish in exile and oblivion. We wish to be uplifted on the wings of eagles and taken to tranquility and everlasting peace! Remember, we must prepare ourselves, ready ourselves for the arrival of our great and holy leader, the scion of David, our king and messiah, Shabbetai Zevi!"

26

Rabbi Yaakov tore himself away from his studies and moved to the window as he watched Velvel, Hershel and many other townspeople hastily return to their homes. Rabbi Yaakov did not like interrupting his studies, especially his early morning session, which was the most satisfying and contemplative of all his daily learning. But ever since his townspeople began their nightly excursions into the forest he could not concentrate. He tried to ignore their stirring, their quiet bustling, but every time he returned to those holy books he found himself gazing blankly into the texts, his mind clearly elsewhere. He could think of nothing but his congregants, and of his desire to participate with them in the secret rituals about which he had heard so much. He wanted to experience that unbounded energy, that euphoria that he observed on the faces of those returning each morning. But Rabbi Yaakov was still not convinced their cause was authentic. He even wondered how almost everyone in the town so readily accepted the news, and he could not yet bring himself to accompany them. He was searching for a sign, some indication, a passage from one of his texts perhaps, that would persuade him to join the townspeople. He knew he did not have much time to remain ambivalent. Soon the town would demand that he publicly proclaim his position and Rabbi Yaakov was hoping to have an answer for them.

Rabbi Yaakov waited for everyone to return to their homes. The streets were empty again and Rabbi Yaakov turned to resume his studies. Soon the synagogue would fill for the morning prayers and Rabbi Yaakov wanted a few minutes of quiet review before everyone arrived. He walked across the study and took his seat at the desk. The study, which was originally built as the town synagogue, was a very large room with beautiful woodcarvings along the walls. The room also contained many of the remnants of the old synagogue. There were stacks of worn-out prayer books neatly piled on shelves which lined both sides of the room, and old, frayed prayer shawls which were carefully folded and stored in the far corners. The original ark, which was only big enough to house two Torah scrolls, still stood in the same spot at the front of the room. The ornaments which had adorned the ark were long gone and it was covered with a large burlap cloth and had not been opened in years. A new, larger, more imposing synagogue had been built immediately adjacent to the old one soon after it became too small to accommodate the many Jews who had moved to Krasnystaw. The old synagogue had been converted into the Rabbi's study. A doorway had been carved out of the north side of the study, which opened to the central hallway of the new synagogue. The new synagogue was a grand building featuring some of the finest design and detail in all of Poland. It had two large arched central doors with wood engravings of two lions. Inside stood a large, beautiful, wooden ark. It was positioned at the front of the synagogue and it was covered with a striking deep blue ornamental curtain. The center of the curtain contained a richly decorated crown with colored stones sewn into the crest. On the bottom of the curtain were embroidered the names of several of the children killed during the 1648 massacres.

Rabbi Yaakov conceded he could not concentrate. He closed his books, left the study, walked to the synagogue through the adjoining door and entered in the rear. Morning services were not scheduled to begin for another half hour but Rabbi Yaakov decided he would spend the remaining time reading Psalms and readying himself for prayer. The synagogue was dark, Reb Berish had not yet arrived to light the candles. Rabbi Yaakov turned toward a shelf which hung on the back wall, reached for a book of Psalms and heard a man crying in front of the ark. He quietly approached and as he drew closer, recognized Reb Fishel the shoemaker. Reb Fishel continued sobbing unaware of Rabbi Yaakov's presence. Rabbi Yaakov assumed that Reb Fishel was another of Reb Berish's proteges performing a different method of contrition and prayer. Rabbi Yaakov continued to watch. He had never seen these fascinating rituals firsthand and was overcome with curiosity. A few moments later, Reb Fishel, still crying, took hold of the curtain and whispered, "I still remember my son, I have not forgotten!" He then released the curtain, sat down in front of the ark and closed his eyes. He continued to weep at the foot of the ark. Rabbi Yaakov was puzzled by Reb Fishel's strange remark and concluded that Reb Fishel's heartfelt display was not a ritual instituted by Reb Berish. Why then was Reb Fishel acting this way? Rabbi Yaakov believed Reb Fishel would prefer to remain alone but Rabbi Yaakov could not stand idly by while one of his congregants appeared so troubled, so despondent.

Rabbi Yaakov cautiously approached him. "Is something the matter, Reb Fishel?" asked Rabbi Yaakov softly.

Reb Fishel heard Rabbi Yaakov's voice and instantly ceased crying, opened his eyes and turned around.

"Rabbi Yaakov?"

"Yes, Reb Fishel, I arrived here a little early this morning to recite Psalms before prayer and could not help hearing you. Is everything all right? Can I help you in some way?"

Reb Fishel was surprised by Rabbi Yaakov's presence this early in the morning. He wished Rabbi Yaakov had not seen him, but he would confide in him. He greatly respected Rabbi Yaakov. He sensed he was genuinely concerned and would keep no secret from him.

"I must apologize, Rabbi Yaakov, for acting inappropriately in the synagogue but I know of no other place I can properly express myself," declared Reb Fishel. "I have been doing this for many years yet this is the first time I have been detected. I always come very early in the morning, before anyone is awake. But with the recent news sweeping through the town there is no time of day or night when someone is not stirring about! I will explain my actions to you, Rabbi Yaakov, and I trust they will forever remain between us."

"You have my word, Reb Fishel, that I shall never reveal what you tell me," answered Rabbi Yaakov earnestly. He moved closer to Reb Fishel.

"Do you see this curtain, Rabbi Yaakov?" Reb Fishel pointed to the curtain draping the ark. "Do you see the name there on the curtain, Yehudah the son of Ephraim Fishel? That is my son, my little Yeedle, and on this date eighteen years ago he was savagely murdered. I cannot visit his grave because he has none. No tomb, no everlasting resting place, no eternal peace. This curtain is the only place his name remains, the only memorial that exists. This is where his soul returns to comfort the living and it is here that I come every year on this date to remember him and mourn my loss. Rabbi Yaakov, he was such a wonderful boy, so happy and carefree, only ten years old, full of so much promise, so much life." Reb Fishel tried in vain to hold back his tears but could not and resumed crying.

Rabbi Yaakov sensed that Reb Fishel needed privacy and turned to leave. Reb Fishel quickly grabbed Rabbi Yaakov's arm and urged him to remain. "I have never told anyone what happened that day. Maybe talking with you will help alleviate the ever-present pain and heartache. Heaven knows I have tried everything else. Please don't leave, Rabbi Yaakov. I need you to stay."

Rabbi Yaakov was curious and despite Reb Fishel's plea, was not certain what to do. Reb Fishel was indeed frustrated and disheartened. But he feared Reb Fishel would later resent having confided in him out of so much desperation and despair.

"I am here, Reb Fishel, but I do not want you to feel pressured or forced to reveal anything to me while you are in this state. Perhaps we should talk tomorrow or later in the week when the memories of your tragedy are not as timely and poignant?"

"Rabbi Yaakov, I am fine," insisted Reb Fishel, wiping away the tears.

Reb Fishel looked up at the curtain. He began speaking but his eyes remained fixed on the name of his son. "It was on this day in 1648, a cold, miserable snowy day. Shortly before noon about a hundred of them entered the town. Someone started screaming 'Cossacks! Cossacks! Run! Hide!' I was at work at the time. Back then my shop was located in the town square. I heard the commotion and ran outside. I saw three Cossacks riding on horses, each one dragging a Jewish girl through the streets. The girls were screaming but the Cossacks continued riding in circles laughing and exchanging jokes. I couldn't recognize the faces of the girls they were covered with mud and snow. I knew that if I tried to help those girls I would be tortured and killed. I raced home, avoiding Cossacks at every turn. When I reached my street I heard wild commotion coming from my home. I saw six horses in front of the house and prayed that my wife, Pesha, had managed to escape somewhere with Yeedle and the Cossacks were merely there looking for food or gold. I did not have much of either and I hoped they would leave shortly. Then I heard a shriek, a shrill scream, a sound that has haunted me ever since. It was the voice of my son and I knew he was in pain. I instinctively rushed to my home and as I entered, I saw him tied up, sitting on a pile of religious books and three men with drawn swords were facing him. I lunged toward him, to tend to him, to help him, but was instantly grabbed and tied up as well. They proceeded to kill my son in front of my eyes. Do you hear what I am saying, Rabbi Yaakov? I was forced to witness the murder of my own son! Yeedle and I cried together, we recited the *Shema*, the exquisite prayer of faith and trust in G-d and His goodness, and then I watched him die. Pesha was visiting a neighbor and was spared the entire ordeal. She has never forgiven herself for leaving our son and has never been the same since. After Yeedle died, I pleaded with them to release his body. I offered them whatever money I had hidden but they refused and knocked me unconscious. I awoke two days later and spent the next week searching the forest, the rivers and the nearby towns for any sign of my son, but I never found him."

Rabbi Yaakov was speechless. He did not know how to comfort Reb Fishel and sought to embrace him, to let Reb Fishel know he could always turn to him for solace and reassurance. Rabbi Yaakov drew closer to Reb Fishel but Reb Fishel gently rebuffed him.

"It is all right, Rabbi Yaakov," said Reb Fishel gently. "I know you are sympathetic and can find no words to express your disbelief. I am aware you feel it necessary to exhibit some sort of gesture of understanding, of friendship, and I appreciate that. Oh, how I wish I could be comforted. How I yearn to be consoled for my loss! I thought missing Yeedle would grow easier with time. That I would learn to adapt to a life that did not include his smile, his kindness and his willingness to make me happy. Instead the reverse has happened. I find myself longing for him now more than ever! He would have married by now and with G-d's blessing would have had children of his own. I cannot accept his death and lately I am plagued with gnawing thoughts of doubt and anger. Why did those atrocities take place? What purpose did they serve? When will my suffering be avenged? When will that Day of Justice finally arrive?"

Reb Fishel walked toward the ark, kissed his son's name on the curtain, wiped away his tears and turned to leave the room.

Rabbi Yaakov stood motionless, gazing at Reb Fishel as he departed, a sad and broken man. He looked at the curtain and he too shed a tear. Reb Fishel had confided to Rabbi Yaakov that his tears were unrelated to Reb Berish and those rituals. They were the ongoing legacy of the massacres of 1648. Rabbi Yaakov did not suffer during the massacres. At the time he had lived in Italy with his family. But Rabbi Yaakov, along with Jews in Yemen, Turkey, the Land of Israel and the rest of the world, were very disturbed by the destruction wrought on their Polish brethren. They did whatever they could to revitalize and rebuild what had been lost. Rabbi Yaakov arrived in Krasnystaw three years later at the age of forty, when he accepted a position as the rabbi. He quickly learned that almost every person in the town had suffered a loss and that some families were entirely wiped out. Most of the townspeople refused to speak about what had taken place, it was simply too painful. Special prayers were inserted into the liturgy for the ninth day of Av, the day of national mourning for the destruction of the First and Second Temples in Jerusalem. Personal remembrances were observed throughout the town, but public discourse about the massacres was rare indeed. In fact, since Rabbi Yaakov had come to the town he had never before

before heard an individual account of what had happened during the massacres. Rabbi Yaakov could not understand the pain of his congregation because he could not appreciate what they had undergone. He tirelessly tried to rebuild the town. He helped countless families cope with their suffering and provided comfort and inspiration to hundreds of townspeople. But the true character of his congregants, their endless longing, their perpetual yearning for alleviation of the pain they carried within themselves, eluded Rabbi Yaakov.

Until now.

Watching Reb Fishel cry so expressively over events that were so distant, yet so real and enduring and listening to Reb Fishel's story of unmistakable anguish, afforded Rabbi Yaakov the opportunity to connect with Reb Fishel, for a moment to become Fishel. In that brief heartfelt period of absolute soul baring, Rabbi Yaakov was able to perceive, for the first time, the suffering, the long terrible agonizing suffering of his townspeople. At last he had come to comprehend that the sorrow, the wounds, the torment ran so deep, and were still consuming them after so many years. He could finally understand them and their needs. He could now bridge the gulf that always separated them. He could share in their collective grief, participate in their personal memorials and wait with them for that day when their hearts could once again sing with gladness and joy.

When would that day come?

How much longer would they have to wait?

The synagogue suddenly grew bright and Rabbi Yaakov turned to the cantor's podium and watched Reb Berish carefully light the large candelabra atop the platform in preparation for the morning prayers. Rabbi Yaakov nodded to Reb Berish who smiled and nodded in turn.

Rabbi Yaakov watched as he lit additional lamps throughout the synagogue, making the dim room even brighter.

Rabbi Yaakov looked beyond the present actions of Reb Berish and saw him not just brightening the room but brightening the world. Reb Fishel's world, Krasnystaw's world, illuminating, enlightening and finding meaning in the horrific events of the past twenty years. Reb

Berish afforded everyone a reason to expect that the darkness, which engulfed them for so long, would soon come to an end. He provided for them a genuine source of tranquility and triumph. Rabbi Yaakov now understood the town's fascination with Reb Berish's rituals and their underlying significance. He had been envious of their dedication and was intrigued by the mysterious nature of their observances, but he now saw that it was much more profound than he had realized. He recognized that a belief in Reb Berish's cause was the one thing, the only thing that could assuage so many years of oppression and loss and defeat and sorrow. It was the only way to vindicate the patient acceptance, the silent acknowledgment of the recent persecutions. Rabbi Yaakov was fully aware there were other tragedies in the past, the blood libels of Blois and elsewhere, the Inquisition, the Crusades and the pogroms, each unspeakable acts of cruelty. Yet the devastation which the Cossacks, in particular their vicious leader, Bogdan Chmielnicki, had unleashed, seemed to Rabbi Yaakov so complete, so utterly thorough and exhaustive that he wondered if the townspeople would ever recover. Reb Fishel and virtually everyone else in Krasnystaw were stuck in the past, mired in the inability to forget, to overcome the feelings of neglect, abandonment and confusion. For the first time in history, Rabbi Yaakov feared the ingrained traits — the distinct qualities of boldness and willingness that exist in each Jew, forged over centuries of persecution and debasement, ready to accept and abide by the decrees of Heaven with zeal and enthusiasm — had finally run their course. Rabbi Yaakov sensed that Reb Fishel's feelings of doubt and despair were surely not isolated and were likely shared by thousands of Jews throughout Poland who had also suffered during the massacres.

Perhaps the ordinary Jew of Poland was incapable of embracing hardship, of rising above the lonely valleys of mourning and death, of safeguarding and perpetuating the heritage as selflessly as Isaac and the martyrs of Blois and the secret Jews of Spain?

Or perhaps the tortures, the shocking displays of cruelty, the beastly and wanton carnage of the Cossacks was so depraved, so inhuman, so utterly unfathomable that to accept them without complaint was simply beyond all human expectation? Rabbi Yaakov feared that everyone had lost so much hope and trust in the future that the future itself became jeopardized. He suspected that without help and intervention, without some miraculous defender, someone who could infuse the people with the will and faith to continue, then dire results would follow. Rabbi Yaakov, like his townspeople, now believed the answer could only come from that old pledge, the ancient promise, the guarantee of everlasting peace and contentment. It had to! From where else would it come? Rabbi Yaakov took one last look at Reb Berish and knew the time had finally arrived.

He ran to Reb Berish and embraced him.

He had become a believer.

Reb Berish was elated with Rabbi Yaakov's transformation, welcomed him enthusiastically and urged him to join the townspeople on their nightly excursions into the forest. Rabbi Yaakov assured Reb Berish that he would accompany them. Reb Berish turned away and continued the preparations necessary for the morning prayers.

Rabbi Yaakov was relieved that his answer had come so quickly and with such stark clarity. He greatly anticipated undertaking the acts of repentance that were necessary to insure he would not be left behind along with the unworthy. He was convinced that his meeting with Reb Fishel was not coincidental.

It was the sign he had been seeking.

27

Reb Zundel awoke to the soft quiet movements of his children and he remained in bed, paralyzed with disappointment. For the past few weeks he had repeatedly warned them not to associate with Reb Berish, or anyone else who participated in those barbaric and blasphemous rituals in the forest, and he was horrified that they continued to disobey him. But Reb Zundel was afraid of seriously punishing or scolding them or forbidding them to go there entirely. He did not want to further distance himself from them. He had heard that Yehoshua Leib's two sons recently ran away from Krasnystaw when they were prohibited from going to the forest and Reb Zundel swore he would not act that harshly. He did not wish to lose his sons, he did not want to become like Yehoshua Leib. Reb Zundel conceded that he and his sons were drifting further and further apart and he would do nothing to widen that rift. Reb Zundel recalled with great displeasure that his relationship with them was steadily deteriorating. They no longer confided in him, rarely spoke to him at all and had stopped accompanying him to the synagogue for evening prayer and late night study. They seemed to always be there already, reciting Psalms or praying. Reb Zundel knew they harbored no ill will toward him, they were merely preoccupied with their cause. He was aware that they slept at odd times so they could rise well before dawn to venture into the forest. Reb Zundel was disheartened by their attitude but would not impose any sort of demands on them or forbid them in any way to continue their visits to the forest. He simply reiterated his displeasure to them numerous times each day, hoping they would ultimately obey him. He was aware his threats were largely ignored but he was afraid to take stronger action, more authoritative control, and he remained in bed knowing this could not continue.

Reb Zundel was particularly distraught by the total dedication his children displayed, their obsession with Reb Berish's instruction and the strange rituals they practiced. What else would Reb Berish demand of his children? What further acts of self-denial and pain could his children inflict on themselves? Could he tear his children away from this madness, from these extreme forms of devotion, and return them to a moderate and balanced life? Could he break the mesmerizing influence Reb Berish had on them, the damaging control he exerted over their souls?

Could he ever succeed in redeeming his children or would they continue to be misled down a path of error, of misguided principles and mistaken rituals?

Reb Zundel fully understood the allure of believing in the messiah's impending arrival. Like Rabbi Yaakov, he knew it would mean so much to those who had suffered for so long. Reb Zundel had himself lost his parents to those loathsome Cossacks and he admitted that when he had first heard the news he was as excited and curious as were his sons. But when additional information about the new messiah was forthcoming, Reb Zundel quickly grew disillusioned. Reb Zundel was not a very learned man. Many years of Torah study had been lost while he had raised his three younger sisters. However, he had heard so many accounts of the messiah's bizarre behavior, some of which clearly violated the Torah itself, that he could not accept him as the savior and righteous son of David. Reb Zundel was certain the rest of the town would eventually come to the same realization. But after waiting almost a month for this to happen, the town's enthusiasm only seemed to grow stronger each day! Reb Zundel knew there had to be others who agreed with him, others who ignored the longings of their own tortured lives and examined the reports about the messiah carefully, objectively. He knew he was not the only man in Krasnystaw who believed the messiah was a fraud. He could not explain why no one sought to publicly discredit him and thought that perhaps they were waiting for Rabbi Yaakov to be the first to claim that honor.

Reb Zundel could not predict how this ordeal would end. He continued to consider the changes that recently affected Hershel and Velvel and did not wish to just sit by and wait to find out.

The sun's rays began to filter into the room and Reb Zundel realized it was soon time to pray. He quickly rose from his bed. He walked toward Velvel and Hershel's room, and saw that they had not gone to sleep after they had returned from the forest. He reminded them they would be leaving for morning prayers in about fifteen minutes.

The furious blizzard had all but ceased. The snow on the ground was quite deep, yet the three of them reached the synagogue quickly. They approached the central doors and were met by Wolf the tailor who arrived at the same moment.

"Good morning, Reb Zundel, good morning, boys," said Reb Wolf cheerily, nodding as he reached for the door.

"How are you, Wolf?" responded Reb Zundel.

"I am well, thank you," answered Reb Wolf. Wolf then turned to Velvel and Hershel. "I visited Betzalel on my way here and he is recovering nicely. I am sure he would greatly appreciate a visit from both of you."

"Yes," answered Velvel, trying to end the discussion without arousing his father's suspicion. "We shall visit him later."

Wolf smiled and entered the synagogue.

Velvel tried to follow Wolf but was detained by Reb Zundel, "What happened to Betzalel? Is he ill?" asked Reb Zundel, pryingly.

The boys sensed their father suspected they were at the forest last night and was not merely curious about Betzalel's illness. Hershel and

Velvel looked at each other and they both froze in silence. They would not lie to him but would not divulge that they had disobeyed him unless directly confronted. Velvel thought of a response and quickly snapped, "He injured himself collecting twigs near the clearing." Velvel grabbed Hershel's hand and turned to rush inside. Reb Zundel nodded and accepted his son's suspicious and curt reply.

"Then you will visit him later, and be sure to mention that I too wish him a speedy recovery," intoned Reb Zundel. The boys quickly agreed and raced inside. Reb Zundel knew there was some truth to Velvel's story, he would not blatantly lie to him. He also knew Betzalel's injury was somehow caused while engaging in one of those strange practices. He shook his head, rolled his eyes and followed Wolf and his children into the synagogue.

The services concluded about forty-five minutes later and as the room began to empty Reb Zundel turned around and called to his son-in-law, Zalman. Zalman sat only three rows behind Reb Zundel, yet Reb Zundel always waited until services finished before conversing with him.

"Good morning, Zalman!" announced Reb Zundel.

"Good morning, Father," answered Zalman, walking toward Reb Zundel.

Zalman was twenty-five and had been orphaned for nearly eighteen years, since three Cossacks brutally murdered his parents. He had been married to Reb Zundel's daughter, Gittel, for almost two years and in another month would be completing his first year as an apprentice to Mordche the blacksmith. Reb Zundel was very fond of Zalman and treated him like one of his sons. Zalman was always welcome at Reb Zundel's home and ever since he was first introduced to Gittel, he had called him "Father."

"Any news, Zalman?" asked Reb Zundel impatiently.

"No, Father, she is the same," answered Zalman.

Gittel was due to have her first child. For the past two weeks Reb Zundel had asked the same question and Zalman had offered the same reply.

"Zalman, the other day Gittel asked me to bring her some apples from the market. I did not see any of good quality until yesterday and I purchased some then. I left the bag in the front of the synagogue. Please don't forget to bring them home. They are quite tasty, I ate some myself!" boasted Reb Zundel.

"I think you should deliver them yourself, Father, that would especially brighten Gittel's day! She is very impatient, she feels the time is very near indeed!"

Velvel and Hershel informed their father they would be going to Betzalel and they promised they too would visit their sister later in the day. Reb Zundel acquiesced and walked home with Zalman.

The walk did not take very long. No house in Krasnystaw was far from any other, and they arrived a few moments later. Zalman entered first and informed Gittel that her father was waiting to see her. Gittel motioned to Zalman, who quickly welcomed Reb Zundel inside. The home was quite small but adequate for a young married couple. It was modestly decorated with some silk curtains, which Zalman bought with the extra money he had earned from some of Mordche's more generous customers. The sitting room was furnished with a table and a few chairs and a shelf near the ceiling, which held several pottery pieces and a few books of the Talmud that Zalman used in his spare time. Gittel was sitting on a chair and was resting her feet on several folded feather quilts, which were on the floor. She saw her father and tried to stand.

"Please, Gittel, do not get up, stay where you are and rest! How are you feeling?"

"I am tired, Father, but I feel all right. Did you bring me some apples?" asked Gittel, hungrily.

"Yes, Gittel!" exclaimed Reb Zundel. "I waited all week for the best tasting ones in the market and I brought you a bagful. Enjoy!"

Reb Zundel suddenly turned solemn and addressed the couple, "I do not wish to detract from the happiness that will soon fill our lives, but I have recently decided something quite important which I must discuss with both of you. It is quite distressing and I will not mention it until after the baby is born and Gittel has sufficiently recovered, but some very significant changes will be taking place in our lives."

Gittel and Zalman heard the solemnity of Reb Zundel's pronouncement and were momentarily concerned and frightened by it, but they were too excited with their own impending news to give it more than a fleeting moment's thought.

"Oh, Father!" cried Gittel, dismissing Reb Zundel's warning. "You always sound so somber, I only wish to hear happy and pleasant thoughts as I rest and anticipate the wonderful new life that G-d will provide for us soon."

"All right, Gittel, we shall talk later. Feel well and call on me if you need me. Goodbye, Zalman."

Reb Zundel departed and began walking home. Zalman and Gittel were alone and Gittel turned to her husband.

"Do you think my father's mysterious decision is connected in any way to the messiah's imminent arrival?" inquired Gittel.

"I am not certain, Gittel, but I hope he does not engage in rash or impetuous behavior. I do not want him to forfeit his chance to accompany us as we enter Jerusalem under the messiah's banner of victory and triumph!"

Gittel stood up and together they quietly prayed for the well being of the recently crowned messiah.

Reb Zundel reached home and was warmed to see his wife, Chana, eagerly awaiting his return. She escorted him to the table where a modest meal awaited him. Seven chairs surrounded the table, which stood in the main sitting room. The room was sparsely yet tastefully decorated. Reb Zundel sold fabrics and usually did not deliver his wares until noon. He spent the mornings either at home or at the synagogue. Chana observed Reb Zundel's quiet demeanor and instantly knew that her sons had defied him yet again.

"Did Velvel and Hershel venture to the forest again last night?" asked Chana sorrowfully.

"Yes, they continue to disobey me and I do not know what can be done about it!" lamented Reb Zundel.

"Do you want me to talk to them?" pleaded Chana. "Perhaps my soft-spoken manner can influence them in some way, convey to them the damage they are causing?"

"I do not think any discussion will be productive, that time has long passed," responded Reb Zundel, abruptly. "Are you aware, Chana, that the problem is far greater than any disobedience they exhibit toward me? I cannot object to their increased Torah study and their fervent and heartfelt prayer, but some of their other penances can cause injury. I fear their very lives may be in danger! Last night a friend of theirs, Betzalel, was hurt and could not attend services this morning. Chana, how long can this continue?" Reb Zundel lowered his head.

Chana was not aware of the gravity of her children's conduct. She had been inclined to excuse Hershel and Yaakov's recent behavior as the curious explorations of teenage boys. She now understood that the situation had far deeper consequence.

"What do you suggest, Reb Zundel? What do you propose to do?"

Reb Zundel stood up and started pacing, "I believe that we should leave Krasnystaw! Pack our belongings and move somewhere else, Vilna or Cracow perhaps, away from Reb Berish and these horrifying rituals. They are ruining this family and they are ruining this town!"

Chana had anticipated that Reb Zundel would respond in this manner. She agreed that it was the only way to break the grip that Reb Berish exerted on their children but she wondered whether it would significantly solve the problem.

"Reb Zundel, I was initially unaware of the severity of the problem and I now wholeheartedly agree that Reb Berish is inflicting great harm on our sons, and we should leave here as soon as possible. But do you think it will be different anywhere else? Do you think this hysteria exists only here in Krasnystaw? Wherever we travel, our sons will manage to align themselves with those town leaders who follow the messiah and they will undoubtedly continue the same observances there. Our sons are clever and resourceful and will surely find new leaders to guide and instruct them. Running away cannot solve this; there is nowhere we can run! Perhaps we should remain here and try to expose Reb Berish and his madness and folly, educate our sons and the rest of the town, teach them that their way is not the way to salvation. We could recruit Rabbi Yaakov to help us."

Reb Zundel acknowledged that Chana's suggestion offered an alternative that was intriguing and could eventually prove successful. Even more importantly, he knew she did not wish to leave. Chana was born and raised in Krasnystaw and both her parents were buried in the town cemetery. She maintained a deep connection to Krasnystaw that she did not want severed. Reb Zundel, too, was born and raised in Krasnystaw and could trace his family's presence there for at least four generations. Yet, he would abandon all that, relinquish his attachment to this small Polish town, to ensure the future of his family. He was convinced that Chana would act with similar readiness but that she truly preferred to remain.

He considered her proposal for the remainder of the day, carefully weighing every one of Chana's words and suggestions, trying to judge whether they could solve the most pressing concerns affecting their children. After many hours he concluded that Chana's suggestion was too risky and although leaving the town afforded no guarantees of success, it did insure that Velvel and Hershel's access to leaders of this bizarre movement would be significantly curtailed. He could not anticipate similar assurances if they stayed in Krasnystaw. In fact, Reb Zundel feared that if they remained, eventually the family would be torn apart.

He returned to Chana shortly before sundown. "I have considered your suggestion, Chana, and I am quite aware of your desire to remain here. I agree that followers of this messiah surely exist in every city and we cannot escape them. However, we must do everything we can to break the grip that has taken hold of Velvel and Hershel and to minimize their familiarity with these leaders. If we move to a large, strange, unfamiliar city, then it will be difficult for them to adapt to their new surroundings. They might find it uncomfortable to continue their observances without the familiar support of Reb Berish and their friends. Perhaps they will lose interest and abandon the enterprise altogether and come to appreciate their mistake." Reb Zundel approached his wife.

"Chana, I am aware you do not want to leave, and I share those sentiments deeply. I too have never lived in any other town and I am likewise intimidated by the immense challenges we will face away from Krasnystaw. Yet I cannot remain here while division and strife destroy this family, as father turns against son, son against mother. I cannot bear to lose our sons the way Yehoshua Leib did. If we continue on our present course of action or escalate the tension and disagreement as you suggest, then I fear they may simply run away! Chana, have you ever wondered why of the many people who perished during the massacres, including our parents, you and I survived? I have always been haunted by that, burdened by the knowledge that we were given a chance to prosper when so many of our friends and relatives were not. I have always believed that there was some deeper purpose, some larger meaning to our survival. I do not yet know that purpose and perhaps I never will but I cannot risk losing the immense gift that has been bestowed to us because of our own insecurities about leaving town. We must rise above the challenges we now face, meet our inadequacies and overcome them. We have raised three children; one of them is on the verge of having one of her own. We cannot jeopardize all that, compromise our future and the legacy we have been entrusted to perpetuate, merely to spare ourselves the personal hardships of leaving our hometown. And Chana, I believe we will only be gone a short while. It shall not be too much longer before this whole ordeal is exposed as one huge fiasco and we can return here! But this must be done."

Chana stood up and drew near to her husband. She knew he was right. She smiled and whispered to him, "We shall leave as soon as Gittel recovers."

About an hour after sundown, Zalman sped to Reb Zundel's home and announced that Gittel had just given birth to a boy. Reb Zundel and Chana could hardly contain their excitement. Zalman informed them the delivery had been smooth and quick and that Gittel and the baby were recovering at home. Reb Zundel, Chana and Zalman hurried to Zalman's house where the widowed midwife, Golda, was tending to the infant while Gittel rested in a bedroom just off the sitting room. Golda assured everyone that the baby was of average height and weight and that he appeared healthy. The midwife pointed out his large wide eyes, which opened every few moments to absorb his new world. Reb Zundel believed the boy would surely grow up to become a wise and learned Torah scholar.

Chana approached Gittel, who was soundly sleeping in her bed. She stirred as she sensed her mother walk into the room. She awoke for a moment, told her mother she was overcome with happiness and resumed her rest. Chana smiled and left the room.

Reb Zundel informed Zalman that he would make the arrangements for the circumcision, which would take place on the eighth day. Reb Zundel suggested that Rabbi Yaakov serve as the *mohel* to perform this delicate procedure. He was quite skilled and gifted and was renowned as an expert *mohel* throughout Poland. Zalman immediately consented and Reb Zundel kissed the new baby and ran to Rabbi Yaakov. Chana lingered a short while longer and caressed the infant while Golda prepared cloths to swaddle the baby and then prepared dinner for Gittel. After dinner, Chana returned home.

"Did you tell them?" called Gittel, half asleep.

"No," answered Zalman, "I could not do it, and anyway, they will know soon enough."

"My father will be quite angry," replied Gittel.

"I am sorry, Gittel, but we have taken a pledge and we cannot violate it simply to appease your father. Now, Gittel, please rest and think of nothing but a healthy and speedy recovery!"

"Yes, Zalman."

The morning of the circumcision was exceptionally cold. It had snowed heavily during the night, and the winds gusted with such force that for the first time in almost a month Velvel and Hershel had decided not to trek to the forest. They knew that Reb Berish would be surprised by their absence but consoled themselves that at least they would not anger their father on this solemn and momentous day.

The synagogue was prepared for the circumcision in the usual fashion. Two chairs were placed in front of the ark, with a small table near one of the chairs. The morning services proceeded and when they concluded, Rabbi Yaakov walked to the table. He placed some utensils, handkerchiefs, a goblet and a bottle of wine on the table and reached for a prayer book. One of the chairs was quite imposing with tall legs and a cushion covered in blue silk. Along the sides of the chair hung ribbons of lace and on the back of the chair were the words "Chair of Elijah" engraved into the wood. The other chair was a simple wooden seat and Reb Zundel approached it and sat down. Virtually the entire town was present, despite the incliment weather. The room turned unusually quiet as the baby was brought into the room. The baby was placed on Reb Zundel's lap. Rabbi Yaakov poured a cup of wine then recited some prayers and proceeded to circumcise the child. The wails of the tender babe quickly subsided as Rabbi Yaakov dipped his finger into the wine and placed several drops on the infant's tongue. Rabbi Yaakov continued to recite prayers and then motioned for Zalman to approach. The child was to be given a name, the concluding rite to this ancient, holy ritual. Everyone in the room naturally assumed that Zalman would name the child after his father, Shloime Yeshaya, who had been dead for eighteen years. This was held to be a sign of deep respect and honor for the soul of the departed.

Rabbi Yaakov, now holding the infant, continued reciting the prayer. He then paused and leaned toward Zalman and listened attentively, waiting for Zalman to reveal the name of the infant, which Rabbi Yaakov would then announce to everyone in the room. Zalman drew near to Rabbi Yaakov, took a fleeting glance at Reb Zundel who remained seated and whispered the name with pride and solemnity. Rabbi Yaakov, holding the sleeping child, grimaced and lurched forward. Reb Zundel instantly stood and caught Rabbi Yaakov before he fell. This startled the as-yet nameless child who began to whimper. More wine was dropped into his mouth and he quickly resumed his slumber. This pause, this break in the ceremony, was highly unusual, and everyone in the room began to murmur and wonder about the delay. Reb Zundel was perturbed by this pause and disapprovingly stared at Rabbi Yaakov. Rabbi Yaakov knew he could not wait any longer. He knew this would cause an unnecessary and deep rift within the town and could lead to much animosity and hostility. But he had no choice, he could not disobey the wishes of the child's father. Rabbi Yaakov braced himself, raised his voice and proclaimed, "Henceforth this child shall be called in Israel, Shabbetai, the son of Zalman."

28

Chana spent the next few days busily packing the family's belongings for their journey. Reb Zundel decided they would travel to Lublin, the largest city in the region, where some of Chana's distant relatives lived. Velvel and Hershel were particularly distraught by the move but they knew it would not happen anytime soon. Gittel had fallen seriously ill and the family would not leave until she recovered. Several doctors examined Gittel and they concluded she suffered some complications following the delivery. It would take at least a month for her to recover. Reb Zundel was quite distressed that he would have to remain for so long. He feared his sons were becoming so attached to the cause that even moving elsewhere would not save them.

Two weeks after the circumcision, Reb Zundel still could not comprehend that Zalman and Gittel named their son after a sinner. A man who created rifts among families, a man who spurned the Torah and its precepts. He was particularly troubled by Zalman's decision not to honor his own father and name the child after him. Reb Zundel had known Zalman's father, Shloime Yeshaya, a tall man with a warm, friendly smile. He remembered the day he was savagely killed by the Cossacks. He had compassion for Shloime Yeshaya's soul yearning for respect and honor, for a namesake to perpetuate his good name.

Reb Zundel blamed Reb Berish for all this. He believed that Reb Berish not only engaged in crude and harmful practices, which injured many of his followers like Betzalel, but pervaded their minds as well and fostered misplaced ideals.

Reb Zundel longed for Gittel to recover so he could leave Krasnystaw as quickly as possible. He even contemplated leaving before she fully recuperated but he knew Chana would never consent to that.

He waited and waited.

Zalman and Gittel fully expected Reb Zundel to express anger and disappointment at their decision, but they were a little surprised by the extent to which Reb Zundel refused to be placated. Zalman discovered from Hershel and Velvel that Reb Zundel would no longer accept Zalman, Gittel or the new child into his home and had vowed never to speak with them again. Zalman admitted he did not expect this drastic reaction from his father-in-law and was certain that it was only temporary. Zalman was convinced that at any moment, Reb Zundel would come to accept the messiah as enthusiastically and wholeheartedly as the rest of the family and that his current stance would quickly be replaced by renewed feelings of affection of love. He was sure that it would happen and that it was only a matter of time.

He too waited.

Reb Berish was confused. The news of the messiah's arrival was generating greater and greater enthusiasm. The weather was less harsh, which was certain to increase participation by those townspeople who had shunned the severe cold. It was the end of February and for the past few days the town had experienced a warm spell. Reb Berish knew the winter was far from over, but a respite from the coldest weather brought more people to seek his guidance and instruction. Reb Berish was terribly distraught by the rift that had grown between Zalman and Reb Zundel. He wondered if the impending news of the messiah was meant to cause such strife between families. Reb Berish had only just begun to realize how many aspects related to the messiah were troubling him lately.

Rabbi Yaakov, too, was perplexed. While more and more people expressed an interest in learning about the messiah and how they could best prepare for his imminent arrival, a sizable portion of the town remained indifferent, even hostile. Rabbi Yaakov was bothered by the growing breach developing in the town and was particularly annoyed by some townspeople who taunted and degraded the opinions of others. Even though Rabbi Yaakov was shocked and disappointed that Zalman had not named the baby Shloime Yeshaya after his father, he hoped the presence of a child with such a glorious and noble name would serve to unite and direct the town toward a common understanding, but that expectation proved elusive indeed.

In fact, Zalman and Gittel's decision exposed a rift in the town that had been smoldering for some time. Following the circumcision, many disputes and quarrels arose about all sorts of matters, from monetary disagreements to marital disputes, all of which were fundamentally rooted in disagreement about the messiah. These arguments were eventually brought to Rabbi Yaakov for resolution.

The first dispute that came to Rabbi Yaakov, about a week after the circumcision, was an argument that erupted between Reb Anshel the cheese maker and Dov Ber the wine merchant. The two men came to Rabbi Yaakov's study seeking a resolution. Reb Anshel refused to pay for wine he had previously purchased from Dov Ber on the grounds that Dov Ber was not a follower of the messiah and hence his wine was tainted and unfit for consumption. Dov Ber furiously disputed that charge and argued that Reb Anshel could not pinpoint any conduct that impugned his character or challenged his observance and allegiance to any of the laws of the Torah, that would render his wine defiled. Reb Anshel pointed out that Dov Ber's refusal to embrace the messiah was the most serious denial of faith and trust in the Torah. Rabbi Yaakov listened carefully as both parties presented their arguments.

Rabbi Yaakov was unsure how to adjudicate their dispute. On the one hand he knew that Dov Ber was an observant man and doubted whether his wine was truly defiled. Yet he did acknowledge that Dov Ber's stance was troubling. If he denied the messiah, what other customs, what additional practices would he refuse to accept? Rabbi Yaakov evaded the crux of the dispute, whether the messiah was authentic, by seizing upon the fact that the sale in question took place before any news of the messiah even reached the town. Rabbi Yaakov ruled that at that time Dov Ber's character had been beyond reproach, and consequently, the wine was acceptable and payment was due. Reb Anshel begrudgingly accepted Rabbi Yaakov's decision and the two men thanked him and left the study.

Rabbi Yaakov knew he could not remain evasive for too much longer.

The following week another argument exploded and Reb Shraga Feivish the scribe, his daughter, Malka, Reb Mendel the innkeeper and his son, Levi, stormed into Rabbi Yaakov's study one afternoon. Reb Shraga Feivish demanded the nullification of the engagement between Malka and Levi. Reb Shraga Feivish stated that he had learned Reb Mendel and Levi both rejected the messiah's legitimacy and he therefore refused to allow Malka to join such a dishonorable family. Reb Mendel, though, demanded Malka's presence at the forthcoming wedding, citing no blemish in Levi or in the family that would permit Reb Shraga Feivish to cancel the wedding agreement. Reb Shraga Feivish of course pointed to Reb Mendel's and Levi's repudiation of the messiah as proof of their discredited family status. To make matters worse, Malka, the bride-to-be, threatened to remain single her entire life if her father would prevent the wedding from taking place. The parties came to Rabbi Yaakov seeking adjudication. Again, Rabbi Yaakov carefully considered all the arguments articulated by each party. Rabbi Yaakov was reluctant to challenge Reb Shraga Feivish's position that all non-believers in the messiah were deemed heretics, not worthy of association. He did not agree with that belief but felt constrained to respect it. Rabbi Yaakov conceded that Reb Mendel and his son were men of sparkling character and that this single stain on their character could hardly disqualify Levi as a suitable marriage partner. Rabbi Yaakov suggested that Reb Shraga Feivish wait patiently and that perhaps over the next few weeks Reb Mendel and Levi would become persuaded of the messiah's legitimacy, thereby ending the dispute amicably. Rabbi Yaakov reminded Reb Shraga

Feivish that the wedding was not scheduled to take place for another two months, more than enough time for even the most ardent disbeliever to become transformed by the truth! Rabbi Yaakov knew his decision would displease Reb Shraga Feivish but he was hoping Reb Shraga Feivish would take his daughter's threat into consideration, follow his advice and agree to wait. Reb Mendel assured everyone that no amount of time would change his beliefs but he would consent to Rabbi Yaakov's decision for Levi and Malka's sake. They all left the Rabbi's study momentarily pacified and they all knew they would be returning to him in a few weeks. Rabbi Yaakov realized he did nothing but delay the situation, but he was beginning to understand that this itself was a significant accomplishment.

Two weeks later, Rabbi Yaakov faced the most serious disagreement of all, the one which caused Rabbi Yaakov the most anguish, the greatest distress, and which finally led him to realize that there was great disunity in the town, far more than he was at first willing to acknowledge. It was the argument between Yechiel the barber and his wife Tzipporah. Yechiel was a follower of the messiah while Tzipporah was adamantly against him. To prepare himself and undergo penance in anticipation of redemption, Yechiel fasted during the week. He only ate on the Sabbath and even then never indulged in hot food and shunned all delicacies. He twice passed out from lack of nourishment and spent many days in bed, reciting Psalms while languishing from hunger. No matter how sick he became he would not relent and his extreme conduct greatly distressed Tzipporah. Their three children had mixed reactions to their father's conduct. The eldest, Raphael, a boy of eleven, was enamored by his father's dedication and sought to emulate his service. The two others, Rochel, aged seven, and Zissel, aged six, were too young to understand the motives of their father but noticed that he was often sick and bedridden. Tzipporah appealed to Rabbi Yaakov, she demanded that Yechiel forego the fasts and sustain his body in a healthy, balanced manner. Yechiel refused and urged her to join him in abstinence of food and all worldly delights. She declined and threatened to leave town with the children and stay with her parents in Warsaw. Yechiel countered that he would deny her a bill of divorce and she would then be unable to remarry. Yechiel demanded that she cooperate with him and likewise refuse all food and drink during the week. He conceded that the children would not have to follow these hardships; even Raphael, who appeared so eager to fast, would be required to eat at least one nutritious meal a day. Yechiel argued that his wife's refusal to accept this proposal was tantamount to a rejection of values set forth in the Torah. He therefore could divorce her without satisfying the monetary obligations of their marriage contract. Tzipporah countered that this messiah was a fraud and on the contrary, her support of him would void her financial expectations! She pleaded with Rabbi Yaakov and insisted that if Yechiel did not put a halt to these afflictions immediately she would leave town. To demonstrate the seriousness of her position, she had temporarily left her home and for the past week had been residing with a neighbor.

Rabbi Yaakov heard the couple shouting their demands at each other and turned away in shame. He admitted he did not know how to advise them. He could not criticize these prolonged fasts. He had recently undertaken similar fasts of his own, although not as vigorous and torturous, and he genuinely admired Yechiel's resolve. But he wanted the family reunited more than anything else and he knew the fasts would have to cease. He recommended to Yechiel that he relinquish this particular form of preparation and accept other, less offensive and dangerous ones such as intense, fervent prayer or repeated immersions in the ritual bath. Yechiel, who calmed down and was sitting quietly, responded that he did not mean to be difficult and unyielding. He was quite distressed that Tzipporah found his dedication so distasteful and futile and he had considered abandoning the fasts. Yechiel explained that he could not choose a different form of penance, however, because Reb Berish determined that his soul required this particular method of self-denial. Reb Berish had reached that conclusion by delving into the mystical teachings of the Kabbalah, those ancient texts full of wonder and hidden meaning, and by peering into the nature of Yechiel's inner being. Yechiel admitted that he was bound to the fasts and must continue them.

Rabbi Yaakov did not fully understand the precise method Reb Berish employed to reach that conclusion but knew that once Yechiel was informed of his manner of service he could not be persuaded to change it. Rabbi Yaakov needed time to sort out the dilemma. He needed to consult other rabbis from the neighboring towns who surely faced similar disputes. He needed to think of a way to reunite the couple. As a gesture of reconciliation he asked Tzipporah to return to her home while he considered how best to solve this perplexing problem. He promised that he would render his decision within the week. Tzipporah agreed and the couple left his study.

Rabbi Yaakov stood up and began pacing in his study. It had been four days since Yechiel and Tzipporah had approached him with their dilemma. Time was running out and Rabbi Yaakov still had not reached a decision or even a compromise to settle their predicament. He traveled to nearby Zamosc and consulted Rabbi Elchanan, an elderly sage, but he could offer no definitive solution. Rabbi Yaakov only had a few more days before the week was over and that family suffered long lasting and irreperable damage.

Rabbi Yaakov sensed that worse conflicts were developing and they would soon occupy all his time and energy. Rabbi Yaakov was also aware that these disputes were far more contentious than others he resolved in the past. They were underscored by an animosity, a coldness he had never seen in the townspeople before. Rabbi Yaakov knew that if some message of reconciliation, of togetherness and understanding was not presented to the townspeople, that if he did not attempt to heal the rifts that were tearing everyone apart, if he did not speak directly to Yechiel and Tzipporah and appeal to their shared dreams and aspirations, then dire consequences would result. Rabbi Yaakov decided he would address these themes on the Sabbath. He sat down, reached for his books and began preparing his lecture.

That Sabbath the synagogue was unusually crowded. Rabbi Yaakov had mentioned to Reb Berish that he could not tolerate the enmity that was growing in the town and wished to end it immediately. Everyone knew of the disputes between Reb Anshel and Dov Ber, Reb Shraga Feivish and Reb Mendel and the unfortunate rupture that grew between Yechiel and his wife, Tzipporah. Reb Berish understood that Rabbi Yaakov would be addressing these problems on the Sabbath and spread word to insure a large attendance. Reb Berish was hoping Rabbi Yaakov could resolve the inner conflicts that recently had been tormenting him. Rabbi Yaakov was certain that Reb Berish's efforts accounted for the large crowd and he was hoping they would not be disappointed.

Rabbi Yaakov also decided that during this speech he would publicly proclaim, for the first time, his allegiance to the messiah. He knew that almost the whole town already suspected as much. Reb Berish had told many of the townspeople and Rabbi Yaakov did make occasional appearances at the forest. He knew his announcement would immediately spark a debate that would be a source of elation and vindication for some and anger and resentment for others. But he knew he could not hold back any longer. The town had a right to know the position of their spiritual leader.

The services proceeded quickly and many of the congregants were visibly anxious. That day the portion of the Torah reading recorded the sin of the Golden Calf. Rabbi Yaakov felt fortunate this particular portion fell on the Sabbath he had chosen to address the town. He believed it would provide him with the material he hoped would end the divisions once and for all.

The Torah was returned to the ark, the majestic ark with the blue silk curtain that bore the names of slain children. Rabbi Yaakov slowly walked to the cantor's podium. He was a man of average height with a graying, almost white beard. He had small eyes and a small head and a pleasant demeanor, which endeared him to everyone. He was well respected and as the past few weeks had demonstrated, was called upon for all sorts of matters. He approached the podium that morning and appeared regal. He seemed to tower over everyone else as he commanded the attention of the entire room. It was uncommonly quiet as Rabbi Yaakov stood at the podium. He looked out at the gathering and saw the faces of his confused and angry townspeople as he drew a deep breath. He began his speech by reminding everyone of those Jews in the desert who had erected a false god, an insignificant lifeless piece of metal. He wondered what could have led a nation, which beheld miracles of glory and amazement, to fall so quickly, to descend to the despair of idolatry. He explained that only a small number of the Jews actually participated in the sin, yet it was treated as one committed by the entire congregation. Rabbi Yaakov continued, "It is quite understandable that history views that event as a national catastrophe, not merely the backsliding of a few unworthy members. It is appropriate that the Talmud and the Midrash emphasize the magnitude of that sin even though a tiny fraction of the people were actually guilty. It is because we are one nation with one set of ideals, one focus, one goal and yes, one Torah. We may have differing opinions regarding the exact moment the Sabbath ends or whether certain legumes may be consumed on Passover or whether a mezuzah should be affixed on the doorpost this way or that. These differences merely enhance our collective body, they do not destroy it. Our differing customs attest to our adherence to the heritage of our fathers and grandfathers within the greater traditions of our people. Our similarities, though, are so universal, so harmonious and account for so much of the details, which dominate our rules and customs that in some sense we are all one family. Yet, we concentrate on those minute differences, those subtle contrasts that have developed over time and distance and allow those few distinctions to blur our purpose and our affinity toward one another. I myself have been guilty of such conduct. The Torah, though, is emphasizing that our brotherhood, our togetherness, the bonds we secure between each other, is a deep and enduring quality of our character. When one falls we all fall, when one is exalted we are all elevated. Therefore, when a few of us sin by creating a golden calf, it is treated by the Torah as if the entire nation did so."

Rabbi Yaakov sensed the crowd accept the clarity of his logic, and he knew they were waiting for him to connect that lesson to the events destroying the town. He grew more serious and continued by mentioning many of the unfortunate tragedies of the past, which always engendered understanding and compassion. They would help emphasize his message about the common bonds shared by all Jews. "No one in this room can deny that the Cossacks affected the lives of every Jew. True, the actual massacres only took place here in Poland, but the consequences, the tragedy was felt and absorbed and mourned by Jews from as far away as Yemen. Our collective nation suffered at the hands of those villains. The same may be said of the blood libels, the expulsions and the pogroms. The hatred, the subjugation was sometimes isolated to a single village, a remote town, yet as Jews and brothers, we all suffered together. In some sense we experienced them as well. Of course, we are separated from those events by time, distance and memory but we are connected to them by our common destinies, our common faith and our common brotherhood."

Rabbi Yaakov was ready to conclude his speech and profess his belief in the messiah. He knew there was a chance it could further divide the town but he could no longer remain silent about his beliefs. He was also hoping that his position as the town rabbi would sway many of the ambivalent members of the audience to follow him in his acceptance of the messiah. He remained strong and determined.

"However, recently a situation has presented itself. You all know what I am referring to, there is no need for elaboration. It has caused much discord, much argument. It has led to many legal disputes and the possible destruction of some families here in town. There have been many disputes over the years, and husbands and wives have bickered before, yet for the past few weeks I have sensed a distinct animosity, a vitriolic attitude that I have never seen among Jews, surely never here in Krasnystaw. I must admit that I am both shocked and saddened by what I have seen. While I fully support and am enthusiastic about his imminent arrival..." Rabbi Yaakov looked out into the crowd as he proclaimed his allegiance to the messiah. He noticed many people nod in disappointment, others in delight and some in surprise. He was relieved nobody stormed out of the synagogue in anger or contempt and was now supremely confident that he would heal the town's wounds, "...yet we may never cast aspersion on someone who does not welcome the messiah."

Rabbi Yaakov knew the crowd received his speech warmly. He continued to speak of unity and understanding. "The news about the arrival of the messiah was initially greeted with skepticism. I appreciate that, I too had my doubts. I am aware that this has caused much disagreement in the town and has led to an unusual degree of conflict. We cannot let this continue. We must remain united and dedicated to a common destiny, a common future and a common redemption. These divisive attitudes will only serve to prolong his arrival or perhaps induce him to abandon us entirely. I am not asking anyone to change how they feel about him or to ignore the stories of questionable conduct we have heard about him. They are valid and need to be addressed. I am merely urging that for our sake and the sake of our future we must approach our differences about this matter with respect, with friendship and with understanding. We may maintain our positions and allow the events of the next few months to vindicate us or to discredit us. But it is quite another matter when we refuse to trade with townsmen who disagree with us or to marry into families of those who disagree with us or to leave our spouses if they do not share our convictions." Rabbi Yaakov made sure to look at all of the disputants who sought his opinion over the past few weeks while he uttered his last request, and stared at Yechiel for a particularly long and uncomfortable moment before resuming his speech.

"I would hate to learn that we all lost a chance for redemption, whenever it may come, because of the selfish sins of the few. That happened once already in our history, I pray it does not happen again. Everyone have a good Sabbath!"

Rabbi Yaakov walked away from the podium and resumed his seat, confident that the terrible and unseemly disputes that plagued the town would now be resolved amicably. He was also certain that all the disputants would reach some sort of understanding and while everyone might not accept the messiah, at least the hostility, the animosity, would cease.

Rabbi Yaakov's speech would prove to be virtually ignored by the entire congregation and the disputes in the town would only grow more vicious and more violent. But there was one man in the audience who absorbed each word of Rabbi Yaakov's speech and was moved by the passion of his message. That man was greatly troubled and confused and now questioned how the messiah he had honored the past two months could truly represent the collective nation when so many people refused to accept him. One man believed he had made a terrible mistake.

Reb Berish left the synagogue that day a bewildered and shattered man.

29

Gittel recovered from the complications following the delivery sooner than the doctors had expected and Reb Zundel made arrangements to leave within the next few days. He sent a letter to Chana's relatives in Lublin informing them they would be arriving within the week. Chana was fully prepared to move. While she appreciated Rabbi Yaakov's efforts, the negative reception his speech had received confirmed that she could not remain in a town so divided and she quickly grew as impatient as her husband. Reb Zundel could not wait to leave. He respected Rabbi Yaakov's endeavors to try to save the town and was quite fond of him, despite his acceptance of the messiah. But he believed that nothing would change and he wanted to leave before his sons grew more distant. Reb Zundel personally spoke with many of the townspeople following Rabbi Yaakov's speech and while everyone had expressed an interest to try to end the conflicts in the town, they all remained so dedicated to their opinions that no conciliation seemed possible. Hershel and Velvel, though, were truly devastated. They knew for some time they would be leaving but now that the moment was upon them they were beside themselves. They understood they only had one or two more nights to spend with Reb Berish in the forest and they were determined to make them memorable and meaningful.

It was early evening and following services Velvel and Hershel went to sleep. Reb Zundel and Chana sat near the large table in silence, both reminiscing their fondest memories.

"I will never forget," exclaimed Reb Zundel, "the moment our eldest, Gittel, was born. It was a most warm and wonderful feeling."

"Yes, Reb Zundel, I too remember it well. We have enjoyed many happy moments in this home. I will surely miss it here," bemoaned Chana.

"I know," echoed Reb Zundel.

Reb Zundel glanced over to the room where his boys were fast asleep. In a few hours they would rise and venture into the forest. It was almost the middle of March, the festival of Purim had just passed, and although that generally signaled the very beginnings of spring, the weather was unusually cold. It had snowed for three days straight and there appeared to be no end in sight. Reb Zundel continued to gaze at his sleeping sons, resting calmly and peacefully. Soon they would be braving nature's fury, battling the cold and the snow to engage in bizarre rituals to honor a false leader. Were those rituals so compelling, so inspiring to drive so many there every night? Or was the cause so alluring, so captivating and mesmerizing that people could not turn away? Reb Zundel was determined to find out. Ever since the news had first reached Krasnystaw he had always been curious about the practices performed at the forest, the strange rituals and bizarre ceremonies, but would never dare go there himself. He did not wish to be seen associating with Reb Berish. He heard varying reports from many townspeople about what took place there, from foolish and adolescent games to miraculous displays of wonder and glory. He always wished he could observe them and satisfy his deep-seated curiosity but feared his reputation would be seriously tarnished. Now, with only a few days left in the town and virtually no chance that his presence there would cause him any embarrassment or shame, he believed he could indulge his overwhelming interest in them and see firsthand the principal reason he chose to leave Krasnystaw. He decided to follow his sons to the forest.

Velvel and Hershel woke and quickly dressed in silence. They sensed that this would be their last excursion to the forest and proceeded with unusual solemnity. They quickly threw on their coats and rushed to the clearing. They did not speak to each other as they marched toward the familiar destination; they were each absorbed with the fulfillment of their final mission. Reb Zundel followed them, gasping and breathing furiously, trying to maintain the pace of his children.

Velvel and Hershel reached the top of the clearing and quickly ran to find Reb Berish for encouragement. Reb Berish was not there but Reb Anshel handed them the thorns and explained that Reb Berish was ill. The brothers lowered their heads and lamented that their last mortifications in the forest would be undertaken without the guidance and care of their mentor and teacher. Reb Zundel followed close behind and kept a careful eye on his sons as they headed for their usual spot at the edge of the clearing. Reb Zundel did not wish to flaunt his presence there and he lowered his head and avoided eye contact. He cautiously followed Velvel and Hershel and moved through the crowds quickly.

Reb Zundel stood behind a large tree and watched from a distance as his children undressed in the freezing temperature. He stood aghast as they proceeded to lie down in the snow and roll around in it with a rapture he could not comprehend. He sought to rush to them, to rescue them from this madness, warm them and take them home, but he was paralyzed by shock and terribly afraid they would spurn him and leave his protective home. He continued to gaze from afar and after a few moments was relieved to see Hershel emerge and quickly throw on some clothes and wait for Velvel. Reb Zundel's horror instantly resumed when he noticed Velvel continue to roll around in the snow. Reb Zundel feared Velvel would contract a serious illness from such prolonged exposure to the severe cold and he wished to reveal his presence there and nurture his son. But he was so afraid that Velvel would mistake his love for reproof, his affections for criticism, and was terrified that Velvel would run away like Yehoshua Leib's boys and that Velvel would be gone forever. He refrained from running toward him and consoled himself that soon his entire family would be residing safely in Lublin. Reb Zundel continued to wait, hoping his children would not be harmed by these escapades.

Reb Zundel continued watching and was delighted when Velvel finally stood erect and covered his frigid body with a shawl. He fully expected his sons to return to Reb Anshel and warm themselves by the fire that burned there before walking home. Reb Zundel realized that he was quite cold himself and greatly anticipated an end to this miserable experience. He continued to watch as Velvel reached for the bundle of thorns that Reb Anshel had given him. Reb Zundel had forgotten about those thorns and could not imagine why they had been handed to his sons but watched cautiously, hoping this night would soon end.

Suddenly Velvel fell to the ground and let out a shriek, a cry for help.

"What's wrong, Velvel?" asked Hershel, who bent down to tend to his brother.

"I don't know, Hershel. I believe I slipped and the thorns have lodged in my leg, I cannot move, please run for help!" pleaded Velvel in obvious pain.

Hershel removed his coat and attempted to wrap Velvel's leg. He lifted the leg and threw the coat underneath to support the leg and to help stop the bleeding. The thorns were still firmly in place and Hershel's jerk of the leg caused the thorns to settle deeper and cause more pain. "Please, Hershel," bellowed Velvel, "I need assistance, summon Reb Anshel or Wolf the tailor!"

Hershel stood up and raced to Reb Anshel.

Reb Zundel slowly approached his son. He could no longer remain idle. He understood he might suffer alienation or rejection from Velvel but that was no longer an overriding concern: If he did not intervene now Velvel could die! He stood in front of Velvel, who slipped into unconsciousness. Reb Zundel lowered his body and with all his might grabbed the thorns and yanked them out of Velvel's leg. Velvel's body jerked from the pain, but Velvel remained lifeless. Reb Zundel threw down the thorns and saw that his hand was terribly cut and was bleeding profusely. He sought to grab Hershel's coat and wrap it around his hand but heard Hershel and someone else racing toward Velvel. Reb Zundel quietly slipped away, undetected.

Reb Anshel and Hershel reached Velvel. Reb Anshel held a knife to cut the thorns. He lowered himself and observed the thorns no longer pressing Velvel's flesh. He looked puzzled. "Come here, Hershel, what is this?" Reb Anshel pointed to Velvel's leg.

Hershel joined Reb Anshel as they kneeled, hovering over Velvel. "I do not understand, Reb Anshel, only a moment ago they were here stuck in Velvel's leg. I cannot explain how the thorns were removed. Perhaps a miracle has occurred!" wondered Hershel.

"Are you certain that the thorns were lodged in your brother's leg?" pressed Reb Anshel.

"I am absolutely sure, Reb Anshel. You can see the gash and wound on the leg and look, there are the thorns!" Hershel pointed to the open wound on Velvel's leg and the thorns on the ground near Velvel.

Reb Anshel observed the thorns, bloodied and torn. He then noticed that Velvel was comatose and tried to revive him. "He lost much blood Hershel. Help me carry him down where he will be taken home. We must pray for his speedy recovery, but I believe he will be well. After all, a miracle has been performed for him!" Reb Anshel sounded jubilant.

"You truly believe it was a miracle?" marveled Hershel.

"How else can we explain what happened here? An animal would not have the strength or the willingness to rip the thorns this thoroughly, and surely Velvel could not have done it. It must have been a miracle! How glorious, Hershel, the messiah has performed a miracle for your brother Velvel! No doubt Heaven was deeply pleased with your brother's acts of penance! Hurry now, Hershel, we must get him indoors!"

They quickly lifted Velvel and carried him to the center of the clearing where some men were waiting to rush Velvel home.

Reb Zundel did not feel badly about leaving Velvel in that condition. He knew Velvel would be taken home at any moment and that if he were found in the area, his presence would further alienate

Hershel. Velvel was being cared for by concerned and trusted friends. He quietly slipped away from the tree, and made his way home quickly, as blood dripped from his hand.

Hershel escorted the men carrying Velvel home. He knew that his father would surely be woken by all the commotion and that he would be so disheartened to learn of Velvel's injury. Hershel realized his father would be disappointed by the blatant disobedience which resulted in this calamity. He would not be encouraged by talk of a miracle, he would surely not believe one had occurred.

Hershel entered the home and was surprised to see his father already awake and dressed, with a bandage covering a noticeably bruised hand. His father looked nervous and apprehensive. The men carrying Velvel immediately followed Hershel. Wolf, who was holding Velvel's feet, entered first. "Hello, Reb Zundel," whispered Wolf. "It is unfortunate that we must meet under such serious circumstances. Your son was injured a short while ago. He is unconscious and needs a bed." Reb Zundel accompanied the men as Velvel was carefully placed in his bed. Reb Zundel covered him with a blanket and nodded as the men quickly left. Reb Zundel turned to Velvel, who remained lifeless.

"Is there anything I can do, Father?" asked Hershel, concerned.

"Well, Hershel, go and fetch another blanket. Your brother is still quite cold," answered Reb Zundel, flustered. Hershel nodded and went to search for one. Reb Zundel remained next to Velvel, waiting for any sign of movement. He realized that the doctor needed to be called. He would send Hershel to summon him as soon as morning services concluded. He knew that none of the local doctors would be willing to come any earlier. He continued to wait while standing over his son and barely noticed that his hand had resumed bleeding.

Hershel returned with a blanket and gently placed it over Velvel. He knew his father was angry and displeased but would not say anything as long as Velvel remained in this condition.

"Perhaps we should expose the wound and determine whether we can apply some sort of remedy before the doctor arrives?" piped Hershel.

"That is a good idea, Hershel. You display an astuteness quite unusual for someone your age. Have you seen this before? Is this what happened to Betzalel?" returned Reb Zundel scornfully.

Reb Zundel did not wait for an answer and ordered Hershel to bring some water and fresh cloths. Hershel hurried to the kitchen and reached for some cloths at the rear of the top shelf of a cupboard. Hershel noticed a small pool of blood on the floor of the kitchen. Where did it come from? It was surely not Velvel's, Wolf and the men carrying him in had not come near the kitchen. It could only have come from his father. That would explain the bandage on his hand, but what had caused him to suffer a wound that produced such heavy bleeding?

Hershel returned to his father and the two of them removed the coverings on Velvel's leg. Reb Zundel was relieved that the bleeding had stopped. Reb Wolf or someone else must have closed the gash before transporting him home. But the wound appeared to be inflamed and Reb Zundel feared the leg would not heal properly. He waited and prayed.

Hershel too sensed Velvel was gravely ill. He could not remember Velvel ever staying in the snow for so long and understood that his body may have been severely abused. He looked at his father, who had closed his eyes in solemn meditation. Hershel felt sorry for him. This was the second instance where one of his children suffered illness.

Was he next?

Reb Zundel suddenly grimaced and opened his eyes. He looked at his hand and turned it in all directions and rubbed it softly until the pain subsided. Hershel watched his father try to maneuver his hand into a comfortable position.

"Father, may I help you in some way to alleviate the pain?" asked Hershel, respectfully.

Reb Zundel turned to his son, "No, Hershel, there is nothing that can be done, it will heal itself in a few days. Thank you for your concern."

Hershel pointed to the hand, "How did it happen, Father?"

Reb Zundel wondered whether he should finally confide in Hershel, overcome his fears of rejection and reveal that he had removed the thorns, that his love for his children ran deeper than their allegiance to a false savior. Perhaps Hershel would rethink the stiff and unyielding impressions he recently had attributed to his father and resume the warm relationship that the past few months had slowly eroded.

But perhaps not.

Reb Zundel was too afraid to divulge the secret. He could not predict how Hershel would react and he could ill afford to take any risks and end up like Yehoshua Leib.

"I cut my hand chopping wood, Hershel, it will heal soon. Now let us pray for Velvel's speedy recovery, and remember, we shall be attending morning services within the hour."

"Yes, Father."

Reb Zundel and Hershel remained seated near Velvel's bed. Reb Zundel once again closed his eyes. Hershel recalled that his father never chopped any wood. He always bought their supply from Shimon the woodcutter. Hershel did not tell his father about the miracle that had taken place but as he gazed at the wound on his father's hand, wondered whether it was a miracle at all.

Reb Berish awoke, forced himself to dress and prepared for morning services. He proceeded slowly, almost reluctantly. For the past three days, ever since Rabbi Yaakov's speech, Reb Berish was overcome with so much despair that he felt lethargic and faint and barely had the desire to leave his home. He was not ill at all. He had merely told Reb Anshel that he was in order to avoid continuing to supervise the practices he now seriously questioned. He had always maintained reservations about the extreme forms of penance and bodily harm that were prevalent among his followers and only encouraged such methods of penance when based on his interpretation of kabbalah and mystical sources. But now the damage they caused was far more severe than he first imagined. He was shocked by Betzalel's injury and the divisiveness in Reb Zundel's family and was saddened to learn that his instruction to Yechiel, which he had based on Kabbalah, now resulted in irreconcilable differences which threatened Yechiel's marriage.

But it was Rabbi Yaakov's words of understanding, of a common allegiance to a familiar and ancient set of values, that spoke to him in a personal and intimate way and demonstrated to him his misplaced eagerness for this cause. Reb Berish was fully aware that many of the townspeople rejected the messiah and the unusual rituals which were practiced in his name. He knew that a lack of harmony, an absence of brotherhood that Rabbi Yaakov stressed, was present every night at the forest. While more and more townspeople found their way there each night, a sizable part of the populace would have no part of it. Reb Berish had believed that it would take time and patience to win over those who remained reluctant or ambivalent. It was a challenge, that Reb Berish had enthusiastically welcomed.

But after analyzing Rabbi Yaakov's lecture, after studying each word, Reb Berish realized that something as universal and pervasive as the arrival of the messiah could not take place amid so much rejection, so much doubt. True, Reb Berish did not know how the messiah should be received, this had never happened before; there were no precedents to review and consider. But he did know that the messiah was destined to usher in an era of peace, relief from oppression, and foster awareness and dedication to the Torah, not create divisions among families and friends. The messiah evoked images of kingship, victory and pride, not discord, doubt and ambivalence. Reb Berish always dreamed of waking one morning to the sounds of music and shofars heralding the new kingdom of the savior. He always envisioned that scene, the happiness, the elation, the joy, the throngs rushing to greet him, comforted by the realization that at long last the terrible, agonizing exile was finally over. Reb Berish was certain that his dream was shared by every Jew, from the saintly rabbis in Safed and Jerusalem to the starving peasants of Poland and Russia. Yet, no one ever imagined the messiah's arrival would be met with hesitancy and reservation and even hostility. Reb Berish could not fathom anything but a total endorsement, a complete acceptance of the messiah. Yes, something this momentous would always initially be greeted with skepticism, that was human nature. But this prolonged and ongoing rejection of this messiah undermined Reb Berish's dream and the dreams of the people. It challenged their longing and diminished their aspirations.

Reb Berish recalled the events of the past few months, all the disagreements, all the strife, all the townspeople who refused to accept the news. Reb Berish knew the same divisions that existed in Krasnystaw were present in many towns throughout Poland. There was disagreement everywhere! This man could not be the messiah, he could not be authentic. The messiah's presence was not meant to foment rifts and separation, which now characterized daily life. A man who lacked universal respect and acceptance could not alleviate the struggles of the Jewish people.

Reb Berish was devastated. All the extremes and excuses of the preparations still practiced by the townspeople were all in vain! He had misled them down a path that was sure to end with heartache, with disillusionment. Reb Berish did not know if he could retain his position as the caretaker of the synagogue and continue his service in a town he betrayed. He was not sure he could even stay in Krasnystaw altogether. True, his motives were genuine but that mattered little to the families that were still pained by his guidance. Would Betzalel's wounds heal? Would Levi and Malka ever marry? Would Yechiel and Tzipporah salvage their marriage?

Reb Berish knew he would not be able to face the angry and disappointed townspeople who invested so much and who waited so faithfully with him to lead them in glory to Jerusalem. He saw the surge in anger and resentment which existed between feuding townsmen, and he believed he would suffer from the wrath and fury of some of the angrier and particularly distraught men in town. He knew that when this ignoble cause finally ended, he would be blamed and ridiculed and possibly harmed.

He decided to leave town by nightfall.

Reb Berish barely closed the door to his home and was immediately greeted by Wolf, who bent over to catch his breath.

"Hello, Reb Berish," said Wolf, rising and inhaling quickly. "Sorry to have missed you these past few days. Are you feeling better?"

"Yes, thank you, I should be ready to rejoin everyone soon," replied Reb Berish apathetically.

"I am happy to hear that, Reb Berish. However, I raced here as fast as I could to report some sad news. Velvel, Reb Zundel's son, has fallen seriously ill as a result of an accident that happened before dawn and I believe he is unconscious."

Reb Berish stared blankly at Wolf, troubled that another youth had seriously injured himself. Reb Berish felt remorseful that his misguided leadership had caused this accident. He felt particularly guilty that this tragedy befell Reb Zundel, a man who had been publicly disgraced at the circumcision of his grandson. Reb Berish knew he would have to visit Reb Zundel, beg his forgiveness for contributing to his sorrow and offer him any assistance and comfort. He did not fear retaliation or harm from Reb Zundel. He was known for his even temperament and fairness. Reb Berish pledged that he would not depart Krasnystaw until he visited Reb Zundel and petitioned him to forgive his error.

Reb Berish suddenly noticed a warm, calm smile suffusing Wolf's face and was startled that he appeared cheerful relating such distressing news. Wolf though quickly eased Reb Berish's concerns. "But something else took place this morning, something which probably saved Velvel's life. It was a miracle!"

Wolf proceeded to relate the events at the forest which such animation and vitality that Reb Berish momentarily longed for the enchantment he had just rejected. Wolf spoke of the wondrous and awesome sight, which Reb Anshel beheld when he observed Velvel lying on the ground free of the thorns that only moments ago were lodged in his flesh. Reb Berish admitted it was a remarkable story indeed but seriously doubted that a miracle had taken place. He was certain there was another explanation. Reb Berish wondered if Reb Zundel, a non-believer in these matters, might have a reasonable answer.

Reb Berish accompanied Wolf to the synagogue as a changed man. He no longer relished his role as leader to so many people seeking guidance and meaning. He was terrified by a new and frightening vision. The exile would continue. The blood libels, the pogroms, the expulsions, the wandering from town to town and country to country. The persecution, the debasement, the inability to live without fear, without peace. It would all continue. For a brief, fleeting moment he had believed the promise of salvation was at hand. He would now have to resume his life subject to the whims and vagaries of Cossacks and so many other zealous enemies. The rest of the nation would be forced to join him in the continued struggles of a hard and mean life. They would renew their daily pining, their perpetual longing and expectation for the arrival of the true messiah. They would continue to wait for the fulfillment of that ancient promise. They would continue to sanctify their lives, to suffer and sacrifice for their beliefs with patience and anticipation.

But for how much longer?

30

Reb Zundel paid close attention as Count Jan Podolski, the most capable doctor in town, examined Velvel. Count Podolski was a fine, caring doctor who understood the workings of the human body better than any man in the region. He had once considered entering the priesthood but his easy grasp of medical knowledge persuaded him to pursue a career as a physician. He took the oath of the doctor quite seriously. Since the very early days of his career, when his fame barely spread beyond the few towns that surrounded Krasnystaw, he swore that he would never refuse to treat any man or woman, even Jews. That attitude offended many Poles who thereupon refused to use his services. Count Podolski did not care. Over the years he had come to realize that even the most hate-filled people sought his medical advice when they had nowhere else to turn.

Count Podolski was a tall, robust man. He had very large hands and keen, piercing eyes. He always towered over everyone in the room and always wore the cape of nobility. He examined Velvel for nearly one hour, moving him about, spending a great deal of time dressing the wound on his leg. He finally finished the examination and turned to Reb Zundel.

"It seems that your son has suffered a terrible shock, which was brought on by extended exposure to the severe cold. Was your son outside without adequate protection for any length of time?" asked Count Podolski.

"Yes," answered Reb Zundel, sheepishly.

"That is what I suspected. Moreover, your son suffered this wound on his leg from some needles or pricks of some sort. He lost considerable blood but the leg should heal in a few weeks. The loss of blood, coupled with the body's inability to remain warm, probably accounted for his rapid loss of consciousness. What was your son doing which caused all of this? It is quite fascinating," inquired Count Jan curiously.

"It is a long, personal and rather embarrassing story which I do not wish to share. Please respect my sensitivity," begged Reb Zundel.

"Of course, Reb Zundel. There is not much I can do for him at this time. It will take some time for his body to regulate itself and resume normal function. He will probably slip in and out of consciousness and when he awakes be sure to give him food. He will undoubtedly be too weak to eat anything by himself; you will have to feed him. Give him hot soup or a thin broth. That should hopefully sustain him while he recovers. I do not know how long that will take, but I am optimistic that within a few weeks he might regain his faculties and his strength and will be able to sit up and talk. I have treated the wound, which should greatly alleviate the stress it was exerting on the body. Make sure your home stays warm and call me if the slightest change occurs."

"Thank you, Count Podolski, thank you for all your help," exclaimed Reb Zundel.

He escorted the doctor to the door and waited until he was out of view. Reb Zundel then turned and continued to gaze at his ill son. By now they should have been on their way to Lublin, away from this dreadful town.

Would they ever leave?

Reb Zundel trusted Count Podolski: His diagnosis was generally flawless and his expertise unmatched. If he predicted it might take a few weeks then the family would wait with optimism. He knew he needed to make sure there was always hot soup simmering on the stove should Velvel momentarily awaken.

Reb Zundel stood up and moved to a window, which looked out on the town. It truly was a wonderful place, full of caring friends and family. Reb Zundel recalled that once, many years ago, the king of Poland sought to expel the local citizens and requisition Krasnystaw as his summer retreat. It was an ideal location, close to the River Bug with its accompanying cool breezes and soft peaceful currents. The town managed to bribe the king's advisers to abandon that plan. The universal understanding and common vision which the town had exhibited then seemed lost now. Reb Zundel also recalled the terrible tragedies which had touched every home over the years: the Cossacks and the wars fought in the nearby Ukraine, which nearly ravaged Krasnystaw. Reb Zundel remembered feelings of kinship and togetherness then as the town united to withstand common enemies. But today the enemies were themselves, brothers, fathers, spouses, even Rabbi Yaakov.

Were there not enough enemies among the Gentiles?

Was there not enough suffering and sorrow at the hands of the nations of the world?

Reb Zundel conceded that Rabbi Yaakov was certainly correct. Without a common goal, without a united mission, without the strength and fortitude to stand in unison, the town's present friction would only increase. There would never be resolution because there would never be common ground on which to agree and eschew any further conflict. The town would sink deeper and deeper into disaster as it slowly tore itself apart. Reb Zundel's own life only reinforced those beliefs. He still had not forgiven Gittel and Zalman and was furious that Reb Berish's methods had left his son mangled and unconcious. Would he remain angry and disappointed forever? Would he ever reconcile with Gittel and Zalman, restore the affection and tenderness and warmth that once had existed between them? Would he ever visit his only grandson? Would he allow Yom Kippur, the Day of Atonement, to pass without renouncing his grudge against Reb Berish?

But there were other disputes destroying Krasnystaw, which were far more serious than his own. Would they ever be settled? Would Krasnystaw ever return to the pleasant and cordial place it once was? Reb Zundel regretted that he had contributed to the general decline of the town's cohesiveness. He felt sorry that he impetuously shunned all contact with Gittel and Zalman. He determined that while he waited for Velvel to recover, he would do whatever he could to try and heal some of the breaches in his own life and in Krasnystaw. He would heed Rabbi Yaakov's advice and try to understand and respect everyone. He knew that meant abandoning his opposition to the new messiah and all those who followed him, including Reb Berish. That would be a most difficult task, one that required him to undo so many months of disapproval and criticism. But Reb Zundel knew he needed to confront and surmount the very essence of the problem. Reb Zundel understood he could never accept or comprehend the harsh penances which the followers practiced, they were too rigorous, too ascetic. But he would try and ascertain, for the first time really, whether or not the man who claimed to be the messiah was authentic. He would visit Rabbi Yaakov and discuss it with him. He would meet with Reb Berish and learn about the texts of Kabbalah, which foretold of his imminent arrival. He would greet them with an open mind and a willing and loving heart, free of the hostility that had characterized him these past few months. He was aware this was a radical change, one that he would never not have contemplated even a few days earlier. But things were different now: His son was on the brink of death, his daughter remained estranged and alienated and Krasnystaw seemed on the verge of collapse.

Reb Zundel felt that he was now embarking on a mission to try to restore Krasnystaw to its former charm and grandeur. He would seek out the truth about the messiah and hopefully encourage others to do the same. He knew that like himself, many others in Krasnystaw had never truly given the messiah in-depth scrutiny. They had heard some fantastic and outlandish stories about him, saw the bizarre rituals practiced in his name and concluded it was nothing but absurdity and falsehood. They had never stopped to question that perhaps the truth was present, but was blurred and sullied by extreme zealousness. They never entertained that the foolishness might lie in the followers, not the leader. He could not deny that adherence to the precepts of the Torah were more scrupulously observed than ever before. The more Reb Zundel thought about it, the more he realized that he had never seriously considered the merits or arguments in favor of the messiah. He had been so obsessed with condemning the ceremonies in the forest, with accepting the rumors of blasphemy and irreverence, that it obscured genuine contemplation, which was now long overdue. Reb Zundel, though, still maintained that he would never accept the idea of bodily harm as the way to penance.

Reb Zundel also knew that he would have to initiate a reconciliation between himself and Gittel and Zalman. He could not demonstrate a willingness to embrace all the townspeople, no matter their beliefs, without first healing the breach within his own family. Reb Zundel pledged that he would offer his apology for his rash and insensitive reaction and express sincere regret for the unjustified flaring of his temper. He was sure they would welcome him and reciprocate with feelings of love and understanding. Reb Zundel looked forward to rejoicing with the grandson he had not seen in almost two months. He would then petition his able and wise son-in-law to further enhance his understanding of the messiah's unique personality and the momentous times in which they lived. Reb Zundel was excited.

Reb Zundel continued to gaze out beyond the town, quite unaware that he had taken the first step, that slow, cautious step, one that he had been avoiding for almost three months, toward a cause that would ultimately end in disappointment and shame.

Hershel suddenly ran into the house and announced that the messiah had safely arrived in Constantinople, where he had been taken to a fortress to await an audience with the Sultan. Hershel was reluctant to impart this news, he did not wish to further anger his father, but Hershel wanted Velvel to hear it. Perhaps the wonderful news would stir his soul and spark his recovery. Hershel emphasized that the messiah was treated in this respectful and dignified manner because the Sultan feared him and was postponing meeting with him, a meeting that would surely result in the Sultan's abdication of power. Hershel reiterated that when the entire world finally acknowledged the messiah's arrival, then those found worthy would join him in the Land of Israel. Hershel appeared exuberant and he could hardly contain his happiness. He was certain he would be among those chosen to leave the exile and reside in glory and radiance in Jerusalem. Hershel also recounted that the ten lost tribes, led by Reuben and Gad, those battle-ready warriors and protectors of the ancient Jews, were marching across the steppes of Asia, on their way to the communities of Europe to salvage the downtrodden people and to protect them and defend them from the local mobs. There could be no denying the end was in sight!

Reb Zundel did not mention to Hershel his newfound tolerance for the messiah. He first wanted to apologize to Gittel and Zalman and reveal his change to them, he owed them that much. But he admitted he was excited. He did not know how Hershel was aware of these events taking place so far from Poland but filled him with anticipation and suspense. What if the Sultan would renounce his power, relinquish his kingdom? What if the lost Jews of yesteryear suddenly reappeared, ready to stand alongside their brethren in unity and love? It that were all true, it would confirm the fulfillment of the ancient promise, forged in blood and suffering. It would signal the actualization of so much waiting, so much patience. It would usher in the arrival of the Judgment Day, the day when all the crimes committed against the Jews would be answered and then avenged. The day when every Cossack, every Crusader, every Inquisitor, every blood libel accuser, every hate-consumed enemy would be called before the tribunal and made to answer for their deeds. The day he would once again face the murderers of his parents and his wife's parents and Zalman's father and Fishel's son and the endless list of victims across time and memory. The day of final retribution, decisive and irreversible condemnation.

Reb Zundel quickly concluded that there was no reason not to believe Hershel's reports, no reason to doubt they were true. While he still shunned the severe rituals in the forest and still retained doubts about the integrity of the man, he was suddenly attracted to the allure and fascination of what it all represented. He tried to remain calm and poised, to methodically analyze the events of the past few months while under the guidance and wisdom of Rabbi Yaakov and Reb Berish. He did not wish to blindly commit himself without first understanding its authenticity and validity, without first reconciling his preconceived opinions with the truth. But he continued to witness Hershel's unabashed excitement and he continued to relish the vindication which might be forthcoming, and the reconciliation within his own family, and he was seized with an ardor that he never experienced before. Reb Zundel could not contain himself, he could not wait for Gittel and Zalman. He moved toward Hershel, embraced him and told him they would wait together, for the messiah and for Velvel's recovery. Hershel smiled and, for the first time in three months, he embraced his father.

Reb Berish reached Reb Zundel's home and nodded to Reb Zundel, who was standing outside enjoying the fresh air. Reb Berish was relieved and greeted Reb Zundel prior to entering the home. He believed it would help ease the tensions he was sure would erupt. Reb Zundel fully expected Reb Berish to visit and inquire about Velvel's welfare, and he was eager to begin learning about the messiah and his ways. He welcomed Reb Berish. Reb Berish bowed respectfully and proceeded into the home.

The two men faced one another. Two men who in the past day had undergone vastly different transformations. "Good morning, Reb Berish, I heard you were ill. Have you recovered?"

"Yes, thank you. I was sick for a few days, but I am feeling stronger now. I did not come here to speak about myself. I came here to offer my sorrow and express my shame that your son remains injured and bedridden. I was informed earlier that he suffered an accident and that he did not regain consciousness. Please forgive me for the grief I have caused," cried Reb Berish.

Reb Zundel stood shocked. He knew Reb Berish would feel sorry about what happened but would maintain it was necessary, even admirable. Was he expressing regret?

"I accept your apology, Reb Berish. Obviously you never intended or even desired for this to happen. Count Podolski left here a short while ago and was confident that Velvel would awake every now and again and would eventually recover," Reb Zundel sounded optimistic.

"I am relieved to hear that," returned Reb Berish. "Count Podolski is the best doctor in Krasnystaw. Velvel should be up and about in no time at all!"

"We continue to pray, Reb Berish."

"Is there any way I can help, Reb Zundel?" asked Reb Berish, trying to offer some evidence of remorse.

Reb Zundel was certain there was no need for Reb Berish's assistance. The only thing they could do was wait, but he thought this a perfect opportunity to engage Reb Berish. "Well, recently I have been thinking about this messiah. Where was he born? How old is he? Where did he study and how did he reveal himself as our savior?" Reb Zundel was eager and looked impatient waiting for a reply.

Reb Berish remained still. Why the sudden interest in the messiah? Was this a trap, a pretext for Reb Zundel to hurl rebuke and contempt toward him? Reb Berish could not fault Reb Zundel if he were to erupt in anger. After all, his instruction led to Velvel's condition. But Reb Berish was hoping he could escape the past he now thoroughly rejected and begin anew, free of the mistakes and confusion that had resulted in so much damage. Reb Berish realized that he could not so easily ignore Reb Zundel's concerns and would have to accept his admonishments and those from other town members as long as he remained there. He looked at Reb Zundel and was startled to see him anxiously awaiting answers. He did not appear angry, hurt or resentful, he seemed calm, almost peaceful. He surely did not look like someone who was asking questions simply to find fault and lay blame. Reb Berish concluded that Reb Zundel was not angry or bitter and harbored no ill will toward him, and that his questions were sincere and heartfelt. That could only mean one thing: Reb Zundel had become a believer.

Reb Berish was surprised by Reb Zundel's sudden change, especially since Velvel was deathly ill. What led Reb Zundel, a sensible and learned man, to embrace the messiah after so many months of resistance? Reb Berish recalled that the townspeople followed this messiah for all sorts of reasons. Some, like Rabbi Yaakov and Reb Fishel, were so disheartened by the prolonged exile that they forced themselves to believe, if only to ease their tortured souls. Others, such as Velvel and Hershel and other young men, were fascinated by the excitement and mystery of strange rituals performed deep in the woods. Others still, like Yechiel, Reb Shraga Feivish and Zalman, were truly convinced of this messiah's legitimacy and sought to honor and glorify him. But what motivated Reb Zundel to change his position now, to abandon his beliefs and accept those he had utterly rejected for so long?

Reb Berish realized that Reb Zundel was waiting for a response, and while he did wish to help him and alleviate his suffering while he waited for his son to recover, he would not bless the messiah. "There is so much to learn about the messiah, Reb Zundel. I do not feel I can adequately explain it all," answered Reb Berish spiritlessly.

Reb Zundel mistook Reb Berish's refusal for humility. "But, Reb Berish, you have led so many of the townspeople all these months, surely you are the most qualified man to enlighten me and teach me and guide me."

Reb Berish remained obstinate. "No, Reb Zundel, perhaps you should seek your answers elsewhere."

Reb Zundel could not understand why Reb Berish continued to refuse to help him. He thought that perhaps Reb Berish was reluctant to have any further connection to a family he had caused so much anguish. "Please, Reb Berish, I truly need your guidance and wisdom, neither I nor my wife blame you in any way for what happened to Velvel. Why are you so opposed to assisting me?" pleaded Reb Zundel

Reb Berish hoped to leave Krasnystaw without revealing to anyone his changed beliefs. He believed that would minimize the commotion and possible anger his departure would cause. But Reb Berish could not deceive Reb Zundel. He could not hide the truth from him, not after all the pain he had caused him. Reb Berish would confide in him, express his sorrow once again and then slip away forever.

"The reason I cannot guide you, Reb Zundel, is because I no longer have positive feelings toward this messiah. I no longer believe he is our savior." Reb Berish lowered his head and turned to leave.

Reb Zundel was shocked. "What led you to change your mind?" demanded Reb Zundel.

"The lecture which Rabbi Yaakov delivered this past Sabbath," returned Reb Berish. "His words of reconciliation, of harmony, made me realize that all the opposition toward the messiah reduced his credibility and cast serious doubt on the success of his eventual arrival. He would never be accepted by all of us and therefore could never represent even some of us. I concluded that he could not be our savior."

Reb Zundel could not believe Reb Berish's reversal. Reb Berish seemed so ready to dismiss it all so hastily, as if he had been seeking to do so for some time and had just discovered a suitable excuse. Was Reb Berish telling the truth? Could a man's beliefs change so suddenly? Were they so vulnerable, so unsteady? Reb Zundel turned those questions toward himself and admitted he did not know the answer.

The two men faced one another. Each was now aware of the other's recent changes. They both understood that their inability to maintain their convictions merely highlighted the serious confusion and doubt which faced each town, each Jew. The dilemmas which confronted everyone were so novel, so unique, and there was nowhere to turn for resolution. They did not involve sacrifice, or martyrdom, or forced conversion or any of the usual struggles which history visited upon the Jewish People. The current difficulty involved only one thing, truth. Was the messiah authentic? Would he lead the people to glory and salvation? Was the exile finally over? These were questions which only time would answer. But in the meanwhile the confusion and discord would surely continue.

Reb Berish resumed speaking. "Please, Reb Zundel, what I have just revealed to you is personal and I trust you will not divulge it to the rest of the town. I do not wish for them to learn of my change and come to hate me when this is finally over and everyone is facing deep disappointment. I shall be leaving now. I cannot remain knowing that I have mislead so many well-intentioned and good-hearted Jews. Be well, Reb Zundel, and I hope Velvel recovers soon. I will continue to pray for him." Reb Berish walked toward the door.

Reb Zundel tried one last time to appeal to Reb Berish's sense of cohesiveness which he knew he also valued, "No, Reb Berish, do not leave. Your secret is safe with me. Stay and together we may try to make some sense out of these strange and confused times, as Rabbi Yaakov insisted, together, together!" Rabbi Zundel stood exhausted and terribly distraught.

Reb Berish, though, approached Reb Zundel and embraced him. He then walked out the door and left Krasnystaw, never to return.

31

The holiday of Passover was only three weeks away. Since most of the town was busily preparing for the festival, it took many days for the news of Reb Berish's departure and speculation about his whereabouts to subside. Many were shocked and disappointed, others were quietly pleased.

Malka was readying herself for her wedding, which was due to take place later that day. Reb Mendel and Levi remained adamantly opposed to the messiah. Malka's father, Reb Shraga Feivish, continually swore the wedding would be canceled, and Malka would never be permitted to marry into that family. Nevertheless, Rabbi Yaakov had convinced him to allow it to proceed. Rabbi Yaakov informed Reb Shraga Feivish that while his reason for cancellation was novel indeed, there were no previous cases of similar revocation, and he would still be responsible to pay for all of the groom's wedding expenses and to return at least one half of the dowry. Reb Shraga Feivish was dismayed by Rabbi Yaakov's ruling but could not dispute it, Rabbi Yaakov was a believer as well and surely sought every avenue to vindicate his claim. Rabbi Yaakov, though, based his ruling on sound legal and halachic precedents and on his overarching desire to foster unity among the townspeople. Rabbi Yaakov could not accept preventing this wedding simply because the fathers of the bride and groom maintained philosophical differences. Rabbi Yaakov wished that Reb Mendel would have embraced the messiah by now but his refusal to do so was not valid grounds for canceling the wedding without any serious financial penalties. To enhance the relationship between the two families, Rabbi Yaakov extracted a pledge from Reb Shraga Feivish as well as from the groom's father, Reb Mendel, that neither of them would act toward the new couple with any animosity or hostility. Rabbi Yaakov did not want another family to experience the shame and heartache that plagued Yechiel and Tzipporah. Both fathers acquiesced to Rabbi Yaakov's pledge, set aside their personal differences and anticipated the wedding with excitement and optimism.

Malka cared little for the disputes of her father and Levi's father and dismissed them as the bickering common before all weddings. Her mother, Fraydel, helped her with the wedding dress, the same one Fraydel had worn at her own wedding. Malka looked quite beautiful. Her long black hair was neatly trimmed under a veil, which hid her face during the ceremony. Her dress was simple yet tasteful, decorated with buttons and ribbons. Like all brides she exuded a glow of happiness and contentment. Fraydel looked at Malka and announced that she was ready. Malka and Fraydel met Reb Shraga Feivish, who was waiting for them in the kitchen, and the three of them exited the house. Before walking toward the clearing where weddings were held, they proceeded to the cemetery to invite their departed relatives to this most joyous and meaningful event. Malka never knew her grandparents. All four had been killed by the Cossacks during the massacres. She was named after her mother's mother, who perished the year she was born. But Malka had always sensed their presence and their influences and was inspired by their sacrifice and their dedication.

Malka approached their graves solemnly. She moved carefully, avoiding the brush and wild shrubs that would soil her dress. Reb Shraga Feivish and Fraydel stood off to the side. They had already visited the day before and remained away from the site to afford Malka her privacy. Malka did not speak, she simply gazed at the gravestones, those harsh reminders of life's frailty and transience. She thought of her grandparents, of all the wonderful and warm stories that her parents had shared over the years. She knew they were special people and wished they could attend her wedding. She truly believed that their spirits would be there in some mystical sense and she was immediately filled with a sense of destiny. Malka perceived that not just her grandparents, but their parents and grandparents as well, would be present at the wedding. Her role as a future mother, the nurturer and provider of Jewish children, was so important, so vital to the continued existence of her people that all of the generations, stretching far back to the great Matriarch Sarah, would be present in some way, to guide her thoughts, provide her the inspiration and the wherewithal to brave any storm, to maintain the heritage despite the challenges and obstacles which would arise. Malka realized that she was the next in line, the immediate heir to a legacy so cherished, so honored and holy, which would perpetuate the traditions and laws of the Torah well into the future. She stood fully ready to accept that role and take her place among the daughters of Israel. Malka was so overcome by the importance of the moment, she could no longer contain her emotions and broke down in tears. Fraydel instinctively started toward her daughter but Reb Shraga Feivish held her back. This was a moment that needed to be experienced alone. Malka quickly ceased crying, contemplated one more time the legacy she would be continuing and turned to face her mother. Fraydel looked at her and smiled warmly. Malka returned the gesture and understood that her mother before her and virtually every bride on her wedding day is overwhelmed with similar feelings of destiny and duty.

All the town weddings took place at the clearing beside the synagogue. It was the only area large enough to accommodate all of the townspeople. The snows had melted to reveal a lush, grassy field. Like Malka and Levi, all couples were married after the cold winter was over. The small hill which led to the clearing was blooming with flowers, and small bushes and shrubs were scattered along the slope. In honor of the wedding, white ribbons delineated a path up to the clearing on the hill. In the center of the clearing stood four poles held by four youths to form a square, covered with a white cloth that served as a canopy. A small patch of cloth hung down near the front of the canopy and was exquisitely embroidered with alternating colors and designs. The poles were laced with white flowers and the top of the canopy was bedecked with flowers and white and purple ribbons. There was enough room under the canopy for about five people to stand, as well as room for a small table. At the edge of the clearing were several tables set with food and drinks.

Most of the town was already there; the men standing to the right of the canopy, the women to the left. Behind the canopy waited three talented violinists hired to entertain the guests and add to the festivities following the ceremony. One of the violinists, nicknamed "Moishe with his bag of tears" had an uncanny ability to play the violin with such skill that he could create the impression that the violin was crying and wailing. It was rumored that if he played long enough the violin would cry so sorrowfully, with such melodic force, that he could provoke the entire crowd to weep as well. In the midst of this sad, melancholy moment, Moishe was known to suddenly stop playing, pause for an instant, then resume playing, this time with the most lighthearted, enjoyable, happy, silly tune imaginable. The unexpected shift in tone and emotion would evoke mirth and laughter from the crowd, some of whom could not adjust to the change as quickly as Moishe and his violin. Many in the crowd found themselves laughing while still in tears! Moishe's nickname was well deserved and he was highly regarded.

When the townspeople arrived at the clearing and saw him waiting to play, they instantly forgot about all their strife and anticipated an afternoon of happiness and enjoyment, celebrating with the newlyweds.

Reb Mendel also hired a troupe of skilled and sharp-witted performers to compose lyrical poems about the bride, groom and their families, to sing and dance, and to stage a skit in honor of the young couple.

Rabbi Yaakov conducted the wedding ceremony. Levi was dressed in his finest clothes and looked older and more mature than his twenty years. He wore a serious expression and walked slowly, contemplatively to his position under the canopy, accompanied by his parents. Malka proceeded past the watching, curious crowd and stood next to Levi beneath the canopy, under the expanse of the immense, all-embracing sky. The couple faced Rabbi Yaakov, who sensed they were quite nervous. He smiled at them, nodded understandingly and reached for a goblet he had already filled with wine. Rabbi Yaakov lifted the cup and recited the blessings. He then turned toward Levi, who placed a ring on Malka's finger. He softly whispered to her, "You are hereby wed to me, according to the Laws of Moses and Israel." Rabbi Yaakov then offered the cup to Levi, who quickly took a sip. It was then passed to Malka who likewise drank and returned it to Rabbi Yaakov. Rabbi Yaakov intoned the remaining blessings, then placed a small empty glass on the ground near Levi's foot. Levi quickly stamped on it and it broke. This ritual symbolized the ancient Temple in Jerusalem that still lay in ruins. It reminded each person to always keep that tragedy and the ensuing uninterrupted exile foremost in their thoughts, even during these moments of supreme joy and elation. Some of the messiah's followers sought to abrogate this custom by pointing out that the Temple's reconstruction was now imminent. Rabbi Yaakov explicitly rejected that idea and preferred to maintain old and revered customs until the messiah himself had invalidated them. The breaking of the glass also heralded the completion of the ceremony. Levi and Malka were now married!

The new couple was escorted to their home not far from the clearing where they remained a short while, barely able to contain their happiness. They waited while some men hired by Reb Shraga Feivish removed the canopy and prepared the area for the festivities that would soon follow. Some of the weeds had already been removed and the ground in certain spots had been leveled. The couple returned about a half hour later and was greeted to cries and cheers of "Mazel Tov," "best wishes" and "welcome bride and groom." Levi and Malka appeared exuberant, almost ecstatic. Malka motioned to Levi, who turned then ran into the center of the crowd to initiate the festivities. "Moishe with his bag of tears" took Levi's cue and began to play a lively, boisterous tune. The two other players joined in creating a wonderful atmosphere of joy and good will. The women of the town moved off to the sides and afforded space for Levi and the men to dance in the center of the clearing. The performers likewise added to the merriment. They juggled hats and scarves while dancing, and performed acrobatics and marvelous stunts of jumping and tumbling, which delighted everyone. The celebration lasted many hours.

It was late afternoon with another hour of daylight left, more than enough time for the actors to perform one last time. Everyone in the town was thoroughly exhausted. Yet, the thought of additional entertainment from those talented and gifted performers was so compelling that no one left while they prepared in the forest just beyond the edge of the clearing. The past few hours seemed a dream; there had been no bickering, no insults hurled and no mistreatment by anyone. Since news of the messiah had reached this small, remote town there had been nothing but strife, disagreement and discord. But today, everyone forgot and for one brief afternoon, the town behaved in a cohesive and loving fashion, and it was difficult to discern that there was any ill feeling at all.

Would this continue?

Rabbi Yaakov was fully aware of the togetherness and congeniality that was evident and he hoped it would continue long after the wedding was over. He too waited for the performance with optimism and excitement.

No one knew the true names of the three performers. They were known only by their titles, Reb Pesach, Reb Succos and Reb Shavuos. Reb Pesach was the leader. He had a long, white beard with a black streak down the center. His distinct appearance was matched by his quick-witted humor and extraordinary ability to always speak in rhyme. Reb Succos was bald and always wore the most outlandish, colorful, funny hats ever seen. Reb Shavuos never spoke, it was rumored he had no tongue, yet his eyes were so wide and scintillating, and he made the most remarkable hand gestures. He did not need to speak to be understood. No one knew where the three of them lived or if they had families, but their fame was widespread throughout Poland.

A short while later the performers emerged from the forest, ready to perform one final act. The crowd stood in a large semicircle and made sure to leave enough space for the troupe to interact with each other. Levi, Malka and their families stood in the front with Rabbi Yaakov. Everyone immediately began cheering as the three performers approached. The final act that they performed was usually the most enjoyable. They already would have gained some insights into the townspeople and learned a little about them and their interests.

Reb Pesach announced they were ready to begin and everyone quickly grew quiet.

Reb Shavuos started pacing back and forth, hurriedly. He looked as if he were waiting for something. He turned his head in all directions, then reached into his pocket. He removed a watch, looked at the time, nodded then shrugged his shoulders. He repeated that about six or seven times, appearing more anxious and more impatient with each check of the time. Reb Succos stood quietly beside Reb Shavuos wearing a warrior's helmet. Suddenly, Reb Pesach appeared with a crown on his head, wearing a purple cloak. The moment he appeared, Reb Shavuos jumped in the air, threw the watch on the ground and began clapping excitedly. The crowd burst out laughing.

Reb Shavuos ran to Reb Pesach and kissed his hand. Reb Pesach acknowledged Reb Shavuos's display of respect and motioned for him to sit down.

"Yes, my son, you have waited quite long
For me to arrive and to sing you my song.
I am the messiah; there is nothing to fear.
I will rescue all the Jews from here!"

Reb Pesach quickly turned to the audience to try and gauge their reaction to his first rhyme. He knew from experience that the first rhyme set the tone for the remainder of the performance and if the audience appeared uninterested or even hostile there was still time to shift the focus of the act and proceed with an alternative one. Most of the audience was surprised that the troupe would parody something so controversial, so holy to some, so worthless to others, but Reb Pesach did not notice anything necessitating a change. He sensed they were curious and interested to see more of this performance. He moved toward Reb Succos and waited for him to speak. "What is your name, messiah?" asked Reb Succos, still wearing the battle helmet. Reb Pesach nodded and eagerly responded,

"Shabbetai Zevi is my name, I am fifty years old.
My prophet is Nathan, a man ever so bold.
Trust me and please listen to all that I say
I have taken the Torah and whittled it away!"

Again, Reb Shavuos clapped excitedly, almost sarcastically. Reb Pesach moved toward Reb Shavuos and looked at him disapprovingly,

"Do not clap, my son,
There is much work to be done
I must avenge all our sorrow
In a few days from tomorrow!
I will summon the sons of the ten lost tribes
To help me vanquish our enemies, we will not offer them bribes."

"I am ready to help and fight," exclaimed Reb Succos, positioning the helmet firmly on his head. Reb Succos bent down and retrieved a stick lying on the ground, then raised it above his head, as if it was a spear, "I am here to wage battle, to purify these lands from our enemies!" Reb Shavuos nodded and immediately picked up three sticks and began juggling them. Reb Succos scolded Reb Shavuos. "This is no time for games, dear brother, the hour of redemption is at hand!" Reb Shavuos maneuvered his juggling next to Reb Succos, threw the sticks in the air and allowed them to fall on Reb Succos' helmet. Reb Shavuos then picked up his watch and pointed to it while jumping up and down. The crowd burst out laughing, thoroughly enjoying the antics of Reb Shavuos, scarcely paying attention to the more serious performances of Reb Pesach and Reb Succos. Reb Shavuos held the watch in front of Reb Succos' face and shook his hand, grabbed Reb Succos' spear and waved it in the air, demonstrating that he too was battle ready.

Suddenly, Reb Succos turned to Reb Pesach. "What will happen when the battle is over, messiah? What shall become of us?"

"I am here to bring you to a different land,
That flows milk and honey, it is wonderful and grand!

But to get there, first you must be rid of your sins.
Roll around in the snow; stick your flesh with thorns and pins;
Experience penances that are harsh and cruel —
Then you may join me, that is my rule!"

Reb Shavuos immediately lay on the ground and began rolling around, mimicking the ritual performed by so many of the townspeople. He jerked his body a few times, as if he was in pain, then stood up and brushed off his clothes. Reb Succos approached Reb Shavuos, "Yes, my brother, you have done well. That it what the messiah demands, did it hurt?" Reb Shavuos nodded vigorously. "Good, continue this practice every night, it will bring you much success, if it doesn't maim you first! Now, I am exempt from such activities, I am preparing the battle!" Reb Succos turned to Reb Pesach, "Will you be accompanying us in battle, messiah?"

Reb Pesach responded,

"I am the messiah, that is quite true
And I have many things to do.
I must change many laws and abolish the fasts
And insure that my kingdom lasts and lasts.
The crown on my head in not just for show,
And to battle the enemies, I cannot go.
I told you before and I will tell you again
You will have an army of thousands of men.
They will punish and strike them, they surely will fall
Is that not the reason you have answered my call?"

Rabbi Yaakov was becoming increasingly uncomfortable due to the rhymes of Reb Pesach. They were insensitive and highly exaggerated, to the point where in his view the character of the messiah was grossly misrepresented. True, the messiah was accused of neglecting and abandoning important precepts of the Torah and it was rumored that he feasted on the Tenth of Teves, a day of fasting and mourning. Many followers and non-followers alike questioned whether the messiah, if he was the true messiah, had the authority to act that way. But the performance of these actors, and Reb Pesach's rhymes in particular, mocked the messiah in a most disparaging, condescending way. Reb Pesach implied the messiah randomly nullified or ignored certain precepts without careful consideration and judgment. Rabbi Yaakov found that insulting. He believed that any part of the Torah that the messiah had chosen was disregarded only following the most penetrating and careful analysis.

Rabbi Yaakov understood these performers did not believe in the messiah. If they did, they would not continue to further ridicule him in this derogatory manner. He stood quietly while they belittled the messiah's authority by mocking the changes he had instituted in Jewish law and custom, and they trivialized his arrival as nothing more than the hopes and wishes of desperation. Rabbi Yaakov was not sure how much more of this blasphemy he could watch. Reb Pesach and the ongoing performance also incensed the other followers of the messiah. Some started to move off to the side and refused to watch. Others were truly enthralled and despite the contempt which the performers displayed, clung to the belief that they would soon end this nasty presentation and admit their unyielding allegiance to the messiah.

Those members of the town who refused to follow the messiah, such as Reb Mendel, Levi and Tzipporah, the wife of Yechiel, found the troupe brilliant. Reb Mendel did not hire them to satirize the messiah; the troupe never revealed their repertoire in advance and Reb Mendel was unaware these secretive men even knew anything about the messiah. But he found their performance encouraging. Three obviously unlearned men believed the whole idea of the man who claimed to be the messiah so implausible that they saw no reason not to parody it. The troupe's presentation exposed the messiah's disrespect for the cherished and holy Torah and revealed the serious sins the messiah already committed. Reb Mendel was certain the performers would convince many of the townspeople to renounce their faith in him and continue to wait for the true messiah with patience and zeal.

Reb Succos removed the helmet from his head and immediately replaced it with a turban. He then announced, "I am the sultan, ruler of the Arab world! Who are you?" Reb Succos pointed to Reb Pesach as he spoke in a stern, regal voice.

"I am the new king of the Jews,

I am here to tell you some wonderful news!" replied Reb Pesach.

"What makes you a king?" laughed Reb Succos, "Is it your crown? Guard, loosen that crown and bring it to me!" Reb Shavuos, now acting as the Sultan's guard, rushed to Reb Pesach and quickly plucked the crown off his head. Reb Shavuos then placed it on his own head and began dancing wildly. "Look!" shouted Reb Succos, "now my guard is the messiah!" Reb Shavuos grabbed Reb Succos' hand and proceeded to dance with him while Reb Pesach stood with his head lowered. After a few moments the two of them stopped dancing and Reb Succos retrieved the crown from Reb Shavuos. He held it and faced Reb Pesach. "This crown is a worthless piece of metal. You cannot even rule over beggars with it if they do not accept your authority. Tell me, messiah, where is your authority?"

Reb Pesach looked up and quickly retorted,

"The Jews have waited so very long
For the savior to come and sing them this song.
And now they have reached the end of the rope –
Without me to save them, they will lose all hope!"

Reb Shavuos immediately bent down and appeared as if he was looking for something. He moved very slowly, examining each spot on the ground, each clump of earth. He continued searching, and it was quite clear he did not find what he was looking for. He eventually bumped into Reb Pesach who remained stationary while Reb Shavuos acted out this latest antic. Reb Shavuos looked up, saw Reb Pesach and instantly wore a face of relief and comfort as if he had been looking for Reb Pesach all along. He jumped up, hugged Reb Pesach and although he did not utter a word, he never did, his expressions were abundantly clear. Reb Pesach represented the hope Reb Shavuos feared had been lost.

Reb Succos folded his arms across his chest, imitating a monarch ready to scold one of his servants. He continued to press Reb Pesach, "Your arrogance is quite surprising. You may not force history, messiah! You cannot insist on the freedom of your People. You cannot make demands of G-d!"

Rabbi Yaakov could not believe Reb Succos just slandered the messiah by hinting that he was unworthy to rescue the Jewish People but would somehow coerce fate nonetheless. He was particularly bothered by their assertions that the only reason the messiah and his movement had any momentum at all was because the people had grown so miserably desperate. He found the entire attitude of these players highly offensive, almost heretical, and would not allow it to continue. He did not wish to interfere with the wedding celebration, or Reb Mendel's decision to hire these performers, but he resolved that if they uttered another word of denigration or humiliation he would demand they cease at once.

Reb Pesach sensed that many in the audience were growing weary of their act, especially Reb Shavuos's enactments of his rhymes. The skit had been going on for almost a half hour and it was starting to become tiresome. Reb Pesach was also mindful that as the plot unfolded more and more people turned away and refused to watch. He knew he only had a few more rhymes left and he was certain the remaining crowd and Reb Mendel, the man paying him for his performance, would not object to a grand and hilarious finale. The play would be over in a few moments.

Reb Pesach turned to Reb Succos and appeared sad and dejected, as if he conceded the illegitimacy of his kingship. Reb Pesach had rehearsed some rhymes, which joked about Reb Succos' authority as the sultan. The performance was supposed to end with both of them arguing endlessly whether a crown or a turban was more befitting a ruler. Instead, Reb Pesach suddenly thought of something else to say, alternative rhymes which further continued the scorn and ridicule. His quick wit allowed him to compose the lines just moments before he actually recited them, surprising the entire crowd, including Reb Succos and Reb Shavuos who were astonished by the ingenuity of their comrade. Reb Pesach could not explain why he chose to offer a different ending to the one they rehearsed but the moment he uttered it, he knew he had made a terrible mistake.

"Well, sultan, if you think I am too bold
After all that you have been told;

That all my efforts have been in vain
To try to force an end to the suffering and pain.
If you insist that I am a fake
And the title 'messiah,' I may not take
And the persecutions will continue for many more years
And the people must endure more pain and tears;
If there is nothing that I can do,
To alleviate the despair of every Jew
Then I want no part of a Jewish life!
No Torah, no laws or libels or strife,
No hatred, no persecutions, crusades or wars
I will abandon my religion and happily embrace yours!"

Reb Pesach approached Reb Succos, removed the turban and placed it on his own head, eerily foreshadowing Shabbetai Zevi's ultimate betrayal. Reb Succos was startled by his cohort's impromptu declaration. Reb Pesach had altered the endings of their performances before, but never with a speech so shocking and facetious and for a moment Reb Succos lost his sharpness and was frozen, unable to offer any rejoinder. He quickly glanced at Reb Shavuos, hoping he could execute one more animated and lighthearted stunt, to distract everyone from the awkwardness that was quickly developing. Reb Shavuos sensed he needed to do something and started clapping.

Rabbi Yaakov was infuriated. He had watched three ignorant men disparage and impugn the holy messiah. He could no longer contain himself, he was filled with so much disappointment and anger. "Get away from here!" shouted Rabbi Yaakov. "We do not want you to perform anymore! We have seen enough heresy for one afternoon!"

Reb Mendel was standing a short distance away from Rabbi Yaakov and quickly drew toward him. "I have paid a very substantial fee for this group of performers and they will leave when they have finished. You may not demand they step away from here one moment before they have completed their performance!"

"I am quite sorry, Reb Mendel, but I will not tolerate their sacrilegious and disrespectful conduct. They have no place in my town!"

Rabbi Yaakov sounded angrier than anyone could remember. He turned toward them again, "Go home! Leave here at once!"

Reb Mendel was adamant, "No, Reb Pesach, finish your act, we are in no rush to see the three of you leave!"

Someone shouted, "Leave immediately, you are not welcome in our town!" Another cried, "Do not listen to that, you may go when you are finished!" Soon almost every member of the town was shouting toward the troupe, ordering them to leave or to stay. The three players were not sure what to do. The longer they remained there they feared they might be harmed.

Reb Mendel raised his voice louder than everyone else's. "Please, I have hired them and I have paid them already. Let them finish and then they will go!" A moment later someone came from behind Reb Mendel and, defending the honor of the messiah, struck him in the back. Reb Mendel instantly fell to the ground and the wedding descended into chaos.

It was midnight, the clearing was empty, the crowd had dispersed after the verbal and physical disputes subsided. It took many hours for everyone to come to their senses and by then it was too late. Too much was said, too many fists were hurled, too many friendships broken. It was surely the worst day in the history of Krasnystaw, far worse than any day Krasnystaw was ravaged by Poles or the dreaded Cossacks. Today, the town finally realized in the most stark and real terms that they were enemies with themselves.

Levi and Malka returned to the clearing. They had stolen away when the eruption began and walked away from it all, it was no place for them. Now they came back and gazed at each other, beneath the sky that earlier had witnessed their union. They understood their new marriage was now sullied by the insensitivity and stubbornness of the town they had known all their lives. Their life together in Krasnystaw would lack the blessings and heartfelt wishes that friends and loved ones always impart to new couples. They would now be forced to live the rest of their lives together under the shadow of strife and discord and disagreement. They would have to live with the knowledge that their wedding sparked animosity that might never subside. It was present on their wedding day and their years of togetherness would be spent combating those horrible and destructive events. Their emotions, their tempers, their disagreements would always be measured by the odious and inexcusable dissension which inaugurated their life together. The heritage and legacy they were destined to develop and perpetuate was now in serious jeopardy. They would forever be judged by this day. It would continue to plague them, test their dedication to each other, raise the specter that they were doomed for marital hostility. They could not remain in the town that brought this upon them. They could not shoulder this challenge while walking the streets and visiting the homes of the town that had desecrated their marriage. They took one last look at the town of their youth, the town they desperately needed to escape. They did not tell their friends or their families and shortly before dawn they slipped away.

32

Reb Zundel sat at the table in the sitting room, his head lowered in shame. He had barely moved the entire night. He kept reliving the events at the clearing. He was the one who had struck Reb Mendel! He could not explain what had prompted him to act in that provocative and confrontational manner. He was so totally incensed by Reb Mendel's attempts to allow the blasphemy to continue that his rage just overpowered him, causing him to lunge at Reb Mendel. He was certain no one in the town knew it was he, nothing was said to him the rest of the evening, and he heard repeated declarations that the assailant was still unknown. Yet, now that it was over, he deeply regretted it. He still maintained that what Reb Pesach had said was unforgivable but he knew he should have behaved with greater restraint, greater self control. What bothered him more than the irreverence of Reb Pesach and the rest of the town who had enjoyed the performance was the horrible schism he precipitated. True, the disagreements among the town members had worsened over the past few months, but it had never fallen to the shocking depths which his zeal had exposed. Reb Zundel understood that his efforts to heal the wounds of the town had ended in miserable failure.

Reb Zundel was unsure what to do. Confront Reb Mendel? Apologize to the entire town? Leave in disgrace without waiting for Velvel to recover? Reb Zundel was numbed by the rashness of his attack and knew that if he did not do something quickly, the town's pain and acrimony would forever rest on his shoulders. He suddenly heard someone stirring quietly. Had Velvel awakened? He rushed to Velvel's bed only to observe him still in a prolonged slumber. A moment later, Chana appeared.

"Were you up all night, Reb Zundel?" queried Chana.

"Yes, Chana, I could not sleep, I could not stop thinking about what happened yesterday," answered Reb Zundel tensely.

"It was truly terrible, but why is it affecting you so personally?" asked Chana, puzzled by the depth of Reb Zundel's remorse.

Reb Zundel knew his wife was unaware of his complicity. She surely would have confronted him if she suspected it was his fault. He considered confiding in her and seeking her guidance but he was afraid she would not understand him and refuse to forgive him. He answered her very carefully, "I am terribly distraught thinking about the man who struck Reb Mendel. Do you suppose he regrets it?" Reb Zundel waited, seeking to discern if his wife would be forgiving toward the aggressor.

"I do not understand why you think about that man at all!" protested Chana. "That man, whoever he is, should suffer the wrath of this town for a hundred years! He has foiled any hope of reconciliation, any harmony that Rabbi Yaakov and people like you were trying to foster here. He will receive no pity from me!"

Reb Zundel was surprised that his wife spoke so adamantly. "I agree he acted rashly and impetuously, but do you think after witnessing what took place that he would do it again if the chance arose?" Reb Zundel sounded conciliatory, almost forgiving.

"I am not sure, Reb Zundel, but I know that he has destroyed this town and no one but the messiah can save it now! Please, Reb Zundel, there is still some time before morning services, try and get some sleep."

"Alright, Chana, I will." Reb Zundel moved toward his bed, still unsure what to do.

Throughout the town everyone was reviewing the regrettable events that followed the wedding ceremony of Levi and Malka. Reb Mendel was so distraught he could barely contain his emotions. The bruise on his back healed quickly but he felt so betrayed, so abandoned by a town he lived in his entire life. He was also agitated that Levi and Malka were nowhere to be found. He even visited his nemesis, Reb Shraga Feivish, thinking that perhaps the couple were secluded there. Reb Shraga Feivish and Reb Mendel agreed to set aside their differences and focus their efforts on finding their children. They would search for close to three weeks, until the night before Passover when a letter sent by the couple was delivered. It said that they had settled in Podolia, near Bessarabia. Both Reb Mendel and Reb Shraga Feivish wondered why they chose to live in a place so remote from their hometown. Neither of them could comprehend that they wanted to escape all the fighting, all the disappointment.

The moment Reb Mendel and Reb Shraga Feivish discovered the whereabouts of their children, they resumed their feud and ceased speaking to one another.

Rabbi Yaakov too, was consumed with disappointment. He truly believed his impassioned speech would generate feelings of understanding and companionship but now realized the town was seriously divided. He blamed the attacker for causing this final eruption but knew full well it most likely would have occurred anyway. Rabbi Yaakov believed the only thing he could do was wait for the messiah himself to come and end all this strife. Rabbi Yaakov again turned his attention to the real cause behind the events at the wedding and every other dispute in town: the messiah. Who was the messiah? Was his arrival supposed to engender this hostility, this hatred among Jews? Why was his arrival delayed for so long? Was he weak? Cowardly? This led Rabbi Yaakov to ask the same question, that nagging question that plagued every thinking Jew. Was the messiah authentic? Rabbi Yaakov believed in him and was not yet willing to forswear that belief. The messiah would arrive soon, of that he was certain, but what was he do to for the town in the meantime?

Was there any hope at all that everyone in Krasnystaw could reach some sort of reconciliation and present a united front to welcome the messiah? Rabbi Yaakov wondered whether his questions would ever be answered. He walked to the synagogue slowly.

About two weeks after the wedding, following morning services, Rabbi Yaakov turned to enter his study and spend a few moments learning Talmud before returning home. As he reached for the door he was met by Reb Zundel.

"Good morning, Rabbi Yaakov. Do you have a few moments for us to speak privately? There is something I must discuss with you," asked Reb Zundel urgently. Rabbi Yaakov was aware Reb Zundel's son was still hovering on the brink of consciousness and presumed he wished to talk about a possible cure or ask if he knew any doctors in Lublin or Chelm who could possibly offer additional remedies.

"Of course, Reb Zundel, come with me." Rabbi Yaakov opened the door to his study and Reb Zundel followed him inside.

Reb Zundel had not been in the study in many months, since before Rosh Hashanah when he had gone there with Chana, Hershel and Velvel to wish the rabbi well for the coming new year. Reb Zundel was relieved that it still looked the same; some things in Krasnystaw refused to change no matter how much time passed. It still contained all the old and worn out religious items from the original synagogue and there were books still stacked throughout the room. The original small ark still stood in the same spot, covered with the same burlap cloth. Rabbi Yaakov sat down at his desk and motioned for Reb Zundel to sit in one of the chairs he hurriedly cleared of books. Reb Zundel took his seat and appeared nervous and anxious.

"Reb Zundel, allow me to inquire about your son, is he improving?" asked Rabbi Yaakov, concerned.

"There is no real change in his condition. He has awakened many times but he is never truly conscious. When he awakens I quickly feed him to sustain his body. He usually falls back into a prolonged slumber moments later," bemoaned Reb Zundel. "But Count Podolski has visited several times and insists that Velvel's chances for a complete recovery remain high. We continue to wait and pray," retorted Reb Zundel, optimistically.

"My thoughts and prayers are with you, Reb Zundel. I heard that without the miracle which occurred his condition would have been far worse!"

"Thank you for your kind words, Rabbi Yaakov, although I hardly believe a miracle took place," snapped Reb Zundel.

"Do not be so quick to dismiss that a miracle saved your son, Reb Zundel. They take place every day, we just don't always see them!" answered Rabbi Yaakov philosophically.

"Yes, Rabbi Yaakov," returned Reb Zundel methodically. "But that is not why I am here. I wish to speak with you about a different matter entirely." Rabbi Zundel sounded mysterious and greatly intrigued Rabbi Yaakov. He was excited that perhaps someone in town wished to discuss something other than the messiah and he could temporarily dissociate himself from that whole issue. Rabbi Yaakov was hoping Reb Zundel's question related to the upcoming Passover holiday, about unleavened bread perhaps, or a fowl whose kashrus was questionable. Rabbi Yaakov felt such questions would be a refreshing change from the repetitive inquires which seemed to occupy the minds of almost every town member.

"Yes, Reb Zundel, how may I help you?" Rabbi Yaakov waited for Reb Zundel's question with great anticipation.

Reb Zundel turned pale and stood up. He had decided to speak with Rabbi Yaakov during the morning services and was still not sure it was the correct course of action. He had not had time to formulate his thoughts and feared that Rabbi Yaakov would misunderstand him and reject him, or worse, excommunicate him altogether. But he decided that he would confide in Rabbi Yaakov and accept any shame or punishment with wholehearted maturity. He would no longer hide from his wrongdoing. He faced Rabbi Yaakov. "I am sorry, Rabbi Yaakov, I am deeply sorry for what I have done. I acted foolishly and impulsively and I have squandered any chance at all!"

Rabbi Yaakov was baffled. "Reb Zundel, what are you talking about?"

"I struck Reb Mendel at the clearing the other day, I started it all!" Reb Zundel turned away from Rabbi Yaakov and began to weep.

Rabbi Yaakov remained seated and stared blankly at Reb Zundel. He did not believe him and suspected Reb Zundel confessed merely to protect his son. "I do not believe you, Reb Zundel, I do not believe a man of your demeaner and temperament could have done it. Are you trying to protect someone, your son, Hershel, perhaps?"

Reb Zundel was shocked. Rabbi Yaakov refused to believe him. "I insist, Rabbi Yaakov, I truly did it. I became so enraged by Reb Mendel's continued endorsement of that performance that I lost all control and instinctively lunged toward him. I truly regret what I have done! Rabbi Yaakov, you have known me for a very long time, and you must know that I am telling you the truth!"

Rabbi Yaakov witnessed the shame and pain of Reb Zundel and realized Reb Zundel was indeed being truthful and was now trying to rectify his lapse. Rabbi Yaakov understood there would be nothing gained by any further reproach or condemnation. Reb Zundel was fully aware of the imprudence of his actions and the continued distress and ill will it engendered. Rabbi Yaakov had all but conceded that following the wedding, nothing could ever heal the town, nothing could bridge the misunderstandings which tore it apart. Krasnystaw was doomed. Reb Zundel's revelation gave him cause for hope. He now saw that an accord was possible. Krasnystaw could be brought back to the way it was before there was any news of a messiah, when the goals and dreams of each townsman were shared and supported by everyone else. Rabbi Yaakov continued to stare at Reb Zundel and knew that he was the answer. Only the man who had precipitated the disastrous calamity could somehow yet salvage them.

"Reb Zundel, you have witnessed the dissension and discord in the town. I am certain you are aware that many fights have erupted, even prior to yesterday's explosion."

"Yes, I was involved in one already, but I have come to an agreement and an understanding with my daughter and son-in-law. There is no longer any animosity between us," said Reb Zundel proudly.

"I am happy to hear that and I would like to see similar changes from all the townspeople," retorted Rabbi Yaakov.

"I agree with you, Rabbi Yaakov. That is the reason I reunited with my family and that is why I chose to become a believer in the messiah. He will not arrive if we are not united!"

"You are quite right, Reb Zundel, and what took place the other day only seemed to pull the town further and further apart."

"Yes, I know, that is the most distressing result of my impulsive conduct," lamented Reb Zundel.

Rabbi Yaakov understood that Reb Zundel truly regretted his actions and was confident he would consent to his plan. He drew closer to Reb Zundel and spoke earnestly, almost desperately. "But you may be able to change all that, appeal to their divisive and confrontational urges. Of all people, Reb Zundel, no one better represents the contentiousness of the town than you. No one better than you epitomizes the stark anger and animosity that has devastated the town. And you are the only one who can plead for a return to understanding and friendship, finally convince them to cease all this hostility and embrace each other with harmony and kindness. I am asking you to confess your deed in front of the entire town and implore them to follow your example of feelings of remorse and regret. You will further sway them to put aside their petty differences about the messiah and to remain united as long as the exile continues. I tried to convey that to them once and failed. But you are different, you are one of them. In fact you best exemplify the violence as well as sincere remorse and they will connect with you, hopefully understand you and ultimately listen to you. Reb Zundel, I believe you are Krasnystaw's only hope."

Reb Zundel saw Rabbi Yaakov's exasperation and acknowledged that the future of Krasnystaw lay with him. He once promised he would act tirelessly to help heal the wounds of the town and now he would honor that promise. It would cause him much embarrassment and shame but he would suffer any disgrace, endure any humiliation. Reb Zundel knew it would be difficult and he pitied Chana, who would also have to bear her share of the reproach, of the degradation and indignity. But he was convinced this selfless act would finally unite the town, finally succeed where all others attempts failed and he was confident Chana would acquiesce. He turned to Rabbi Yaakov. "Yes, Rabbi Yaakov, I will do it!"

Rabbi Yaakov was ecstatic. "Thank you, Reb Zundel. We have taken the first step in restoring the town!"

Suddenly there was a loud, almost violent knock on the door. Rabbi Yaakov hurried and instantly opened it. Hershel rushed in and ran to Reb Zundel. "Come quick, Father, Velvel has recovered!"

Reb Zundel sped back to his home overcome with excitement. It had been so long since Velvel fell ill and so much had changed. He had reconciled with Gittel and Zalman, was now a believer in the messiah and was about to set aside all feelings of personal pride and family honor for the sake of the town. Surely Velvel would be delighted with all these changes!

Reb Zundel burst into the house and ran to Velvel's bed. Count Podolski was busy examining Velvel who was sitting up and coughing softly. Count Podolski motioned for Reb Zundel to wait until he finished and resumed his examination. Velvel looked pale and sleepy but Reb Zundel was so relieved that Velvel had recovered, he barely gave any thought to his weakened condition. He could not wait to speak with him and tell him all that happened while he was incapacitated. After about a half hour Count Podolski announced that Velvel would soon recover fully and that he needed additional rest before he could leave the bed. Reb Zundel would now be permitted to speak with him. Reb Zundel thanked the Count and escorted him outside.

Reb Zundel rushed to the bed, eager to embrace his son. He lowered himself and softly placed his arms around Velvel's body and whispered that he was happy to see him.

"Yes, Father, it is wonderful to see you as well. Has anything happened here in town over the past few months?" asked Velvel, lethargically.

Reb Zundel smiled. He was eager to inform Velvel of the many new developments which recently took place. He sat on a chair near the bed and told Velvel everything that happened since his accident. He was confident Velvel would be excited by all the news and waited anxiously for his response.

Velvel began speaking but quickly grew tired and could not raise his voice at all. Reb Zundel found himself unable to hear his son. Reb Zundel bent down and placed his ear near Velvel's lips to allow Velvel to speak softly. Velvel sat up and positioned himself in front of his father. He leaned forward and whispered to him, "Father, please do not be disappointed. You are a good and sincere man. I understand your enthusiasm and excitement, I once felt the same way. But now I know the messiah is false. He will not rescue us, he will not save us from this exile. I have spent the past two months on the brink, tottering between life and death, between sleep and awareness, and I possess insights now I never dreamed of. I perceived truths that are unmistakable, indisputable. I experienced a calmness which any healthy person can never imagine. In that moment of absolute clarity I fathomed his falseness, his blasphemy, his insincerity. That man is no messiah and his followers are doomed to disappointment and sorrow. Please, Father, do not be angry with me. I understand why you cling to him, I once felt the same way. I fully appreciate the lure of his attraction and I do so wish that he could rescue us from here and bring us to Jerusalem in glory and triumph. But he is not the one. We must wait a little longer, we must continue to brave the world and all its hatred until the true messiah, inspired by G-d, filled with a deep sense of respect and understanding for the Torah, will come and rescue us. I am sorry, Father."

Velvel felt too weak to remain sitting and slouched down to resume his rest. Reb Zundel was stunned by Velvel's transformation and wondered if perhaps he was unaware of what he just said. Perhaps he had not yet recovered all of his mental faculties. "But Velvel, only a short while ago you were such a fervent believer in him! Could you have changed your beliefs so quickly? Do you realize what you are saying? Are you still suffering some effects of the injury? Yes!" exclaimed Reb Zundel, "That must be the answer. Rest awhile and we shall discuss this again when you regain more of your strength and are refreshed and coherent." Reb Zundel sounded desperate.

"There is nothing the matter with me, Father. I have had over a month to consider this change. It was not sudden at all. I apologize again for disappointing you." Velvel grew solemn and with great effort, sat up once again. "Life brings many unexpected events, Father. I disappointed you when I believed in the messiah. Now I disappoint you because I no longer believe. I imagine this town is now full of disappointment, doubt, frustration and hesitation, and those feelings will surely increase following the messiah's downfall."

33

News quickly spread that Reb Zundel would soon be addressing the entire town. Everyone understood that some sort of discussion or speech was necessary. The town was estranged and no reconciliation seemed possible, but everyone questioned why it fell to Reb Zundel to try. The town was as yet unaware of Reb Zundel's role at the wedding. They assumed he was selected because he was a distinguished member of the town and he might succeed where Rabbi Yaakov had already failed.

Most town members were eager to hear from Reb Zundel, a man well liked and respected, and regardless of how he felt about the messiah, would engender understanding and compassion. Everyone was fully aware of Reb Zundel's recent transformation. This only added to his stature as a man of integrity, willing to change and adapt to new ideas if he truly believed in them. Even the opponents of the messiah were hopeful that Reb Zundel could somehow speak to them as well, encourage them to tolerate each other and finally end the animosity and antagonism infecting the town. They too were shocked by their own conduct and understood that what had happened at the wedding was unacceptable.

Reb Zundel was thoroughly confused. He agreed to speak to the town, atone for his precipitous and violent nature and especially apologize to Reb Shraga Feivish and Reb Mendel for ruining an otherwise glorious day. He also believed that only he could best save the town from further upheaval. But Velvel's revelation worried him. Was Velvel speaking the truth? Had Velvel seen matters with clarity and precision while he lay unconscious? Was the messiah indeed an imposter? Was Velvel's prediction plausible? Would the frustration reach unmanageable proportions? Reb Zundel was unsure. He realized that Velvel had been dead to the world for quite some time and could have spoken sheer nonsense. He also realized that when the soul wavers between life and death it often glimpses truths that are withheld from ordinary men. He wondered whether Velvel spoke as a messenger, sent to warn the town to avoid all contact and familiarity with the messiah or any of his followers. Perhaps the truth lay in his own home and he was oblivious of its presence! Perhaps Velvel was that sign, that omen and signal that everyone was waiting for! Perhaps he awoke at this particular moment to provide encouragement and strength to all those divisive townsmen.

Reb Zundel needed to question Velvel further, discern how Velvel could state with such authority that the messiah was a fraud and ascertain what had led Velvel to that conclusion. Reb Zundel knew he could never question his son alone. He knew nothing about the mystical place Velvel's soul resided while his body lay unconscious. He did not know where to begin examining the truth of his assertions. He wished Reb Berish were still in Krasnystaw. He would know best how to question Velvel, interpret his responses and facial expressions and discover if he spoke the truth. Reb Zundel suddenly grew excited and apprehensive. He needed to find someone sufficiently skilled in the mystical teachings who could speak with Velvel and travel with Velvel to that place between life and death where all is absolute and the truth cannot be questioned. Who to turn to? Surely not Rabbi Yaakov, he was well versed in mysticism and Kabbalah but he would too quickly reject Velvel's insights as the rambles of illness. Reb Zundel knew he could only confide in his son-in-law, Zalman.

Zalman was very pious and well-versed in many mystical teachings. Also, Velvel would feel quite comfortable talking with him. Reb Zundel was confident that even though Zalman firmly believed in the messiah he would objectively listen to Velvel. If he believed Velvel spoke the truth he would then acknowledge his error wholeheartedly. Reb Zundel knew there was a possibility Velvel's declaration might be the unfortunate machinations of a mind that had been oblivious to everything for over a month. But Reb Zundel could leave nothing to conjecture, he needed to be absolutely certain. He hurried to Zalman.

Rabbi Yaakov greatly anticipated Reb Zundel's efforts to save the town. He heard that Velvel had recovered and was sure that would encourage Reb Zundel to speak with greater affection, no longer hindered by the burden of the incapacity of his beloved son. Rabbi Yaakov even decided to relinquish the podium on the Sabbath before Passover, the time of the traditional "Great Sabbath" lecture, and allow Reb Zundel to speak during that most coveted and honored time of year. He believed that gesture would further emphasize the importance of Reb Zundel's speech. Rabbi Yaakov was confident Reb Zundel would succeed where he had not.

There was only one thing that continued to trouble him. He had learned that two days earlier Tzipporah, the wife of Yechiel, had left Krasnystaw with their three children. She had issued an ultimatum whereby she promised to leave town if her husband did not abandon the fasts by the first day of the month of Nissan, two weeks before Passover. That day came and went and she implored Rabbi Yaakov to urge Yechiel to grant her a divorce. Rabbi Yaakov consented to meet with Yechiel and order him, on pain of excommunication, to forego the fasts for the sake of marital unity. Rabbi Yaakov arrived at the home and was shocked to see Yechiel in bed starving, too weak to object or even to talk with Rabbi Yaakov. Rabbi Yaakov explained that Yechiel could not grant a divorce in his condition, he was barely conscious. He informed Tzipporah that he would order Count Podolski to the home immediately and begin the process of nourishing him back to health. Tzipporah agreed and waited for the doctor.

The following day, Tzipporah returned to Rabbi Yaakov and informed him that she could not tolerate the situation any longer and she was leaving. She explained that Count Podolski had examined Yechiel and discovered the primary reason for his condition was not his refusal to eat but his recent habit of consuming vinegar and soap, which further damaged his digestive system and harmed him irreparably. Tzipporah explained there was no longer any hope her husband would return to his senses. She bade the Rabbi farewell, thanked him for his tireless efforts to reunite them and left with her three children.

Rabbi Yaakov spoke with Count Podolski, who explained that Yechiel was gravely ill. He related that he would continue to treat him but was unsure if he would be successful. Rabbi Yaakov thanked him and urged him to continue the treatments. He clung to the hope that perhaps Tzipporah would return.

Rabbi Yaakov conceded this was the one dispute he could not resolve, the one disagreement he could not settle amicably. He was greatly distressed that Yechiel had harmed himself to such a grave extent and was even more upset that it led to the dissolution of a family. Rabbi Yaakov considered it a grave tragedy and believed that only the conciliation efforts of Reb Zundel could prevent further calamities from taking place. Rabbi Yaakov now attributed even greater importance to Reb Zundel's speech.

Reb Zundel held his grandson while he waited for Zalman. The child was sleeping but Reb Zundel continued to embrace the babe, unwilling to part with that innocence, that glow of contentment. He cherished these moments and bemoaned that he did not experience enough of them.

Suddenly Zalman entered and indicated he was ready. He did not know why his father-in-law needed him so urgently but had readily agreed to help him. He gently took the child from Reb Zundel and quietly laid him down in the crib. The two men left and proceeded to Reb Zundel's home. "Zalman, did you have an opportunity to visit Velvel since he recovered?" asked Reb Zundel, seeking to inform Zalman about the nature of this visit.

"Gittel and I visited him the other day. He looks quite strong. I am sure he will be permitted to leave the house in a matter of days!"

"I believe you are correct. Count Podolski will be visiting tomorrow and if Velvel exhibits renewed strength and vigor he will no longer be confined to his bed." Reb Zundel sounded anxious and relieved. Suddenly Reb Zundel turned serious. "Did you discuss the messiah with Velvel when you visited him?"

"No, I did not mention it on purpose; I did not want to excite him and possibly weaken his condition," answered Zalman.

"That is admirable, Zalman. However, I must insist that you now speak with Velvel about *him*. Velvel has much to say which is interesting and frightening. I am not learned and skilled enough to know whether he speaks the truth, that is why I invited you. I need you to speak with Velvel, to listen attentively to him, to question him and delve into the nature of what he says. Then I need to hear your opinion," said Reb Zundel nervously.

Zalman stopped walking and turned to Reb Zundel, "What are you talking about? What has Velvel said that you do not understand? Why do you need me?" Zalman looked puzzled.

"You will soon find out."

The two men entered the home and Reb Zundel led Zalman to Velvel's bedside. Velvel was sitting up resting quietly. "Hello, Zalman," whispered Velvel. "I believe I am a bit stronger since the other day. I hope to be up and about by the end of the week. I hear Father will be speaking this Sabbath and that is something I do not wish to miss! I am certain Count Podolski will grant me permission to attend services this Sabbath," said Velvel with pride and admiration.

"Yes, the whole town is talking about it," beamed Zalman. "I heard that Rabbi Yaakov will permit your Father to speak during the afternoon, when the rabbi generally delivers his lecture in honor of the "Great Sabbath." What your Father has to say must be quite important!" Zalman then turned to Reb Zundel, "Why were you chosen to address the town?"

"I am not sure myself," answered Reb Zundel avoiding the truth. "But I hope the town will find it inspirational and interesting. I have begun working on it already. I only have four days left! Now I shall leave the two of you alone while I resume my preparations for the speech." Reb Zundel turned and left Velvel and Zalman together. He sat down at the large table. He was able to glimpse the back of Zalman, who was bent over and listening intently to Velvel. Reb Zundel waited.

One hour had passed before Zalman approached Reb Zundel. His face was white and he appeared crestfallen. Reb Zundel quickly stood up and Zalman embraced him and began to cry. "Why did you bring me here? Why did you insist that I speak with him? Why did you destroy my expectations? He speaks the truth! There is no doubt about it, he speaks the truth! What will happen now? More waiting? I cannot accept that! Oh, why did you bring me here?" Zalman continued to sob.

Reb Zundel understood the torment of his son-in-law; he had had a similar reaction when he had first spoken with Velvel. But Reb Zundel knew that Zalman would come to appreciate that he was brought there not merely to confirm if Velvel was correct but also to become aware of the truth before the pain would become too great to bear. Zalman, who was a more ardent follower than either Velvel or Reb Zundel, found the news particularly difficult to accept, but even he could not deny it. Velvel had seen things. Those deathly ill are privileged to many secrets, and Zalman was convinced beyond all doubt that this messiah was a fraud. Reb Zundel suspected this would happen and sought to comfort Zalman. "Are you certain, dear Zalman, could you have possibly made a mistake?"

"There is no mistake," wailed Zalman. "Your son speaks only the truth, his mind is clear and precise! He has revealed to me many secrets, all of which confirm the messiah is false. I am so sorry the redemption will be further delayed, but what am I to do, it is the will of G-d!" Zalman thanked Reb Zundel and ran home to share the news with Gittel.

"What is the matter?" asked a concerned Gittel as she observed the ghastly look on the face of her husband.

Zalman was unsure how to tell her. She would be so heartbroken, so despondent. He knew he could not keep it from her but he wished to tell her while she was calm and relaxed and would have the ability to focus and concentrate. "Where is Shabbetai?"

"He is sleeping and Golda is watching him. We may talk without fear of interruption. Zalman, what is wrong?"

Zalman confided to Gittel all that had transpired at her father's home. He did not reveal the specific secrets which Velvel had disclosed, she would not understand them. But he stressed that he believed the messiah was false. He observed Gittel's eyes begin to well with tears and quickly sought to calm her. "Do not be distraught, Gittel. I too cried when I first spoke with Velvel but I have had some time to make sense of it all and I now see it as a blessing. It was far better to learn of it now than at some later date! We shall overcome this unfortunate setback as well and continue to wait for the true redemption."

Gittel trusted her husband's judgment but admitted it would take time for her to come to terms with this revelation. Zalman agreed that it could not happen overnight, it would take months, perhaps years.

Golda had been listening carefully as Zalman and Gittel spoke and she had heard every word. She was a follower of the messiah and did not believe anything Zalman said. She was not swayed by Velvel's assertions at all. In fact, she now suspected that Rabbi Yaakov was not a follower himself but an imposter, one who denied the legitimacy of the messiah's kingdom. She believed that he had asked Reb Zundel to speak on the "Great Sabbath" to further belittle and besmirch the messiah's holy name. To further sway the town to abandon hope in him, to continue where Reb Pesach had left off. She had come to this ridiculous conclusion because it was the only way she could maintain her faith in the messiah without yielding to the intelligence and lucidity of Zalman's argument. She truly believed that Rabbi Yaakov and Reb Zundel and now Zalman and Gittel were involved in one concerted effort to destroy the belief in the messiah and to frustrate his imminent arrival. She quickly spread word to her friends and neighbors. Within a day, the town was seething. They too naturally believed her story and were especially concerned that Reb Zundel harbored a false prophet who denied the messiah's legitimacy.

But they reserved their most vitriolic hatred for Rabbi Yaakov.

34

Two days before the Reb Zundel was scheduled to address the town and end the strife forever, Reb Zundel awoke early in the morning and headed directly for Rabbi Yaakov's home. He did not know what to do. Zalman's confirmation of Velvel's startling statement further confused and troubled him. He had agreed to address the entire town, to appeal to their sensitivities, in an effort to unite them before the messiah's arrival. The town still required serious healing, of that there was no doubt, but the reasons were now significantly different. There was no longer any pressing need. In fact, when the messiah would ultimately be proven false Reb Zundel was sure that most of the healing would take place spontaneously, without any outside intervention, as all the townspeople would understand by themselves that they acted improperly and needed to rectify the way they treated each other. Reb Zundel believed each town member would quietly and methodically undergo a personal introspection aimed at remedying months of vitriol and animosity. But until that happened, Reb Zundel was now thoroughly reluctant to possibly further stoke the fires of divisiveness, especially since he no longer believed in the messiah.

He reached Rabbi Yaakov's home to see Rabbi Yaakov exit and proceed toward the synagogue. "Good morning, Rabbi Yaakov," called Reb Zundel, running after him. "I must speak with you, it is quite urgent."

Rabbi Yaakov sensed Reb Zundel was having second thoughts about speaking before such a large crowd during such a momentous time of year. "Is it about your speech this Sabbath?" Rabbi Yaakov hoped it was nothing more than nervous reluctance.

"Yes, Rabbi Yaakov, it is quite serious."

"Alright," said Rabbi Yaakov. He was wary due to Reb Zundel's rejoinder. "We shall discuss it as soon as we reach my study." Rabbi Yaakov hoped he could help Reb Zundel overcome any apprehension he might be experiencing and prayed that Reb Zundel would not change his mind. The future of Krasnystaw rested with him.

The two men entered the synagogue and proceeded to the door-way leading to Rabbi Yaakov's study. Rabbi Yaakov opened the door, looked into the room and stood aghast. The room had been vandalized. Many of the old prayer books were strewn about the room, the old prayer shawls were torn and scattered, the rabbi's desk was turned over and the bookshelves were thrown down. It was obviously done with malice aforethought, but why? Neither Rabbi Yaakov nor Reb Zundel could imagine why anyone would have done such a thing. Neither of them was aware of the preposterous rumors swirling around the town. Reb Zundel quickly offered his assistance.

"Let me help straighten out the room. My dilemma can wait until later."

"Thank you," returned a bewildered Rabbi Yaakov. "I am truly at a loss for words. I cannot express my disappointment, my utter disillusionment with the spiteful and hateful people who committed this terrible atrocity. Obviously, they are unhappy with me, and that is something I can tolerate, but to damage sacred articles, there is no excuse! What led them to do this, Reb Zundel? Are they so full of hate, so unwilling to abide by me and the togetherness I am trying so hard to develop? This town has finally gone far enough! I no longer care for them or their problems!" Rabbi Yaakov moved to collect the many prayer books left scattered throughout the room. Reb Zundel could not think of anything to say to comfort Rabbi Yaakov. He felt the same way, but he could not remain silent. He needed to appeal to Rabbi Yaakov's sense of compassion, urge him not to leave the town. They would desperately need his guidance soon.

"I understand your frustration, Rabbi Yaakov. I have never heard of actions so blasphemous, so intolerable, yet please do not speak in anger. Let us hope only one or two townsmen were responsible for this. We shall discover who they are and then refer them to the *beis din* in Lublin and allow them to pursue the matter with all the authority and prestige they possess."

Rabbi Yaakov knew that Reb Zundel was correct and that he had spoken hastily. "You are right, Reb Zundel, I am just so exasperated by this town. Can it ever be saved?"

The two men spent the next hour cleaning the study. They returned the desk and the bookcases to their original locations, removed all the prayer shawls and books from the floor and returned them to their places. There was still about a half hour till morning services began and they were almost finished. Suddenly Rabbi Yaakov noticed something odd, something he had not seen since he came to Krasnystaw over eighteen years earlier. The burlap sack, which covered the old ark, was nowhere to be found and the door of the ark was ajar. Rabbi Yaakov cautiously moved toward the ark, overcome with curiosity. Reb Zundel too was curious and likewise moved toward it. Rabbi Yaakov pushed the door wide open and observed a Torah scroll inside. He carefully lifted it out of the ark and placed it on his desk. The Torah was covered with a beautifully fashioned decorative cover in the Spanish style. He called to Reb Zundel and together they removed the cover. Beneath was an old, worn out cover fraying at the bottom. The two men stared at the many words written there and read all about Rabbi Gavriel and Juan de Ciudad's grandfather. They continued to read the letters that looked newer and bolder. They read about Juan de Ciudad's remarkable journey from Plasencia to Huesca in 1465 and Juan's spiritual rebirth, which culminated in Juan's pilgrimage to Jerusalem. The narrative continued to recount that in 1492, when the Jews were expelled from Spain,

Rabbi Yechezkel, a distant relative of Rabbi Abraham Bibago, fled to Naples along with many other Jews and took the Torah with him. The narrative concluded on the back of the cover that when the Jews were forced out of Naples in 1541, Rabbi Pinchas, the nephew of Rabbi Yechezkel, settled in Krasnystaw.

"Is this Rabbi Pinchas the young, the first rabbi of Krasnystaw?" asked a bewildered Reb Zundel. "I have heard of him."

"Most probably. He died at a very early age. Not much was known about him and there is no one alive today who knew him," returned Rabbi Yaakov.

The two of them continued to examine the cover and reread the amazing travels of this Torah. Finally Rabbi Yaakov removed the cover and Rabbi Gavriel's Torah lay in front of them.

The Torah was quite old and the parchment had yellowed. Rabbi Yaakov unrolled it carefully and the two men beheld the Torah scroll.

Rabbi Yaakov and Reb Zundel could not turn away. Although it was old and some of the letters had cracked, it was the most beautiful scroll they had ever seen. The age of the scroll had not diminished the magnificence of the words and letters, which filled the numerous columns in remarkable symmetry. They marveled at the singularity, precision and detail of each letter.

Reb Zundel suggested they continue to roll the scroll to insure the rest of it was written in the same meticulous fashion. Rabbi Yaakov readily agreed, astonished that this precious masterpiece had remained hidden for so long. They continued to look at it, read from it and were infused with warmth by its beauty and depth. For a few moments they were lost in an endless world of knowledge and perception. All thoughts of the messiah, the town, the fighting and the recent destruction of the study faded into the background. They were captivated by the scroll's stark grace, mesmerized by the sheer brilliance and charm of each letter.

But they both knew the scroll meant much more than that.

Four hundred years.

They were quite aware this Torah had seen much: libels, expulsions, Crusades perhaps and, judging from the Torah's cover, the

Spanish Inquisition as well. Yet, the Torah remained so beautiful, so steadfast. True, it was inanimate but its magnificence stayed untarnished despite the harrowing travails it surely must have experienced. While Jews everywhere were coping with hardship, the Torah was there with its everlasting legacy, to provide comfort and meaning. They realized this discovery was no accident: nothing ever was.

Rabbi Yaakov looked up at Reb Zundel who nodded understandingly and then proceeded to help Rabbi Yaakov return the scroll to the ark. It was time for morning services yet both men seemed unable to move. They were so overwhelmed by the scroll, so inspired by its splendor and craftsmanship. The scroll represented the enduring quality of the Torah itself. It exemplified the perpetual and singular mission of the Jewish People, the bearers of the Torah. The scroll reminded them that no matter the obstacle, no matter the hardship, the Torah would prevail and triumph. It could be disregarded and ignored but it would not go away. It would always be there for someone to draw upon, to return to after so many years of neglect and abandonment. The heritage that lay within that scroll, the history of that scroll, of the Torah itself, was so overpowering, so profound, so everlasting that Rabbi Yaakov and Reb Zundel immediately felt consoled and reassured. They both understood that the problems destroying the town would pass, they would eventually yield to the reliability and constancy of the Torah. The strife would become unimportant, inconsequential and would surely fade in the face of the beauty and elegance of the continuing legacy. They knew this Torah was the answer, far better than speeches or lectures. They turned and left the study anxiously awaiting the Sabbath.

The Sabbath soon arrived and everyone was anxiously anticipating Reb Zundel's speech. Virtually the entire town came to the synagogue to hear what they all believed would be words of reconciliation and understanding. Everyone knew that after what had happened at the wedding, and the recent vandalizing of the Rabbi's study, that serious healing was necessary but they all doubted whether Reb Zundel would be successful. Most showed up simply to hear what he had to say and out of respect for his valiant efforts.

The synagogue was quiet as they waited in hushed expectancy. Reb Zundel approached the podium. Rabbi Yaakov hurried to his study and returned a moment later carrying Rabbi Gavriel's Torah scroll. Many people, especially those non-believers in the messiah, were shocked: A speech did not call for the reading of the Torah. What blasphemy were they contemplating?

Reb Zundel quickly calmed their fears. "I am sure you are wondering why Rabbi Yaakov has brought this Torah here and I shall explain. Rabbi Yaakov and I found this Torah hidden in Rabbi Yaakov's study shortly after he discovered the inexcusable damage that was perpetrated there. The Torah has probably been in the study for over one hundred years and no one ever realized it before. This is a very unique Torah, it is quite old. The history of this Torah is woven on the front and back of the cover and I will now read it to all of you."

Reb Zundel then read all of the narratives sewn onto the cover, beginning with Rabbi Gavriel in Blois and concluding with the famous Rabbi Pinchas. When Reb Zundel was finished he removed the cover and neatly placed it on the podium. Rabbi Yaakov then announced that he wanted each person to approach the podium and gaze into the Torah scroll. Some were hesitant at first but others immediately sensed the importance and significance of the moment and cautiously moved toward the podium. One by one they saw the Torah and one by one they returned to their seats, changed. Each was overcome with the same feelings that Rabbi Yaakov and Reb Zundel experienced when they first looked into the scroll. Reb Shraga Feivish caught a glimpse of his enemy, Reb Mendel, sobbing softly as Reb Mendel returned to his seat. He promised that he would visit him later in the day; their feud had gone on long enough. Many made similar promises about Rabbi Yaakov or others they had avoided recently. Everyone in the room felt refreshed, invigorated.

The room was very quiet. Everyone was deep in thought marveling at the scroll, which they agreed was the most beautiful they had ever seen. But more importantly, they were all absorbing the same message that the Torah unmistakably revealed, a message of harmony and understanding. They had all come to the same conclusion about their destiny and the role this Torah, every Torah, plays in that destiny. Everyone in the town was no longer despondent and discouraged. They were now assured that whatever might happen to the messiah, their lives would ultimately find contentment within the heritage that was larger than them. They no longer feared the future. They no longer embraced the hatred, the disappointment, the endless confusion and doubt. It all seemed so petty, so temporary.

They left the synagogue that afternoon arm in arm with each other as friends, brothers and neighbors, now confident and ready to brave the uncertainties of tomorrow.

Paris, France 1944

[A Jew] believes that if something happened, it was meant to be.

– Lodz Chronicle, August 25, 1942

35

Pierre and Claude dug furiously, trying to pack all the explosives underneath the tracks as quickly as possible. Dawn was fast approaching, they did not have much time. The train carrying supplies, arms and ammunition for the German army was scheduled to cross the area in less than two hours. They worked on opposite ends of the track, removing earth, inserting small sticks of dynamite, at even intervals then concealing the explosives with the loosened earth. They intended to damage a stretch of track fifty meters long. This operation would have gone much faster if additional men accompanied them but that was too dangerous. No more than two resistance members went out on a mission at any one time. The recent German reprisals against resistance groups all over France, especially in Paris, necessitated these extra precautions. Pierre and Claude's group had suffered the loss of three of their most courageous fighters when they were caught at a railway station in Paris one month earlier. Since then the group instituted restrictions to prevent the capture of too many members of the group at any one time. Pierre and Claude found themselves preparing the explosives without assistance and they were exhausted.

Claude and Pierre always worked together. They were cousins and were both in their mid-twenties. They had joined the resistance together one year earlier, shortly after the fall of Paris. They were Jews and shared a deep-seated and well-deserved hatred for the Nazis. They were likewise thoroughly disillusioned with the French government, which had prematurely surrendered and allowed France to be occupied by the Germans in so cowardly and disgraceful a fashion. They had taken to the forests shortly after the surrender, to try and restore the dignity and respect of their homeland. They joined a resistance movement and remained committed to a free and unoccupied France. For the past year they had participated in all sorts of subversive and underground activities, including blowing up convoys, destroying various Nazi headquarters and disrupting rail lines. Their targets were carefully selected to avoid detection by roving German patrols or zealous French citizens prepared to betray their countrymen for additional rations, often as little as an extra slice of bread and some milk.

The site of this particular mission had been determined several days earlier when the resistance group had learned through intercepted communications that a large shipment of arms and supplies would pass through the outskirts of Nantes, a large Atlantic seaport in western France at the mouth of the Loire River. The outlying fields of Nantes were deserted grasslands where people seldom traveled, a perfect location to plant explosives without exposure. Pierre and Claude's superior, a tall bearded man named Leopold, urged caution and stealth. This train was carrying an unusually large amount of supplies, and its destruction would significantly inhibit the German war machine. He warned them not to fail and to avoid getting caught at all costs.

After nearly two hours of meticulously and fastidiously inserting explosives, Claude announced, "I am finished, Pierre. Do you need help on your side of the tracks?"

Pierre looked up and replied, "No. I will be finished in another moment. I only have two sticks left. As soon as I bury them we can retreat to the forest, prepare the detonation devices and wait for the train to arrive!"

A moment later Claude stood up and motioned to Pierre. The two men raced to a nearby forest, placed their explosives apparatus on the ground and looked out toward the tracks. They had a clear view of about one hundred meters of track surrounded on both sides by meadows of tall grass. Pierre confirmed the detonation devices would be disengaged when the first car of the train passed an odd looking rock which hung down a slope on the near side of the forest. That would ignite the fuses at an ideal moment and cause the most damage to the train and the supplies it was transporting. Pierre pointed toward the rock and Claude nodded in agreement.

The men waited. This was the hardest part of their job, even more difficult than carefully placing deadly explosives into the ground. The anticipation, the expectation, seemed an eternity and it only allowed them time to question and second-guess their judgment and skill. What if the fuses did not ignite? What if the sticks of dynamite became moist from the earth and fizzled out before they exploded? What if they were caught before the train arrived? What if the engineer sensed something was amiss and stopped the train, inspected the tracks and discovered the explosives?

Claude could not stand the idleness, the stillness of the tension, and sought to divert his attention from the monotony of waiting. He whispered to Pierre, "Remember our first mission, just one week after Paris fell?"

"How could I forget?" returned Pierre. "Our parents begged us, pleaded with us, not to abandon Paris and Marshal Pètain's cunning wisdom for the dangers of resistance fighting. But how could we stay and watch that old, senile man sign a death sentence dooming the entire country, especially the Jews?"

"We were commanded to blow up a theater in Paris and we did not even know how to ignite the explosives!" exclaimed Claude.

"Yes, but back then we could roam free without fear of arrest or capture. I remember that for the first few months those arrogant Germans could not believe that ordinary Frenchmen sought to undermine their control here. They ignored our missions and we were able to prepare for strikes without fear of exposure. We did not know how to handle explosives and the rest of the group came to our aid and assisted in the attacks."

"But it is different now," continued Pierre. "The Germans seem to be everywhere! Somehow they anticipate our every move and over the past few months have captured almost half our original group! Imagine, Claude, this is our biggest operation in months and only you and I were sent to execute it!"

"I know it was too risky to send others to help us but it's the least we can do for our country!"

Pierre nodded in agreement. "But let us hope we can continue these operations before we are finally caught!"

Claude turned away, ignoring Pierre's gloomy chatter and they continued to wait in silence.

One half hour later the two men heard the faint distant hum of a locomotive and knew the moment had arrived. Pierre positioned himself directly in front of the detonation devices and motioned for Claude to do likewise. The consistent, steady rumble of the train grew closer and louder and both men knew in a few minutes it would all be over. They glanced to their right and saw puffs of smoke rising above the trees and an instant later saw the train itself. It was a standard cargo train with eight to ten cars. Swastikas were painted on the sides of some of the cars and two German flags protruded from the face of the front car.

Claude and Pierre watched with surprise as the train reduced its speed and came to a complete stop a few hundred yards before the spot they had chosen for detonation. They knew the sticks of dynamite were well hidden and a cursory scan of the area would not reveal them. But Pierre and Claude did not see any German soldiers exit any of the cars and wondered why it stopped at all.

"Maybe there is some sort of malfunction," whispered Claude, terrified the mission would fail and the Nazis would catch them.

"Then how come no one got off the train to inspect the engine? It does not look like anything is wrong with the train and I see that the engineer in the locomotive has not moved!"

"Perhaps someone exited on the other side of the train and we cannot see them," offered Claude, halfheartedly.

"I thought of that, but then why didn't the engineer accompany him? This sudden halt is very strange. I am frightened, Claude."

"Me, too," admitted Claude.

An instant later the train resumed its course and both men panicked. It was obvious there was nothing wrong with the train. Then why had it stopped? Claude was gripped with an overwhelming terror. He told Pierre there was no time to wait. An instant later the two men detonated the explosives and then raced deeper into the forest.

A dreadful explosion ripped through the soft, quiet, deserted field and the train and rail lines were instantly shattered and mangled. The explosives continued to erupt further down the line, burying the train in an infernal mass of steel and earth. The train and virtually all the supplies and ammunition were completely destroyed. Most of the men inside, soldiers sent to guard the shipment, were instantly killed.

The mission was a success but Pierre and Claude saw five German soldiers racing toward them. They turned and ran for their lives. Pierre and Claude were well ahead of the soldiers but they were far from safe. They enjoyed a sufficient lead but they were tired and losing momentum. They soon began to hear shouts and threats, which grew closer and closer.

"Stop now!"

"You cannot escape!"

"You will pay for your crime!"

The shouts were repeated over and over. They increased their pace to stay well ahead of their pursuers. The cousins continued to run and at last saw the outline of the city on the horizon. They knew they had almost reached Nantes where they would blend in with the residents of the city and hopefully escape capture.

They raced into the city, exhausted, and tried desperately to catch their breath, wipe the sweat off their faces and regain their composure and appear as ordinary citizens. They did not possess identification papers or passports and if the S.S. guards stopped them they would be arrested, regardless of whether they were suspected of bombing the train. They found a remote alley near the town square and rested there briefly. They emerged refreshed and relaxed and walked aimlessly through the town avoiding all police officers and German soldiers. They joined the bustle of the streets of Nantes and soon became lost in the crowds.

A short while later they saw a commotion just outside a small café and, mildly curious, approached with caution. They observed an argument erupt between the owner of the café and several S.S. guards who were denied drinks because they had no money. Claude and Pierre breathed a sigh of relief. If news of their feat had been spread to all police stations and army posts the S.S. guards would not have time to visit the café. But their time was severely limited. Every pro-German in the area would be looking for them and would shoot first and ask questions later. They turned away from the café, found a hiding place and waited for nightfall to return to the group.

It was eight o' clock in the evening and the streets were deserted. Everyone in Nantes had heard of the bombing and they were surprised to hear that the invincible Germans had suffered a major blow. Medics and firefighters had rushed to the site as soon as they had learned what happened. The fire was contained and all the bodies were removed from the wreckage. The Germans imposed a curfew on the city and no one was permitted to leave their homes after seven, but everyone in Nantes knew that was merely the Nazis' way of exerting control when nothing else could be done. Even the Germans believed that the attackers were long gone by now.

Pierre and Claude passed the Palace de la Cathédrale and proceeded out of the city with extreme caution. They were not permitted to be on the streets and their presence there would surely lead to arrest. They walked close to the shadows of buildings, avoiding the street lamps and certain exposure. As they turned away from the palace they saw a group of men dressed in German uniforms approaching. They gasped in terror and quickly turned around, moved and stood up against a building, hoping to blend in with the structure and avoid detection as the soldiers turned the corner. The men approached and Pierre and Claude could hear their conversation. They were slurring their speech, speaking incoherently and were completely unintelligible. The soldiers turned the corner and swaggered and swayed as they walked. Pierre and Claude realizing that they had nothing to fear from these drunkards and waited until they were out of sight. They left Nantes to joined Leopold, their leader, and his group of resistance fighters somewhere well hidden deep in the forests of France.

36

They were packed inside the train until there was barely room to stand. For four days the Nazis had rounded up as many Jews as they could and forced them on to the train. Each of the cars was overflowing and many of the elderly were feeling faint. Rumors circulated that the train would be departing shortly, and that afforded some relief to the hungry prisoners. Maurice Andeau was shoved into the third to last car late one night in early November 1942. He pushed his way through the cramped, dense crowd, headed toward one of the windows and immediately began planning his escape.

Maurice still could not believe he had been caught. He had managed to be elusive and to remain free for the past two years, never falling into the hands of the Germans. His capture could have been avoided so easily if Maurice had simply moved out of the way instead of running at the sight of those policemen. That was over a month ago and Maurice could still not accept he had done something so foolish, so impulsive.

The train was unbearably hot even though it was almost winter. The throngs of people and the minimal circulation of air contributed to sweltering temperatures within the train. Maurice managed to remain near the window and saw the strong metal bars which took the place of the usual frame with a glass pane. How would he get out? He could not crack off the bars, he did not have any tools with him. He continued to examine the window. He could fit through the two bars if they could somehow be bent or removed. He pulled on them but they were firmly bolted into the frame of the car. Maurice did not know the train's destination, nobody did, but he sensed the journey would end in misery and disaster and he did not want to stay and find out. He continued to inspect the window, dreaming of a way to escape.

The train filled with more and more people and Maurice, sweating profusely, wondered how many more could be stuffed inside. Soon there would be no room to breathe. He recognized several neighbors from Paris, and classmates at the Sorbonne. Maurice had not seen them in two years, and was surprised how much everyone had changed. The physical deterioration was obvious. They all appeared weak and malnourished. But worse than that, they all wore expressions of grief, of hopelessness, of despair and of desperation, which revealed an inner breakdown as well. Maurice studied the tired, pinched faces of the old women, the frightened, vulnerable children clinging to their parents, too afraid to cry or ask for food. Maurice quickly realized that had he remained in Paris he would have likewise suffered along with them. He always had doubted whether he had made the right choice to leave Paris and face the war alone, away from home. Gazing into the abyss of abandonment and dejection on the faces of his fellow Jews, he knew he had made a wise decision.

Maurice clearly remembered the day. It was October 1940, a few months after the fall of Paris. The country was divided into two zones and the Germans now occupied Paris. Maurice was studying at the Sorbonne. He was twenty-five and would earn a doctorate in French history in three years. Maurice was fascinated with France, the country his family had lived in for over four hundred years. He diligently studied the heritage and history of his homeland and was especially sensitive to the many unfortunate past instances of French anti-Semitism. Maurice was not a religious Jew and he considered himself a Frenchman first, but he did admire and respect those Jews who still clung to the traditions of the past. Maurice's parents had died during the 1930's. They had never taught him any of the observances and ceremonies of the Torah. Maurice had not attended synagogue in over ten years and rarely thought about his Jewishness at all.

Maurice entered the classroom on the third floor shortly before noon, sat down near the front and waited for the professor to arrive. The professor, a tall, bearded historian named Klippenberg, was an expert on Napoleon. Maurice was unsure of Klippenberg's background, but believed the professor came from Belgium. Maurice greatly respected his knowledge and passion for history. The other students quickly filled the room and waited patiently. The professor was always early and his absence began to raise suspicions. Someone shouted that he was ill. Another asserted that he had fallen and broke a leg. About twenty minutes later one of the administrators of the university entered the room. He was a tall distinguished-looking man with a long moustache and an even longer pipe. Clad in a finely tailored navy blue suit he was quite formidable. He informed everyone that Klippenberg would no longer be teaching the class. He had been dismissed because of the new law.

"What law?!" shouted Albert Pateleu, the smartest student in the room.

"The Statut de Juifs, the law of the Jews," answered the administrator stoically. "The law was passed yesterday. It forbids all Jews from engaging in many of the professions, including public service, teaching, journalism, theater, radio and the cinema. This institution cannot blatantly violate that law and this morning all the Jewish professors, including Klippenberg, were summarily dismissed."

Maurice had not known Klippenberg was Jewish and was surprised the university would so quickly rush to enforce this outrageously discriminatory law. Besides appeasing the Germans, what function did the law serve? Maurice took great pride in his French heritage and could not accept that France would violate the rights of so many citizens in so brazen a fashion. True, the country was at war and many civic luxuries were curtailed or denied altogether and suspected spies were deprived of basic liberties, but all Jews were not enemies, or were they?

"It is about time we got rid of those Jews!" contended Marie Lambré, a quiet, soft-spoken student who rarely voiced her opinion. "Who knows what sort of propaganda and anti-French rhetoric Klippenberg has been spouting the past few months!" she continued.

Many of the other classmates applauded and echoed Marie's scorn for Klippenberg. The administrator took a few puffs of his pipe and quietly slipped out of the room. He proceeded down the hall to inform another class of their professor's absence.

Many in the room continued to praise the new law and welcome its enactment. Maurice looked around in disbelief. He had never heard this kind of talk from his classmates before. Of course Klippenberg was not a spy and there were no specific charges leveled against him. He had never uttered a single word which could be construed as disloyalty or criticism toward France. Yet all the students were so eager to discredit him, so quick to brand him a traitor, to deride his Jewishness, to express their satisfaction at his dismissal. Where did that rash, almost irrational attitude come from? Klippenberg was one of the most respected teachers at the Sorbonne. How could his Jewishness suddenly evoke such visceral contempt and disdain? Maurice understood that his classmates and friends could not have transformed overnight and these sentiments had been seething beneath the surface for quite some time. Maurice suddenly felt quite alone and wondered if he would soon be subject to their rancor and contempt. He remained quiet and still while his classmates continued to tarnish and besmirch the reputation and honor of Klippenberg.

But Maurice was troubled by something even more frightening. The laws would not stop there, they never did. Maurice knew history well and was quite aware that governments frequently passed discriminatory laws in stages, which served to minimize any public outcry. Maurice only had to look at the slew of boy-cotts and anti-Jewish laws enacted in Germany over the past seven years. He correctly understood that if the Germans did not force the French government to pass this legislation, they would have done so anyway to demonstrate their willingness to appease their German occupiers. Maurice thought about this newly en-acted law and admitted it was harsh and unfair yet restrained. It did not mandate physical harm or imprisonment. It merely re-stricted Jews from the most public professions. It was a precautionary measure which, during wartime, could be justified for many reasons. But Maurice knew that slowly, ever so slowly, more laws would be passed which increasingly restricted the free-dom of Jews. The laws would further curtail their employment opportunities, seize their property and ultimately exclude the Jews from all facets of French society. Maurice also knew the very lives of Jews could be in danger and he wondered how he could escape it all.

Half of Maurice's classes were postponed, others were held with substitute professors who tried to bridge the gap left by the absence of so many faculty members. Maurice left at about four o'clock. All of his later classes had been canceled.

Maurice passed a garden that stood in front of one of the smaller buildings. He noticed four students huddled together and recognized three of them from Klippenberg's class.

"Good evening," offered Maurice.

None of the students responded, they merely waited until Maurice walked past them. When Maurice was about six yards away, one of them shouted, "We do not want you here, Jew! We do not want you in our university. Stay away, along with Klippenberg and the other Jewish vermin infesting this institution! It will become very dangerous for you to remain here! Heed our warning, Jew, do not return!"

Maurice heard snickering which quickly grew faint and un-derstood that they were laughing at him. He immediately turned around and saw them running away. They were already far down the path, out of earshot.

Maurice stood frozen, unsure whether to chase after his classmates and engage them further or ignore them entirely. His hesitation afforded them a chance to slip away. Even if he ran now he would never catch them. Maurice remained standing, so shocked and disturbed by the harangue he could scarcely believe it had been expressed at all. It was his first personal encounter with anti-Semitism and Maurice admitted he felt betrayed and ashamed. He realized they considered him less of a Frenchman, indeed less of a man. Maurice was not a practicing Jew and had no particular affinity toward any Jewish customs or rituals but he was a student of history and understood the age-old heritage of his religion. He knew better than most the suffering and persecution of his ancestors. While he remained ignorant and uninterested in the practice of his religion he always had maintained a certain pride, a distinct appreciation for Judaism; a secular, detached and vague appreciation. His respect for Judaism was similar to an Englishman's regard for the British Crown or a spectator's marvel at an accomplished athlete; esteem and admiration with little or no consequence on everyday life. Yet for Maurice that all suddenly changed. His clouded, obscure and distant feelings toward Judaism were now sharpened. For the first time his Jewishness was the central focus of his emotion and consciousness. He was now forced to examine his Jewishness and to confront it. What did being Jewish mean? Why were Jews subject to persecution and oppression? Why was he humiliated and threatened? Why was he Jewish? Maurice could not explain it but the diatribe affected him, touched him. Of course Maurice was aware of France's long history of mistreatment toward the Jews, of the infamous Dreyfus trial where much of the French military elite was found to be anti-Semitic. That episode troubled Maurice deeply but that was actually at the root of the problem. Maurice had been so confident that his French countrymen were beyond all that. Now he realized he was terribly wrong and that no matter how much time and healing passed he could never become an accepted member of French society. He knew he had only one place to turn. The student's diatribe awakened his soul, a dormant, uninterested, distant soul. It initiated a spark, a flicker of yearning, a need for increased knowledge and awareness. Maurice did not have an opportunity to further explore these feelings. He was too distraught by what he just experienced.

Maurice was sure Jean de Muelle, a serious and conscientious student, had uttered it. He recognized his voice and he had been one of the students huddled near the garden. Maurice had known him for almost three years. They met at the Sorbonne and Maurice always found him a sensible, intelligent student. Jean and Maurice were not particularly friendly but Maurice never said or did anything that might provoke Jean to lash out in that manner. Jean's warning was contemptuous and it only further compounded the feelings of isolation and rejection that Maurice had first encountered earlier in the day.

Was his life in danger? Could he risk returning to class? Was there any class worth returning to? Was Jean merely playing a cruel joke or was the warning serious?

Maurice knew of similar taunts which German and Austrian Jews suffered almost on a daily basis. But this was France, educated, enlightened and progressive, free of the malicious attitudes of the past. What prompted these ordinary and sensible Frenchman, understanding and unbiased individuals, to suddenly advocate the exclusion of Jews? Why the instant threats and warnings and the embracement of such enmity and scorn? Was the desire to appease the despised Nazi occupiers so overwhelming that it blurred an otherwise sensitive and caring reaction? Or did the Nazis awaken the true French spirit, one of collaboration and anti-Semitism, which had been suppressed by years of ritualistic and insincere homage to brotherhood? Was this war an opportunity for the French to abandon the liberty equality and fraternity they espoused and resume the centuries long persecution of the Jews?

Maurice tried to disregard it but knew he could not. The conclusion was obvious: He would leave France. The more Maurice thought about it, the more he realized this was not really his first encounter with anti-Semitism. This was the most vicious but there were others. He now remembered those polite, yet impolite glances, those subtle looks of superiority and those seemingly off-hand yet intentional slurs of the Jewish faith and its unique rituals. Maurice had been oblivious to all of that, but now it all made sense. He had been so foolish, so blind to sentiments that were always present. These reminisces only reinforced his decision to leave. Maurice was not troubled by his decision, there was nothing for him in France anymore. Except for his Uncle Bernard, his father's only brother who Maurice visited often, and some distant cousins, he had no relatives in France and no familial obligations forcing him to remain. He knew it would be difficult, much of Europe was at war and the Nazis were everywhere. But he could not return to the Sorbonne and realized it was only a matter of time before it became impossible for Jews to live comfortably in France. Maurice decided to leave and escape while he still had the chance.

But first he would visit his Uncle Bernard.

Maurice reached his uncle's house and softly knocked on the door. No one answered. Maurice turned the knob and discovered the door was unlocked. He entered and saw his uncle resting on the sofa. The home was very opulent. The living room was decorated with many antiques, some of which dated back to Louis XIV. The room was quite large and it was covered with a plush oriental rug. There were three sofas upholstered in pure Irish linen placed in a semicircle. They were each flanked by two small end tables draped in red and gold damask. The walls were hung with various works of art, including portraits, scenes of the countryside and some modern abstract works, all painted by French artists. A rich deep mahogany mantle adorned the fireplace at the far corner of the room. The mantle was strikingly designed with flowers carved into the wood. Atop the mantle rested Bernard's most prized possessions: the three medals he had received for his service and extraordinary bravery in the Great War, including France's most distinguished award — the Medal of Honor — and a faded grainy picture of Bernard's smiling wife, Henriette, who had died in 1930.

Maurice's entry startled his uncle, who awakened from his mid-afternoon nap. Bernard Andeau was groggy and disoriented but regained his composure after a few moments. Bernard was semi-retired from a very lucrative furniture factory he owned on the outskirts of Paris. He did not have any children and Maurice had no interest in succeeding his uncle as the president of a company founded by Maurice's great-grandfather. He found the business too uninteresting, too mundane, too stifling. Maurice was an intellectual and could never envision himself inundated by deadlines, receivables and inventory. Bernard understood that his nephew's future lay elsewhere and designated a distant cousin, Albert, to replace him.

Bernard was a strong, robust man, nearly fifty-five years old. He had fought with distinction during the Great War and suffered a permanent injury. He took great pride in his French citizenship, considered himself one of the most patriotic Frenchmen in all of Paris and, like Maurice, barely gave any thought to his Jewish roots.

"It is nice of you to visit, Maurice. What brings you to my home?" asked his uncle, who stood up, now fully awake.

"You did not hear what has happened, Uncle? You do not know about the new law?" Maurice sounded troubled.

"What are you talking about?" responded Bernard calmly.

"The French government passed a law yesterday forbidding Jews from working in many professions," snapped Maurice. "A number of the professors at the university were dismissed this morning!"

"Are you certain?"

"Yes, Uncle, one of the administrators came to our classroom to tell us and I heard people speak of it on the street."

Maurice informed Bernard about the particulars of the law and the extent of its reach. Bernard sat down on one of the sofas absorbing the news. He was deeply disturbed and annoyed. Except for his religion, which was determined at birth and which carried no significance for him whatsoever, he was no different than any other Frenchman. How could that one distinction provoke such intolerance, such unfair and exclusionary legislation? He was quite aware that France was under occupation. He fully expected the Nazis to impose these rules here, they had passed many similar laws in Germany. But he could not understand the motivations of his own countrymen who appeared eager and ready to exclude so many citizens for so spurious a reason. France was a country of tolerance, of acceptance, of equality. It granted citizenship to all peoples and wholly rejected the shameful discrimination of its past. Could his country so quickly fall again to the depths of hatred and tyranny? Was the German influence so alluring, so powerful, that France would so willingly succumb to their heinous designs? True, the legislation only involved the loss of income, not bodily harm or death, but would it stop there?

"I am quite troubled by the law and I cannot accept that our country would dishonor so many of its patriotic and productive citizens," proclaimed Bernard. "It was probably enacted to confuse the Germans, to make them think we hate the Jews as much as they do. Perhaps that will earn us extra rations of butter and cheese. I believe that within a few days the law will be ignored everywhere and your Jewish professors will once again resume teaching."

Maurice did not share his uncle's optimism and maintained that the law heralded misfortune and oppression. Maurice conceded that France might have acted to appease the Germans. But the swiftness of its passage demonstrated a French willingness to assist the Germans, support them in their endeavors, comply with whatever demands they might later insist upon with regard to the Jews. Maurice predicted additional laws would be enacted that would further alienate and exclude the Jews. Who knew where it would end? Maurice understood that his uncle's stubborn French pride and respect for his country prevented him from objectively evaluating the depths of French indifference. Bernard still clung to the hope that France would ultimately vindicate these wrongs.

Maurice moved toward his uncle. "I disagree, Uncle, this war has exposed the evil in everyone. You may believe France is better than the rest of Europe, but what will you say when you are forbidden to attend the theater or the university, when the police will not respond to your needs and neither you nor Albert will be permitted to remain open for business?"

"That is preposterous," thundered Bernard. "I fought for this country! I held the lines at the Marne in 1914 and lost a finger!" Bernard moved his left hand in front of his nephew to show his missing index finger. "I received the highest Medal of Honor bestowed upon soldiers! I sacrificed for this country and I cherish it dearly. I am no different than any other Frenchman. I will not be treated like an outlaw or a criminal!"

Maurice persisted. "But we are different, Uncle, we are Jewish. I never fathomed the significance of that distinction until today. I am not certain I fully understand it now, but our religion occupies the minds of the French more than we may know. You can remain oblivious to the new law or try to excuse it and minimize its significance, but new laws will keep coming and our freedoms here will be dramatically reduced." Maurice held his uncle's hand. "I have decided to do something about it."

Bernard saw the determination and conviction of Maurice and instantly feared he had joined an anti-government organization. "What are you going to do, Maurice?" asked Bernard, nervously.

Maurice had decided on a course of action. He was still unsure if it was the prudent decision and he would continue to doubt it for two long years. "I am leaving Paris, Uncle, I am leaving our home," announced Maurice. "I am not sure where I am going, but I cannot remain here, I do not wish to witness the downfall of my country. I will probably go to Spain or to Switzerland, countries which are likely to remain neutral for the duration of the war. Restrictions to those countries are relaxed and a visa can be obtained legally or at least purchased in the black market for an affordable price. You may come with me, Uncle, and together we can seek a new home and wait out of harm's reach for the war to end."

Bernard was surprised with Maurice's decision and was disappointed that he would not stay and fight for changes to alleviate the harshness of the new law. He also believed Maurice would be in far greater danger away from the familiar surroundings and comforts of Paris. He hoped he could change his mind. "But Maurice, where will you live? How will you support yourself? You may starve!"

"I have thought of all that, Uncle, and I do not have the answers, I am just impelled to leave, to avoid further encounters with French apathy, to free myself of this allegiance to France that I now seriously question. I am resourceful and I have some money. Please, Uncle, do not worry about me."

"But what about your studies, Maurice? What will become of them?" asked Bernard in desperation.

"I have thought of that as well. I cannot go back to the university. It is quite dangerous there. My studies will have to wait. It is another consequence of this dreadful war."

Bernard understood he could not persuade Maurice. "Please be very careful, Maurice, and try to write me every month."

"Yes, Uncle."

Maurice drew near to Bernard, hugged him and left the house.

37

The moment he left his uncle's house he raced to his apartment, threw a few essential belongings into a sturdy French military backpack given to him by Bernard, purchased a strong yet rusty used bicycle and began his journey. He steered through the streets of Paris quickly yet cautiously, wondering if he would ever return to this glorious city. Maurice hoped to return: It was still his home and he was entranced by its artistic achievement and architectural beauty. He wondered if one day the French would finally abandon their alliance with hatred and intolerance and welcome him and all Jews wholeheartedly. It was too dangerous to pedal once it became dark and Maurice walked with the bicycle until midnight, when he finally reached the outskirts of the city. As he turned and lost all view of the city he stopped and waved au revoir one last time.

Maurice continued to walk for another hour until he was so tired he could barely move. He wanted to get to Switzerland as quickly as possible, before the snows came, but understood that if he did not rest and take care of himself properly he could become ill with no medication or doctors to help him. He turned off the side of the dusty, rarely used road and found a small patch of grass, where he lay down and quickly fell asleep.

The journey was tiresome and difficult and Maurice reached Switzerland about two weeks later. He was exhausted. He took along enough food and bought some bread and cheese in the black market in Dijon, about three quarters of the way to the Swiss border, but the journey was so tiring. He almost collapsed from exhaustion as he crossed the border but forced himself to continue, until he reached a town where he could find some food and recover from the trip.

He avoided the border police and arrived at Le Brassus, a small quaint village near the Orbe River just inside the Swiss border. Maurice looked disheveled, unkempt and half-crazed. He smelled, his clothes were filthy and torn and he walked slowly, unevenly, as if he was drunk. Maurice's appearance would surely have prompted one of the villagers to summon the police but there was a war raging; people with a bedraggled appearance passed through this border town all the time and no one even acknowledged his presence in the town square. Maurice stopped a man who was walking briskly, "Please, sir, where might I find an inn?"

The man pointed to the right and continued walking.

Maurice quickly turned and followed the direction for two short streets. He found the inn, entered, purchased a hot meal and rented a room on the top floor.

The room was small and very plain, it only had a bed, a small, circular table and a narrow closet. The showers and bathrooms were situated at the far end of the hall and were shared by all the guests. Maurice was pleased with the room, it was far better than the conditions he had endured during his journey. Maurice knew the next few weeks might prove difficult. He would have to find a job and he had no marketable skills. He also knew he could not do or say anything which would raise any suspicions that he was Jewish. He did not know if that would matter in this neutral country but he did not wish to take that chance. A few moments later Maurice was asleep.

The following day, Maurice secured a job working in a bakery, a job he would hold for two years. He was offered the job when he volunteered to fix a flat tire on the bakery's truck that was stuck in front of the inn on the way to a delivery. The driver, a devious looking man named Peter, refused to fix it, claiming his boss should have purchased new tires months ago and that he was not surprised one finally tore. Peter called Leonhard Zürenmantt, the owner of the bakery, from a telephone at the inn, informing him that the truck had a flat and he would not fix it. Leonhard, a short man with a large head, arrived about a half hour later and pleaded with Peter to repair the truck. The two men began shouting and soon it escalated into a heated argument. Many people gathered to watch the two men quarrel including Maurice. A few moments later Leonhard, frustrated with Peter's obstinacy and disobedience, told Peter he was fired and he never wanted to see him again. Peter instantly ceased speaking, dropped the keys to the truck, turned around and walked away from Leonhard. The crowd quickly dispersed. The truck remained in middle of the street and Leonhard appeared helpless. Maurice immediately offered his assistance. He admitted to Leonhard he was not very adept at fixing flat tires but hoped that his eagerness and willingness to help would enable Leonhard to overlook his inexperience and give him the job.

"What is your name?" asked Leonhard curiously.

"Maurice Andeau."

"I am Leonhard Zürenmantt, are you French?"

"Yes, Mr. Zürenmantt," answered Maurice, surprised he would care at all.

"Why are you here in Le Brassus?" continued Leonhard.

"To escape the war."

Maurice purposely avoided mentioning he was Jewish. He did not know if this man would care but knew nothing could be gained by informing him. If confronted would he lie and deny it? Would he claim he was a Christian to avoid further mistreatment, to escape the destiny of his people? Would he ever pursue those yearnings which were kindled the moment Jean lashed out at him? Would he attempt to understand his rich and complex religion? Or would he forsake it all, continue to pursue his studies and deny his heritage? Maurice was unsure and waited for the owner of the bakery to respond.

"I need a worker in my bakery, Mr. Andeau. Are you interested? I need someone to drive the truck around town, clean the bakery each evening and help bake bread each morning. As you can see from my recent dispute with Peter, I require someone immediately. I will pay you a fair wage based on the number of hours you work each week."

Maurice liked Leonhard. He seemed honest and respectable and knew he might not find another job this easily. "I accept," declared Maurice. "But, Mr. Zürenmantt," he joked, "will I be required to fix all the flat tires on the truck?!"

Leonhard chuckled and promised to install new tires within the week. Leonhard was relieved he found someone to replace the incompetent and sly Peter but wondered why someone as intelligent and witty as Maurice would accept this menial, unproductive job.

The tasks Maurice was required to perform in the bakery did not require much skill and Maurice mastered them within a matter of weeks. He studied the town map and could deliver goods anywhere in Le Brassus. The job did not pay much, just enough to cover his rent for the small flat he shared with three other workers from the bakery, his food and other basic necessities. Maurice did not care. He was away from the war, the battlefields, the surrenders, the remarkable Nazi victories and the persecution. He was free to walk the streets without fear of being arrested at any moment. He all but forgot about his stirrings toward Judaism. The town had no synagogues and he never divulged his Jewishness to anyone. He often wished he could write to Bernard and urge him to join him in neutral Switzerland but he knew that was too dangerous. He also knew that his stubborn uncle would never admit that he had made a mistake by remaining in Paris. He would have written back insisting that life in Paris remained tolerable and enjoyable and he would not leave the comforts of his home. But Maurice knew the real truth, he read the newspapers and was aware that legislation persecuting the Jews was passed with a consistent and sinister frequency, and he hoped Bernard was safe.

Maurice spent the next two years working in Zürenmantt's bakery. Over that time he saw many new faces in the town, some French, some Czech, occasionally Poles and Russians, and he assumed they were either Jews or political refugees. Most merely passed through on their way to England or America. Others remained and took humble jobs similar to the one Maurice did, working diligently and unassumingly.

In September 1942 everything changed. The Swiss police abruptly issued an Instruction, an official decree, that race alone could no longer distinguish someone as a political refugee. That meant all the Jews fleeing to Switzerland to escape the terrors of France would be denied entry. Overnight the Swiss haven was transformed into a closed, sealed country. Jews were refused entry by the thousands. Others already in the country were apprehended and escorted to the border where the French militia stood waiting for them. Maurice grew terribly frightened. Would he be caught and returned to France? Should he leave Le Brassus and travel deeper into Switzerland, away from the border and the zealous Swiss police? But Maurice understood that he could not leave, he could not steal away in the face of the new police Instruction. That would only confirm that he was Jewish and that he had no legal right to remain there. He would surely be hunted and pursued by the Swiss authorities. Maurice did not know the hinterland of the country well enough and would most likely be caught. He realized he had to stay and hoped he would be overlooked. Perhaps no one suspected he was Jewish or perhaps Mr. Zürenmantt would demand he was essential to his business and protest his removal.

The streets became emptier and emptier. By the end of September only three of the ten bakery workers remained. The

Swiss were methodical and thorough, questioning all the new-comers who had entered the country since the war broke out. It was only a matter of time before they would interrogate Maurice.

Would he lie?

Would they believe him?

On the last day of September 1942 Maurice arrived at the bakery shortly after dawn. Leonhard was already there and he was ashenfaced. He waited for Maurice to enter then ran to him. "Maurice, you are the only one left. I don't know if the rest were Jews or political prisoners or ordinary Swiss citizens uncomfortable with recent events here in the town, but they are gone. Soon you will be interrogated. I always suspected you are Jewish. Why else would an intelligent French student suddenly leave his home and settle in a foreign country, working a menial job for minimal wages? If I am wrong I apologize." Leonhard observed Maurice turn away and knew he was correct, Maurice was a Jew.

"I do not want you to go, Maurice, I like you, I have always liked you and I do not want my business to close down. I don't care that you are Jewish, I never cared about that sort of thing. Here, take this. I don't know," his voice trailed off, "but it could save you!" Leonhard handed Maurice something wrapped inside a handkerchief, nodded with embarrassment and left the bakery.

Maurice felt gratified that Leonhard displayed such positive feelings toward him, it was encouraging. He looked at the hand-kerchief. What was inside? He carefully unwrapped it, saw the item, shuddered and dropped it on the floor. Maurice picked it up and held it again. It was a cross, a large black steel cross, suspended from a brown leather necklace often worn by monks and priests. Leonhard was obviously suggesting that if he wore it, he might not be questioned or expelled from the country.

What to do? Maurice had entertained this dilemma before and admitted then he did not know the answer. He decided he would not wear it now, not yet. He put it in the handkerchief and placed it on one of the tables in the bakery.

That night Maurice was walking home and noticed a group of men and women running toward him, followed close behind by a band of Swiss policemen. The policemen were shouting, "Stop Jews, stop at once! You are violating the law! Stop! You cannot escape, stop! Stop!" Maurice froze momentarily as the group of Jews drew closer. They were running furiously and would not slow down or change their direction. He realized that if he remained still he could be trampled. He only had a few moments to decide on a course of action. The Jews were so close he could now see their exhausted, terrified faces. In another moment they would be upon him! He glanced in all directions then inexplicably sped off to the side only seconds before they reached where he was standing. One of the Swiss policemen mistook Maurice for one of the Jews being pursued who broke away in an effort to save himself. He immediately tore away from his colleagues and chased after Maurice. Maurice was unaware he was being followed and was overtaken by the officer and knocked to the ground. The rest were caught a short while later.

Maurice was placed in a cell in a Swiss police station along with the seven other Jews he was suspected of deserting. The other Jews explained to the Swiss authorities they did not know Maurice and he surely did not escape France with them. The Swiss police refused to believe them. The police surmised that Maurice was their leader and they would say anything to try and save him.

The cell was a long narrow room enclosed by large steel doors. There were three benches in the cell and two small beds. Maurice sat on one of the benches, rubbing a small bruise he had sustained on his head when he was thrown to the ground. He then observed the seven Jews all huddled together. They seemed to be part of one extended family. Some were quite young, one did not look older than thirteen. One of them noticed Maurice staring at them and approached Maurice. "Why did you not simply stand out of the way? Why did you run and induce them to follow you?"

Maurice was plagued by that same question, "I do not know, I felt I had to do something, I panicked and ran. If I would have moved to the side, they would have thought I was just another Swiss citizen and they would have ignored me," bemoaned Maurice.

"Yes, your capture was unfortunate indeed."

"What do you think will happen now?" asked Maurice hesitantly.

"We will surely be sent back to France, and I dare not think what will be in store for us there," answered the man.

"Oh, how foolishly I have acted," wailed Maurice.

The man and Maurice continued talking. Maurice learned that he was Meir Kaplan, an Orthodox Jew from Paris. The others were his family, two brothers, an aunt and three cousins. Maurice was introduced to them and found them a very determined, hardened bunch. They had been on the run for over two months. They had escaped Paris only days before the July roundup.

"What's a roundup?" asked Maurice sheepishly.

Meir glanced at his eldest brother, Ezra, a tall skinny man of twenty-seven. Ezra deferred to Meir who turned to answer Maurice.

"The Nazis gather all the Jews of one city or town. They literally round up all the Jews, place them on trains and send them away. It is a vicious, horrid scene. The brutality, the savagery, the violence which takes place cannot adequately be described."

"Where are they sent?" followed Maurice.

"No one knows, somewhere in the East but even that has not been confirmed."

Maurice could not believe what he was hearing. It sounded so sinister, so macabre. "I do not understand. Nazi soldiers enter homes and physically remove Jews?"

"If the people do not choose to come willingly then they are forced to do so. I know what I am saying sounds impossible but it is true. My parents were taken by the Nazis. Who knows if they are even still alive!" Meir gasped, withheld tears and continued. "Let me explain, Maurice, the French supply the Nazis with lists of

Jews. Initially the lists were of immigrants, then they included natural born Frenchmen as well. The Nazis use those lists and demand the surrender of a specific number of Jews. If the number falls short, they begin searching for Jews themselves. My entire family planned to escape together but my parents and my uncle were apprehended on their way to our rendezvous point. My cousin, Tzvi," Meir pointed to one of the men in the cell, "witnessed three S.S. officers stop them and interrogate them. Tzvi knew they would never be released and came to the rendezvous point without them. We still do not know where they are!"

Maurice stood up in the cell and approached the steel doors. He could no longer listen, he no longer wished to listen. Maurice closed his eyes. He tried to imagine how it happened. How could the Nazis know who was Jewish? How could they trust their enemy, the French? How could they be sure they were not seizing Catholic Frenchmen or Germans? The whole enterprise seemed so chaotic, surely doomed to fail. True, the Nazis were harsh but how could they insure success in an endeavor that required the cooperation of so many factions over which they had no control? And for what purpose? Meir's account of the roundup defied standard military protocol. Why would the Nazis expend valuable and battle-ready men on such vague and non-military exercises?

But Maurice gazed at the faces of Meir's family and could see their pain. Where were Meir's parents? The rest of the family? Surely Meir was not fabricating a story. Were the Nazis actually gathering Jews onto trains to ship them someplace? Was that possible? They were in control of the country, but wouldn't they be met with resistance? This was far worse than Jewish professors and actors losing their positions.

Did no one try to stop them?

Maurice talked with Meir at length and discovered that while they were the same age they had very little in common. Meir's entire family were observant Jews. They adhered to all of Judaism's laws and customs and worshiped in the synagogue daily. Meir wore a skullcap but he had lost it while running from the Swiss police. Maurice had worn a skullcap once, when he turned thirteen and celebrated his bar mitzvah, and had not entered a synagogue since. Maurice learned they did not live far from each other in Paris, yet they shared so few of the same goals and aspirations. But Maurice liked Meir, he was smart and caring and cunning. He remained optimistic despite their predicament and continued to explore ways of escaping.

Later that evening Maurice was placed in a Swiss police van along with Meir and his family and driven to the border where they were all released and arrested the moment they touched French soil.

The French military truck drove for hours. Where were they going? Back to Paris? Maurice sat in the cramped, stifling truck along with Meir, his family and about forty-three other Jewish refugees banished from Switzerland. Nobody spoke, everyone was too cold, too unsure, too afraid. Maurice heard soft murmuring emanating from Meir's lips and realized he was praying. Maurice too thought of praying, opening his heart, pouring out his emotions in heartfelt supplication. But he felt so removed from that sort of sentiment — the thought of worship was so foreign to him, he was so detached from holiness, from anything sacred — that he could not bring himself to pray. He realized that regrettably he had no one to whom to pray.

The truck drove through the night and finally stopped the following morning. Everyone was ordered out of the truck and marched to a camp a few hundred yards away. The prisoners followed obediently and proceeded through the cold bitter frost of the early morning. The prisoners walked in a strict line toward an unknown destination. Someone suggested they were in Italy, another believed they were in Lozère. Maurice was unsure but sensed they had not left France. They proceeded toward the entrance of the camp and as they entered, someone toward the front of the line courageously asked one of the guards where they were.

"The Rivesaltes camp, in the Pyrénées-Orientales region of the country," answered the guard abruptly.

Knowledge of their whereabouts quickly spread through the line. Maurice had visited this part of France once with Bernard. They were near Perpignan, close to the Spanish border at the southeastern tip of the country. Why were they brought here?

Maurice entered, not knowing what to expect. He had heard of the prison refugee camps while in Le Brassus but never saw pictures of them and had no knowledge about anything specific that took place in them. He was very disturbed by the physical appearance of the camp. It was squalid, filthy and foul smelling. The camp consisted of two long rows of barracks with two levels of bunks on either side. The men were housed in the barracks to the left, the women in the other one. The compartments were so small there was barely room to sleep. There was no heat and the barracks were cold, but they were also humid and reeked of human sweat. The blankets and pillows were threadbare, the beds flat as cardboard. Most of the bunks were in disarray, there were clothes and other personal belongings strewn everywhere.

Yet outside in the large yard, which stretched all the way to the heavily guarded main entrance hundreds of yards away, life seemed normal, almost happy. Maurice observed that outside no one seemed to mind the camp at all. Families were permitted to stay together, children were able to laugh and play with one another. He learned there was adequate food to eat and medical facilities were available. The conditions were horrible but they were far outweighed by the emotional support and familial encouragement which were present everywhere. Maurice quickly realized that with the security and warmth of the family, the tenderness of a mother's unwavering love, the strength of a father's unshakable determination, the comfortable familiarity of a spouse's devoted heart, they could soar beyond the impenetrable gates of Rivesaltes, of French oppression, and escape from the squalor, the stench and the misfortune. Maurice envied them. True, he was fond of Meir and his family but they could not substitute for his own family, Uncle Bernard and his stubborn optimism. Maurice conceded he missed him terribly and wished he could speak with him and draw strength from his experience and advice. He knew he could never survive alone, he would have to gain inspiration and encouragement from the families that surrounded him.

He turned to the front of the yard and studied the faces of these content and gratified strangers. He saw two children playing cheerfully with a small rag shaped like a ball held together by a fraying piece of twine and smiled warmly. He approached them and joined their game. The youths exhausted him but he would not stop, he relished every moment, it was fresh and cheerful. He developed a rapport with them, a relationship with them, a relationship he desperately craved, one that could help him cope with this camp. When they finished, Maurice thanked them and embraced them. He learned their names and promised to continue the game the next day. That night Maurice slept serenely, peacefully, barely aware of the cramped conditions or the frigid temperature. Yes, with friends to occupy the time, the camp was tolerable indeed.

But within a month everyone would be uprooted again, and this time their lives would be completely torn asunder.

38

Meir and Maurice spoke almost every day sometimes for hours at a time. Meir always claimed that if not for his family he would try to break out and escape the camp. He could not abandon his brothers and cousins and was sure they would be caught if they all escaped together. But he urged Maurice to escape, pointed out the weaknesses of the French positions surrounding the camp and assured him success if he followed his instructions. Maurice ignored Meir's suggestions. He believed he would never get past the first hundred yards if he could even break out at all.

The two men formed a warm, deep relationship. Maurice spent much of his time with Meir and his family. He dined with them, slept in the same compartment with them and sat quietly watching as they prayed together. The Kaplans prayed three times a day. The family did not have any prayer books. They relied on their memories and prayed slowly, contemplatively.

Maurice grew inspired by their devotion, their sincere service, and sought to join them. Their prayers, their faithful acceptance of their plight, their unyielding adherence to their beliefs rekindled within Maurice those old barely ignited embers that were virtually extinguished after two years of indifference and neglect. Maurice had briefly been drawn toward Judaism, the old noble religion of his ancestors, but he had never nurtured those feelings, he never developed the sensitivity and awareness he once craved and he remained ignorant and uncommitted. Now, observing the holy prayers of his friends, he was moved again to turn in their direction, to turn toward G-d. This time there would be no distractions, he had nowhere to go and all the time in the world.

One afternoon while walking in the yard Maurice interjected, "Meir, I wish to pray with you and your family."

Meir had been expecting this. He had seen the longing in Maurice's eyes as he watched him pray with his family and was ready for a response. "You cannot start there, Maurice, you must go back to the beginning."

"What do you mean, Meir?" asked Maurice innocently.

"I am happy you show interest, Maurice, and I want to help you but you must approach it carefully and with restraint. Before you learn how to pray you must first learn to Whom we pray! Come Maurice, I shall teach you."

Maurice understood he had acted impulsively, that it would take time and patience to learn the prayers and their meanings. He was fully ready for that challenge and with Meir as a teacher and guide he was certain he would master it properly. He zealously followed Meir toward the barracks.

Maurice was a student again. He had no textbooks, notes, pencils or study guides, just the words and passion of his teacher, Meir. Maurice was sharp and attentive and grasped many difficult concepts with relative ease. Meir was impressed with Maurice's intelligence and analytical skill and was satisfied with the progress of their studies.

Maurice greatly respected Meir. He was honest, conscientious and patient. Meir answered all of his questions, even the most elementary and repetitive, with care and respect. Maurice continued to learn from Meir and wondered how he could ever repay him.

One week later, the two men were walking in the yard, reminiscing about their first meeting. "You have repeated this to me many times, Maurice, but I still cannot understand why you ran the way you did. It only resulted in your being arrested!"

"Like I have told you Meir, I simply do not know what came over me." Maurice suddenly turned serious and faced Meir. "But there is more, Meir, something I have not yet confided to you. My boss at the bakery, a caring and decent man, gave me a cross to wear around my neck, to appear Christian and avoid being caught and thrown out of the country. I was thoroughly confused. I could not bring myself to wear it and I was not even certain it would protect me. Generally only priests wear crosses and I feared I could be exposed as an imposter. I could have kept it my pocket and produced it to any Swiss officer who stopped me but I could not bring myself to do that either. I left it on a table in the bakery, still undecided and still confused. If I had carried it home with me that night, the guard who had stopped me would certainly have released me. He would have concluded I ran in fright and would have apologized for mistaking me for a Jewish refugee. I might have been caught later, but I would have been spared that night! Imagine, Meir, then we never would have met!"

Meir listened to Maurice's story and nodded in agreement. Maurice was correct, if he had produced the cross he would have been saved that night, and with his wit and intelligence would probably still be safe and secure in Switzerland. But Maurice's decision meant much more to Meir than that. He recently had grown quite fond of Maurice and viewed him as one of his brothers. True, he was not religious, but he exhibited an appreciation and respect for Judaism which Meir found impressive and refreshing. Meir understood that if not for the war they would never have crossed paths. Meir believed their friendship was more than a coincidence, more than an arbitrary and unintentional encounter precipitated by the ravages of the war. He sensed there was importance and meaning to his relationship with Maurice, which needed to be maintained. Meir turned to Maurice, "I am proud that you withstood the temptation to conceal your religion. It was courageous and admirable of you. But it was not an accident we were thrust together, nothing ever is. I do not think we shall be staying here in Rivesaltes too much longer. I overheard two guards talking about some trucks that will be arriving soon. I have no idea where we will be taken but we must remain together. You are part of my family now and when I plan my family's escape, I want you to come with us!"

Maurice blushed, genuinely honored that Meir regarded him with such esteem, but dismissed Meir's obsession handily. "Thank you, Meir. You are kind and what you said means a great deal to me, but you must stop this nonsense. Don't you realize that we cannot escape, there are guards everywhere! Your family lives in a fantasy thinking you will rescue them!"

"That may be true, Maurice," returned Meir unconvinced, "but promise me that when we do escape, you will join us!"

Maurice studied Meir and for the first time realized that his future was somehow bound together with Meir's, that they shared a common destiny, a mutual fulfillment of their dreams. He could not explain it but could not deny it either. "Yes, Meir," answered Maurice, "I will join you."

Meir thanked Maurice and returned to the barracks. Maurice sensed Meir was long aware of their shared destiny and was slightly annoyed that it took him all this time to realize it as well.

Five days later the studies between Maurice and Meir ceased. Early in the morning, the central gates of the camp opened and six army trucks drove in. German soldiers exited the trucks and followed French officers toward the barracks. The French officers began yelling, ordering everyone to appear in the yard immediately. It was shortly after sunrise, and most of the prisoners were still inside. Some were not yet awake. The barracks were full of commotion. "They have finally come for us!" declared an old man. "I knew this freedom would not last for too long!" The man was not yet fully dressed but ran outside anyway, dutifully complying with the French authorities.

Maurice observed that everyone moved with an urgency, a seriousness that frightened him. What was happening? Why were they being summoned outside?

Maurice dressed, stayed close to Meir and his family and followed everyone out of the barracks. In the yard, French officers directed the prisoners, both the men and women, to form long lines. One of the French guards produced a list and started taking attendance. He called the names of each prisoner, in no particular order, including the children. About two hours later the guard finished and announced that everyone was present.

It was a cold, brisk autumn morning and many of the prisoners were visibly uncomfortable standing outdoors for so long. They were all too afraid to speak up and remained standing, waiting to be taken indoors. Maurice and Meir stood side by side during the entire ordeal, not speaking to each other. Meir's family stood nearby, desperately looking to Meir for some sort of encouraging gesture or facial expression, to assure them they faced no immediate danger but Meir remained stiff and preoccupied and barely moved a muscle. His eyes remained fixed on the trucks that stood at the entrance of the camp. He knew the prisoners would be placed on them and he was thinking of a way to escape.

After the roll call was completed the prisoners were ordered to march toward the trucks. The trucks were all the same size and were all covered with an identical green camouflage canvas. The inside of each truck was likewise identical. There were old wooden benches that hugged the sides of the truck, as well as a bench that stood in the front, directly behind the cab. The center of the truck was an open area where the prisoners were forced to stand. The benches could comfortably sit about twenty people and another thirty people could be squeezed into the standing area.

The prisoners arrived near the trucks in an orderly, almost militaristic fashion. They looked like a finely rehearsed procession as they neared the area where the trucks waited. Once there, the organized lines quickly turned to disarray and confusion. The German soldiers awaiting them began directing people onto the trucks, with no particular structure or plan. The precision and meticulousness which brought the prisoners the few hundred yards from the barracks to the trucks was suddenly shattered by the utter terror which seized the prisoners as they were commanded to enter the trucks. A few German soldiers stood in front callously ushering the prisoners toward the trucks, giving no regard to any families who wished to remain together. Children started to cry as they were pried from their mother's protective arms. Mothers shrieked in horror as their children were ripped from them. Any strong or assertive movements to reunite with family were immediately met with the threat of a machine gun or of a beating with a club. The prisoners continued to proceed at a faster pace than the guards could handle them. The guards were forced to act in a swifter and harsher fashion to prevent the complete collapse of a methodical evacuation of the camp.

There was chaos everywhere!

Some of the prisoners, sensing the separation of family that awaited them, began swapping their own children with those of their friends, hoping the Germans would sever these feigned families and unknowingly reunite true ones. Others stood dumbstruck, numb with longing and defeat and were beaten with the butts of guns into the trucks.

Maurice stayed with Meir and his family. They were close to the back of the line and Meir was furiously thinking of a way to insure they remained together but realized that it would be impossible. He suggested that his family disperse within the procession and enter the trucks individually; as a family they would certainly be separated. Meir hoped the family would enter the trucks seemingly at random and possibly reunite with each other inside. He knew there was virtually no chance that all seven of them and Maurice would find themselves on the same truck. He was optimistic that perhaps they would be scattered on two or three trucks. Meir's youngest brother, Hillel, a quiet, reserved boy of eleven, was snatched first and placed on the truck furthest away from the line. The two women, Meir's Aunt Chaya and his cousin, Rivka, were grateful they had been assigned to the same truck. They clutched each other and kept a careful and watchful eye for any other members of their family. Ezra and Tzvi were rejoined on a different truck while another cousin, Yehudah, a wiry boy of eighteen, was one of the last prisoners forced on the same truck as the two women. Maurice stood a few yards behind Meir appearing as if he did not know Meir at all, hoping he would randomly be sent onto the same truck. Meir was directed to a truck, that contained none of his relatives. He boarded the truck anxiously looking for his brothers and cousins and was disheartened to discover he was alone. A moment later the door of the truck was forced shut and he heard a German shout, "This one is full, let it proceed." Meir pushed to the back window of the truck and saw Maurice still standing in the yard, being directed by a German to enter a different truck. Meir then heard the truck's ignition start and watched as it turned around and exited the camp.

Maurice entered the truck and noticed Meir's brother. Hillel, sobbing uncontrollably. Maurice comforted him and disingenuously assured him that everything would be all right. Maurice heard the other trucks begin to exit the camp and a moment later his truck started to move. Where were they going now? He peered out the back window and saw the Rivesaltes camp for the last time. Maurice looked around the truck, did not recognize anyone except for Hillel and understood that once again he was alone. Who knew if Bernard was alive? His friend Meir was now out of reach. Would he ever see them again? Would he ever go home again? Would the war ever end? Maurice looked at Hillel, who had stopped crying. He heard faint noises emanating from Hillel and noticed that he was praying softly. Maurice could not hear the prayers and did not understand them anyway. But they sounded so uplifting, so full of confidence, so encouraging. Hillel was surely far more frightened than Maurice. He was a young boy and this ordeal was very terrifying and strange. Yet he found the conviction, the determination to cry to G-d, to beseech Him to protect him and sustain him. In a great hour of need, a young Parisian boy knew where to turn. Maurice felt humbled by Hillel, embarrassed by the profane and secular world of which he was a part, a world which foreclosed these tender and compassionate moments of simple faith. Maurice continued to look at Hillel and saw a hundred generations of tradition and history. He saw the blood libels, the Crusades, the Inquisition, ghettos, expulsions, mistreatment and suffering. He also saw the Talmud, the great legal, ethical, halachic and moral book of the Jewish People. He saw Torah scrolls written with meticulous precision and detail. He saw the dedication and sacrifice Hillel and his ancestors displayed to honor and study those holy works and he remembered the hardships they had endured. He knew all this from his history lectures but he had never experienced it, he had never lived it. Maurice did not know where the truck was headed but he knew what he had to do. He expressly disobeyed the direct instructions of his teacher Meir and asked Hillel to teach him how to pray.

39

The train was hot and stuffy, and the small window, which Maurice continued to examine, did little to circulate air within the car. Maurice stared at the two parallel bars, which stood as the main obstacle to freedom. How could they be removed? He pulled on them again but they did not yield at all. Maurice had not seen Meir in almost a month but found that he had absorbed his passion for escape and remained glued to the bars, thinking of ways to remove them.

The past month had been very difficult. The trucks had taken them from Rivesaltes to Drancy, a small detainment camp outside of Paris. Maurice was imprisoned there until earlier in the day, when he was removed and forced on the train. The moment he arrived at Drancy he was separated from Hillel and did not see him or Meir or anyone else from Meir's family. The conditions were much more uncomfortable than at Rivesaltes. There was very little to eat, there were no beds or doctors and most families were torn apart, which only increased the anxiety and longing. All the prisoners there seemed to pass the days with oblivious preoccupation and frightened expectation. Escape was not possible: The grounds were heavily fortified and guarded and movement within the camp was curtailed. Maurice knew he would be moved again; Drancy lacked many of the facilities necessary for prolonged imprisonment such as sturdy barracks and work detail. In addition, none of the prisoners Maurice spoke with in Drancy had been there for longer than a few months, and he understood the camp was only a temporary way-station in a longer journey.

Maurice was certain the car would soon be closed, there was no more room for any additional prisoners. He felt a sudden tug at his sweater and looked down. An old frail woman with wisps of tangled white hair stood gazing at him. The woman looked familiar, surely a neighbor from Paris. Perhaps under better conditions he would recognize her. She pulled at his sweater once again. "You do not recognize me, Maurice?" she asked softly.

Maurice studied her face intently. She was pleasant looking but her eyes revealed an inner sadness, recent sorrow and pain. He examined her another moment, and then remarked, "Mrs. Levy?"

"You do remember me!" she cried while breaking into a smile, which made her uncomfortable, as if she had not smiled in a very long time.

Mrs. Levy, Maurice did not know her first name, was once married to Charles Levy, a tall, brave man who was in the same regiment as Bernard during the Great War. Bernard and Charles rarely visited each other but they exchanged correspondence frequently. The last time Maurice saw Mrs. Levy was at Charles's funeral in the winter of 1938.

"Yes, Mrs. Levy," said Maurice calmly. "It is comforting to see familiar and loving faces during these desperate and unfortunate times. Have you seen my uncle recently?"

Mrs. Levy grew pale and serious. "You have not heard what happened?" She looked away hoping to avoid Maurice's obvious curiosity.

Maurice nodded and sensed something terrible had transpired. He did not know for certain but Mrs. Levy's sudden change of expression was foreboding indeed. Mrs. Levy refused to meet his eyes. "Please, Mrs. Levy," begged Maurice, "please tell me about my uncle."

Mrs. Levy turned around, faced Maurice and saw him visibly distraught. She could not deny him the truth no matter how painful. She dropped her head and very softly began to speak. "It was two days after Bastille Day and the Jews of Paris were being rounded up by the police at the behest of the Nazis. Officers went to each Jewish home in

Paris informing them where and when to appear for relocation. An officer came to Bernard's house and told him he was required to be at a police station near the Vèlodrome d'Hiver in the Rue Nelaton not far from the Eiffel Tower by eight the next morning." Mrs. Levy paused, took a deep breath and continued.

"I was also directed by the police to go to that same police station and I arrived there at about seven thirty. Bernard was there already, dressed in his old cavalry uniform. It barely fit him but he wore it anyway with pride and honor. About ten buses were lined up in front of the police station and as the Jews arrived they were told to enter the buses and wait quietly. As each bus filled it quickly drove away. Bernard refused to enter any of the buses. He stated that he was a French war hero, produced his three medals and insisted that he could not be told to relocate for no reason. He stood there defiantly, refusing to listen to the French officers.

"One of the officers, sensing Bernard's uncompromising obstinacy, sought to appeal to him rationally. He approached Bernard and explained that he and all the Jews of Paris were being moved for their benefit, to spare them the unpleasantness of the ongoing war. The officer believed his answer satisfactory and thought Bernard would now acquiesce and enter one of the buses. As a gesture of friendship and understanding the officer moved toward him and held out his hand to escort Bernard toward the line of buses. Bernard ignored the officer and started laughing loudly and sarcastically. The officer was shocked by Bernard's rudeness and lunged at him demanding an explanation. Bernard turned toward the officer and explained that he found it difficult to believe that the Jews, who were subject to two years of continuous discrimination and mistreatment, were now the only people in Paris worthy of being spared the horrors of the war. He urged the officer to stop insulting him and instead invent a more believable and plausible explanation. A crowd was quietly gathering and the officer knew he had to act fast. It was obvious he was incensed with Bernard but calmly asked him again if he would enter a bus and again Bernard refused. The officer immediately grabbed Bernard and dragged him into the police station. I could see Bernard through a window in the station, arguing furiously with the officer and two Nazi soldiers. A few moments later I saw Bernard throw up his hands and turn to exit the station."

Mrs. Levy stopped. She was crying softly and wished to stop speaking. Maurice sensed her hesitation, "Please, Mrs. Levy, please continue. I am aware it is difficult but I must know what happened!"

"All right Maurice, I just need a moment." She regained her composure and resumed. "Bernard started walking toward the door. One of the Nazi soldiers removed his gun from his holster, and fired at Bernard. I saw Bernard fall to the ground. Everyone outside heard the gunshot but we were all so frightened and shocked that no one moved toward the station to see if Bernard was alive. Everyone just quickly turned and entered the buses. One of the officers on the bus later told us that Bernard was dead."

Mrs. Levy covered her face with her hands and succumbed to her tears.

Maurice too began to cry but he knew he could not allow his emotions to overpower him, to drown him and plunge him into inaction and cause him to give up trying to escape. He thanked Mrs. Levy, wiped away his tears and silently mourned the loss of his uncle.

About a half hour later the door of the car was locked then sealed shut. It was very crowded and although Maurice tried he could not see the faces of those standing at the other end of the car. He wondered if perhaps Hillel or one of Meir's other relatives was on the same car and if he would ever see any of them again.

The next morning a loud shrill whistle shattered the still quiet autumn air and the train began to move. It traveled slowly at first but once it gained momentum it proceeded at a quick and steady pace. Maurice did not know the train's destination and did not know how long he would be on the train, but he realized that if he did not escape soon he was surely doomed.

Maurice had already been in the car for over thirty hours. Others had been there much longer. A small waste bucket stood on the floor in the corner of the car near where Maurice was standing and was slowly starting to overflow. Maurice turned away from the bucket and its foul smell of human waste and leaned against the wall of the car. It was not yet noon but Maurice was very tired, he had not slept in over a day. The train was no longer hot and stifling: The speed of the train and the breezes entering through the small window, were sufficient to cool the entire car. Maurice was standing in an uncomfortable position and was surrounded by people everywhere but he soon fell into a light sleep. He dreamed of Uncle Bernard, his defiant obstinacy, his naive belief in the vindication of the French government. He had been dozing for nearly an hour when the train suddenly turned sharply, the car jerked to one side and Maurice was awakened. He was still disoriented from his slumber and did not yet realize that Meir Kaplan was standing in front of him.

"We do not have much time, Maurice," cried Meir excitedly.

Maurice rubbed his eyes and stood in disbelief. "I cannot believe you are here, Meir! When were you placed on this car? I have been here almost two days."

"I was shocked to see you over at the other end of this car! In fact, I was not sure it was you and I pushed my way to this side to make sure it was you. I was forced on the train early this morning, soon after dawn. I believe I was one of the last prisoners on the car, they closed the doors shortly afterward." Meir turned serious. "Have you seen any of my relatives, Maurice?" asked Meir desperately.

"I left Rivesaltes with your brother Hillel but we were separated the moment we reached Drancy. I have not seen anyone from your family since," offered Maurice apologetically.

"That is what I was afraid of," bemoaned Meir. "I have been searching for them since we left Rivesaltes as well and I have not seen any of them."

Meir quickly continued, "But we cannot dwell on the past, it will only discourage us and dampen our spirits. Right now we must concentrate on escaping from here."

Meir had not lost any of his obsessive determination, which Maurice found reassuring and encouraging. It was good to see Meir again. "I have been thinking about that as well," answered Maurice. "The only way out of here is through that window and the bars are firmly bolted into the frame of the car." Maurice pointed to the window.

"I see, Maurice. You are quite right, that window is our only way out. We must find a way to bend those bars."

Maurice chuckled. "Those bars are probably solid steel! How do you propose to bend them?"

"I do not know. There must be something we could use, some material which could soften the metal, enabling us to bend it." Meir looked at Maurice, "You are the student, you should know all about this sort of thing."

Maurice blushed, "I never excelled in science. I only studied history. I apologize but I never heard of bending metal before."

Meir looked around the car, searching for something to work the metal. It was difficult to concentrate with all the noise and commotion within the car. There were the terrifying cries and wails, children screaming for water, mothers trying to hush their shrieking, sick babies. Some old men kept predicting they were destined for death, others were guessing torture.

Meir looked out at one hundred people and another nine hundred in the other cars who were so terrified, so unsure of the future, so full of despair and anguish. They were all Jews, most of them were still wearing the Yellow Star, which the French government had required since June, and Meir was overwhelmed with pity and remorse. Where was the train headed? To a work camp? Then why take the elderly and the infirm? Meir could not fathom what was in store for them and was determined not to find out.

Meir continued to think and scan the room, and a moment later his eyes lit up. He pointed to the corner and watched as Maurice recoiled in horror. "The waste bucket?!" cried Maurice.

"Yes, Maurice. The substances in the bucket should soften the metal if we apply it for a long enough time."

"How do you suggest we do that?" asked Maurice, unsure if he wanted to hear the answer. "I will show you. Come, Maurice, we have much to do!"

Meir squeezed to the corner of the car, removed his sweater and submerged it into the bucket. He stood as far away from the bucket as he could, the stench was overwhelming. He then returned to the window and rolled the sweater until it was a long, circular, snake-like garment. He pushed one end of the sweater around one of the bars and pulled it back into the train so that the thick, bulky center of the sweater hugged the bar. Maurice understood what Meir was doing, removed his own sweater and copied Meir's motions. The two of them began pulling their sweaters back and forth in a pulley-like motion, rubbing the bars with the foul and odious contents of the bucket.

Onlookers gawked with curiosity. Some demanded they stop, if any of the guards saw what they were doing everyone in the car would surely suffer. Others cheered them and spurred them to act quickly. Meir and Maurice ignored the warnings and encouragement of their fellow prisoners in the car and continued to work the metal, desperately trying to soften the bars.

One hour passed, then another, then still another. The train proceeded on its journey eastward but Meir and Maurice continued to pull the ends of the sweater to and fro, rubbing and relaxing the bars with each motion. They stopped once, after about three hours, to submerge the sweaters into the repulsive bucket again, after the sweaters turned dry from the friction caused by the repetitive pulling. The two men were tired, their entire bodies smelled from the refuse of the bucket and their arms ached but they would not cease. After five hours of almost continuous action Maurice felt a slight movement from the bar. He stopped, placed the sweater on the floor and pushed the bar with his forefinger. The bar moved a trifle and Maurice stood surprised, wondering whether the sweat and waste attached to his finger created a false illusion. He wiped his hand dry, pushed the bar again, this time more forcefully with his open palm, and watched with fascination as the bar wobbled with definitive symmetry, as if the bar seemed to possess an almost rubber-like quality.

"Look, Meir," shouted Maurice. "You were correct, the bars are starting to bend!"

Meir was captivated by the display and likewise put aside his own sweater to test the progress of the bar he was engaging. He pushed his bar and it also moved slightly.

Meir tried to move both bars far enough apart to allow someone to squeeze through but they would not yield that much.

"We are almost there, Maurice, a few more hours and we should be able to escape!"

They picked up their sweaters and continued their work with increased enthusiasm. For the next three hours they pulled with all their might, scarcely aware that the sun was setting and they had spent the entire day absorbed in this endeavor.

Their renewed efforts further sparked the interest of many of the prisoners within the car. Some insisted they would not allow them to leave, the Nazis would know some people had escaped and the rest would suffer unfairly. Others said they wished they could leave with them but some were too frightened to jump mid-journey, some still clung to the misguided belief they faced no harm, and some were too despondent, too full of hopelessness and resignation, unable to rationally consider the harsh reality which engulfed them and they remained frozen with despair and grief.

Shortly after sunset they stopped. They had softened the bars considerably and the bars could now be moved and manipulated as easily as a clump of clay.

"It is time, Maurice," announced Meir solemnly.

Maurice stood in front of the window and sensed imminent freedom. He turned around and gazed upon the wretched, jaded faces of the prisoners he was leaving behind. What would become of them? Of the prisoners in the next car? Of the prisoners still in Drancy? Of the Jews in the rest of Occupied Europe surely placed in cattle trains and transported to some unknown destination?

Maurice sighed, slowly turned away and faced the window.

"We have been softening the metal for almost eight continuous hours, let us hope our job is done!" said Meir anxiously.

Meir carefully perched his feet in the corner where the wall met the floor. With all his strength he pushed the bars and slowly watched as they moved further and further apart until the space between them was wide enough for them to escape. Meir then cautiously stuck his head out the window and observed large floodlights positioned near the roof casting light on the entire length of the train. Armed Nazi guards stood at steady intervals in special compartments within the train and their upper bodies were leaning out of carefully constructed windows, scanning the area illuminated by the floodlights. Meir instantly withdrew inside the train.

"What is the matter, Meir?"

"There is a problem," said Meir regrettably. "The sides of the train are lit up and are carefully watched by the guards. If we leave the car we will certainly be seen," he explained.

Maurice nodded, peered out the window to assess the situation for himself and thought for a moment. "We can make our escape when the train takes a sudden sharp turn. I believe we are the fourth or fifth car in the train and that will give us a few extra seconds where we can escape. When this car enters a turn the train will be in an awkward position and the floodlights will necessarily bypass the side of the car. The side of the car will become darkened, the guards will not be able to see us and our escape will go unnoticed!"

Meir stared blankly for a moment, thinking about Maurice's suggestion, then nodded in full agreement. "For someone with little science background you seem to understand a great deal about light and angles and the movement of trains," joked Meir.

The two men waited impatiently, carefully trying to anticipate a sharp, sudden turn. They had already discussed how they would jump and hopefully cause as little damage to their bodies as possible. They agreed that after exiting the car they would immediately curl up and try to force their bodies to roll away from the tracks and protect themselves from the impact of the fall.

Mrs. Levy quietly approached Maurice, fully aware that he would soon be gone. She handed something to Maurice. He looked at it and saw it was an object wrapped inside a handkerchief. He remembered that Leonhard Zürenmantt once handed him something concealed within a handkerchief, quickly slipped it into his pocket and thanked her. "It was once an object of scorn and degradation, but for you it will be one of honor and heritage. I want you to have it, Maurice. Now please, run and may G-d watch over you!" She sadly turned and walked away. Maurice wanted to call her back but she was too far-gone and he could not turn away from the window. "Farewell, Mrs. Levy," he whispered.

"Now, Maurice," shouted Meir. "Now is our chance!"

The train made a sudden sharp turn and everyone in the car fell to one side. Meir cautiously peered out the window and watched as the cars of the train folded as it turned, and observed that the side of their car grew dark. The floodlights completely skirted the car and it could not be seen by any Nazi guards. Meir quickly motioned to Maurice. Meir then jumped out the window and Maurice followed an instant later.

The two men landed and rolled down a small slope beneath the railroad track and remained motionless until the train was safely out of view.

"Are you hurt?" asked Meir, as the train disappeared in the distance.

"I do not think so, some slight bruises from the fall but nothing that appears too serious. I will wait another moment, then walk around and make sure I am all right. Are you hurt?" he returned.

"I also have a few scratches and cuts but I expected that much."

Meir and Maurice lingered a few more minutes, confident the train was far enough away and they were now out of danger. They stood up and checked themselves and confirmed they did not endure any serious injuries. They were healthy and free! They smelled terribly and were tired and hungry and lost but they had finally escaped! Meir instinctively clapped his hands, overcome with relief they were out of the grip of those hated Nazis. Maurice turned to Meir and glanced disapprovingly at Meir's clasped hands. Maurice raised his arm and pointed toward the train and the roughly one thousand Jews still trapped inside. Meir understood, ceased clapping and lowered his head in silence and shame and sorrow.

40

Meir and Maurice ran through the forest seeking a safe place to sleep. They would have to take turns, one of them had to remain awake in case wild animals or roving patrols spotted them. They found a small patch of level ground directly in front of a large tree and Meir quickly went to sleep. Maurice agreed to stand guard for three hours, then wake Meir, who promised to relieve him.

The serene quiet of the forest was soothing and Maurice was exhausted. He feared he would fall asleep as well. He knew he needed to remain awake, occupy himself with something interesting, but he had nothing. He thought of searching for food but feared he might get separated from Meir and become lost in the woods. He wanted to remove his shirt, it smelled awful, but it was too cold and he did not want to get sick. He then remembered the handkerchief Mrs. Levy had given him and he quickly retrieved it. The handkerchief was likewise dirty but he quickly opened it to see the contents inside. Maurice peeled away the handkerchief and threw it on the ground. He observed the contents and although he had seen others on the train, he now had time to study it and think about its implications. It was quite dark and except for the light of the moon there was no other illumination, but Maurice was able to discern what he was holding. It was a yellow, star-shaped cloth with the word *"juif"* imprinted on the front in bold black letters. Maurice held it up to the moonlight and continued to gaze at it. He was not quite sure why Mrs. Levy gave it to him, perhaps to remind him of his background as he ventured into an unknown future. Maurice knew all about the yellow star, the humiliation, the inferior status it represented. It was an old way of disgracing the Jews, forcing them to display their religion for all to see and ridicule. The star or badge had been in existence for hundreds of years and had only recently been reinstated as French policy.

Maurice stared at the word again.

Juif.

The word simply meant "Jew" but its underlying connotation was far more sinister. The yellow star was an odious reminder of centuries of mistreatment and debasement. Requiring each Jew to wear it signified a retraction, a regression from all the equality and brotherhood that France had manifested for the past one hundred and fifty years. This was far worse than the betrayal Maurice felt when Jean thundered at him at the Sorbonne over two years ago. Those were the diatribes of one man, this was an act sanctioned and endorsed by the French Government! After the incident with Jean, Maurice knew that for the duration of the war he could not remain in France, he was not welcome there. But what about when the war ended? Could he ever return? Could he ever resume life in Paris with the knowledge that deep in their hearts the French did not consider him an equal?

Where then could he go?

Maurice continued to remain standing, certain that if he sat down he would fall asleep. There was only a half hour left to his watch and in about another four hours the sun would rise. Maurice wondered if Meir had planned where to travel next. They could not remain in the forest: Winter was fast approaching and without shelter and an ample supply of food they would surely die. Maurice returned the yellow star to his pocket, still unsure why Mrs. Levy had given it to him, and resumed his position behind the tree. He awoke Meir precisely one half hour later and was asleep within minutes.

The sun's rays were beginning to break through the thicket of trees and Meir heard a sequence of sounds. They did not sound like the movements of an animal, they were more methodical and deliberate. Meir bent down to wake Maurice. "I hear something," he whispered. Maurice was still half asleep and saw the blurry visage of Meir hovering over him. "Wake up, Maurice," demanded Meir. "I hear noises!"

Maurice jarred his head and lay wide awake. He saw the seriousness and dread on Meir's face and immediately stood erect. "What is it?" asked Maurice.

"I am not sure, but they seem to be coming from over there," returned Meir, pointing away from the tree.

"I hear it too," cried Maurice. "Should we run away?"

"I do not think so. I am not even certain our presence here is known, those movements could be routine patrols or French civilians looking for food. If we do run we will surely reveal our position. I think we should wait and see if they turn away."

The sounds grew louder and louder and finally Meir and Maurice heard the command from within the forest, "Do not move! You are surrounded! If either of you reach for a weapon you will be shot instantly! Slowly, slowly place your hands in the air!"

Meir and Maurice had no weapons and if they tried to run they would surely be shot. Were they Nazis? Thieving French peasants? They both knew that it did not matter, they had no choice but to comply. Meir nodded to Maurice and they placed their hands well above their heads. An instant later ten men pointing machine guns emerged from the forest. Meir and Maurice were completely surrounded. Meir realized they were not an army unit: They had no uniforms and carried at least four different makes of machine gun. They were also unkempt and dirty, hardly adequate representatives of a standing army.

The ten men approached cautiously. Two of them, Pierre and Claude, drew closer.

"Who are you?" demanded Claude, speaking French.

Maurice motioned that he would allow Meir to speak. He was more cunning and quick on his feet, he would know what to say. Meir was unsure who these men were and was afraid to admit he was Jewish. He suspected they were some sort of resistance group. Who else would carry guns in the forests of France! He concluded they were not Nazis; the man spoke French and the Nazis would have shot on sight. He decided to divulge as little as possible until he could trust them. Claude was waiting for an answer.

"We were prisoners and we escaped from the train," answered Meir vaguely.

Claude, Pierre and the other eight men suspected that Meir and Maurice might be Nazi spies sent to infiltrate their group. They accepted Meir's response with skepticism. "That hardly seems plausible. How did you escape?"

Meir related how they broke out of the train and offered his foul and soiled shirt as proof of their success. Claude sniffed it and recoiled in disgust. Would the Nazis go to this extent to penetrate a resistance group? Was this man telling the truth?

Meir sensed the men were starting to believe him and wanted to stress that he was not lying. He knew there was one thing he could say which would convince them he was sincere. He knew there was a possibility it would backfire but he wanted to secure their trust and decided to take the risk.

"My friend and I are Jews," offered Meir.

Claude, still aiming a machine gun at Meir and Maurice, retreated a few paces and conferred with Pierre and three of the other men. They huddled together and spoke quietly. The rest of the men continued to aim their guns at Meir and Maurice. Claude noted that it was highly improbable a Nazi would voluntarily admit he was Jewish and agree to wear such repulsive and putrid clothes. Pierre countered that this exceptional and surprising behavior perhaps demonstrated the lengths the Nazis would go to discover their whereabouts.

Claude and Pierre were confused. They wanted to believe these men were not spies but they needed more proof. They decided to search them, tie them up and take them back to their headquarters for further questioning from Leopold and the others. If they turned out to be Nazi spies they would be killed there. Pierre barked the orders to one of the men who immediately put down his gun and began searching Meir and Maurice. Claude reminded the man to be especially thorough, transmitters could be hidden in many places. The man, who now smelled almost as bad as Meir and Maurice, completed the search and reported that both men possessed neither weapons nor communication devices. Meir and Maurice's hands were then firmly tied behind their backs and they were forced to march with the men, guns still drawn, toward the headquarters.

Meir was convinced the men were resistance fighters. They moved with bravery and perseverance yet exhibited strains of fear and worry, normal conflicting emotions for partisans in hiding. Meir was intrigued by them. Where did they come from? How many were there? How long had they been in the forests?

Maurice also understood that these men were resistance fighters, similar to the ones his uncle warned him about. He too was fascinated by men his age who exhibited such courage and who risked their lives to help destroy the Nazi war machine. He realized these men might hate Jews but they undoubtedly hated the Nazis more. But Meir and Maurice were both preoccupied with the same overriding concern, how to convince these resistance fighters they were not the enemy. They were able to converse with each other while they walked toward the headquarters and they each suggested many arguments they would employ to sway their captors but they both understood that none of them were especially persuasive.

The walk lasted about one hour. Neither of them knew where they were and they were both very tired. They came to the edge of the forest and Maurice and Meir observed a small farm adjacent to a large barn a few hundred meters away up a small hill. The ten men raced to the barn single file, dragging Meir and Maurice along the way. They reached the top of the hill and stood in front of the barn door. The door opened and a short, husky man stood in the entrance. "Why are you back so soon?" he asked pensively. "Did you lose anyone?"

"No, thankfully we are all here. We caught two prisoners," responded one of the fighters. "They could be spies, call Leopold!"

The short, husky man nodded, turned around and disappeared inside the barn. A moment later a tall, bearded man appeared and Maurice stared at him for a moment, then broke out in a smile and breathed a very long sigh of relief. "Professor Klippenberg!" he shouted.

Leopold exited the barn and approached Maurice carefully. "Maurice Andeau? Is that you?"

"Yes, Professor," said Maurice excitedly.

Meir turned to Maurice, "You know this man?"

"Yes, he was my history professor at the Sorbonne. He was dismissed shortly after the fall of Paris, October of 1940, I believe."

"You always had a way with small facts, Maurice," broke Klippenberg, "and you are correct. I stole away to the forests soon after my dismissal from the university. I joined a small band of resistance fighters, people like myself who knew we could not remain in Paris. We are called the Maquis and we are dedicated to defeating our sworn enemy, the Nazis." Klippenberg pointed to Meir, "Is he with you?"

"Yes."

Klippenberg eyed Meir and Maurice. He observed their foul clothes, their exhausted, scared faces and their slim builds. He knew they were not the enemy. He turned to Claude, "Release them, they are not spies. We have nothing to fear from them."

Claude was relieved his dilemma was resolved quickly and painlessly. He motioned to one of the men who then loosened the ropes and untied them. Klippenberg waved his hand, inviting Meir and Maurice inside, and they followed Klippenberg into the barn.

The barn was not a barn at all. It merely had the facade of a barn but was a large two-story house equipped with a food storage area, a room for meals and many rooms for sleeping. Meir could not guess how many people lived inside but observed at least thirty beds. Upon closer inspection, Meir realized they were not beds at all, merely bundles of straw in large burlap sacks strewn here and there. It was still more comfortable than sleeping out of doors on the rocky hillside. He quickly understood that the appearance of a barn was intended to disguise the headquarters of the resistance group. The structure was long and narrow and each room seemed to have its own function and purpose. In one room Maurice saw piles of guns, grenades and explosives. In another room he saw a list of twenty-five names on the wall. In a third room he observed what looked like a communications center with varying machines of all sizes. Most of the rooms, though, merely contained beds and Maurice wondered how long it had taken to convert the barn and how many more resistance groups were scattered throughout France.

Klippenberg led them to a washroom where they could wash and clean up. They were given a change of clothes and then escorted to the common eating area where they were served a hot, tasteless yet filling broth and some dry, barely edible bread. Maurice and Meir were starving and ate non-stop while listening to Klippenberg.

Klippenberg informed them about many of the attacks which the Maquis carried out and recalled some of their more daring successes, including the destruction of a German train carrying arms near Nantes. Klippenberg watched as the two men listened with fascination, hardly aware that while they and thousands more were languishing in work camps and prisons, other Frenchmen were risking their lives to free the country and the world from the terrible tyranny, from the scourge of the Nazis. Klippenberg observed their wide-eyed interest in the Maquis and continued to highlight their successes, hoping to entice them to join the group. He was fairly certain they had nowhere else to go and was confident they were excited by the prospect of helping to defeat the enemy. Klippenberg also knew they could be lured by the decent supply of food, shelter and clothing.

Klippenberg desperately wanted them to remain, he could use two smart and cunning fighters and he already envisioned a great future in store for Maurice. Klippenberg rose and carefully placed his left hand on Maurice's shoulder and his right hand on Meir's. The two men looked up at him and saw the seriousness and solemnity on Klippenberg's face.

"Meir and Maurice, we need you," he began. "We need intelligent and courageous men in the Maquis and we are all impressed that you have already outsmarted the Germans and proved your bravery and will to fight. We desperately need your help if we are to continue our efforts. You would be provided with ample food and shelter. I do not want to mislead the two of you, the activities we engage in are dangerous and are undertaken at a risk to life. I believe you already saw the list of our casualties, a list of the men we have lost, a list which grows longer each day! But we have struck the Germans many times and we are doing whatever we can to inhibit the Nazis from inflicting any more damage here in France. You can make a great contribution to our cause, you can fill the empty shoes of some of the unfortunate losses we have suffered. Furthermore, you already know the whereabouts of our hideout and could reveal the location under torture." Klippenberg finished, knowing there was not much else he could say to urge them to remain. He stood up and walked to the far end of the room. Before exiting he turned around, "You need not make a decision immediately. Think about it and talk it over and I will see you again later." Klippenberg proceeded to the door and left the room.

Maurice and Meir remained seated. They were alone, yet they somehow felt at home in the barn, comfortable and unafraid among the Maquis. Meir never met Klippenberg before but found him warm and encouraging. The rest of the resistance fighters were also friendly and welcoming. Meir and Maurice were treated as if they had been there for the past two years.

Meir looked at Maurice, who seemed to already know what he was going to say. "I also think we should stay," jumped Maurice. "I know you believe it is the right decision and I agree with you. We will be fed here, even if the food is meager, and you must admit that the accomodations here are better than the forest. Of course we will be involved in dangerous missions but if we can inflict more damage on those Nazis then I will accept the danger carefully and with caution!"

"Yes, Maurice. We really do not have any alternative."

Klippenberg was delighted with their decision and was present when Meir Kaplan and Maurice Andeau were installed as members of the Maquis in early November, 1942. They were informed that the word Maquis meant "scrubby underbrush," reminiscent of the hills of Corsica, the traditional hiding place of outlaws. Maurice and Meir were quickly trained in the ways of the Maquis. They were given false passports and citizenship papers, in the event they were ever stopped and searched. They were instructed how to fire a gun, how to ignite explosives and how to camouflage themselves in the forest. They were initiated into the small yet cohesive group and vowed never to reveal their location or the names of any of the members, even on pain of death.

Meir and Maurice were satisfied. They had a place to call home and were working to defeat the enemy. They felt comfortable living with the other members and soon befriended them all. The rest of the group came from all over France and they represented varying philosophies and ideologies. Some were communists, others socialists. Except for Meir, none of them were observant Jews. Several of the Jews were staunch Zionists while others had no connection to their heritage and seemed no different than any other Frenchmen. Yet the entire group managed to put aside their individual opinions and create a cohesive, unified resistance group that was among the most successful in the forests of France.

Meir felt fortunate. He missed his family and feared the horrors they were undoubtedly experiencing but continued to thank the Almighty for the amazing good fortune He bestowed upon him. Meir fully understood that their escape from the train and subsequent encounter with the Maquis was only due to His watchful and caring eye and he wondered why they deserved this special treatment at all. Although Meir was friendly and cordial to all the members of the Maquis he rarely associated with them and spent most of his spare time alone. The boredom and tedium of waiting for the right target with little chance of exposure led many of the members to read together, engage in endless conversation or to take long walks dreaming of a future peace and a secure France. Meir did not harbor any ill will toward any of the Maquis but he declined to join them, he considered it a waste of time, and often walked or sat alone trying to fulfill as many of the laws of the Torah as he could. Although none of the other members were observant they sometimes joined him in heartfelt prayer.

Maurice too was overcome with relief. Since he had left Paris over two years ago he had survived one pitfall after another, always moving, never remaining steadfast in any one place. But now he felt some stability, he had a home and many friends and an important purpose and meaning to his life. He concentrated on his new and exciting endeavor, learning the skills of covert attacks in an effort to defeat the Germans, and excelled rather quickly. He could not wait to participate in his first secret mission and was assured by Klippenberg that it would come within the next month.

But Maurice scarcely gave any thought to those earlier feelings of purpose and meaning that were first ignited over two years ago. He abandoned the learning, the slow methodological awareness he first began with Meir at Rivesaltes. He was too enthralled by the excitement of the Maquis and exerted all his energies trying to mature into a seasoned and experienced resistance fighter. Meir noticed Maurice's disinterest in Judaism and after he was rebuffed by Maurice several times believed any further instruction would prove fruitless. Meir watched with sorrow as Maurice drifted further and further away and became more and more a part of the secular, irreligious Maquis, conversing with them, drinking with them and dreaming about the future with them. Meir recalled that he once considered Maurice his brother, cared for his safety as much as his own family and believed they would remain lifelong friends. But now Meir was unsure. They still spoke often and were cordial toward each other but the gulf separating them, which Meir had briefly and unsuccessfully tried to bridge, was only growing wider and wider.

Would Maurice ever return?

41

The cold weather came within a few weeks, making the search for firewood as important as the search for food. This was Klippenberg's third winter in the forests and he was fully prepared to brave the severe and harsh weather. The barn was insulated with furs stolen from the Germans in Lyons and they had been stocking up on firewood since August. The group continued to grow steadily and after Meir and Maurice joined, another ten members were accepted. At least half the group was out at any one time, carrying out attacks or searching for food. Klippenberg were very busy arranging and orchestrating a new series of attacks, all in Paris, and was hardly seen during the day. It was late December and most of the group were tired and cold. Meir and Maurice had been with the Maquis for almost two months and had yet to see any real action. They waited patiently and trained with the more experienced members of the group. One morning after breakfast Klippenberg approached Maurice and asked him to remain after everyone else departed. The room was soon empty and Klippenberg and Maurice were alone. Maurice wondered why his professor requested this private meeting and waited anxiously. Klippenberg paused a moment then began, "As you know, Maurice, in a matter of days our fighters will be sent to carry out various acts of sabotage and I am sure you wish to join them."

Maurice turned white when he realized that Klippenberg was telling him he would not be one of those sent out. His face fell in obvious disappointment and Klippenberg sensed Maurice's displeasure.

"You are quite astute, Maurice. You have discerned that you will not be sent and that is true. Please let me explain. I know you, Maurice, and I know where your talents lie. It would be a waste to place you in obvious danger when you can better serve our cause here."

Maurice was intrigued but unsure of what Klippenberg had in mind. "What do you mean, Professor?"

Klippenberg drew closer to Maurice, "I remember how clear and sharp your mind was, how easy it was for you to absorb information. You are very smart and I need you to assist me with the intelligence and communication aspects of our operation. It entails a meticulous and persistent system of intercepting, then decoding, then interpreting various enemy signals. It is not the most glorious or heroic part of the Maquis but it is surely the most important. It enables us to plan and coordinate our attacks with the least possibility of failure or capture. I have been thinking about this for a long time, ever since the first day you arrived here. I waited before telling you because I wanted you to receive the necessary basic training, but this is where you belong, Maurice."

Maurice understood Klippenberg's reasoning and was fully aware of his own capabilities. Although he would have preferred to venture out with the other members on daring missions he knew such desires were merely immature yearnings for adventure, which had to yield to common sense. He knew Klippenberg only had the best intentions for him as well as the group and would not argue with his professor. "I understand your argument, Professor, and I accept. I will stay here, learn the communications systems and try to amass as much information about the enemy that I can. I will not disappoint you." Maurice sounded confident, ready to accept this new burden with enthusiasm and determination.

"Good, Maurice. The group shall be leaving tonight after I instruct them about their missions. Then your communications training will begin."

Shortly after midnight, Klippenberg called together four members of the Maquis: Meir, Claude, Pierre and Ernest, a Zionist from a small town near Paris. Klippenberg supplied them with guns, explosives, heavy coats and boots. He provided them with compasses and maps that clearly indicated the selected targets. Klippenberg urged them to proceed with caution and to abandon the mission if they sensed their presence had been discovered or if they suspected the slightest danger. He informed them that they would be joining other resistance groups stationed throughout France and that further details would follow once they arrived at their destinations. He reminded them to strike quickly and quietly and cheerily told them he expected to see them in about three weeks. He bid them farewell and prayed for their safe return. Meir and Ernest left within the hour, Claude and Pierre a few moments after them.

Both groups traveled toward the same destination but they took different routes; Klippenberg's rule permitting only two members to travel together at any one time was still strictly enforced. Meir and Ernest reached the outskirts of Paris within a week and immediately began planning their attack. Meir liked Ernest, who although younger than him was quite smart and very dedicated. Ernest had been with the Maquis for over a year, far longer than Meir, but he appreciated Meir's maturity and respectfully deferred to Meir, and only objected to Meir's authority when Meir was clearly in error. During their journey toward Paris, Meir learned that Ernest was an ardent Zionist and that after the war he planned to immigrate to Palestine, something that Meir never really considered. Ernest was not religious but he did attend synagogue at least three times a year and could speak Hebrew fluently. Meir suspected that Ernest's lack of religious affiliation was primarily due to his upbringing rather than any philosophical objection and wondered what might become of Ernest if he studied the Torah with proper teachers and was taught with a passion he had never before experienced . Meir recalled that he had once entertained the same thoughts about Maurice and quickly set the matter aside.

It was early morning on the twenty-fifth of December and the streets of Paris were deserted. Meir thought it was an ideal moment to strike but they were firmly instructed to wait until sundown, when they would meet the other resistance members. Meir wondered why Klippenberg was not concerned by this upcoming gathering of so many resistance members assembling at one location and thought that perhaps other leaders had insisted it take place. As instructed by Klippenberg, they moved quietly through the streets to their predetermined destination, a small, dark alley near an abandoned warehouse not far from Porte De Clichy, and rendezvoused with other resistance groups that had been coordinated to meet. Meir and Ernest were introduced to the famous Abraham Lissner, a Jewish communist and leader of several resistance groups. He had engaged in hundreds of attacks and his fame was widespread throughout the Maquis network in France. He welcomed everyone and inquired about their previous successes and failures. Lissner spoke briefly with Meir and the other twenty men gathered in the remote alley on the western end of Paris. He did not want the meeting to last too long, it could arouse suspicion. After introducing himself to all the resistance fighters gathered there, he asked for everyone's attention.

"The next few days we will engage in crucial and significant attacks," Lissner announced. "The resistance groups have been relatively quiet the past few weeks and except for the grenades we threw at the German army in the Place de la Nation two weeks ago, we have engaged in very limited activity. The Germans probably think they have succeeded in destroying the resistance movement, that they have defeated the small yet potent network which has inflicted much damage, and they carry a more relaxed, self-assured attitude. Well, tonight and over the next few days we will demonstrate that our fight is far from over and that no matter how many of our resistance members may fall, our movement will continue to thrive and the enemy will receive no respite from us!"

Everyone nodded in agreement, still marveling at the passion and dedication which Abraham Lissner displayed. Suddenly he called toward Meir and Ernest, "I believe you two are from Leopold Klippenberg's Maquis, come with me!"

Meir and Ernest wondered how their identities were already known but along with three additional resistance fighters, they followed this mesmerizing and zealous leader. It was shortly before midnight and they swung around to the Arc De Triomphe, then down Avenue Foch, easily blending in with the shadows. "There it is," whispered Lissner. He pointed to a truck with at least twenty German soldiers inside. "That truck is our target tonight, get your explosives," he ordered.

Ernest opened his coat and removed a small cloth sack, which had been hidden within the folds of his coat. He opened the sack and retrieved four grenades. He gave two of them to Meir and retained two for himself. The other three fighters quickly secured their explosives as well.

"Is everyone ready? Follow me closely," directed Lissner.

They proceeded toward the Porte Dauphine where the truck remained idle. It was very dark and from where they were standing they could not be seen. They were about forty meters from the truck and Lissner shrieked, "Now!" Some of the soldiers inside the truck heard the cry and instinctively stood up with their guns drawn looking out into the darkness, but it was too late. A barrage of grenades entered the truck and it exploded an instant later.

The next day Abraham Lissner and other resistance fighters including Pierre and Claude were in the Eighth Arrondissement near the Arc De Triomphe. They threw a grenade into a restaurant frequented by Germans on Avenue Hoche between Rue de Courcelles and Rue Beaujon.

Maurice proved an adept and skilled communications decoder. He learned how to intercept signals from as far away as Berlin and to maintain contacts with many other resistance groups throughout France. Klippenberg marveled at Maurice's quick learning, his superior handling of the decoding machines and his ability to transmit them to other groups. He always knew Maurice was smart but he was genuinely surprised by the extent of Maurice's brilliance and intelligence. Klippenberg was happy he finally found a suitable protégé and he knew he made the right choice in keeping Maurice at headquarters. As the winter wore on Maurice absorbed everything there was to know about communications until he was as skilled and adept as

Klippenberg. Klippenberg joked to Maurice that he was becoming so proficient, soon his own services would become obsolete!

Meir, though, continued to carry out various acts of sabotage and matured into a skilled and cunning soldier. He became an expert marksman and could handle the most delicate explosives with the greatest of ease. Maurice remained in the communications room with Klippenberg and hardly spent any time at all with Meir. Meir and Maurice rarely spoke except for exchanging instructions concerning the various missions.

Toward the end of March, as the severe winter slowly melted away, the Germans increased their efforts to destroy the resistance groups. They had spent the winter updating their communication equipment and were able to intercept and decode many of the messages sent by the Maquis. Claude and Pierre were captured near a train station in Toulouse. They were on their way back to the headquarters following an unsuccessful attempt to blow up a German train carrying supplies. A Nazi soldier grew suspicious when Pierre and Claude turned in the other direction after noticing the soldier staring at them. Within seconds Claude and Pierre were surrounded. They offered the soldiers every excuse they could think of and almost succeeded in convincing them they were peasant farmers on their way back home. A thorough search of Pierre's pockets revealed coded instructions from Maurice. Pierre refused to answer any questions and they were immediately handcuffed. They were taken to a nearby police station and were brutally beaten. They were told they would continue to be beaten until they divulged the location of their hideout. Pierre and Claude suffered hours of cruel tortures but would not break the oaths they had taken when they joined the Maquis. The following morning their half-conscious bodies were taken outside and they were hanged.

Ernest and three other members were shot while trying to escape from a failed ambush of a convoy of German soldiers and arms in Grenoble. The convoy was merely a trap to lure resistance fighters there and they had no chance of escaping. Klippenberg feared that the barn, the hideout deep in the woods of Northern France, would shortly be discovered. He thought of abandoning the barn and moving south, or perhaps leaving France altogether and resuming operations in neutral Spain. The other members, including Maurice, quickly disagreed and insisted they would face greater danger if they ventured into the unknown. Klippenberg relented but feared they were making a mistake.

It seemed as if every mission now ended in failure. The Maquis lost twenty men in a three-week period and although they gained an additional thirty men, mostly young Jews who had remained hidden during roundups, the losses were troubling indeed. Meir and Maurice had been with the group nearly half a year and except for Klippenberg, only four other original fighters were alive. Maurice's role as Klippenberg's top assistant met with approval and he was revered throughout the group as an essential component of their entire operation. But with the deaths of so many of the senior members Meir, too, was now regarded as an important mentor and teacher. Meir did nothing particularly outstanding to earn his elevated rank but he was forced to step into the void which had been created and which needed to be filled. Meir was selected as the only available member with the experience necessary to instruct the new recruits in the use of explosives and weapons. Meir knew he was not skilled enough to provide extensive training but he was quite aware there was no else to serve that function and hoped the new recruits would not suffer from his inexperience. Meir proved more adept than he first realized and adequately prepared the new members of the Maquis, some of whom never even had held a gun.

Meir and Maurice had risen high in the ranks of the Maquis and except for Klippenberg, they were the most senior members of the group. The two rarely spoke and when they did it was only a casual greeting or information relevant to the Maquis. They no longer discussed philosophy or Judaism or anything else which had once sparked their friendship. Maurice never prayed with Meir or tried to learn the Torah with him, and Meir never made any overtures to revive the awareness and understanding he once craved.

But they never forgot the debt they owed each other.

It was mid-April and the weather was comfortable and calm. The snows all melted and the first buds of spring were sprouting everywhere. It was well past midnight and everyone in the barn was asleep. Meir crept away from the barn trying not to wake anyone and proceeded down the hill that he had climbed the day he first came to the Maquis. He descended the hill many times since that day, roaming throughout France attacking the Germans. But this night was different. Meir had nowhere to go and he moved lazily as he nodded to Alain, the young sentry who stood armed and ready at the checkpoint halfway down the hill. The moon was full and Meir followed its light. He walked quietly, contemplatively. He passed through the plains at the foot of the hill, then walked out to the adjoining forest. He carried his gun and remained alert and attentive. He suddenly heard a noise and froze. Alain was too far away and heard nothing. He sensed it was not an animal and he did not think it was a Nazi, they rarely traveled alone. Meir believed it was either a resistance fighter or a peasant from one of the surrounding villages. The person approached quickly and Meir grew terrified and turned and aimed his gun steadily. Meir now suspected that perhaps it was a group of Nazis. He knew he could never defeat a group alone but he would not surrender without a fight. The person drew closer and an instant later Meir saw the face, aided by the moon's light, and immediately lowered the gun. "Maurice," whispered Meir, relieved. "It is me, Meir."

Maurice smiled and moved toward Meir. "I feared you were a Nazi. What are you doing here, Meir?"

"And I feared that you were a Nazi! I came here to escape," answered Meir solemnly.

"Are you leaving the Maquis, Meir?" asked Maurice, cautiously.

"No, of course not, Maurice, I just wanted a quiet place where I could be alone and meditate about the emptiness, the longing which has recently overwhelmed me."

"What do you mean, Meir?" asked Maurice tenderly. "I understand you miss your family, we all lost loved ones, Meir, but you are not alone among the Maquis!"

Meir looked up. "You are right, Maurice, but that is not what is troubling me. Tonight is Passover, that unique and meaningful day. It is a day full of custom and ceremony, yet I approach it now empty-handed. I have no unleavened bread, no wine, no bitter herbs, and no prayer book to sing hymns. I already recited whatever prayers and songs I can remember but I have no way of sanctifying the day, of performing the rituals and ancient ceremonies. I am disheartened by that." Meir sighed.

Maurice looked puzzled as if he did not comprehend Meir's predicament. "I see, Meir, but we are in the midst of a war. You cannot expect such luxuries."

"I hardly consider some unleavened bread a luxury," interrupted Meir, annoyed by Maurice's quick dismissal.

"That is quite true but you have forgotten how fortunate you are. Think of the Jews languishing in Warsaw or Lodz or Kovno or Pietrkow or those Jews we left on that train. You have heard the rumors, Meir. You have heard what is being done to our people, you must be thankful you are not among them and that you are not hungry."

Meir conceded that Maurice was right. He was not hungry and he suspected that if he had remained on the train he would no longer be alive.

Maurice continued, "Furthermore, I do not understand how you can celebrate the holiday now anyway. Where is the freedom, the royal trappings that the holiday promises? Where is the subjugation of the nations, the supremacy of the Jewish people?" Maurice grimaced.

"Meir, you know there has never been a time in history when the Jews were more crushed and tyrannized. There are ghettos, forced labor details, mistreatment and cruelty and those rumors, those horrific, incomprehensible, terrifying rumors about camps and mass graves. How can you wish to celebrate a holiday which commemorates our deliverance from bondage? We are more enslaved than ever before and the threat of death is constantly looming over us!"

Meir was not surprised by Maurice's attitude, it was one commonly adopted by those who never experienced the essence of the holiday, who never shed a tear for the sorrows of the past, who never smiled for the promise of the future, who abandoned the trust and faith that one day there would be vindication and salvation. No, Maurice could not understand the void, the emptiness that a barren Passover represented and for a moment he regretted telling him at all. Nor was Meir disturbed by Maurice's analysis. Meir knew like so many before him that all the traditions of the Torah, the commandments of Moses, needed to be embraced and cherished no matter the obstacle or the dire plight of the Jewish people. He understood from the long list of martyrs who tragically filled the pages of history that he could not abandon the heritage, there was no lapse, no abrogation of the fate, which connects the Jews to the Torah. To the contrary, the centuries of persecution and debasement and misfortune merely reaffirmed than attachment. True, the current condition was far more severe that at any other time in history but that merely served to further motivate Meir to cherish the observances with greater fervor. The suffering, the ghettos, the rumors, merely strengthened Meir's resolve and increased his desire to fulfill the commandments, to reaffirm his pledge to the Torah and to demonstrate his dedication.

He knew that Maurice would not understand and he feared he never would.

Maurice offered that he had taken a late night stroll, something he did almost every evening since the weather turned warmer.

Meir and Maurice started toward the barn as a heavy silence separated them. Suddenly they heard a truck in the distance. An instant later they heard it stop in front of the barn and they heard men shouting in German exit the truck. They could not be seen, they were safely hidden in the forest, far from the hill, but they instinctively moved deeper still, behind some trees to avoid any detection from possible roving patrols. They knew what was about to happen and quietly waited for the inevitable, praying that somehow disaster could be averted. They heard an exchange of gunfire that was intense at first but grew increasingly weaker until finally all was silent. They heard the Germans enter the truck again and drive away.

The two men waited silently in the forest. The hours passed but they would not venture up the hill, not until they were certain there were no Nazis lurking near the barn. The first rays of sunlight could be seen breaking over the horizon and they both realized that soon it would be morning. They were now confident it was safe to return. The Nazis would not turn once it became daylight where they could face an ambush or a sniper attack. They proceeded slowly, cautiously, reluctantly up the hill. They reached the checkpoint midway up the hill and saw no sign of Alain or evidence of any struggle. They both believed they knew what happened to Alain and continued toward the barn, hoping somehow their worst fears would be proven wrong. Maurice conceded that while he recommended to Klippenberg not to move their headquarters, he always harbored a belief their location might become known to the enemy, how could they remain undetected forever? As Maurice lumbered toward the barn he viewed himself a failure, as if he alone could have prevented this, that he should have anticipated the Nazis were close to discovering them and he should have organized an escape before they arrived. He presumed that everyone inside was no longer alive and continued to blame himself for incompetence and carelessness. Maurice observed that Meir likewise wore an expression of dread and inevitability, which confirmed Maurice's fears. Before they reached the barn they noticed two Nazi soldiers lurking near the back entrance. They quickly turned and ran back to the forest.

"What are those soldiers doing there?" asked Meir trembling.

"They are waiting for more of us to return, there were not that many of us inside last night, they surely know our operation was bigger than a handful of men."

"How long do you think they will remain here?"

"I am not certain," answered Maurice. "But we must stay here until they lose patience or realize that somehow the others were alerted and that no one will return."

They waited in the forest for two days, sneaking up the hill every few hours to check if the guards were still there. They were tired and hungry but they continued to wait. On the third day, shortly after dawn, they moved as close as they could without being spotted and saw the two guards make a careful search of the area surrounding the barn. A few hours later the guards left. Maurice was sure the guards were instructed that if no one returned by the third day they could as-sume the area was abandoned and they could leave. They waited another few hours, then cautiously climbed the hill. On their way up Meir turned to Maurice. "I have been wondering, why didn't the Nazis burn down the barn? Why didn't they destroy our headquarters in ac-cordance with all the warnings we have heard from them?"

"I do not know," offered Maurice. "Perhaps the Germans have in-formation there are other resistance headquarters nearby and burning down our barn would have alerted them of their presence," he guessed. "Or perhaps we were their second destination tonight and if we would have seen a fire in the distance, we could have escaped to safety," lamented Maurice.

In front of the barn they saw the body of Alain clutching his weapon near the entrance. It was quite obvious what had transpired. The moment Alain had heard the truck come to a halt he raced to the barn and was the first to be killed. Inside the barn Meir and Maurice saw the rest of the Maquis, including Klippenberg, all shot dead. All the members were shot wherever they had been standing. It had hap-pened so fast, the Germans had the element of surprise, possessed superior numbers and strength, that no one had had a chance to mo-bilize or escape. Klippenberg was killed in the communications room and all the equipment had been demolished. Gilbert and Alexander died in their beds, Louis and Oliver in the common eating room and Joseph in the ammunition room. Meir and Maurice searched the en-tire house and were grateful that only seven members had been in the barn at the time of the raid. Maurice then recalled that the rest of the group, about twenty-five men, were out on various missions. "We are lucky we arranged many attacks these past few weeks, we only lost seven men," said Maurice comfortingly.

"Yes, Maurice but the damage that has been done is devastating in-deed. How will we ever recover?"

"I am not sure, Meir. We must wait for everyone to return here, I am confident we are still safe here. I can no longer send any commu-nications and I am certain the Nazis will not return. When our Maquis is united once again, we will plan our next course of action. Perhaps we can join Abraham Lissner and his band of resistance fighters. Our own members should all be returning within the next few weeks. Until then we must wait patiently."

Meir nodded and agreed they had to wait for the rest of the group. He followed Maurice back outside, there was much work to be done.

Meir and Maurice could not think of the loss, of the damage and destruction they just experienced. They could not properly mourn their friends, contemplate the absence of Klippenberg and the others, they did not have the time. They needed to bury all the bodies before the local peasants observed unusual movements and invited the Nazis to return. Meir and Maurice worked at a furious pace. They were both exhausted, they had barely eaten or slept for almost three days, but they would not yield to their fatigue. They spent the entire day burying Leopold Klippenberg and six other Jews who were killed by the Nazis on Passover night, 1943.

Maurice quickly fell asleep but Meir lay awake. He was very tired but he could not close his eyes. He reviewed the events in his mind countless times and while he was thankful he was still alive, he was terribly saddened by what transpired. But there was more, something unnatural, something terrifying which haunted him. He first raised the question the moment he escaped the train from Drancy and was still without an answer. But now he realized it was the second time in one year that he and Maurice were saved from disaster together. It was obvious that they were no longer close, yet they seemed bound by an amazing destiny which continued to thrust them inexplicably into each other's arms.

What else was in store for them?

42

Maurice and Meir waited. Slowly and sporadically the members of the Maquis returned to the barn. Within a month all but two of the twenty-five resistance fighters sent out in April returned. None had heard what had happened in their absence and were all saddened to learn of the destruction and the loss but, like Maurice, they had always feared it might happen. Maurice suspected the two remaining members, Albert, a student from Rheims and Kurt, a German born silversmith, were both dead. He could not send any signals to try and ascertain their whereabouts or learn if they were caught by the Nazis, and agreed to wait another week in case they had been unexpectedly delayed.

Nobody dared question what the group would do next, they all knew Meir and Maurice would not decide on a course of action until Albert and Kurt were accounted for. Some of the members thought of returning to their homes, hoping some of their relatives were still alive; they thought of leaving the Maquis altogether and conceding defeat. Others thought of escaping France and the failed resistance movement, escaping to Palestine or perhaps America, before they too met Klippenberg's fate.

Maurice realized that the group was losing interest in continued resistance operations and the Maquis was unraveling, slowly falling apart. Maurice would not speak with the men about it, would not try and convince them to remain until Albert and Kurt returned or were confirmed dead. He knew that any discussion about their future together without knowing what had happened to Albert and Kurt was inappropriate and would be met with apathy and disdain. He confided to Meir that he could not wait forever and he would try to send a signal and possibly risk having the group's whereabouts exposed to learn the fate of the two missing men. He needed to put an end to all the doubt. Meir agreed with Maurice's move but admitted their safe return was now highly unlikely.

Four days later Kurt and Albert quietly entered the barn, surprised to find so many resistance fighters there. The group greeted them with amazed shock and disbelief. Everyone had come to believe Albert and Kurt were not alive and their return filled them with joy and encouragement. Kurt and Albert's survival reminded the despondent group that it could be safer for them to continue hiding in the forests and midnight alleys of France then to remain in one fixed location. It reinforced for them one of the cardinal truths of war, that life and death, survival or defeat could not be predicted or explained. Klippenberg, who rarely held a gun, was dead while twenty-seven of the fiercest partisans and resistance fighters in all of France managed to overcome and survive one obstacle after another. The group understood their leaving the Maquis would not mean that they would escape death or capture. They could run and hide but that would not insure survival. Who lived and who died was beyond their comprehension, beyond their control. It was even beyond the control of the enemy, as many of them recalled close brushes with Nazi soldiers that ended safely. Albert and Kurt demonstrated a reality repeated endless times during the war which the depression and sorrow had temporarily blurred. Most of the group now reconsidered their earlier thoughts about leaving the Maquis and waited with anticipation for Maurice's decision.

Maurice learned that Albert and Kurt had arrived and hurrried to greet them. "We are happy to see you," exclaimed Maurice, startled. "We feared you were captured!"

"Yes, we are lucky we are alive. We experienced many encounters with the Nazis and we managed to survive them all! We did not expect to see you all here, we feared so many were dead," offered Albert. "We were almost captured near Paris but we were saved by Lissner's men. We were accompanied to Lissner's headquarters and were there when Lissner intercepted a communiqué that three underground resistance bases in the Artois region were ambushed and everyone inside them was killed. I never even knew there were other resistance headquarters in this area but Lissner confirmed there were many resistance groups nearby. We could not know if our group was one that was attacked and if anyone survived, and we could not risk sending a signal, which the Nazis could intercept. Lissner suggested we wait a few weeks until the Nazis had withdrawn their strong presence in the area and then travel back here and ascertain if anyone survived. We have to return to Lissner with the information. We assumed a few of you would have been out at the time and would still be alive but we are happy to see that so many managed to survive that night!"

"Yes, it is fortunate indeed," returned Maurice. "All of us have now returned! We must carefully consider our options."

"That is true," admitted Albert, who was bothered by one additional detail. "But how did you and Meir manage to survive the Nazi ambush that night, if the two of you were not sent out last month?"

Maurice turned to Meir, who understood Maurice was equally tormented by their miraculous absence from the barn when the Nazis appeared. "We were walking together in the forest at the foot of the hill when they arrived. We were out of harm's reach the entire time and we buried everyone three days later." Meir interrupted, "Yes, and since then we have been waiting for all of you to return."

Meir was unsure whether the men were still ambivalent about continuing as resistance fighters. Any doubts which Meir himself harbored quickly disappeared the moment he saw Albert and Kurt. He was confident the rest of the group was likewise revitalized by their return but he wished to consolidate the group and perpetuate its importance and significance, to provide them with the feeling that their task is necessary. Meir knew the best way to accomplish that was to elect a new leader, one who would inspire the group to continue their important, irreplaceable work. "Before we consider a course of action," announced Meir, "I suggest that we nominate Maurice Andeau to replace Leopold Klippenberg as our leader. Are there any objections?"

The room was silent; Maurice was the obvious choice and everyone knew it. Meir waited a moment, knowing no one would offer any opposition to his proposal. He enthusiastically proclaimed, "It is settled, then, Maurice has been chosen as our new leader."

Maurice nodded in respectful acceptance and moved to the front of the room. "I am sure we are all distraught by what has happened here. I have had a month to absorb and accept the loss, but some of you have only known about it for a few days. I fully understand the sentiments I have heard recently about abandoning the Maquis and if anyone wishes to leave they may do so at any time, no one will be held here against their will. However, I believe we should continue our resistance operations. I am not certain how we will accomplish that, now that we have no communications network, but I do not wish to give up and admit defeat. Perhaps we can join with another group somewhere and continue under their guidance, within their network."

Maurice conceded he was unsure how he could contact another group and stepped away, discouraged.

"Maurice!" called Albert. "I believe there is a solution to our dilemma. Our group has been invited by Lissner to join him near Paris. He knew that we could no longer carry out any acts of resistance here and that our inaction could lead to our dissolution or worse, our capture. Lissner estimated about ten survivors; he will be delighted to learn there are twenty-seven of us!"

"Does he have need for us?" asked Maurice cautiously.

"Of course. He loses men every day. The Nazis pursue him relentlessly and we would greatly enhance his operation, we already possess training and experience. He informed us he would not be remaining in the Paris region for too much longer but he promised to wait for us until the end of June. Maurice, we are dedicated to you and to this group and we shall follow you wherever you take us but if you decide not to join with Lissner, we must return to him and inform him of your decision."

Maurice nodded and thought for a moment. He looked around and saw the anticipation on the faces of his men and knew they were excited about joining with Lissner. It was obvious to him there really was no other alternative. Maurice felt relieved his first decision as leader would be fully supported by the entire group.

"I understand, Albert, and I think we should join him, there is nothing for us here anymore. Without a communications network we can never learn where the Germans are and we can never strike them effectively. We received a devastating blow last month and the only way we can recover is if we join with Lissner and continue with him. I am aware Lissner's network is vast. We might not be able to maintain our cohesiveness, our comradery, in his large resistance network but we cannot worry about these small details during this terrible war."

Maurice surveyed the room and everyone nodded in agreement. Everyone wished to escape the barn and the tragic memories it held for them. Everyone anticipated a fresh start with Lissner, despite their concerns about losing their unique identity within Lissner's larger group. Everyone looked forward to a more sophisticated and more complex resistance operation, and hoped for a speedy end to the war.

The Klippenberg Maquis left their headquarters, the barn hidden deep in the Ardennes Forest, in early June 1943. They traveled south toward Clairvaux and then shifted northwest, looping around Les Tourelles not far from Paris. The group could not travel directly to Paris, there were too many Germans roving there. The weather was pleasant and the journey was long but tolerable. They only moved during the night and took turns standing guard while they slept by day. Nearly one month later they reached Lissner's headquarters, a barn located just outside Les Tourelles.

Albert and Kurt gave the password Lissner had given them and the group was then led into the barn. Once inside they all marveled how much it resembled the one they had just abandoned: there was an ammunition room, a communications room and many bedrooms. They were escorted to the dining room where Lissner sat, reviewing maps. Lissner arose, surmised Maurice was the leader and approached him first. Lissner was then introduced to the rest of the group.

Lissner remembered that Meir had assisted him with the attack of a truck the previous December. Maurice had never met Lissner before and was immediately captivated by his forceful and magnetic personality. Lissner expressed his condolences for the loss of Klippenberg and the other men killed that night and vowed that their deaths would be avenged.

Maurice spoke on behalf of the group and expressed their desire to participate in the destruction of the German army in France. Lissner then excused himself to the group, told them their meal would be served momentarily and motioned for Maurice to follow him. Lissner and Maurice walked toward the far end of the barn and entered the communications room. The room was similar to the one Maurice operated with Klippenberg but it was larger and more sophisticated.

"This is the center of our operation, Maurice. This is where all our information is gathered and analyzed. I am sure you are familiar with all this equipment. Klippenberg informed me of your talents!"

Maurice studied the machines carefully. They seemed to be quite sophisticated and up-to-date. He concluded that Lissner probably received communications from all of Europe! He moved closer and examined them again. "These look far too technical for my elementary training," admitted Maurice.

"They are not very different than the machines you are familiar with," returned Lissner encouragingly. "They are larger and their reach is extended, but they are essentially the same machines you utilized in the Ardennes. When we have an opportunity I shall demonstrate how they operate."

"I am looking forward to that," replied Maurice.

Lissner moved away from the machines and drew closer to Maurice. "Within the next few weeks I will be orchestrating scores of attacks throughout France. The attacks will be swift, fierce and deadly. Some of the attacks will be carried out simultaneously in different parts of the country to highlight to the Germans, to demonstrate to them in a clear and explicit manner, that we possess a strong, united, cohesive resistance movement. Your men will prove vital to this plan; in fact I do not think it could succeed on the grand scale I envision without them!"

Maurice listened intently, wondering why Lissner was informing him again about his planned attacks. Maurice already promised Lissner that his men were available for assistance.

"I want to stress," continued Lissner, "that many of your men might be captured or killed. These attacks will be highly confrontational and the men will be exposed in ways they never experienced before. Some of the attacks will not even be carried out secretly and I want your men to appreciate the risks involved."

Maurice nodded and assured Lissner his men that were willing to face any danger and would accept any hardship in their fight against the hated Germans.

Maurice turned to rejoin the men.

"There is one more thing," called Lissner. "Any of your men who succeed and remain alive will not return here when their missions are completed. They will remain in the different regions to which they are being sent and receive further instructions from me and the local resistance leaders who are in constant contact with the headquarters here. I have determined that we would be squandering our resources to wait for the men to return here merely to send them back the following week! This decision has been carefully studied and we have determined it is the most efficient way to maximize our men and our efforts."

Maurice could not deny the benefits of Lissner's decision but he was terribly distraught. "No one knows when this war will end," countered Maurice. "It could drag on for years and my men could find themselves scattered throughout Europe. I also might be forced to leave here and could end up in Spain or Switzerland or even America. I might never see my men again!"

Lissner understood that Maurice's concerns were heartfelt indeed and surmised that Maurice had no other family and loved these men as brothers. But Lissner could not change strategic and thought-out plans based on research and experience simply to appease Maurice's emotions.

"You are quite right, Maurice, you might never see these men again," returned Lissner coldly. "The war has torn apart much of France and the rest of Europe but what can be done? Do you think I am making a mistake?"

"Of course not," answered Maurice. "I agree that your decision is efficient and it would be foolish to act otherwise. I just thought that after all that has happened to the group we might be fortunate enough to enjoy some consistency, some normalcy, some sort of permanence, an end to all the wandering and uncertainty. I am fully aware that I have no right to demand that now and I am only alive because of the miracles that took place for Meir and myself but I am weary of this dreaded war and I momentarily spoke selfishly. I am sorry. I will wish my men farewell and continue to hope we will all meet again in peace and health."

Maurice turned and left the communications room and walked back to his men waiting in the dining room.

The next few days were busy and tense. All the members of Maurice's Maquis, including Meir, received instructions and maps highlighting their destinations. Some were sent only a few kilometers away, others were sent to the farthest reaches of France, to Marseilles and Bordeaux. Maurice spoke with each member before they departed, bid farewell to everyone, reminded them of the training they had received from Klippenberg, urged them to remain alert and attentive at all times and hoped they would meet again when the war ended.

One by one Maurice's men left to engage in resistance operations throughout France. The men likewise felt the same bonds of brotherhood and kinship as Maurice and they all knew they might never see each other again, but they accepted their far-flung missions with duty and honor.

At the conclusion of the week all of Maurice's men were gone, except one. Meir was still waiting for his assignment, he knew it would come any day and waited anxiously. Meir was by far the most skilled and daring of Maurice's men and Lissner was saving him for a dangerous task, one that required his particular savvy and expertise.

The following day Lissner informed Maurice that he received a communiqué from Toulouse, in Southern France, requesting an expert marksman and someone especially skilled with explosives. The famous 35th Brigade, that amalgam of immigrants, displaced persons and homeless resistance fighters, was planning an enormous attack and needed only the best fighters to help coordinate and arrange the strikes. Maurice immediately understood that Meir's assignment was now at hand and that Meir would be leaving by the end of the day.

Meir was informed of his assignment and readily accepted. He was not told the details of the mission but was confident that the strikes, if successful, would be far-reaching and damaging. He immediately began preparing his small backpack of food, clothes and weapons. Lissner provided Meir with maps and the name of resistance leader in Toulouse who was expecting him. Lissner reminded Meir to remain cautious and brave and hoped they would yet see each other after the war.

Meir and Maurice were alone. Maurice knew he could not allow Meir to leave without a final farewell. Maurice was uncertain whether Meir would survive the remainder of the war but was certain that even if Meir did survive they would never see each other again. Maurice did not know where he would be in six months and admitted the chance of ever finding Meir again was too remote to consider. But he could not allow Meir to leave without embracing him and thanking him for all his determination and perseverance, which had enabled him to survive. Meir also wished to see Maurice one last time, he too owed much to Maurice, and as they approached each other they were both aware of a certain distance, a coldness that separated them. This distance had existed for quite some time but they could avoid it no longer. They were forced to confront each other.

"I am sorry you must go," said Maurice, breaking the silence.

"Thank you, Maurice. I do not wish to leave but I must do my part to end this dreadful war," returned Meir tenderly.

"Do you think we shall see each other again, Meir?" asked Maurice, already certain of the answer.

Meir had not given it much thought but quickly concluded it was highly unlikely. "I do not think so, Maurice, we shall be separated by great distances and this war could drag us further and further apart. I will miss you, Maurice, you have been a wonderful friend and I could not have survived without you. I do regret that we did not have the opportunity to become closer in certain respects."

Maurice understood Meir's reference and readily agreed. He did not want to dispute with him now. "As do I, Meir," answered Maurice.

The two men embraced and wished each other well. Maurice remained at the door of the barn until Meir was no longer in view, believing he would never see him again, and then turned to meet with Lissner and begin training with those advanced and superior communications machines.

But Meir's farewell wish and his regret continued to haunt Maurice and he somehow knew it was not over, not yet.

They would meet again.

43

Within a few weeks Meir reached Toulouse and was introduced to many of the members of the Brigade. They were unlike the men who had fought with him in the Maquis. These men were battle-hardened, several of them had been combat soldiers for ten years during the Spanish Civil War. These were not students or artisans who fled their homes and escaped to the forests, these men were soldiers, warriors. They possessed a fierceness, an intensity for battle that he had never seen before. True, Meir had engaged in many attacks and had trained men to carry out many others, but he had never relished the role. He merely did his job to help defeat the Germans. But these men were different, they were bold, almost violent and they frightened Meir.

Meir quickly learned that the Brigade members were seething over the execution of Marcel Langer. He had been their undisputed leader and had recently been executed. Langer had been captured back in February when he was caught with a suitcase full of explosives at a Toulouse railway station. He was tried by a French court, found guilty of transporting explosives and was guillotined in July 1943. The Brigade quickly wired Lissner, requesting skilled and able men who could help carry out various strikes against the Germans and those Frenchmen who were responsible for Langer's demise. Meir learned he was only summoned to the Brigade to help them execute their plans for revenge, retaliation and punishment. These were not the motivations which had kept Meir a resistance fighter these many months, and he realized he did not want to stay. He did not wish to remain among men who relished their roles as aggressors and promoted violence to a terrifying degree. They did not merely wish to see an end to the war but a ruthless, almost barbaric destruction of the enemy. They did not seem satisfied by any mention of a German surrender, however far-fetched that sounded, because it denied them victory on their terms and it prevented them from fulfilling their obsessive, almost fanatical schemes. Meir too engaged in damaging and devastating attacks, but notions of retribution and recrimination never inspired him even as he accepted that his entire family was probably no longer alive. Meir viewed this Brigade as a group with misconceived ideals that were only further skewed by the prolonged war. Meir did not want to evolve into one of them, adopt their unmerciful and unfeeling beliefs, and he knew he had to escape their influences.

Yet there was something else troubling Meir, something equally distressing to him. Although Meir could not know for certain, he believed he was the only practicing Jew in the Brigade. Many of the members of the Brigade were not Jewish, and the Jews among them were irreligious, some were even hostile toward Meir. Meir had hoped he could finally meet other practicing Jews and develop a relationship with them and try to rekindle once again the passion for further growth which the war had all but extinguished.

But where could he go? Meir knew that leaving would only raise other, more impossible-to-solve dilemmas. What would he eat? How would he protect himself? Meir realized he would have to remain with them, at least for a while. Perhaps if France fell to the Allies he could venture out alone and search for his family or a new place to call home with like-minded friends. But not yet, it was still far too dangerous. Meir concluded that he would have to remain for a while and assist the Brigade in their attacks but he would have little to do with them while at their headquarters. He would not make any attempt to befriend them or converse with them needlessly. He would be polite and cordial toward them but would avoid becoming one of them.

Meir sensed the group did not particularly care for him either. They taunted him about his peaked cap, the one he always wore and they ridiculed his refusal to eat meat. But most importantly they resented the three quiet, soft prayers which Meir recited each day with closed eyes and open heart. They believed Meir valued the efficacy of prayer more than the certitude of guns and grenades. They could not tolerate such simple and plain faith and they continued to demean him. Meir hardly minded their contempt for him, if they did not like him they would never befriend him and he would never follow their repulsive lifestyle.

But there was one man who set aside all these petty and irrelevant disagreements. Armand Costegue, the new leader of the Brigade was a brilliant and keen strategist. He knew he could not waste precious time disputing religion and ethics. Armand was not Jewish and did not care if any of his men practiced Judaism or anything else for that matter. He always told his men that when the war was over he would gladly meet them at any café in Paris and remain there for hours sipping cognac while debating the world's problems. But as long as the war raged he would hear none of it. He even rebuked a few of his men who had spent one night harassing an ignorant Spaniard and neglecting their duties. Armand was a serious soldier and while Meir found him to be a little extreme, he admired his determination and commitment to defeating the enemy. Armand needed Meir's expertise in carrying out many of the attacks intended to avenge Langer's death.

Shortly before noon a few days after Meir arrived, Armand approached him. Meir was inside one of the smaller buildings, a converted stable that served as the living quarters for him and twenty other men. Armand entered and quickly motioned for Meir to follow him outside. They walked a few moments until they reached the main house and entered. The main house, an old neglected farmhouse, was the center of the Brigade where Armand worked and slept. Meir was accompanied to the "planning room," a large room at the far end of the house. It resembled Klippenberg's communication room where he would often review matters with Maurice, but it did not contain any sophisticated machinery, merely a long table surrounded by chairs and piles of maps and books. Meir correctly concluded the room was utilized by Armand to plan and outline their maneuvers and attacks.

Meir looked at Armand and noticed he was tall and broad. He sported a thick moustache and small round glasses. His hair was neatly combed and he was so fair-skinned he could easily pass for a German. Meir surmised Armand came from the North, far from the Mediterranean Sea.

Armand turned to Meir. "Come with me, Meir, I have much to discuss with you," offered Armand warmly. "I hope you will be as effective here as you were with the Maquis."

"Yes, Armand. I hope I can make a difference here," answered Meir coldly.

"Is everything all right, Meir?" asked Armand sensing some unease in Meir's answer. "Is it my men? Do they frighten you?"

"No," returned Meir, avoiding the topic entirely. "I am merely growing tired of this war."

"That is understandable, Meir, but you will help us end it that much sooner. You know there are rumors of an American and British landing here in France within the year! They will liberate this country and continue on to Germany. They will not stop until Berlin itself is razed to the ground. The end is rapidly approaching, Meir! Another few years and we shall again be free!"

"But will we still be alive when that happens?"

Armand did not respond to Meir's gloomy rejoinder and turned the conversation to the attacks they were planning. "I am organizing a series of attacks that will include the destruction of rail lines, factories, bridges and military installations. I need your help coordinating this multi-pronged approach. Take a look at this map."

Armand produced a map of Toulouse and the surrounding regions, Gascony, Langfeudoc-Roussillon, even the northern edge of the Pyrenees Mountains. The nearby cities chosen for strikes such as Toulouse, Blagnac, Muret and Montauban were clearly marked. Armand explained that he wished to engage in attacks on four or five targets at the same time. That would not only surprise the Germans but also confuse them and delay their response, affording the resistance more time to continue their strikes in a second wave of attacks. Meir studied the map carefully and was impressed with Armand's plan. Conducting an attack in two stages was a brilliant idea. It would allow for a sustained, continuous strike and hopefully cause much damage. Meir observed that Armand had planned the second wave of strikes in the exact locations where the first ones were engineered. A double assault on the same targets would surely accomplish their goals.

"I must admit I am impressed, Armand. These strikes are well conceived and with proper execution will prove successful. I have a few suggestions which I believe will help facilitate the steady movement of the men and provide for a more streamlined and efficient attack."

Armand and Meir spent the next few hours reviewing the intricacies of the attacks. They detailed the number of fighters needed for each strike, the weapons each man would carry and rendezvous points where the men could meet while the Germans were regrouping, or if they became lost. Meir advised Armand to forgo the attacks at Montauban, it was too far away and if any problem developed it would take too long to send additional men. Meir agreed to lead a group sent to blow up a major headquarters in Toulouse. It was a very dangerous and complicated mission and he wanted to be there to insure success.

The next few months saw a relentless, almost daily assault by the 35th Brigade against many enemy installations throughout the regions near Toulouse. The Germans suffered terrible losses while the Brigade lost only a few dozen men. The great triumph of the Brigade came in early October 1943, with an attack which resulted in the death of Monsieur Lespinasse, the chief French prosecutor of Marcel Langer.

Meir was exhausted. He had been fighting for over two months with hardly any respite. He was proud of his successes and the tenacity and determination of his men, but he was still terribly bothered by the brutality and violence which motivated and guided the Brigade's every move. Meir hated those sentiments and could not wait to leave.

Maurice remained with Lissner and continued to become more adept at handling the vast communications network of the resistance movement. In mid-November he uncovered three fraudulent communications deliberately sent by the Nazis to try and expose some of the resistance groups. Each of the transmissions urged various groups to respond to these feigned calls of distress. Maurice traced the origins of the transmissions and determined they were not sent by any resistance group in France. Maurice's methodical and patient dissection of all transmissions enabled him to discover they were frauds and helped save the lives of scores of men. News of Maurice's skills and intelligence spread throughout the resistance network in France. Maurice even received a communiqué from General Charles de Gaulle, the undisputed leader of all Free French forces, thanking Maurice and commending him for his extraordinary service to France during this unfortunate time of war.

Maurice appreciated the warm sentiments of General de Gaulle but knew that he did not deserve all the credit. Klippenberg as well as Meir and Lissner were likewise responsible for his ability as well as the opportunity to offer any assistance at all.

The months dragged on. It was already 1944 and still the war had no end in sight. The Allied invasion had still not come and the Germans were still everywhere. Maurice thought of Meir often and received several communications from Armand detailing Meir's whereabouts.

In late January, Lissner informed Maurice they were abandoning the headquarters.

"We must leave here, Maurice, and soon! I have learned that the Allies will begin bombing the region. They will not bomb Paris itself but they will bomb the surrounding areas, Trappes, Juvisy and Villeneuve Saint Georges. The intelligence reports I have read indicate that the Allies wish to prevent the German 15th Army from securing the area near the Pas-de-Calais in preparation for the impending invasion. They will begin a bombing campaign within the month and they have notified General de Gaulle that nothing can be done to insure the safety of the resistance groups."

Maurice was not surprised by Lissner's announcement. He had intercepted similar reports and understood that shortly they would be forced to disband.

"You are aware, Maurice," continued Lissner "that we will not be able to continue our communications network. Our departure will signal the end of an operation that has continually provided information to various resistance groups for over three years. I regret that all the groups throughout France will be forced to rely on their own inferior and often misleading information. Nonetheless, this move does auger the beginning of the end of the war, we must be thankful for that!"

"Yes," agreed Maurice. "While I am also fearful for the resistance groups that will be left languishing in the forests, I am comforted that any confusion or danger they might face should only last a number of months until the Allies arrive." Maurice was bothered by one additional problem. "What shall happen to all the equipment here?"

"That is a good question," conceded Lissner. "Obviously we cannot take any of the machinery with us, it will no longer serve any purpose. The equipment, which contains the most sensitive and classified information in this building as well as the nearby headquarters always in frequent contact with us, must be destroyed. I have already informed Francois and Georges that they must destroy anything that could serve to benefit the Nazis should they happen upon the buildings once they are abandoned. I also told them we shall be leaving the day after tomorrow, and perhaps they will join us."

Lissner sighed deeply, "This is a turning point in the war, Maurice. Today we shall begin a new venture. We must prepare for our escape and strengthen our continued belief that the war shall soon end."

"But where are we going?" asked Maurice.

Lissner stared blankly at Maurice for a moment as if he had never given any consideration to their eventual destination and was dumbfounded by the question. Maurice knew that Lissner had a detailed plan which would enable them to remain hidden for at least two years. Maurice concluded that the very question startled Lissner because it highlighted the immediacy of their sad departure.

Lissner composed himself and responded. "First we shall travel to Corbeil, then west to Chartres. We shall remain in the Loire valley for as long as we can. I wish to remain close to Paris yet far enough away to avoid the bombings."

Maurice was pleased. He too hoped to remain close to Paris, the city he had not returned to in over three years.

"I miss Paris dearly," offered Maurice. "I miss the shops, the cafés, the theater and most of all my home. I am so anxious to return!"

"I understand, Maurice. Hurry, prepare for our journey, and let us pray that we may return to our liberated capital soon!"

Lissner and Maurice left their headquarters on the first of February 1944 and arrived in Corbeil a few days later. They heard frequent and steady bombings in the distance and heard planes flying nearby but for now they were safe. They quickly blended into a city filled with chaos and excitement and knew there was too much commotion taking place for anyone to question them or demand passports or papers of nationality. Maurice and Lissner did carry forged documents but they did not wish to be stopped at all. They did not want to be forced into offering concocted, farfetched and contrived stories to explain their recent arrival in the city, and remained cautious and alert.

Maurice was on the move again. He had left his uncle and Paris in 1940, had lived two years in Switzerland, was a prisoner in two French internment camps and spent the remainder of the war in the French resistance movement. Now he was leaving all that and venturing elsewhere, where would he travel next? Maurice did not know, he put all his trust in Lissner. But Maurice did know that like his other wanderings during the past few years, this one too would only be temporary. Maurice realized that while so much had happened to him since he left Paris, so little had changed. The world was still at war, he was still on the run, still spurned by his own country and still unsure of his future.

Ah, the future.

Maurice had spent much of his adult life pursuing a distinguished career as a lecturer and professor. Yet he had long ago conceded that he could never teach at the Sorbonne or any institution that rejected and denounced his People, that so quickly excluded Jews at the first sign of trouble. His friend, Meir, as well as living in France for the past few years, had taught him at least that much. He knew he could never hold any public position in France without sacrificing his loyalty and fealty, however shaky, toward his religion. But he was a student of history, consumed by the decisions of great men, sweeping changes in thought and outlook, cataclysmic battles and conflicts that shaped the destiny of the mightiest empire and the lowliest peasant. He still desired to finish his doctorate, his life's dream, the honorable and noble discipline, which he had pursued for as long as he could remember. He recalled the passion and fervor which had inspired him to strive and excel in this endeavor, almost as if he were born and destined for it. But all that was over, the central focus of all his emotion and energy, his very reason for being was shattered along with so many Jewish communities in France. His foiled dream, his aimless future, was just another consequence of this dreaded war. In truth, this had bothered Maurice for quite some time but this recent move, another significant change in his life brought the dilemma into sharper focus. What would he do with his life? He knew French history better than any of his classmates at the Sorbonne but how could that serve his interest now? The war would not last forever. What would become of him when peace was finally declared? Maurice had no alternative plan to pursue, he had nowhere else to turn. He had been raised on French honor, French history and a strong and firm allegiance to France. He had spent his entire life caring about nothing except perpetuating those sentiments by honoring and glorifying the French past. What would he do when the war ended? Would he leave France? Would he forsake the very essence which had once defined him? The heritage of his parents and grandparents was now exposed as a vacuous, vain and ignoble life. Would he ever seek out Meir, if he was alive, and begin anew somewhere with him?

Maurice did not yet realize it but this journey away from the headquarters was a journey of his conscience, of his soul, and bottled up within him, the soul of his lost generation.

And the journey was almost over.

44

Meir stood guard outside Armand's house for the last time. He had decided he would leave in the morning and had informed Armand of his imminent departure. Armand had known Meir would be leaving soon and accepted the news with sorrow and resignation. He could not convince Meir to remain, although he had tried. Even Armand understood the conditions were just too much for Meir to bear. The group treated Meir with such hostility and contempt, always deriding and mocking him, that Armand often wondered why Meir did not leave sooner.

Over the past eight months, though, Meir thought of leaving many times but some unforeseen event always prevented him from doing so. For the majority of the time the severe winter made extensive travel alone virtually impossible. Meir knew he would never survive hiding in the forests without a source of food and shelter, and waited patiently and longingly for the snows to thaw. Early spring saw a quick resumption of renewed resistance attacks, which occupied all his time and energy. By the time Meir had a free moment to consider leaving he realized that Passover was only a few days away. He was aware that there were no Jewish communities left where he could join with others to celebrate the holiday properly. Armand managed to barter for some bitter gourds and potatoes but could not secure any wine or unleavened bread. Meir appreciated Armand's efforts and admitted that this Passover was far more meaningful than the previous year; at least he was able to fulfill some of the holiday's rituals. Yet the holiday was still largely devoid of significance particularly because Meir could not recall from memory the complete texts of some of the prayers and songs that he had remembered only one year ago. How deficient and faded would his memory become if another year would pass without returning to those sacred texts?

Or another?

Or still another?

It was shortly after Passover in late April 1944, and Meir knew it was time to leave. There was nothing holding him back anymore. He stood outside Armand's house plotting his journey home. Meir had heard rumors of the continuous Allied bombings near the Loire valley but he nevertheless concluded he would travel there first and then move toward Paris. Meir heard rumors the Allied invasion was expected within the month and wished to be in Paris by the time the city would be liberated.

He waited anxiously for dawn to arrive.

Meir saw Armand emerge from the house just as the first rays of the sun were breaking over the horizon. "Hello, Meir," called Armand softly.

"Good morning, Armand," returned Meir.

Armand drew close to Meir. "I am sorry you are leaving, Meir. You are a brave soldier and you have served this Brigade with distinction and valor. I know you do not agree with many of our practices but your integrity and decency has left its mark on the men; they will not soon forget you. I understand that you cannot stay and I wish you well on your journey."

Armand approached Meir and embraced him. "Do not fall into enemy hands, be cautious and attentive!"

"Yes," answered Meir, thankful at least someone in the Brigade expressed concern about his welfare. "I will continue to remain alert and avoid the enemy at all costs and I will pray for my safe return to Paris."

Meir turned and reached for his backpack. Armand bid Meir farewell and quickly returned to the house. Meir did not wish to waste any more time and slipped away from the headquarters and began traveling north.

Meir traveled at a furious pace. He rarely stopped to rest and reached Limoges a few days later. He continued northward and passed Châteauroux, Levroux and Valençay. By the first week of May, Meir had reached the Loire River and knew that at the speed he was traveling he would arrive in Paris shortly.

Maurice and Lissner left Corbeil and continued to move southwest. They heard frequent explosions and saw Allied planes flying above the western slope of the region. Lissner presumed the larger cities, Tours, Chinon and Montréuil-Bellay, were being hit. Lissner and Maurice believed the Allies were trying to rid the region of all enemy soldiers to prepare for the eventual Allied landing, most likely at the Pas-de-Calais. Lissner and Maurice did not fear they were in any danger, they were many miles away from the actual bombing sites but they moved cautiously and quickly. They traveled west to Chartres then south toward Bonneval, Cháteaudun and Vendóme. While resting near the outskirts of Vendóme they heard bombs fall on what they believed was nearby Trôo and Montoire and feared the bombing campaign was now moving in their direction. They decided to shift eastward to get away from those threatening planes and they hastily traveled down until they reached the small town of Blois near the banks of the Loire River. Maurice had never been there but knew the town well.

"It is interesting to point out, Abraham," offered Maurice, "that the first blood libel on Continental Europe took place in this town."

"I was unaware of that," responded Lissner. He had little interest in the matter.

"Yes," continued Maurice. "I believe it happened in the year 1171. Theobold the Good, a vicious, petty and vain man, ruled the region.

His seat of power was in Chartres, in Il de France, the town we just passed the other day. He accused the Jews of Blois of murdering a Christian child, using the child's blood for some evil religious purpose then discarding the body in the Loire. Even though the corpse was never found, a corrupt and biased tribunal investigated the matter and concluded that the Jews were guilty. Almost all forty Jewish members of the town were killed here, burned alive in a building constructed by the Crusaders. A few of the townspeople managed to buy their freedom, but no Jews ever returned to live here."

"That is a sad story," agreed Lissner. "It is a shame the world has not yet wiped its hands clean from these vile displays."

Maurice knew Lissner was referring to those rumors which were all but confirmed, that thousands, perhaps millions of Jews were dead, towns were completely destroyed, regions of Europe were now completely free of Jews. Maurice had once stood in a cattle car destined for a similar fate. He knew better than Lissner the abject torments which were inflicted in the process, and he believed those rumors implicitly.

Lissner turned away, looking for shelter, and Maurice stood atop a small hill overlooking the town.

Blois.

It was quite true that except for the libel of Norwich, England, this was the first. It was the first in a long history of mistreatment, persecution and death. Europe's very essence, her glorious and noble character, was haunted by the blood of the Jews that flowed through the generations. It was everywhere: France, Spain, Italy, Russia and of course Germany. There was no escaping it and this war only reinforced the collaboration of Europe's most vaunted citizens. The indifference of some, the halfhearted participation of others and the outright assistance of still others all spoke to that same hatred that was ignited here, that first exploded here in an unquenchable crusade that was still ongoing. There were exceptions, countries or individuals who withstood hatred's lure, but they were too isolated and too insignificant to make a real difference. This recurring hatred was so pervasive, so irrational. It consumed men, aroused armies and clouded judgments. It had plunged the world into the present abyss of madness and destruction and it had remained there for the past five years. The Jews were at the center of it all. That was true in 1171 and it was equally true today. For the first time Maurice realized that while the world had hardly changed its attitudes since then neither had the Jews, at least those Jews who still followed the Torah. They still adhered to the same ancient principles and still clung to those same pristine beliefs.

And it was those beliefs which so infuriated the rest of the world.

Maurice stood transfixed and scarcely heard Lissner calling him.

"Maurice," hollered Lissner. "I have found a small shack a little further downstream. It appears to be abandoned. We can venture there and rest while we pursue our next course of action."

Maurice obligingly followed Lissner. A few moments later they arrived at a dusty, uninhabited shanty. It did not appear very sturdy: The exterior consisted of dangling or broken rectangular slats of wood unprofessionally affixed. There were no lights or candles lit inside, the windows had not been cleaned in years and untamed vines covered most of the structure. Maurice assumed the house was originally built as a place for farmers, water carriers or field hands to rest before resuming their assignments. It was a small and isolated house, surely no one ever lived there on a permanent basis. Maurice was happy Lissner had found it. If they could enter without altering the barren and desolate facade no one would ever think it was occupied and they could remain there in safety. They looked in all directions and quickly yet carefully approached the front door. The door was not locked and they entered. Inside, the front room was dark, the shades were drawn at each window and they could scarcely see if there were any furnishings or supplies. They were both able to discern another door at the far end of the room directly in front of them and began walking toward it. Suddenly they heard a voice from the left side of the house: "Place your hands in the air or I will shoot without hesitation!"

Lissner and Maurice immediately raised their hands, then looked toward the direction of the voice. They saw the outline of a man protected by the darkness, pointing a gun at them. The man was half concealed behind a large beam, which ran from the floor to the ceiling. No doubt he had heard them enter and had run behind it for protection.

Maurice and Lissner froze with terror. Was the man a French peasant? A Nazi? What would happen to them? Could they escape from him unharmed? They could not claim they were innocent travelers, they carried guns in their backpacks. If their bags were searched they would be suspected of being spies and would surely be killed.

The two men did not move and stood transfixed by the glint of steel, which was only a few feet from them.

Maurice wondered if they could somehow overpower the man, wrest the gun from him, tie him up and flee without a trace. Maurice was certain Lissner was contemplating the same thing and watched as Lissner deftly moved in front of Maurice. "Do not move, I will fire this weapon! What are you doing here?" the man barked.

"We are here to rest," offered Lissner earnestly. "We pose no threat to you and we have no intention of harming you. We merely thought this place was abandoned. If this is your house we will leave at once."

The man did not budge and kept the gun directed squarely at the two intruders.

Maurice was fairly certain the man was not a German. A German would have already shot them and though the man only spoke very briefly Maurice did not detect an accent. Maurice knew he would not further jeopardize them by reiterating Lissner's sentiments. Hopefully the man would believe them and dismiss them unharmed.

"My friend speaks the truth," confirmed Maurice. "We did not know you lived here. We apologize for the intrusion. Please let us go, you have nothing to fear from us, we would never reveal your presence here."

Slowly, very slowly, the man lowered the gun and emerged from behind the beam.

It was Meir.

"Maurice! I apologize for frightening you, I did not recognize you until you spoke." Maurice looked relieved and quickly embraced his old friend. Meir then turned to Lissner. "It is good to see you as well, Abraham. It has been almost a year."

"Yes," echoed Lissner relieved. He too then embraced Meir. "Neither of us recognized your voice. What are you doing here?"

"I left the Brigade a few weeks ago. I'm returning to Paris to search for my relatives and I stopped here to rest. I only entered this house a few hours ago!"

The three men spoke in the darkness, reminiscing about their past experiences together and their activities over the past year. For a while it seemed as if Meir and Maurice had never parted, they had so much to say and were so genuinely happy to be reunited.

The hours passed and they had hardly moved. Lissner noted that it was getting late, the sun would soon be setting and night was approaching. He offered to go outside and search for food, possibly berries or some vegetables, before night fell and movement became dangerous. Maurice and Meir agreed and watched as Lissner slipped out the front door.

Maurice and Meir were alone. They continued to speak of the different paths their lives had taken over the past year. Suddenly Meir remarked, "It was foolish of us to send Lissner for food without first searching this place. It might contain some perishables left here by roving soldiers. We should open one of the shades and search it thoroughly."

"I agree," said Maurice. "But I do not want anyone outside to suspect our presence here!"

"That is a valid concern," confessed Meir. "But I watched when Lissner left. There does not seem to be anyone close by and it will only be for a few moments."

"Alright."

Meir suggested they first enter the lone room at the far end, as he had not been inside it either, and concluded that any provisions would likely be there. They opened the door and observed a small room with nothing inside but an old, sturdy and durable table. Maurice immediately walked toward a window at the back of the room and slowly opened the shade. Daylight streamed into the room, revealing nothing but dust and dirt. "There is no food in here," announced Maurice."

"Yes, but what is this?" Meir pointed to the wall behind the table. The wall revealed a narrow crack, which ran from the floor almost to the ceiling. They studied it carefully and also observed two hinges, one near the floor the other near the ceiling, embedded into the wall about two meters from the crack. Meir and Maurice concluded it was a door that probably led to a closet concealed in the face of the wall. "There appears to be some sort of compartment, some hidden cubicle here behind the table. Help me move away the table, Maurice."

Maurice and Meir lifted the heavy table and moved it to the far corner of the room. Then they approached the wall and, using their fingers, pried open the door. Inside was a small empty closet. There was a shelf toward the top and it held what looked like piles of clothes. Meir reached up and while moving the clothes felt something else, something he could not identify. He perched his feet and reached for the item. The moment he realized what it was he immediately called for Maurice's assistance. "You hold the top of it," instructed Meir. "I have secured the bottom."

The two of them carefully retrieved the item and carried it to the table. It was a Torah scroll wrapped with a plain blue cover.

"If I am correct, that is a Torah," remarked Maurice. "What is it doing here?"

"I do not know," conceded Meir, "The cover of a Torah is generally embroidered with a dedication, including the names in whose memory and honor the Torah was written or purchased, but this cover does not reveal anything at all." Meir tugged at the cover in disappointment and noticed another cover underneath.

"But look, Maurice, there is another cover! Let's remove this one, maybe the one underneath has writing on it." Meir removed the outer cover and they both stood gaping at a very old cover almost fully embroidered on the front and back with Hebrew words. Maurice could not read it and asked Meir to translate it for him. Meir pointed to the top of the cover and began by reading about the tragedy that took place in Blois, Juan de Ciudad's wanderings, and the Torah's journey to Poland. He further read how the Torah helped save the town of Krasnystaw in 1666. Meir continued reading about Rabbi Shlomo, a great-grandson of Rabbi Yaakov who left Krasnystaw with his entire family in 1824 because of hostilities which broke out with the Gentiles there. They were on their way to live with relatives in Paris. The last words sewn onto the Torah's cover read, "Let us hope we shall reach our destination."

Maurice shuddered and realized that like himself this Torah was still lost, still waiting for a permanent home, for direction and for an end to the ceaseless wandering. At last, Maurice understood that it was never too late.

"What do you think happened, Maurice? Why was the Torah left here?"

"I am not sure," answered Maurice, still shaken by what he had just seen. "Perhaps it was placed here temporarily for safekeeping during a riot or some other sort of encounter with enemies, and no one ever had an opportunity to return here and save it, or perhaps someone on the journey fell ill and they could not travel. There could be many reasons why it was left here. I'm sure we could spend all day thinking of different possibilities and never really know the true story."

"You are right, Maurice. Let's stop all this speculation and remove the cover and see this Torah scroll!"

The two men stood gazing at the table and the scroll which lay there. Maurice was suddenly overcome with the belief that he had been destined for this since he first left Paris in 1940, as if all his travels and experiences since then were nothing more than a prelude to this moment, to what lay within the scroll, within the Torah. Maurice stole a quick glance at Meir and then smiled. He was ready.

Meir slowly and delicately unrolled it and revealed the most beautiful scroll he had ever seen. It was very old, the parchment was yellow and some of the letters were cracked or faded. But the singular beauty of the text, the craftsmanship and attention to detail was still marvelous to behold and Meir could not tear himself away.

Maurice too was enthralled by this hidden find, this wonderful treasure of Jewish lore. Maurice had seen many old manuscripts and documents during his history lectures but he admitted this was by far the most elegant and the most graceful.

Maurice continued to gaze upon the words he did not understand, he continued to examine the holy scroll. It was so old yet its core, its substance, remained pure and pristine, undaunted and unsullied by the passage of time. It had survived crusades, pogroms, libels and history's other assorted persecutions, each of which had targeted the Jewish People. Indeed, the Jews had survived those tragedies as well and it was this Torah, the Torah, the sublime principles and beliefs of the Torah, which enabled the Jews to survive, which afforded them the courage and conviction to survive. There was something about the Torah and the teachings which lay deep within it that infused ordinary Jews with the love and respect to endure any adversity with patience and forbearance, to remain dedicated to its precepts despite the unnatural and life threatening hardships which continued to plague them.

Maurice conceded he was quite removed from that heritage. He had no connection to the Torah and he could not relate to it. He had never studied it, never sought to understand it and never followed any of its commandments. He had experienced some brief stirrings over the last four years to try to comprehend and absorb an understanding of Judaism but those feelings always disappeared as quickly as they surfaced and they had never amounted to anything. Maurice had already come to realize that his life before the war was empty and futile and hopeless, built on generations of false pursuits, misguided scruples and erroneous assumptions of tolerance and brotherhood. This war, Europe's latest expression of its own base failings and inadequacies, shattered the foundations upon which his entire existence was based. The carnage, the pervasive intolerance, the sickening rumors, exposed his yearnings, his dreams, his hopes of success, all instilled in him by his parents who were likewise seduced by the allure of French society and culture, as nothing more than a failed quest for self fulfillment. Maurice understood that now there was no turning back, he could never resume that life when the war ended. He had challenged his past, his family's deluded preoccupation with a civilization whose true substance had been revealed to the world and he rejected it implicitly. Maurice realized that his entire life had been a dreadful waste.

But there was always time for change.

Maurice reached into his pocket and withdrew the yellow star given to him by Mrs. Levy in the cattle car. He had carried it with him since that day and had guarded it zealously. He always assumed she gave it to him to remind him of his past, of his heritage, however that heritage had been interpreted. But he no longer needed the imposition of European force and oppression to identify himself. He no longer required these secular, even negative reminders of a bygone world. Mrs. Levy had nothing else to give him. She too had been raised like his family and this relic was the only association of her Jewishness which she safeguarded and which she could then pass to the next generation. Even her heritage was measured and influenced by French governmental conduct! Indeed, she took great pride in her gesture and believed it was admirable and noble, and until this moment so did Maurice. That, conceded Maurice, was his greatest mistake of all.

All that was now over. He would begin a new life, a more cherished and meaningful life, guided by the principles of the Torah, by the timeless, ageless beauty which this Torah represented. It would not be easy, there was much to master but Maurice would not give up, he would not allow anything to stand in his way. He threw the yellow star on the floor and said goodbye to that world. He then bent over, kissed the Torah and began to weep.

"I am sorry! I am sorry!" proclaimed Maurice. "I did not know any better!"

Maurice continued to weep in front of the Torah.

Meir was startled by Maurice's sudden display of emotion and did not know what to do. He was not sure why Maurice was crying or why he was apologizing. He sought to comfort Maurice and try to calm him.

"What is the matter, Maurice? Why are you crying?"

Maurice turned to Meir. "You were right all along, Meir. You were right! You told me years ago that you considered me part of your family, like one of your brothers. I was flattered by those sentiments but did not truly take them seriously. We were so very different and as the war progressed we drifted further and further apart and I was certain we would remain apart. I could not explain the significance of the events we experienced together, the escape from the train, our survival the night Klippenberg and the others were killed and I thought they were just remarkable coincidences. I dismissed your beliefs that we shared a destiny together, that our experiences together foretold greater purpose, but you were right! We are bound together by an amazing fate, which I cannot explain but which has placed us in this room together with this sacred Torah. It is so beautiful, Meir. So enchanting, so majestic. I see that now. It is in this Torah, in the Torah where my future awaits." Maurice moved closer to Meir, "You were once my teacher, Meir, but I abandoned you. I am now ready to return to you and finish what we started so long ago. I am your family and it is with you that I belong."

Meir stood aghast. Since that first day when they ran into each other in a forgotten town in Switzerland, Meir always knew there was something special about Maurice and somehow they would remain lifelong friends. Meir, too, began to weep; his waiting, his longing to forge their friendship with significance and lasting resolve had at last come to be. He approached Maurice and embraced him.

"Welcome home."

AFTERWORD

This novel is a work of fiction. However, I have tried to blend historical accuracy and fiction to emphasize the ordinary Jew within the larger backdrop of history. The famous names, places and historic events of the past are common knowledge to us all but their impact on ordinary Jews, on the struggles and triumphs shared by ordinary Jews, is rarely addressed. This novel attempts to fill that void. I have chosen the Torah, the clearest expression of Jewish identity, as the moving force behind all events from broad governmental resolutions and global battles to decisions which affect even one lone individual.

As I have explained, several of the characters as well as various subplots are based on real people and events.

Part One: Blois, France:

There was a blood libel in the town of Blois in 1171 and virtually all the Jews in the town were killed. Theobold, Alix, Pulcelina, Yitzchok and Rabbi Baruch were real people who played an integral role in that tragedy.

Part Two: Huesca, Spain:

Juan and his son were real people who traveled to Huesca in 1465 to learn about their heritage and to study the sacred Jewish texts.

Rabbi Isaac and Rabbi Abraham Bibago were the spiritual leaders of Huesca at the time and did not at first trust the motives of Juan de Cuidad. Juan did manage to convince the brothers of his sincere beliefs and he was circumcised at the age of fifty before emigrating to Jerusalem. The fanatical priests in Huesca, of whom Father Ramon is representative, heard that a Jewish religious ceremony involving *conversos* had taken place and spent the next twenty-four years hunting down those involved. Rabbi Isaac's participation was eventually proven in 1489 and he was sentenced to death. Rabbi Isaac was informed that if he accepted the Cross, the church would put him to death before submitting his lifeless body to the flames, thereby saving him from the tortures and pain of the fires. Facing pressures that cannot be comprehended today, Rabbi Isaac converted, was "mercifully" strangled and then burned at the stake.

Part Three: Krasnystaw, Poland:

There were many towns throughout the Jewish world where people were swept up in the fervor of the arrival of the messiah during 1665-1666. The belief that the arrival of the messiah was imminent led many to engage in the extreme forms of penance and fasting depicted in the story. Many fell sway to the charismatic Shabbetai Zevi, and the strife between these opposing factions affected the entire Jewish world. Shabbetai Zevi ultimately embraced Islam, revealing himself as a fraud. While Krasnystaw is the name of an actual town in Poland, all of the characters mentioned are fictitious, but the attitudes and sentiments of many of the characters and the actions undertaken in the name off the false messiah Shabbetai Zevi are well documented.

Part Four: Paris, France:

Likewise, all of the characters in the last story are fictitious with the exception of Abraham Lissner, the Jewish French resistance fighter, and the renowned 35th Brigade. In addition, each of the specific locations concerning acts of resistance are documented.

On November 5, 1942, a train left the Drancy camp with one thousand Jews packed on board. During the journey, two people escaped from one of the cars in the remarkable manner described in the book. Alas, the train continued on and would eventually reach its final destination deep in the hinterland of Poland, near Cracow, close to the banks of the Vistula River. Of the 998 French Jews who remained on the train, 771 were gassed immediately upon their arrival at Auschwitz-Birkenau. The remaining 227 were assigned to work as forced laborers, and only four of them would ultimately survive the war.

The challenges we all face today are surely different in scope and degree than those faced by Jews of the past. Yet there are many factors which remain the same and which are repeated with regular frequency. If there is one recurring thread, one principle which is the undercurrent of all history, indeed of all mankind, it is the Torah. We may not know which new and difficult issues will present themselves in the future, but like ordinary Jews of the past who faced their challenges with fortitude and faith, we know that with the Torah we too can succeed in all our endeavors.